ALL HE
DESIRES

ALL HE DESIRES

C. C. GIBBS

FOREVER

NEW YORK   BOSTON

Copyright © 2014 by Susan Johnson
Excerpt from *All He Wants* copyright © 2013 by Susan Johnson
All rights reserved. In accordance with the U.S. Copyright Act of 1976, the scanning, uploading, and electronic sharing of any part of this book without the permission of the publisher constitute unlawful piracy and theft of the author's intellectual property. If you would like to use material from the book (other than for review purposes), prior written permission must be obtained by contacting the publisher at permissions@hbgusa.com. Thank you for your support of the author's rights.

Forever
Hachette Book Group
1290 Avenue of the Americas
New York, NY 10104
www.HachetteBookGroup.com

Printed in the United States of America

RRD-C

First Edition: November 2014
10 9 8 7 6 5 4 3 2 1

Forever is an imprint of Grand Central Publishing.
The Forever name and logo are trademarks of Hachette Book Group, Inc.

The Hachette Speakers Bureau provides a wide range of authors for speaking events. To find out more, go to www.hachettespeakersbureau.com or call (866) 376-6591.

The publisher is not responsible for websites (or their content) that are not owned by the publisher.

Library of Congress Cataloging-in-Publication Data

Gibbs, C. C.
  All he desires / C.C. Gibbs.—First edition.
    pages cm
  ISBN 978-1-4555-2829-5 (trade pbk.)—ISBN 978-1-4555-2830-1 (ebook)—ISBN 978-1-4789-8301-9 (audio download)
  I. Title.
  PS3607.I2254A78 2014
  813'.6—dc23
                                                              2014013990

ALL HE
DESIRES

ONE

London, May

Dominic frowned. "What?"

Kate took a small breath. "I don't suppose I could have a written guarantee that all the bad stuff is over?"

"You can have a written guarantee in every language known to man," he said, hoping to end his least favorite conversation in the world. "Framed in fucking diamonds."

A trace of a smile tipped the corners of her mouth. "That sure?"

"Totally. Two weeks at the most and we get married." He held up his hand and grinned. "Word of God."

Kate set the last tiny newborn outfit on the pile of baby clothes beside her on the antique Anatolian carpet, looked across the tumble of torn wrapping and empty boxes at a man known for the brevity of his relationships, then blew out a small breath. "One more question, okay?"

"Go for it." Dominic's blue gaze was open, without secrets. "Ask me anything."

She lifted her chin in a little defensive gesture. "Are you really excited about the baby? Or are you just doing your duty? I'd completely understand if this isn't your thing…I mean… well, all these lovely gifts aside, you and babies…with your lifestyle." Kate shrugged. "It's a major shift in your life."

"I *like* kids."

Dominic's bland disclaimer brought to mind his easy rapport with his nieces and nephews in San Francisco. "Still," she pressed. She had a tendency to overanalyze everything and Dominic Knight, billionaire and world-class playboy, was the least likely candidate for fatherhood she knew. "Raising a child is a serious commitment for at least eighteen years, probably more with college and maybe graduate school and—"

"I know what I'm doing, Katherine." Seated on the floor on the other side of the mass of crumpled wrappings and discarded boxes, Dominic Knight suppressed a smile at the notion that he might be accepting this child out of either some benighted courtesy or ignorance. "And I don't make a practice of being dutiful," he added, his blue-eyed gaze on the beautiful redhead wearing kitten print pajamas who'd casually turned his life upside down. "Particularly when it involves marriage and fatherhood. I'm beyond excited about our baby. Try to remember it the next time you question my motives." Then his smile broke through. "And knowing you that will be five minutes from now."

She sniffed. "We can't all be totally confident twenty-four/seven."

His smiled widened. "Please. Says the lady who's always right."

"I am brilliant, aren't I?" she said with a grin.

"Definitely, baby. You're my genius hacker." He winked. "And you've made my life a helluva lot more interesting."

She laughed. "How diplomatic. By interesting, you actually mean you like a fight now and then."

His eyelids drifted lower, the teasing gleam in his eyes filtered by his absurdly long dark lashes. "Especially with you, baby." He glanced at his vintage Cartier Santos Dumont watch. "I don't have any appointments till noon tomorrow so we have plenty of time. And my appointments can be canceled if necessary."

"How very accommodating of you," Kate said softly.

Dominic smiled faintly. "We try."

Suddenly the image of countless females being accommodated by the incredibly beautiful, sexually talented Knight Enterprises CEO filled Kate's mind and brought the teasing game to a screeching halt. "But you're accommodating only me from now on, right?" she said, challenge in the obstinate jut of her chin.

"Only you," he readily agreed, when he would have found such limitations incomprehensible a few short months ago.

Leaning back against the flax-colored sofa, her green gaze shimmering with delight, she smiled at the man she loved. "So," she murmured, with delicate impertinence and a little dip of her head. "Have I really tamed the premier playboy of the Western world?"

A lazy flicker of a smile. "I didn't think you liked it tame?"

His words hovered palpably in the sudden silence.

Spiked through her body, a flame hot and riveting.

Pooled in seething delirium deep down inside her.

"Meaning?" she whispered, finding it hard to breathe.

"Meaning, why don't we find out what you do like?" he said gently, coming to his feet in a graceful flow of toned muscle, having patiently waited through the unwrapping of countless boxes for her to finally read his mind. He held out his strong hand with its dusting of dark hair, his long fingers faintly splayed.

A shiver of pleasure raced through her. Broad-shouldered, lean hipped in jeans and a faded blue Peace T-shirt, Dominic's dark, brooding beauty was breathtaking: the long silky black hair, the bad-boy scorching blue eyes, the high cheekbones and fine bone structure, the arrow-straight nose, the mouth saved from outright sensuality by the contradictory don't-mess-with-me firmness. The whole package transcendent male perfection.

And when he leaned down and his hand closed around hers, she trembled at the glut of prodigal sensation, at the feverish need coiling in the pit of her stomach, at the blazing hot desire streaking up her spine. Agitated and restless, she said on a suffocated breath, "I'm sorry. But it's been so long I don't think I'm going to last."

Drawing her to her feet, he slid his hands under her arms, lifted her over the pile of boxes, and set her down. "Then let's go take care of you."

"You don't have much time." Her voice was shaky. "Just so you know."

He shot her a grin. "Do we have time to get into bed? Otherwise"—he glanced down at his erection straining his jeans—"he's good anywhere. Just say the word."

"Jesus, don't ask me to make a decision now!"

He smiled at her familiar, breathless rush to orgasm, and swinging her up into his arms, swiftly strode from the reception room and down the hallway. Moments later, walking into her bedroom, he covered the distance to the bed in four long strides and lowered her to the white quilted coverlet. Quickly unbuttoning and unzipping his jeans as she frantically squirmed out of her pajama bottoms, he dropped, fully clothed, between her pale legs, and on easy terms with expeditious sex, deftly guided the head of his dick to her slick sex.

"Oh, God...hurry, hurry—"

He heard her sharp intake of breath as he plunged into her succulent body, but his erection was only partially submerged when she suddenly climaxed.

Dipping his head, Dominic inhaled her soft breathy moan. "You *were* in a hurry," he whispered, his smile warm on her mouth. "We'll make it last a little longer next time— and the time after that, because I'm not going anywhere. I'm staying"—he gently flexed his hips—"right here for as long as you need me."

She softly sighed as his rigid length slid deeper, raised her hips into the heavenly sensation, and, when he responded with well-bred grace, forcing himself deeper still, she uttered a low languorous purr of contentment.

He smiled. "Good?"

Another weightless, dreamy pleasure sound, a faint wiggle.

"Not quite enough? More?" Moving with masterful finesse, he drove into her soft yielding flesh, the pressure like silk on silk, smooth, fluid, exquisitely sensual.

"How's that?"

"Ummm..."

He knew that lush, primitive utterance, had missed hearing it the last ten weeks, smiled at the thought of fucking himself to death to keep that velvety growl humming in his ears. The audacious thought had no more than crossed his mind than he rebuked it. *New ball game, dude. No roughness.* Dragging in a breath of restraint, giving himself a mental shake for good measure, Dominic absorbed their new reality. But he needed some guidelines. "Baby, look at me," he said quietly, touching her cheek.

Kate lifted her green gaze, a tiny flicker of unease visible. "No orders, Dominic," she whispered. "Please?"

On his best behavior since she'd only just allowed him back into her life, he said, "No orders, just a question, okay? Tell me if—" He hesitated, taking a small breath. "I don't want to hurt anything...the baby, you, whatever might get hurt. This is all new to me...so you're the one who has to say no. Tame is fine if that's what you need. Understand?"

"Everything's normal. Nothing's changed." At his lifted brow, she held his gaze just long enough to emphasize her certainty. "Really, I'm perfectly fine." Morning sickness aside, but it wasn't morning. "So don't worry about it."

Long past intimidation of any kind, even from the willful mother of his child, he politely smiled. "Just in case, that's all I'm saying. You tell me. I'll listen."

"How about I tell you to move a little?" she said pertly.

He didn't know whether to laugh or be pissed. She constantly shook up the established role of women in his life. Not to mention his life in general. On the other hand, he'd been in command of a global empire too long to accept orders from her or anyone. "Ask me nicely and I'll be happy to move."

She scowled.

He moved just enough to make his point.

After she stopped shuddering, she gave him a squinty-eyed look.

"Come on, baby, compromise. Neither of us likes orders." He grinned. "Just ask me even semi-nicely. We both want this, okay?"

She rolled her eyes, but every sentient nerve in her body was zeroed in on the immensity of Dominic's gorgeous dick filling her to excess, his pulse throbbing through the compressed network of veins in his engorged erection, matching her own hectic heartbeat. And damn him, he could outlast her by a week or more so really...what were a few words in exchange for a mind-blowing climax? "Please move, semi-nicely. Is that enough for a compromise?"

"Absolutely," he whispered, kissing her tenderly, withdrawing slightly, and seeing the moodiness return to her gaze, quickly added, "We're here, baby. This is for you." But he drove back into her slick, yielding body, slowly, carefully, because one of them had to be sensible and that usually meant him. When he reached the ultimate depth and ever so gently nudged her taut flesh, her lashes drifted lower and the fretfulness faded from her eyes. She sighed softly in blissful satisfaction.

He smiled. There. That was the sound he was waiting for.

She was happy, gratified. Without roughness or violence.

But these next few months were going to be an exercise in self-denial and prudence. Not that having Katherine back wasn't an awesome tradeoff. And what the hell, vanilla sex was the norm for most people. Maybe he'd even get used to it.

His priorities established, he ushered in the new construct of making love, a strange, radical concept for him, separate from fucking, unique to this small, voluptuous woman beneath him, enveloping him, warming his dick and his heart. Unselfish, super indulgent, he smoothly slid in and out of her as she grew wetter and wetter, told her what they were going to do later after she'd climaxed again, how he was going to keep her up all night, how he was going to give her countless orgasms to make up for the long weeks of their separation. "Just tell me when to stop," he murmured, nibbling her ear lobe, relishing the taste of her.

His deep, commanding voice warmed her senses, his nipping teeth made her shiver, made her breathless with longing, his massive dick, her fatal addiction, her greedy pleasure. And as he skillfully penetrated and withdrew, mindful of pleasing both her clit and her G-spot, she clung to him, rising to meet each exquisitely placed stroke until, increasingly frantic, she forced the rhythm.

He smoothly altered his pace, intent on indulging her. Fully capable, not to mention accomplished at this game.

How had she ever thought she could live without him, without this sweeping pleasure that was rich with lust, soft with the magic of love, the quintessential metaphor for having her cake and eating it too? "Don't ever stop," she panted, lifting into his downstroke, sliding her hands lower, under his loosened jeans, splaying her fingers over his taut ass and holding on tight. "Not ever, not—" She squeaked as he broke her grip.

"Pay attention, baby." His deep voice was teasing. "This means I'm not stopping." And having withdrawn, he pushed in again, all the way into that sweet spot that always made her gasp.

"Oh God . . ." She could feel her bones melting, her brain turning to mush, her body liquefying into a puddle of hot passion and need. "More, more." She ground her hips into his erection, reaching for the next wave of feverish rapture. "More!"

"Like this?" he whispered.

"Oh God, thank you," she panted in abject gratitude because her climax was beginning to ignite, all flash and dazzle, as he touched her quivering pussy to the core.

He felt the first tiny flutter tremble up his dick and smiled. "Here we go, baby." And plunged in again, deeper, gloriously, delectably deeper.

Surging upward, needy, ravenous, oh so close, she made lurid contact with his down thrust and suddenly the building hysteria broke, and her orgasm began to sweep hot and seething through her body. The raging ecstasy slid red hot up her spine, coloring the entire world in glowing bliss, electrified her brain, and, just as she was about to explode, she momentarily tensed. Then her wild scream rose into the high-ceilinged room, bounced off the pale, butter cream walls, gave potent, gloating voice to ten long weeks of sexual deprivation while she came and came and came . . .

Already pouring into her sleek, drenched sex, Dominic was deaf to her cry, too intent on his own powerful, shuddering, heart-jolting climax.

After a prolonged, rampaging tidal wave of mutual bliss, his guttural grunts and her screams slowly faded, the silence punctuated only by labored breathing. Until at last a hush descended.

Lengthened.

The two people on the bed still cushioned in a velvety euphoria.

Finally, half dazed and warmly aglow, still inexplicably overwhelmed with desire, Kate whispered, "I warn you, Dominic, I may never get enough of you."

It took him a fraction of a second to lift his head from the mattress near her shoulder. And another second to normalize his breathing. Then, resting on his forearms, an ingrained, habitual position for a man his size, he smiled down at Kate. "I'm here anytime, baby." Still resting inside her, his dick only nominally diminished, he shifted his hips in confirmation. "Just ask."

Reaching up, she slid his dark, tumbled hair behind his ears and grinned. "Perfect. Because you're mine," she said. "Don't forget it."

"Back at you, baby." He brushed her grin with his fingertip. "And I don't share. Don't *ever* forget that."

"Why would I want to?" She lazily stretched in a languorous motion that brought her lush pajama-clad breasts into contact with his chest. "I've never been so happy, so filled with lust and love."

When she looked all warm and sexy, when her plump breasts were resting lightly against his body, when her comment about never getting enough paralleled his own libidinous impulses, he suddenly felt the need to firmly underline the perimeters of their relationship. Or more pertinently for a man of his controlling temperament, to decisively mark his territory. Lightly touching the flawless forty-two-carat emerald-cut diamond on Kate's outstretched hand, Dominic said quietly, "This ring means we stay together. Today, tomorrow, forever. All of us. You, me, the baby. Nothing and nobody gets in the way. Got it?"

She nodded, gulping down the tears that had risen in her throat…"I cry…all the…time now," she hiccupped. "Especially…when I think about the baby. You're going to be revolted…at how clingy…and weepy I've become."

"After seventy-two days"—he turned his wrist to glance at his watch—"ten hours and twenty-three minutes without you." He shook his head. "Uh-uh, babe. No chance."

She bit her lip as her tears spilled over.

"Hey, hey, everything's good from now on." Bending his head, he licked away her tears, then grabbed the quilt and wiped her cheeks. "We're not going to fuck this up. We're going to make each other happy. And speaking of happiness," he murmured, leaning back enough to reach the buttons on her pajama top, "let's see this new baby-making body of yours."

TWO

Dominic's blue gaze was warm with pleasure as he freed the top button on Kate's pajama top. "I feel like a kid at Christmas who gets to open his special present."

"Then if you'll undress for me"—Kate's voice was lazy with contentment—"we'll both get a special present."

His grin was wickedly sexy. "That'll take two seconds."

"Be a dear and reword that," she murmured. "So I'm not reminded of the blur of women in your past."

He looked up into her sardonic gaze and his fingers stilled. "How about I take my time undressing? This is all about what you want." *Because I already have what I want?* "Just let us know the schedule."

Kate sighed softly. "Lord, I'm even more jealous than before. I'm going to blame my crazy baby hormones." She smiled faintly. "Tell me you don't mind or I'll burst into tears again."

He laughed. "Whatever you do is fine, baby." Then his voice went soft. "If there are nine circles of hell, I was in the tenth without you, okay? Nothing you can do will even begin to replicate that fucking misery. So jealousy, tears, whatever—hit me with it, I don't care."

Her smile was sunny again. "Really? I have carte blanche?"

"Damn right. You're nurturing this baby for us. You're

allowed anything. You want something, let me know. I'll find it for you. You need a shoulder to cry on, I'm here. You have a craving for something, it's yours." Framing her face in his palms, he dipped his head. "Because I'm good at getting what I want," he whispered.

"And you want me."

"You have no idea, baby. And just as soon as the divorce comes through, we're getting married."

She wiggled her hips.

"Are you trying to change the subject?" But his dick got the message loud and clear and swelled noticeably.

"I am," she purred, not wanting to even think about his problem marriage. "And for your information, pregnancy makes me even sexier."

He stared at her. "It does?"

"No doubt in my mind."

He exhaled softly. Even with Max watching over her during his absence, there was the possibility someone had been missed. Drawing in a breath, he carefully said, "I'll ask this only once and I apologize in advance because I have no right to ask when we weren't together, but did you—"

"Only my vibrator—or yours, actually," she interjected, because he was trying so hard to be understanding.

He blew out a breath. "Sorry. It shouldn't matter but it does."

"Tell me about it," she muttered, shoving him away as jealousy instantly soured her mood again.

He wouldn't have had to move; he was more than a hundred pounds heavier than her. But considering their very recent détente, he did. Smoothly rolling away, he rested beside her in a lounging pose, his head propped on his hand. "Come on, baby, the nightmare's almost over," he said softly. "I haven't looked at another woman since we've been apart. Not even a glance. You should tell Nana we're getting married."

"Don't change the subject. I should whip your ass," she said, although after Dominic's sweet earnestness, her tone was less grumpy.

Encouraged, he smiled. "If that changes the subject, be my guest."

She grinned. "Really?"

"Fucking A. I don't want to talk about this clusterfuck I just went through or even think about it." In a deal that had gone bad, he'd agreed to a temporary marriage to ensure Katherine's safety—although she was unaware of her danger. He wanted to keep it that way. "But seriously," he added, "you should give Nana a heads-up. I'll send a plane for her, but still, she might like some warning."

"I can't call her and tell her that you're married, and I'm pregnant with your baby, but you'll soon be divorced and then *we* can get married. It sounds too much like a scam. Not to mention that I'd like to see your divorce papers before I call her. Nana will have her shotgun loaded and pointed at you when she gets off the plane unless everything's settled. You met her. So that can't be a surprise."

"She didn't seem unreasonable," he said. "We got along."

"Jesus, did you charm her too?"

He grinned. "You mean I actually charmed you?"

"To the extent that we'll soon be parents," she noted sardonically, running her hand over the slight rise of her belly.

He grinned. "That worked out then." Placing his hand very gently on her stomach, he took a chance, kissed her cheek, and gave himself a mental high five when she didn't balk. "But if you prefer, call Nana when everything's resolved."

"Jeez, Dominic, you make it sound as if you forgot your umbrella and as soon as someone brings it to you, life's back on track."

"The degree of difficulty doesn't concern me, so long as we get our lives back." A muscle twitched along his jaw, a sudden chill invaded his eyes. "And I promise you, we will."

"You sound like you did with those bankers in Singapore. Can you stop? It's scary."

He ran his hand over his eyes in a literal gesture of nullification. "Sorry," he said smoothly, the cold belligerence extinguished from his gaze. "And now if you can wait a few minutes before you whip my ass," he added, cupping her small belly in his large palm, "I'd like to say hi to our baby." Bending low, he murmured, "I'm your daddy. We're going to have fun, you and me and Mommy. You're going to be the center of our world, did you know that? And if you want a pony you can have one," he playfully added, then looked up and rolled back. "The baby can hear me, right?"

"I think so. I almost had a pony once but Gramps balked at cleaning the stall. Did you have one?"

"Uh-uh. I never wanted one, but maybe the baby will take after you. Did you hear that?" He brushed his palm over Kate's belly. "Your mommy wanted a pony." He glanced at Kate. "I think we'd better get some baby books. We have some reading to do. In fact, let me call Melanie. She can overnight some to us." He pulled his phone from his jeans pocket and started dialing his sister in San Francisco.

"Now?"

"It's early afternoon in San Francisco. If she buys them today, we'll have them tomorrow. We can't shop for them or the paparazzi might see us. If some of my staff buy them, we're no better off. So Melanie's safe." He grinned. "Instant gratification. I want to learn about babies. Not that I didn't help Melanie with her first two, but when it's not really your job, you just do what you're told. This is *our* baby. I want to know *everything*. Hi, Mel. We need some baby books. All you can find. Send them overnight. No shit, I'm excited. Why wouldn't I be? Yeah, yeah, cute. How about its better, okay? Like a hundred times better. Don't give me any more grief. Just send them. No, you can't talk to Katherine now because I'm talking to her. Yeah, actually talking. Good-bye." He ended the call and tossed his phone on the bedside table.

"What's a hundred times better?"

"Nothing. Mel was being clever, that's all."

"Tell me."

"It's raunchy."

"Now I really want to know."

He made a face. "It was a long time ago."

"Jesus, Dominic. Do you ever want to touch me again?"

"Watch it, baby. That's not negotiable."

"Maybe I have something to say about it."

"Not as much as me," he said in a soft growl.

She sighed. "I couldn't anyway. This pregnancy makes me so horny. But I *could* be too tired for sex. I *am* tired a lot."

"Oh Jesus…okay. But don't get pissed. It's just surfer

slang. When you're surfing in waves that should kill you and you're in the jaws of a wind tunnel that should destroy you and you know you can't control it, you just let go. You lay into the warp and ride it clean through a cannon blast of green spit. And when you come out the other side alive, we call that kind of ride the next best thing to a three-way. That's all." Or that's all he was going to tell her. She'd freak at the real three-way stuff.

"That's not so raunchy. It's cute."

"Glad to hear it." *Really glad.* He was off the hook. "So." He pointed at her pajama buttons. "May I?"

"It's always a yes, damn you. Sometimes I wish I had more control."

He smiled, looked up from sliding a second button free. "I like that you don't."

"Still, it's always too easy for you. It always has been, I expect. I hate to be one of the crowd."

It stopped him for a flashing moment, the thought that he'd do any of this for anyone but her. Risk his life, offer an open-ended bribe of millions to the low-life Gora, who'd threatened Katherine, and marry Gora's horny little mistress who was looking to augment her family's bank account. "You're one of a kind, baby, not one of a crowd," he said gently, back to his unbuttoning. "I've never asked anyone to marry me before. I've never considered having a baby with anyone before. I've never been in love like this before. Would you like that in writing? On a billboard somewhere. I could do a press release. In all modesty," he said with a small smile, sliding the last button free, "it would be a worldwide news flash."

"I want it in skywriting," she said, deadpan, before she grinned. "And thank you. For someone who always had more than my share of confidence, this baby is screwing with my head. It's really strange."

"It doesn't matter. I like you strange or any way at all. Ummm...This I like a lot," he murmured, having brushed aside her pajama top. "They're bigger." He looked up. "When did that happen?"

"Are you sure? I haven't noticed."

"I'm sure, baby. You've been working too hard if you haven't noticed these." He slid his hand under the curve of one large breast and gently lifted. "We're going to have to fly Mrs. Hawthorne over to see that you have some bras that fit."

"No."

"Later then." He sat up and cupped her other breast.

"No, not later either." They'd had this fight before in Hong Kong.

"Then you're going to have to wear some bulky sweaters, because these aren't for public display." He moved his fingers and very gently squeezed her swollen nipples. "These are for me."

"I'm guessing the baby gets first dibs on my boobs. Oh, God, that feels good."

He looked up, smiled. "Then I'll settle for seconds. Apparently, parental self-sacrifice starts early."

"Even earlier than that." She raised her brows. "My breasts are incredibly sensitive now and I'm practically in heat twenty-four/seven. So I'm going to need your personal attention—like constantly."

"Jesus." He breathed. "My dick heard that. Are you sure it's okay?"

"Don't you dare even think that," she hissed.

"My mistake. Although, we should talk to a doctor just to make sure."

She glared at him.

"Tomorrow. Not now. A female doctor. I didn't like Clifton."

"You're not undressed yet," she said, ignoring his comments, only half-listening, her attention focused on her impatient desire, on the steady throbbing between her legs, particularly on Dominic's opened jeans and his obvious erection beneath his blue-and-white-striped boxers. "I'd like the two-second undressing if you don't mind."

"Would it matter if I did mind?" he said with a grin, ripping off his T-shirt.

"I *am* going to whip your ass if you don't hurry." Then she drew in a shaky breath, her eyes filled with tears, and she whispered, "I've really missed you."

He was undressed in less than two seconds. So grateful for the love radiating from her eyes, he would have given her the world wrapped up in a bow and delivered by pixies if she'd asked.

But the one thing he knew she needed he delivered. Quickly settling between her legs, he smoothly entered her, driving in more gently than usual despite her protestations that everything was fine.

Her fine and his were still in contention.

"Dominic! Please!" she cried, hot-headed and hot-blooded, hurriedly wrapping her legs around his hips, her arms around his back, dragging him closer.

He carefully moved deeper, ignoring, or rather disregarding, her nails sinking into his back. It wasn't possible to actually ignore them.

"I'm going to cry if you don't let me come!"

So he compromised, not because her tears disconcerted him, but because he wanted to please her. And in lieu of added depth he flexed his stiff, thick dick upward and rubbed it back and forth over her pulsing G-spot. "We're seeing a doctor tomorrow," he said, rough and low. "Say yes or I'll stop."

"Yes, yes, yes...oh yes." She sighed, her nails relaxing against his back. "Do that again."

"This?" His pain level blessedly reduced, he obliged her with his well-trained dick and steel-hard thigh muscles, pressing gently against her G-spot and clit, once, twice, several more times, before moving slightly in and out, side to side, then back to her favorite entertainment site while she panted and gasped in wonder and delight, softly moaning in rising hysteria.

And he did what women around the world loved him for, over and above his money: he fucked like an artist, with natural talent, an almost indecent technical competence, and the well-honed gift of accurately gauging female arousal.

Like just about *now*, he decided, sliding his long, slender fingers over the curve of Kate's hips, under her soft, round ass, and lifting her so his rigid erection pressed hard into her throbbing cushiony mound of tightly concentrated bliss.

"Oh God, oh God, oh God..."

He watched with a faint smile, and a well-behaved, disciplined dick, as nearly breathless now, she careened at volatile, breakneck speed over the orgasmic edge and climaxed with only the tiniest of screams.

Which served as musical background to his own satisfying climax.

"Don't move," he whispered, a few minutes later, unwrapping her legs and setting her feet on the bed. "We need some towels."

"I can't move." She breathed, her eyes still shut. "I may never move again."

Her sweet naïveté always pleased him. Sex was so fresh and new to her. Every climax was received with unalloyed delight. "So I don't have to worry about you escaping while I'm gone?" he said, rolling off the bed.

"You don't have to worry about me ever escaping. That should frighten the hell out of you."

She still hadn't opened her eyes, her voice syrupy with content.

"On the contrary, baby," he said over his shoulder as he strode away. "It saves me the trouble of dragging you back."

The sound of his voice faded away as he walked into the bathroom.

Instantly feeling deprived of his warmth, as if the light of the world had dimmed, she suddenly opened her eyes, sat up, and cried, "Dominic!"

He appeared in the bathroom doorway, holding a stack of white towels. "I'm here, baby." He didn't take exception to the panic in her voice because he knew too well that feeling of loss. "I'll always be here. In fact, I'd like to tie you to my wrist if you'd let me," he added, walking into the bedroom. "We have to talk about that."

Falling back on the bed, she felt her heart rate begin to slow. "Everything's suddenly so intense, superemotional, bordering on hysteria. I'm jumpy and misty-eyed over everything and nothing at all."

"It's just the baby. We'll talk to a doctor tomorrow, get some basics on prenatal moods, read those books from Mel, and just be happy about all these new changes you're going through. I don't care how jumpy you get, so long as you're within eyesight. You're not the only one flipping out." Tossing all but one of the towels at the foot of the bed, he sat beside Kate, used the towel for her, then him, dropped it on the floor, lay down beside her, and pulled her into his arms.

"You really spoil me," she murmured, snuggling closer. "I could get up and wash. I shouldn't be so lazy."

"I like to spoil you. Don't worry about it." This from a man who wasn't in the habit of spoiling women. From a man who had a staff at all his homes so he didn't have to bother with mundane practicalities.

"Are you tired? I'm a little tired." Her voice was already sliding into sleep.

He glanced at the clock. *Christ, it wasn't even nine.* "I'm good, baby, but we need to talk about when we're going back home. You're going to need more and more sleep. And if we wait too long, it won't be safe for you to travel."

Kate's eyes flew open and she came awake. "I can't go back to the States yet. I still have three months on my contract with CX Capital." She sighed. "And Joanna expects me to do my share with our clients."

He was careful to keep his voice neutral. "Do you want the baby to be born here in London?"

"I don't know. I haven't given it much thought."

Maybe someone should. "I can get you out of your contract," he offered. "I can also find Joanna a replacement for you."

"Could we talk about this later?" Her eyes were drifting shut again. "I'm too tired to think."

"Sure, baby. Go to sleep." It looked as though he was going to have plenty of time to work in the evenings. Which wouldn't be all that bad, since he was planning on spending as much time as possible with Katherine—once he talked her into going home. Because any contract could be broken; certainly, CX Capital could find another forensic accountant somewhere in the world. Maybe not someone as good as Katherine, but that wasn't his problem. As for Joanna, Kate's partner, he could pay her enough so she could hire whomever or however many others she wished to take over Katherine's job. Again, not an equivalent in terms of ability, but fuck if he cared.

Dominic was in love for the first time in his life, but that didn't mean he was undergoing a personality change. He still expected to control his world and the people in it. As for Katherine, he was willing to compromise. To what extent depended entirely on her.

Once she was fully asleep, he left the bed, pulled on his jeans, picked up his phone from the bedside table, and walked into the reception room. Dropping into a chair, he punched in a name and waited while his cell rang and rang and rang.

"Am I interrupting something?" Dominic said when Justin finally picked up.

"We're at the symphony. I walked out into the corridor."

"I won't keep you then. I'll talk fast." At Dominic's request, Justin had not only set up Katherine's consulting assignment in Singapore, but had also arranged for her CX Capital position in London.

"Take your time," Justin said. "It's some benefit. They're droning on about the foundation's financial goals."

"How hard will it be to break Katherine's contract?"

"Not hard. Why?"

"We're having a baby. This is for your ears only. I'm caught up in some complicated problems right now, so none of this is public information."

Justin knew better than to ask. If it was complicated for Nick, it was marginally legal. "So are congratulations in order?" he asked, knowing Dominic's track record.

"Yes, very much in order. I'm marrying Katherine. And I'd like to take her home before it's too dangerous for her to travel. She, on the other hand, doesn't want to break her contract. I'm hoping to change her mind. If and when that happens, could you take care of things for me at CX Capital?"

"Not a problem. Bill will be sorry to see her go, but he'll live. By the way, I'll be expecting a wedding invitation. I never thought I'd see the day," Justin noted drolly. "No offense."

"None taken. I wouldn't have placed any bets on me remarrying either. The actual wedding plans are up to Katherine, though. If she decides to invite more than family, I'll send a plane for you and Mandy. Speaking of Mandy," Dominic said pleasantly, "you must be a new daddy by now. How're Mandy and your daughter?"

This Nick who asked about babies and children still threw him for a loop. After the briefest of pauses, Justin said, "The baby was born three weeks ago, and mother and daughter are doing fine. Also, the nurse and nanny have been a help. Mandy's actually getting enough sleep to enjoy a night out."

"Then you'd better get back to her. What did you name the baby?"

"Don't ask. It's a family name."

"Yours or Mandy's?"

"Her grandmother's name. Beatrice."

"That's not so bad."

"I guess. The baby's cute as hell though, so that'll help even with a name like Beatrice."

"So she looks like her mom, you're saying," Dominic said sportively.

"Thank God, yes. And seriously, I'm happy for you and Katherine. Kids are great."

"I'm beginning to understand that. It's pretty fucking exciting. Enjoy your night."

Justin stood in the corridor of Royal Albert Hall after the call ended and let the stunning news settle in his brain. Not only was the man he'd thought least likely to marry about to marry, but Dominic Knight was, in his own words, *pretty fucking excited* about having a child. He wouldn't have bet a penny on either eventuality ever occurring. Dominic's previous relatively brief marriage aside, he'd always been the poster boy for serious kink and vice.

THREE

Dominic walked over to the liquor cabinet, opened the door, and was pleased to see that Katherine hadn't tossed out all his whiskey. In fact, no one had touched a single bottle in the months he'd been gone.

Pouring himself four fingers of a fifty-year-old Ardbeg, he dropped into a sage green easy chair, sipped on the fine spirits, and mentally ran through his schedule for the coming days. Then, comfortably relaxed after the world's most incredible whiskey had warmed his senses, he set aside the empty glass, picked up his cell, and made one of the calls on his agenda.

It was late for a business call, but he'd find out if he was overpaying the wedding planner enough to have her pick up.

"This is after business hours, Mr. Knight," she said, crisply.

Apparently I'm paying her enough. "I apologize, Mrs. Hastings. But I'd like to set up an appointment at my place tomorrow evening. Any time after seven. My fiancée often works late."

"I'd prefer a daytime appointment."

"I'm afraid that's not possible." He wasn't going to argue with her. His CFO, Roscoe, had wired an initial eighty-thousand-dollar consulting fee to her account. That should pay for an evening appointment or two.

He calmly waited as the silence lengthened. It wasn't as though she was the only wedding planner in London.

"Very well, Mr. Knight," she said coolly.

"I appreciate your cooperation, Mrs. Hastings." His voice was smooth as silk. "You have my address in Eaton Place. And if I might ask a small favor. My fiancée is temperamental. If you would do your best to overlook her occasionally pithy comments, I'd be grateful. She means a great deal to me. I wouldn't want her unhappy."

"Certainly, Mr. Knight. I'll do my best."

"I know you will. Olivia Roche has nothing but good things to say about you. You apparently made her wedding memorable."

"They were such a nice young couple. Both from fine, old Sussex families."

Dominic understood that her professional association with and national pride in the British aristocracy prompted her statement. He was fine with that. But he objected to her condescending tone. "Max is my ADC. He's an exceptional employee. You'll see him tomorrow." He very rarely made a point of his wealth, but in this case he did. With Katherine's emotions being rather unpredictable, he wanted Mrs. Hastings to understand the value of *his* patronage, aristocratic quarterings or not. Ignoring the wedding planner's offended sniff, he added, "Would it be possible to bring a dress designer with you? I understand it's short notice, but Miss Hart might like to look at some bridal gown designs."

"That's not possible," the wedding planner replied, tartly. "The best people are already fully engaged and committed...most, years in advance of a wedding. Some-thing off the rack will have to suffice."

He didn't say what was on the tip of his tongue, which was that "suffice" doesn't work for him. And he didn't give a shit if the designers were engaged a thousand years in advance.

"If you *could* find us someone suitable, they could name their own fee of course," he said instead in the super affable tone he reserved for the intractable. "Would that help?" In his experience, the unspoken but implied *I'm one of the wealthiest men in the world* generally greased what-ever wheels needed greasing.

Mrs. Hastings's voice was tight with constraint when she spoke, each obstinate word drawn out kicking and scream-ing. "Let me see what I can do, Mr. Knight."

"Excellent," Dominic said pleasantly. "I knew I could count on you. Sevenish tomorrow, then. Have a nice eve-ning." He hit End, set down his cell, and slid into a lazy sprawl. It wasn't as though he didn't understand the time pressures. He was willing to pay whatever was required to expedite the arrangements. He thought he'd made that clear to Mrs. Hastings before. Perhaps now the message was crystal clear.

He expected results.

In the next two hours, he answered e-mails, talked to Max numerous times, explained to his major domo, Mar-tin, that they would need refreshments for their evening appointment with Mrs. Hastings, and, finally, gave his sister a call to ask her about arranging a wedding, in the event that he was required to know something other than how to write a check.

But his first question had nothing to do with weddings. "Did you sleep a lot when you were pregnant?"

"I did. Early to bed, naps in the afternoon. You didn't notice?"

"I was sixteen. You weren't a surfer babe. Why would I notice?"

"Katherine's sleeping, I presume."

"She fell asleep at nine p.m. I was just wondering if I should be concerned?"

"It's pretty normal. And she said she's working long hours. That's probably not optimum in her condition."

"Don't tell me, tell her," Dominic muttered. "I'm trying to talk her into breaking her contract and coming home."

"Losing your touch?" Melanie teased.

He snorted. "I never had it with her."

Melanie laughed. "Finally met your match?"

"I wouldn't say that." Kate wasn't the only one with more self-confidence than needed. "Well, maybe. She's damned competitive, and stubborn as hell," he grumbled.

"Just like you. Seriously, Nicky, you have to know that you're incredibly stubborn, even pig-headed, on occasion." She didn't bring up his years of struggle with their mother, but she was thinking it. "Just don't be an ass. You're lucky to have Katherine in your life."

"I know," he said simply. "In fact, that's why I called you. We're seeing a wedding planner tomorrow and I need some advice."

"Have you told Katherine yet? I know how you work, Nicky." At the small silence she snorted disgustedly. "Christ, you haven't told her. What the hell's wrong with you? Haven't you figured it out yet? She's not like all the other women who smile and do what they're told. You want my advice, listen up. First, you'd better be really sweet when you mention the appointment. Bring Katherine breakfast in bed. You, not someone on your staff. Then *ask* her if she minds seeing the wedding planner."

"She still might say no."

"After watching you in action for a decade or more," Melanie said drily, "I'm guessing you can change her mind if you really try. Your record number of three-ways wasn't just about you being a great surfer."

He blew out a breath. "Right. Okay, so first, breakfast in bed. Then ask her. Thanks, Mel. Oh, what about the dress designer? Will Katherine's pregnancy be an issue? Or actually, how much of an issue will it be?"

"I'm sure you're paying the designer enough, Dominic. That means it's not an issue for anyone but Katherine. And if I were you, I'd make sure Katherine knows it's not an issue for *you*. Pregnant women like their men to be helpful, encouraging, and superkind, and you've cultivated none of those qualities. So I suggest a crash course in devotion."

The phone line crackled with muzzled shock. "Devotion?"

Melanie sighed. "Bring Katherine home, Nicky. I can run better interference for you at close range. But get your act together," she ordered brusquely. "Remember, you're miserable without her. She makes you happy."

"Okay, okay, I got the message." He dragged in a breath. "Seriously. Devotion?"

"You can sit home every night jerking off instead. I'm just saying you have choices." She listened to her brother's low grumble for a three count before she went on with her sisterly advice. "And devotion's not about buying Katherine expensive things."

He sighed. "That's what she says."

"Then you already know that."

"It doesn't mean I understand it." Expensive gifts had always worked in the past. Worked extremely well, as a matter of fact.

"It's about doing things for her," Melanie explained.

Besides fucking her when she wasn't sleeping, which seemed to be Katherine's only current request? "Like doing what exactly?" Gifts and fucking he knew; the rest sounded tricky.

"Pay attention to what Katherine likes in books, music, entertainment." *I know the answer to the last one.* "And be sure to ask her about her favorite activities. Whether she enjoys time with her friends for girl talk or maybe yoga. I know I do. Oh, and don't forget to find out if she prefers sleeping late in the morning, because there's nothing worse than someone waking you up when—"

"Jesus, stop. This is getting complicated. Look, I'll start with breakfast in bed and then wing it."

"There you go, baby brother. I'm sure you'll do fine. Women like you, you know."

"Thanks for the reminder. I was beginning to forget."

She laughed. "As if."

"Still...I'm trying not to screw up. I missed Katherine like hell when she was gone."

"Tell her that. Just tell her what you're feeling. And don't micromanage her life."

Would two out of three work? "Okay, thanks, Mel. Hopefully, we'll see you soon."

FOUR

B reakfast in bed was an excellent idea. It set the proper mood that he was caring and kind, helpful and devoted. And once Katherine finished eating, Dominic carried her into the shower and sat her down on the wall bench to wash her. While she half dozed, he quickly soaped and rinsed her off with the shower hose. Then, sliding behind her, he pulled her between his legs and started shampooing her hair.

"Oh God, that's heavenly," she whispered, languorous moments later. "What are you doing?"

"Shampooing your hair."

"And something else too…oh jeez, ummm—that's incredible. I'm getting really hot…sexy…" She felt a warm flutter at the base of her spine that vibrated upward in heated urgency, then down again, and a thrilling hot, deep throb settled deep in her sex.

"It's just a little massage, that's all." Years ago, when he was still living with Melanie, she'd often say to him, "Remember girls like this or don't like that, so pay attention," and he'd always listened. It was like learning a new language, making it easier to navigate in a foreign land. And he'd perfected the art of physical contact over the years. Touch generated a subtle current, small, flowing fingertip circles, slow gliding strokes encouraged a rhythm of desire.

A sublime arousal, an erotic hunger warmed her senses. "I never knew you could come...just from—"

"This?"

"Oh God, oh God..." Her voice trailed off in a soft breathy sigh and she slid over the orgasmic brink in a whisper of bliss.

He let all the sumptuous pleasure wane before he murmured, "We should go soon." He'd been watching the time. "Can you do that?"

Eyes shut, she nodded.

A brief moment passed before Dominic decided to have the conversation about Katherine quitting work later. Wedding planning first. He rinsed her off, toweled them both dry, and led her into the dressing room.

Standing nude in the small room lined with mirrored closets, still slightly drowsy, Kate slid her hand over her tummy. "Please, something comfortable. I don't suppose I could wear sweats."

Dominic smiled. "You could if you worked for me."

"Right now, that sounds really tempting."

His smile broadened. "Could I get that in writing?"

"A few more orgasms, who knows?" she replied playfully.

"I don't give up. You know that, right?" The teasing was absent from his voice. He turned and started flicking through clothes in one of the closets.

She took a small breath. "I can't cave completely, Dominic. I need my own life."

He spun around. "I'm sorry. Your own *life*?"

"You know what I mean."

"Tell me," he said, standing perfectly motionless. "I'm not sure I do."

"I don't want to be owned. I don't want to be a part of Knight Enterprises, where you call all the shots. You can stop scowling. I love you, okay? We'll work it out."

He slowly exhaled, reminded himself to be patient, and told himself that Katherine's hormones were all over the place now. Mostly, he warned himself not to screw this up. "You're right," he said softly. "We'll work it out." Half turning, he reached for a hanger and held it out. "How about this? No waistline. Good?"

"Whatever you think. I don't care. You know that."

"You *are* fun to dress, baby." He slid the black silk tunic dress embroidered with an Impressionist design of colorful flowers off the hanger. "Who knew?" he said, smiling. "You've added a whole new pleasure to my life."

"You, on the other hand," she murmured, gazing at Dominic's naked perfection, "have added a *world* of pleasure to mine. Come here...Anytime you want to quit work, baby, I'm on board." He tapped his watch. "It's your call. Just say the word."

She scowled. "Spoilsport."

"I don't have to be." He lifted his brows. "So..."

"Oh hell," she muttered. "So nothing. I have to go."

"Come home early," he suggested, walking to the dresser, taking out black lace bikini panties to go with the dress. "Just let me know and I'll be here," he offered, moving toward her.

"I can't," she said with a sigh.

He was encouraged by that sigh. Perhaps she'd see the

light sooner rather than later. "Too bad. Maybe some other time." Tossing the dress on a chair, he sank slowly to his knees. "Lift your foot," he murmured. "Now the other one." Sliding the black lace panties up her legs, he adjusted them on her hips, then glanced up. "We should go shopping for maternity clothes."

She groaned.

He rose to his feet. "We'll have someone come to the house. Better?"

"Not really," she grumbled. "Maternity clothes are gross."

"Have you looked at them?"

"No. Have you?"

"I thought about it," he said, picking up the dress.

A small smile twitched at the corners of her mouth. "And?"

He grinned. "I lost my nerve."

She laughed. "So what are we going to do?"

"If you don't want to wear maternity clothes, you could just lie in bed naked." He grinned. "I'm good with that."

"Ummm...tempting." She ran her fingertips down his sculpted abs. "Maybe we could try it out now," she purred.

"Keep purring like that, baby, and you're not going to make it to work."

"Do we have a little time?" she asked, hope in her voice.

"You don't, but I do. My schedule is flexible." He held her gaze. "You decide. We're always ready for you."

She shot a look at his beautiful erection and exhaled a low grumbly sound that matched her pout. "Damn," she muttered. "This sucks."

Unzipping the back of the dress, he held it out.

She grimaced. "This really sucks."

"I agree."

"Don't sound so damn calm when I'm unraveling."

"Look, baby, you know how I feel about this; I don't want you to work. I want you with me every minute. I'm just trying not to make waves this morning." His brows rose. "Clear?"

She groaned. "Okay, okay, just do it."

"Meaning?" he asked carefully.

"The dress, the dress . . ."

"Just checking." Sliding the tissue-silk-lined dress over her head he turned her, zipped up the back, swiveled her around, and pointed at a chair. "Sit. I'll get some shoes."

But he quickly pulled on boxers and his suit pants before he returned with the shoes because, her libido aside, she wanted to go to work. And he didn't feel like taking the blame if she opted for a quickie that would make her late. There was no doubt in his mind what he wanted and he'd make it happen. Just not this morning.

"You're dressed." She pouted.

"Baby, you can't have it both ways."

"What if I want to?" Wearing only steel-gray dress pants, he was raw, unfiltered masculinity. Broad and powerful as an ancient fortress, his swarthy skin rapped an urgent tattoo on her psyche; heat and desire gathered inside her, fingered all her nerves.

He sighed softly, held out green wedge sandals with one hand, and pointed to the bed with other. "I already told you what I want. You decide what *you* want."

There was a small silence.

Then she lifted one foot.

Rome wasn't built in a day, he thought, and with his childhood, he'd developed a significant level of patience. Kneeling, he slipped on the shoes, buckled the straps, and, standing, pulled Kate to her feet. "Tired?" he murmured because she'd briefly shut her eyes and sighed.

"Always."

"Call me and I'll come get you if you can't make it through the day."

She smiled. "Thanks, but I'm okay once I start working. My adrenaline kicks in."

"We should talk to a doctor so we're not flying blind with all the changes you're going through. Why don't I find one today?"

She shrugged.

Since that wasn't a no, he said, "What now? Your phone, your messenger bag?"

"Yes and yes." But she didn't move.

He smiled. "Give me a hint."

"They're probably still in the kitchen where I dropped them."

Five minutes later, Dominic exited the flat, carrying Kate, her messenger bag slung over his shoulder. Jake, who was leaning against the car, waiting, quickly opened the back door and greeted them with a smile.

"Morning, boss. Miss Hart. Good weather for a change."

"It's great weather," Dominic said.

Kate smiled at the driver, who came from the same mold as all Dominic's security: dangerously buff and imposing. "Morning, Jake."

"We're running a little late," Dominic said as he slid into the backseat with Kate.

"I can make up time. Nine. Right?"

Dominic nodded, Jake shut the door, and seconds later, he pulled away from the curb.

Since the wedding planner appointment had been only briefly discussed that morning, Dominic did a quick double check as she was exiting the car at CX Capital. "You're okay with the seven o'clock appointment?" Her blank look wasn't reassuring. *Shit.* Maybe he shouldn't have asked again.

"Oh that—sure, fine. If you really think it's necessary."

"It won't take long," he said blandly, sending a silent thank-you to his sister. "Call me when you want a ride home." Giving Kate a kiss on the cheek, he handed over her bag lunch, which had been packed by his chef.

"Is six thirty all right? I have a heavy schedule today."

"Six would be better. You'd have time to eat."

"Six fifteen? And a sandwich is enough."

He wasn't going to stand outside CX Capital and argue with Katherine about her need to eat a more healthy diet for the baby. "Six fifteen it is," he said with a smile. Then he watched her cross the sidewalk and saw all the men stare at her in her short-sleeved flower print dress that showed off her boobs and legs. *Shit. A suit with a long jacket tomorrow,* he decided. Clenching his fists so he didn't punch anyone, he waited until she disappeared through the revolving doors before getting back into his car.

As his driver shut the door, Dominic leaned forward and opened a compartment that served as a desk.

Sliding behind the wheel a few moments later, Jake turned to Dominic. "Where to, boss?"

"Just sit here a minute. I have to write a quick note. Then drive to some messenger service. I need this hand delivered."

A short time later, Joanna Thorpe, Kate's colleague at CX Capital and also an associate in their small accounting firm, was handed an envelope by a bicycle messenger dressed in full bike rider regalia—red and white spandex, helmet, fingerless gloves.

As she fumbled in her purse for a tip, the young man shook his head. "The bloke already gave me fifty bloody pounds. Save your money." And with a cheerful wave, he walked out of her office.

Her name, *Ms. Joanna Thorpe*, was written in a vigorous scrawl on the front of the envelope and when she turned it over, the dark blue monogram on the flap explained the mysterious delivery. With the exactness of an accountant, she carefully slid her thumb under the flap and eased it up. Then she slowly drew out the card. Someone watching might have thought she was worried about a bomb threat.

After placing the note on her desk, she meticulously lined it up in the center of her work space before reading:

Ms. Thorpe,
    Would you do me the favor of meeting me at Le Gavroche for lunch at noon? Please don't mention this to Katherine. I'll explain.

                                    Sincerely,
                                    Dominic Knight

Grateful for the privacy of her office, Joanna reread the short message. She examined the expensive notepaper, running her finger over the engraved monogram top center on the heavy handmade card stock, and briefly debated her loyalties.

Then, with a glance at the clock, she put the note in her desk drawer.

As it turned out, Dominic's message was opportune.

She had a thing or two she wanted to say to Mr. Dominic Knight.

A moment later, standing in the doorway of Kate's office, Joanna smiled and pointed at the lunch spread out on Kate's desktop. "That looks good. Do you want me to bring you coffee, tea, or anything when I come back?"

Kate held up a small glass container of chilled rice pudding. "I have a chef now." She pointed to the red canvas bag on her desk. "And a Prada cooler."

Joanna grinned. "You help keep the economy going."

"Isn't that nice of me? Public spirited and all."

"He might as well spend his money on you." Joanna had heard it all in the months of Dominic's absence. Not at first, but eventually. "Things are going well then?"

"Yup." Kate held up crossed fingers. "Sometimes it seems too good to be true."

"When it comes to luck," Joanna said crisply, her view of the celebrated Dominic Knight dubious after Googling him, "he's lucky to have you."

Kate grinned. "That's what I keep telling him. You know what—bring me an iced tea. It'll help keep me awake."

FIVE

Dominic was already seated when Joanna was shown to the corner table by the maître d'. Pushing his chair back, Dominic came to his feet and put out his hand. "Dominic Knight. Thank you for coming." He'd seen photos of Katherine's business partner, but she was more formidable in person. Tall, blunt cut black hair, average looks, slightly overweight in a well-cut burgundy suit. Unsmiling. The word *grim* wouldn't be out of place.

"Joanna Thorpe," she said coolly. "But you already know that."

"Yes, I have a competent staff." Warning off the maître d' with a glance, he pulled out her chair himself and seated her. Moving around the table, he spoke quietly to the man who now approached the table, then sat and smiled politely over the sparkling crystal, china, and cutlery. "I appreciate your giving me some of your time. I've ordered, if you don't mind. I thought it would give us more time to talk."

"About Kate." She kept her voice level, telling herself she wouldn't be distracted by Dominic Knight's dark male splendor. He was breathtakingly handsome, powerfully muscled beneath his fine steel-gray Savile Row tailoring, and very charismatic. She wasn't the only one in the room watching him.

"Yes, about Katherine," he said, his voice pitched low.

He glanced down for a moment, as though gathering his thoughts, then looked up. "I'm concerned about her. She's overworked. She has been for some time. It worries me."

"Why?" Blunt and direct, accusation in her tone.

He found it difficult to open his private life to a stranger. "Let's just say because we're good friends."

"Good enough *friends*," Joanna said, visibly bristling, "to know Kate's pregnant? If not, I don't see what we have to talk about." She began to rise.

"Please." He put out his hand to deter her. "I know about Katherine's pregnancy."

Joanna resumed her seat, but her gaze was razor sharp. "Then are you a good enough *friend* to do something about it?"

Dominic smiled faintly. "Is this where I say I'm going to make an honest woman out of Katherine as soon as possible?"

"Yesterday, last week, last month, might have been better."

His dark brows lifted. "She's discussed this with you?"

"No, she hasn't said a word. But I would have been blind not to notice her morning sickness."

"As I understand it, Katherine didn't realize she was pregnant until recently."

Joanna shrugged. "I could have told her. But it was none of my business."

"Speaking of business." Dominic stopped, glanced up, and nodded, and the sommelier poured them both champagne. When he left, Dominic raised his glass. "To what I hope is a mutually agreeable business arrangement." He drank half the champagne, set down the flute, leaned forward slightly, and said quietly, "I have a proposal for you. I'd like to buy out Katherine's share of your business. I'd also be willing to augment that sum with enough additional capital so you can hire as many people as you need to make your operation thrive. My motives are purely selfish, so please be liberal in your estimates. I want to take Katherine home, but she thinks she can't leave either CX Capital or you."

"That's very generous. What does Katherine say about it?"

His gaze narrowed. "Does it matter?"

"Yes." She gave him a critical look. "It's a simple question."

"Then the simple answer is she doesn't know."

"That's what I thought. So what will Katherine say when she finds out what you've done?"

He exhaled softly. "She fell asleep at nine last night. She shouldn't be working such long hours. I'm just trying to hasten the date of her departure. As for what she'll say"—he shrugged—"I'll find out if you agree to my proposal."

"I can tell you now: she won't like it."

He smiled tightly. "No offense, Ms. Thorpe, but that's not your problem. And consider, I'm offering you an opportunity to expand your business. Also, keep in mind, Katherine will eventually leave. If not now, when her contract with CX Capital runs out, and then once the baby makes demands on her, she'll rethink her career."

"How do you know? Many mothers work."

Dominic straightened one of the knives to the right side of his plate before his lashes lifted completely, revealing the cool blue of his eyes. "I prefer not arguing about Katherine." His smile wasn't really a smile. "Let's just say, I don't think she'd mind if an opportunity arose that allowed you to buy out her share. You see, we're both very happy about the baby."

"Why didn't you say so before?"

"I suppose because I don't know you."

His flinch had been almost infinitesimal. "And it's none of my business."

"That too," he said, holding her gaze. "Now, rather than prolong this embarrassing conversation, I'd like to offer you the details of my proposal."

"Certainly," Joanna said, feeling much better since he'd said he was pleased about the child.

"Thank you. First, I'll cover whatever amount you offer Katherine for her partnership. That money would be over and above what you need from me for Katherine's half of the business. The cost of hiring new personnel would be an additional amount. Just give me a total sum."

"I'd have to think about it."

"I understand." He sat back as their food was placed on the table: grilled scallops with clam minestrone, filet of Scottish beef with wild mushroom and red wine shallot sauce, a cheese soufflé with double cream, a variety of colorful vegetables. "I didn't know what would appeal. Please help yourself." Then he smiled a genuine smile, because he knew she was going to take his offer. *"Bon appétit."* And he began cutting his filet.

Quickly finishing the small piece of meat, Dominic set down his cutlery. "I'd appreciate your discretion in this matter. The tabloids follow me from time to time and I'd rather they not be privy to any of this. I don't want Katherine followed or in any danger. So if you were to agree," he said politely, "and once you decide on a figure—and please, I begrudge you nothing—e-mail my ADC. I'll give you his e-mail address. Max will see that you get a check. As for what you say to Katherine about your new business plan, that's up to you."

Joanna had finished her cheese soufflé while he'd been speaking.

Dominic waited for the server to take her plate. "If you have any questions, please don't be shy."

"Do I look like I'm shy?" She reached for the beef.

"If you don't mind my saying it," Dominic said with a very faint smile, "you look as though you'd like to cut out my spleen."

"Heart," she corrected, looking up from slicing her filet. "If you had one."

"Actually, I've discovered I have a heart. I was startled at first, then alarmed. Now I'm quite content, happy." *For the first time in my life.* But that he *didn't* say to a relative stranger.

She held his gaze over a forkful of beef midway to her mouth. "You'd better not be lying about marrying Kate. She deserves someone"—Joanna looked him up and down with a scowl—"who knows her worth. Kate is a remarkable woman, brilliant in fact."

"I'm well aware of that. There were serious reasons why we were apart for the last few months." He fixed his gaze on her. "I was miserable."

For the shortest instant, she saw the exhaustion in his eyes, then he smiled a dazzling smile that turned female heads at the adjacent tables as well, because it was impossible to ignore Dominic Knight's spectacular beauty.

"I hope we have a deal," he said into the thick silence.

After that heart-grabbing smile, Joanna wondered if any woman ever said no. But feeling guilty for her shameful response to his smile, she said briskly, "I have a question."

"Ask me anything," Dominic said politely, having seen women respond the same way since he was fourteen.

"Did you send us any clients?"

"Not directly, no."

"Indirectly?"

His shoulder lifted in the smallest of shrugs. "I know a lot of people. I personally own a great number of companies. But you and Katherine did excellent work. I'm more than happy to continue recommending your firm."

Thanks to his cool composure, she'd regained her equilibrium. "I don't know if that's necessary," she said.

"It can't hurt." He smiled. "Unless you don't like making money."

She was silent for a moment. "Why would you do that?"

"Why not? You're first rate."

"And you know that because...?"

He made a sound somewhere close to a sigh. "Because I saw that I'd been paying way too many taxes on my North Sea wind farm. I'm not averse to paying my share. I make enough. But those taxes were bloody high. So thank you."

"That was yours? Windjammer Acquisitions?"

He dipped his head.

"It was Kate who noticed the discrepancy."

"Don't be modest. You would have too."

Joanna smiled. "True."

"So are we good?" he murmured, holding her gaze.

She nodded. "On one condition."

"Which is?" Despite his indolent tone, his gaze was cool.

"Kate has to be aware of and willing to take my offer," she said in prim rebuttal to his indolence. "Not coerced or convinced. Willing."

He smiled faintly. "Surely you know Katherine well enough to understand she's not likely to be coerced by anyone. So? Are we agreed?" Dominic put out his hand. "Shake on it?"

Her hand was dwarfed by his. And if she didn't like Kate so much, she'd be envious of her future. Dominic Knight was absolutely stunning.

And willing to make her rich.

"I hope you like chocolate," he said smoothly, sitting back, recognizing that glazed look in a woman's eyes, careful to keep the conversation businesslike. "I know Katherine does. Truffles in particular." He couldn't help but smile at the memory of her eating truffles at the Ritz-Carlton bar in Hong Kong their first night together. "Have you noticed?" he said quickly and caught the waiter's eye.

"I have. Although you'd be hard pressed to find a woman who doesn't like chocolate."

"Good," he said, as the water put dessert plates with a rich chocolate mousse before them. "And the cheese trolley here is excellent." He smiled. "Would you like to see it?"

"No thank you."

"Coffee? Cappuccino? More champagne?"

"Coffee."

"One coffee, one cappuccino, Eduardo." He pushed his dessert plate away and relaxed in his chair. "I'm very grateful for your cooperation, Ms. Thorpe. I can't thank you enough."

"You're welcome. Thank you as well for your generosity." She smiled for the first time. "Would you like your name on the business?"

"You're not serious?"

"Of course not."

He laughed. "So you have a sense of humor after all."

"And you're not a complete prick."

"Depends who you talk to. But as long as you don't think so, I'm satisfied.

"And should you ever need further capital, don't hesitate to contact me. I'll tell Max to remember your name. He's my gate keeper." He nodded at the dessert she was eating. "How is that?"

She waved her fork at her nearly empty plate.

"Would you like another?"

"Why not?"

Before he raised his hand, a waiter appeared. "We'll have another," Dominic said, pointing. "And bring me a port, Taylor 1966." He glanced at Joanna. "Could I interest you in a port? I'm celebrating."

"Yes, as matter of fact. I have reason to celebrate too. And now since we've shaken on our deal and you can't back out—"

"You don't know that," Dominic interposed, his voice suddenly cool.

"I do. You want this more than I do." Joanna met his blank gaze and smiled. "You'd do anything for Kate, wouldn't you?"

He didn't immediately answer. "Probably," he said finally. "What do you want?" There was a brutal edge to his voice.

"You can be frightening, can't you? But I survived an alcoholic father. I don't frighten easily."

"I had parents who shouldn't have had children. We could compare notes. But that doesn't answer my question. What do you want?"

"Kate's happiness."

"I can guarantee you that," he said crisply. "And?" In his world there was always something more.

"And what if she wants to go back to work after the baby's born? Will you allow it?"

"Surely you know Katherine does as she pleases," he said, his expression unreadable.

"With you—I'm not so sure. I'd hate to think she was giving up her career simply to please you."

"If Katherine wants to go back to work, I'll take care of the baby. I won't have my child raised by hired help and indifferent strangers." A muscle twitched along his jawline. "Does that erase your concerns?"

She abruptly sat back. "You'd do that?" she said in disbelief.

His faint smile displaced the grim set of his mouth. "You don't think I can feed and diaper a baby?"

"No."

"Then you'd be surprised. And before that frown turns into a scowl, let me make it clear—I don't have children. But I helped raise my sister's first two. I was sixteen, I didn't mind taking orders from her, and it turned out, her babies liked me and I liked them."

"My word," Joanna exclaimed softly.

"Does that shoot my badass image all to hell?"

"Absolutely."

"Good. So don't worry, Ms. Thorpe, I'll take good care of Katherine and our child. You can count on it." He leaned forward slightly to emphasize his point. "I just need you to help me get Katherine home."

"I'll do my best."

"Then you have my deepest gratitude," he said, sitting back and bestowing another of his dazzling smiles on her. "Ah—here's our port."

The rest of lunch turned out to be pleasantly congenial, but then Dominic was on his best behavior, out to charm Ms. Thorpe, careful not to put a foot wrong.

He could charm with the best of them if he chose.

He often did for less substantive reasons.

It was no hardship today—he was getting exactly what he wanted: Katherine's exit from London.

SIX

That night Dominic had dinner served in his library rather than in the cavernous dining room at Eaton Place.

"You have to eat something, Katherine," he said gently, pushing away his appetizer of prawns and noodles, a faint frown creasing his brow. "Would you like me to feed you?"

She sat up in her chair, took a deep breath. "Sorry, I'm really lazy."

"You should be resting." Rising from his chair, he walked around the small table set near the windows overlooking the garden, lifted Katherine from her chair, and sat down with her in his lap. "If you don't like prawns, try the lasagna. I had Nana send her recipe."

Her eyes flared wide. "You called her?"

"We didn't talk long. I just wanted the recipe. You told me it's your favorite."

"You didn't mention the baby, did you?"

Reaching for the lasagna, he half turned to meet her gaze. "Why would I do that?" He drew the dish closer. "Tell her when you're ready."

Kate exhaled.

He smiled, spooned out a portion onto a plate. "You know as far as Nana's concerned, you can do no wrong."

"Still...small town gossip being what it is."

"As if Nana gives a shit about gossip. Come on, baby,

relax. See if Quinn did justice to Nana's recipe. Whenever you tell her about the baby, she's going to be pleased." He picked up a fork and scooped up some pasta. "Open up now. There you go. What do you think?"

"Hmmfff," she said, chewing and smiling.

"It *is* good. I had some already."

Dominic fed Kate the lasagna, then he coaxed her into eating half a bowl of peaches and cream. And when she finally shook her head no, he said, "Thanks, baby. You did well. Don't forget you're eating for two now. You have to make some adjustments to your pizza and candy bar menu." He smiled. "I'm amazed you're so healthy."

"We don't all have chefs."

"You do now. So get with the program."

She grinned. "And if I don't?"

"Maybe we'll have to put up a chart and give you stickers when you eat right."

"Or you could give me orgasms when I eat right."

He laughed. "Better yet. There's a win/win."

She reached up and slid her finger over his bottom lip. "Like maybe now? I haven't seen you all day..."

He dragged in a breath. "The wedding planner will be here any minute."

Wrapping her arms around his neck, she looked up and whispered, "Can't she wait? It won't take long."

He sighed. "Don't do this, baby." Easing one of her hands from around his neck, he turned it, kissed her palm, then folded her fingers and held them lightly. "If you give Mrs. Hastings ten minutes, I'll give you whatever you want the rest of the night." He smiled. "That's a good deal."

She groaned, slowly undraped her other arm from his neck, and sat back. "Okay, but I need a kiss at least."

He dropped her hand. "Just a kiss. That's it."

"Don't you trust me?" She looked up at him with wide-eyed innocence that couldn't have been improved upon by rosy-cheeked cherubs.

He smiled. "Not when you look at me like that." Dipping his head, he kissed her like he'd kiss an elderly aunt—no hands, on the cheek, short and sweet. Then he swept her from his lap, set her on her feet, and rose from the chair. "Come on, baby," he cajoled, brushing his fingertips down her arm. "Ten minutes and I'm yours."

"I'm supertired, and feeling really amorous," she murmured. "Just ten minutes, right?" She grinned. "Say yes."

Fortunately, he'd already warned Mrs. Hastings that Katherine might be moody. "Maybe we can make it less than ten minutes," he said, sliding his fingers through hers. "You just have to okay a few things with the wedding planner. Then look at some bridal gown drawings so the designer can get started."

"Or you could pick out the gown while I'm talking to the wedding planner. That would hurry things along." She suddenly smiled. "I won't embarrass you. I promise."

"No way you can embarrass me, baby. Never. I just want to get this train out of the station."

"You're way too nice." She squeezed his hand. "Thanks."

"It's easy to be nice to you." He drew her close. "You're my world."

"Oh God, I'm going to cry again."

"Hey, hey, it's good." He dropped a kiss on the bridge

of her nose. "Nothing to cry about." He smiled. "You don't have time anyway."

She sucked in a breath, sniffed, exhaled. "Will the designer be shocked when you ask for an adjustable waistline?"

"Nah. They're paid not to be shocked."

"Something simple then. No train, no veil, nothing I can trip over."

"We'll check it out together. Fast." Releasing Kate's hand, he buttoned his shirt collar, snugged up the knot on his loosened tie, fastened the buttons on his suit coat, then took her hand again and smiled. "Let's do this."

In a corner of the large, Adam brothers–style drawing room, two women were seated side by side on one of a pair of facing sofas upholstered in blue striped silk. Since Belgravia hadn't been developed until the second half of the nineteenth century, the house hadn't been designed by the Adam brothers. But it was faithful to their neoclassic model: from the sky blue curved walls to the Grecian pilasters, painted ceiling medallions, and pastel carpet—the decor one of elegant lightness.

Martin was arranging a large silver tray with a tea service on a table between the sofas when Dominic and Kate entered the room.

"Thank you for coming," Dominic said as they approached the women. "I apologize for the late hour. We won't take too much of your time." He introduced Katherine to Mrs. Hastings, and she in turn introduced the young woman seated beside her. Martin poured tea and sherry for the women, tea for Kate, and a whiskey for Dominic, before serving colorful, frosted tea cakes to everyone. That accomplished, he quietly withdrew.

"Since it's after hours, if we might get right down to business," Mrs. Hastings said briskly the moment the door closed on Martin. "I found a small chapel nearby." She looked at Dominic, one hand at her throat in a calculated gesture, her three-strand pearl necklace a badge of class. "They had various hours available so I reserved them all. For the next month, you said."

Dominic turned to Kate. "I thought someplace close would be easier. Is that all right with you?" He glanced at her plate. "Martin didn't give you any of the chocolate cakes. I had them made for you."

"I'm fine," Kate said, blushing.

"You sure?" They might have been alone for all the notice he gave their guests. He smiled and his voice softened. "There's truffle filling in them."

"Please, Dominic." Her voice trembled. Dominic might be indifferent to their audience, but she was fully aware of the starchy wedding planner's shocked expression.

He finally became aware of Kate's unease. "Maybe later," he said casually, leaning over and kissing her cheek. "So do we have your approval on the chapel?"

"You decide. Really," Kate murmured, her cheeks bright red, looking as though she'd rather be anywhere else but here. "None of this matters to me. We could get married in a closet in our underwear for all I care." She wasn't big on ceremony.

"In that case, my only concern is privacy, Mrs. Hastings." Dominic turned his bland gaze on the slender, gray-haired woman with pursed lips sitting ram-rod straight opposite them. "No reporters, no paparazzi."

"We'll do our best, Mr. Knight," Mrs. Hastings said, swallowing her distaste for Dominic Knight's casualness. Americans had no sense of decorum. "With the reception here, as you stipulated," she added, forcing a smile because Mr. Knight was equally casual about her fees.

"Yes. It would better ensure privacy. You can discuss the menu with my chef at your convenience. If Katherine has any requests we'll let you know. Our wine cellar is adequate I think, decorations and flowers are up to you as well as licenses and consular help, should we need it. As for a guest list, why don't you plan for fifty and we—"

"Fifty?" Kate said in a tiny squeak.

"Or fewer," Dominic added with a smile for Kate. "You decide."

"I thought maybe just us."

"And Nana. And Melanie and her family." He dipped his head. "What about your roommate, Meg? She might like to come with one of her, er, friends. And Nana might want her bridge group here."

"Oh God, did she say that?" Kate could see Jan Vogel's pursed lips already.

"No, but you have to at least consider it," Dominic said quietly. "The ladies have been playing bridge and sharing their lives for fifty years. Look, none of this has to be decided right now." He took Kate's hand in his. "Does it?" he said, looking to Mrs. Hastings for confirmation.

The wedding planner knew what was required of her. "Not at all," she said, trying not to choke on her words.

Did he think she was a magician, that a wedding just *happened*?

"Good. Problem solved," Dominic said pleasantly. "Now why don't we look at some dress designs?"

Mrs. Hastings had supplied a long list of the designer's important clients along with her bona fides. But regardless of her credentials, Abigail Strahan looked like an avant-garde art student. She had a wide pink streak in her sleek blond hair, wore a short black T-shirt dress, black-and-white-striped tights, and high-heeled Victorian boots in purple leather.

Kate immediately liked her and her warm open smile. "I need something loose," she said as Abigail placed a folder on the table between them

"We're having a baby," Dominic interjected with a smile.

"I saw that," Abigail said. "Congratulations."

Mrs. Hastings's mouth pursed so tightly her lips went white. Kate didn't notice because she was leaning forward as the designer spread out her watercolor drawings. Dominic noticed, but saw the wedding planner immediately moderate her expression to a more acceptable half smile. *Smart woman.* He didn't care whether she approved or disapproved of his life so long as she carried out his orders. Of course, the most vital was complete confidentiality. No paparazzi.

Mrs. Hastings appeared fully capable of discretion.

"I like your dress." Abigail gestured at Kate's embroidered tunic. "It's perfect with your pale skin and coppery hair."

"Thanks. Dominic bought it. He's the one with taste. I'm lucky."

"But you're the one who makes the clothes look good. He's the lucky one."

"No argument there," Dominic said, sliding his arm around Kate's shoulder and leaning over to kiss her cheek. "I'm the luckiest man in the world."

Kate blushed.

So he kissed her again, always captivated by her sweet naïveté. She was unique in his sophisticated world, a far cry from all the women he'd known, completely natural, fresh and artless, irrepressibly eager for sex. His constant wet dream. Shifting slightly to disguise his rising erection, he dropped his arm from Kate's shoulder and quickly turned his attention to the discussion of wedding gowns.

"This short swingy dress would be easy to wear." The designer pointed at a drawing of a cream silk dress, with a stand-up collar, small cap sleeves, and a shirt-front neckline buttoned with three silk-covered buttons. "Or this chiffon would disguise your tummy."

"That's not necessary," Dominic said. He turned to Kate. "Don't worry about that. Once we're married, the whole world can know for all I care."

"Maybe I don't want the world to know just yet."

He quickly raised his palms. "Forgive me, baby. It's your call."

The women ignored Mrs. Hastings's sniff.

Dominic looked at her, his brows creased. "Problem?" he said.

"No, no, I have...a little touch of...a cold," she stammered, taken aback by the arctic chill in Dominic's eyes.

Calmly turning back to the drawings, Dominic pointed at a simple sleeveless, A-line design in ivory shantung. "I like this one. And it has a matching coat in case the weather doesn't cooperate."

"I like the one with the collar," Kate said.

"Then get it." He smiled at the young designer. "How soon can you have the dress finished? I don't know if Mrs. Hastings mentioned it, but the price is unimportant. So if you need to hire extra seamstresses, please do."

"I could have it finished in two or three days."

"Perfect." He smoothly rose from the sofa, held out his hand to Kate, and pulled her to her feet.

"I will need some measurements," Abigail said.

Kate sighed. "Now?"

"If we send this dress back with you," Dominic said, indicating Kate's tunic, "would that help?"

"I'll still need a final fitting."

"After that? How much time would you need to complete the dress?"

"A day, no more."

He dipped his head so his eyes were level with Kate's. "One fitting, that's not so bad. You can do that, right?"

"Sure."

"That's settled then. We'll send the dress down in a few minutes. It was a pleasure to meet you, Ms. Strahan. And as always, Mrs. Hastings, you've been most helpful. Whatever questions either of you have can be addressed to Martin. He'll arrange for everything from this point on. I'll send him in."

"Thank you," Kate said. "It was nice meeting you both. And I love your dress designs," she added with a smile for Abigail.

"Maybe we could talk Ms. Strahan into doing some maternity clothes for you." Dominic draped his arm over Kate's shoulder. "We're both novices in this department. Think about it at least," he said when Abigail hesitated. "Katherine thinks maternity clothes are gross. Perhaps you could change her mind."

"I'll think about it. But it's not my area of expertise."

"I'll have Martin give you my number. Please call anytime." He turned to Kate, dipped his head. "Is that okay with you, baby?"

"Yup, yes," Kate quickly corrected, grinning at Abigail. "I like the simplicity of your designs."

"You've impressed my fiancée, Ms. Strahan. She normally has no interest in clothes. I do hope you'll call me."

As Dominic and Kate walked away hand in hand, Mrs. Hastings murmured, "I wouldn't refuse if I were you. The man has no qualms about paying any price."

"He's in love with her. He wants to make her happy."

"Umph. That may be, but he wants what he wants more. Men like Dominic Knight are ruthless. I wouldn't want to be his wife when it comes to the divorce. He won't be so accommodating then. And they all divorce. They find some new toy and move on."

"Yet you plan weddings for men like him."

Mrs. Hastings offered up one of her rare smiles. "Divorce is excellent for my business. Some of these titans of industry have been married four times. And always with considerable fanfare. Actually, I'm surprised at the modesty of Mr. Knight's wedding."

"I don't think his fiancée is interested in fanfare."

"Perhaps. And he's been married once already. Did you know that? It was a large affair, worldwide coverage—really quite spectacular. In fact—ah—here's his man now."

SEVEN

I forgot to mention, Justin's wife, Amanda, called today and invited us to dinner tomorrow," Kate said as they moved down the hallway. "It's casual, thank God. And she apologized for the late invitation, but with the new baby she said it's hard to schedule ahead. Is that okay with you?"

"Sure, whatever you want."

"I already talked to Joanna. So I don't have to go into work on Saturday."

Dominic smiled. "Good. I'll have you to myself Saturday."

"And I'll have a day of vacation."

"You could have more." He glanced at her. "You know that."

"We'll see," Kate said, with a flicker of a smile. "Don't get pushy."

Had Joanna already spoken to her? "The offer's always open. That's all I'm saying."

"If I decide to become part of Knight Enterprises"—Kate twirled her hand at Dominic in a gesture of genuflection—"you'll be the first to know, Mr. Knight. As a matter of fact—and don't take a victory lap yet—but you're beginning to wear me down."

"Gotcha, no victory lap, but that sounds *really* good," Dominic said with a wicked grin. "Not to mention deference from you, addressing me as Mr. Knight. It looks as though you might be a model employee, Miss Hart."

She laughed. "As if that's what you want."

"I do from everyone but you. I run a tight ship. But you're allowed anything. You know that."

She gave him a flirty smile. "I am your favorite, aren't I?"

"In every possible way. So while we're on the subject," he said carefully, "if you should decide to come on board, we could run Knight Enterprises together. Equal partners. You'd have the same veto, the same authority, the same command structure. All you have to do is say yes."

"That's crazy," Kate said on a caught breath. "I don't know the first thing about—"

"Sure you do. You know business where it matters—the bottom line. How the money comes in and goes out, how much, how often, whether the margins are good or bad. And I can teach you the deal-making. So no false modesty. You can do anything and you fucking know it."

"You sound like Gramps."

"I'll take that as a compliment."

"It is," she said quietly, swallowing hard.

He saw her eyes mist over and quickly scooped her up in his arms. "I can't ever take his place, baby, but I love you the same way. Unconditionally," he murmured, dipping his head and kissing her lightly as he strode down the corridor. "And no pressure on the job offer. I just wanted it on the table. Whatever you decide is fine with me. Now," he added, turning the conversation to a less emotional topic, "what time is our dinner with Justin and Amanda tomorrow? Eight?"

She smiled. "You should be a diplomat."

"They don't make any money. And I'd probably punch out the first person who gave me shit. But thank you," he said with a grin, "for your wildly misplaced belief." He recognized the hall porter with a faint nod as he moved toward the double staircase rising from the large entrance hall.

"The invitation *was* for eight," Kate said, acknowledging Dominic's question. "But I asked if we could come at seven. I get tired so early now. Amanda said that was fine with her since, even with a nurse and nanny, she's sometimes short of sleep."

"We'll make it an early night then." Dominic began smoothly ascending the right bank of stairs. "I'll pick you up at five, we'll come home, change, and then drive to wherever they live." Which he knew wasn't far.

"You're sure you don't mind going?"

"Nope. And since they just went through a pregnancy and birth, maybe we can learn something. I don't think it matters if we tell them, so long as they don't broadcast the news."

"You sure?"

"You trust Justin, right?"

"Of course." Kate grinned. "I'll take notes then."

"We'll both take notes." He turned at the first landing and moved up the second, shorter, tier of stairs. "Which reminds me, Max talked to Liv and she recommended a woman obstetrician, so I called and made us an appointment."

"I suppose we have to."

"It might be good idea. I don't like being clueless."

"True," she said with a sigh. "When?"

"Next Monday." His shoes were noiseless as he strode down the plush hall carpet. "Three thirty. It was the latest appointment I could get. It's her last one of the day."

"Speaking of getting things," Kate purred, as Dominic came to a stop at a set of double doors. "You said if I gave the wedding planner and designer ten minutes I would have you all to myself tonight."

"I meant it, baby." Opening one of the levered latches with his knuckles, Dominic shoved the door open with his foot, carried Kate in, set her on her feet, and pulled the heavy door shut with a soft click.

"Wow." She scanned the huge room: cream-colored walls, sleek, painted furniture, a large canopied bed hung in mint green silk, ceiling murals of cavorting nymphs in an Etruscan landscape—a wall of glass doors, opening on a balcony with a view of the gardens. The golden glow of sunset lent a luminous quality to the air.

"No kidding, wow." He never tired of looking at her. "You're beautiful, baby," he murmured, thinking how she'd redefined his life, how she'd actually given him a life. Then she turned and smiled that smile that always made him feel like the luckiest man in the world.

"Keep that thought," she said, "as I get fatter and fatter. I warn you, I'm going to need constant flattery. I've never been fat before." Her gaze took on a faint kick-ass glint. "And I don't mean the kind of smooth-talking you've been handing out for years."

"Don't worry. That world's long gone, baby. Just tell me if I'm doing it wrong."

Meeting his blue-eyed gaze, she grinned. "There's one thing you never do wrong."

He glanced down. "He heard you."

"Oh my God, Dominic," she whispered, her gaze on his rising erection lifting the fine wool of his suit pants. "We have to stop talking. I need him *now*. My crazy new hormones are on some rocket trigger and—"

"I've got this," he said brusquely, spinning her around, unzipping her dress, and pulling it off. "Get into bed." He slapped her butt. "I'll be right back." Striding across the room, he opened the door, walked out, and swiftly traveled down the corridor to the top of the stairs.

"Heads up!" he called out. When the hall porter looked up, Dominic pitched the dress toward the man. "Give it to Martin," he said loud enough to be heard twenty feet down. "And tell him I don't want to be disturbed."

"Yes, sir." Suppressing his smile, the young man picked up the dress. "I'll tell him," he added, although he was talking to himself by then.

Dominic was already halfway down the upstairs hall, stripping off his suit coat with one hand, loosening his tie with the other. Entering the bedroom a few moments later, he threw the clothes on a chair, jerked his shirt off over his head, dropped it, and unbuckled his belt. Intent on his expeditious undressing, he didn't look up until he heard a soft whimper.

Kate lay in the center of the bed, lush and succulent, searingly desirable, earth mother and Venus rolled into one as she indolently reclined against a mass of crisp linen-covered pillows, the quilt in a crush at her feet. She was even more voluptuous in pregnancy, her breasts a lavish gift to the eye, the curve of her hips slightly more rounded, the small rise of her tummy always stealing his breath away.

"Dominic." Her eyes were half shut, her voice breathy with need.

He emerged from his lover's trance. "Two seconds, baby." Kicking off his shoes, he unzipped his suit pants with a swipe of his hand.

"Oh…God…"

Kate's cheeks were flushed, her pale flesh pinked from head to toe with arousal—her hands pressed over her mons as though to contain her ravenous desires. "Don't you dare come without me," Dominic growled. "Damn it, Katherine, open your eyes."

Her lashes slowly lifted. "Then you'd better fucking hurry," she said, her eyes hot with longing, the boundaries of the world narrowed to her wanting him—*this second.*

"Now that I have your attention," he murmured, grinning as he shoved his pants and boxers down his hips.

"I don't know about you, but he"—she pointed at his massive erection, fully visible again as he stood upright—"has my attention. I thought about this all day long."

"Then open up, baby," he said gruffly.

She shivered as a hard jolt of lust shot through her senses, his brusque command triggering a flood of audacious memory.

"I saw that," he murmured, kicking the last of his clothes aside. "But I can't get in unless you open wide."

She instantly spread her legs.

He came to a stop at the side of the bed. "You have to do better than that." He flicked a glance downward. "Or he won't fit."

Quickly sliding her hands downward, she slipped her fingers over her slick pouty flesh and eased her sex open.

"More, baby," he said gently. "Unless you don't want him."

She moaned softly as his deep voice, the soft threat or shameless promise, stoked her raging desire.

"I'm waiting," he whispered, then smiled faintly.

Because she'd slid her fingers deeper and opened herself in a lush offering of ripe, carnal pleasure.

"That's a girl," he said softly. "You get a reward when you do what you're told." Leaning over, he delicately stroked her exposed clit, watched it swell into a hard little bud. "Uh-uh, don't move your hands," he warned as she began panting, and tapped her clit hard enough to make her squeal.

Her eyes snapped open. "I have a simple request," she said between tight teeth.

He smiled faintly. "You always do. Maybe I want to play for a couple seconds."

"And maybe I don't," she grumbled.

He ran his finger up his rock-hard dick. "He does."

She unconsciously licked her lips at the splendor of his engorged, upthrust erection pulsing against her stomach.

His grin was insolent. "You like?"

Half breathless, frantic and feverish, it took her a moment to reply. "You know I do."

It had never mattered before—the degree to which a woman wanted him. "Good," he whispered, gracefully lowering himself between her outspread thighs, guiding his rigid dick to her cleft. "Don't ever forget," he added, taut and low.

"Never, never..." Her voice trailed off in a sumptuous moan as Dominic slowly slid into her wet, welcoming heat.

"Jesus." He shut his eyes against the flood of fierce pleasure swamping his senses.

She whimpered, beyond speech with rapture bombarding every shuddering nerve in her body, with feverish lust driving her toward orgasm. Tightening her arms around his neck, she slid her feet over the backs of his thighs and opened her body completely to him.

"Ummm...nice," he whispered, his breath light on her lips.

He felt her faint smile and marveled at how small a gesture accorded him such inexplicable pleasure. But she was wet and wild and almost immediately forcing the pace. He kissed her gently. "In a hurry, baby?"

"Now, now, now," she panted. Helpless, shivering, she'd been waiting all day. For this, for him, for the feel of him, the sublime, hard, thick feel of him plunging, pressing, stroking. Driving all the way inside her. Yesyesyes. *Oh, too much*—no, *just* right...oh God, oh God, Jesus. God! Suddenly, she was choking on pleasure, shuddering, surging. Screaming.

He watched her, politely waited until her breathing turned into a soft, blissful sigh, then whispered, velvety and low, "More?"

She nodded, unable to find sufficient air to speak.

He smiled and continued to indulge her wild, greedy, orgasmic desires, until he finally whispered, "Enough, baby.

We're going to stop. You're trembling." Then he deliberately climaxed. Calling a temporary halt to her demands.

Staring up at him, she pouted a little. "What if I want more?"

"You can have more. Just not right now. Neither of us knows what's permissible until we see a doctor. Let's not overdo."

"I feel fine."

"I don't want to argue about this," he said quietly, rolling up into a seated position.

"I don't either. I'm not one of your employees who has to take orders," she said, a trifle hotly.

He bit back his reply, slowly inhaled. "I know who you are, Katherine. I'm just concerned about your health."

"Why don't you let me worry about that."

Another taut moment of self-control. "I'd feel better after we talk to the doctor," he said with exquisite restraint.

"And I'd feel better after another few orgasms."

He frowned. "Don't be childish."

"Be a fucking tyrant with someone else. I'm not interested."

He looked away for a moment, as though questioning, debating, curbing some impulse. All three as it turned out. Then he slid his legs over the side of the bed, reached back, and lifted her up as easily as he'd pick up a book from a table.

"What are you doing?"

Before her breathless statement was complete, she was facedown over his spread legs, his hand firmly on her bottom, holding her in place. "How many times have I threatened to do this? Do you know?" He held her down as she struggled to get up.

She twisted to look up at him. "Stop this, Dominic. I mean it."

"Six," he said, as if she hadn't spoken. "And you deserved it every time."

"No, Dominic, don't." She tried to resist as his hand slid between her legs and forced her thighs wider.

"Keep your legs open," he said sharply, flicking his finger over her clit with delectable precision.

She gasped at the shameless rush of pleasure. At the outrageous lust melting through her senses. Powerless against the disturbing desire.

"You have to learn, Katherine. You can't always have your own way." His hand came down on her bottom with a hard, brutal slap.

She hissed in shock. Her bottom quivered, the pain stinging. Then a shameful flutter stirred between her legs and she tensed against the impermissible arousal. Felt the delicious shivering ripple, the dissolving wetness in her sex.

"Answer me."

Another hard spank, the imprint of his hand etched on her pale flesh, on her confused libido. Then his other hand was on her clit, a finger perfectly placed and her soft, helpless moan rose into the silence of the room.

"I can't hear you," Dominic growled. Another sharp, smarting spank; his touch on her clit, in contrast, expertly delicate. "Do you understand?"

She gasped, filled with desire, with humiliating, hot, urgent need, her skin still tingling from his last punishing slap on her tender ass, her climax rising, coiling, making her pant.

"You have to speak, Katherine, or your bottom is going to be sore tomorrow." His hand came down again on her burning flesh. "Tell me you understand who gives the orders." Another spank, the whiteness of her bottom pinked and hot, the marks of his fingers like a brand on her skin.

"You do, Dominic, oh God, oh God," she breathed as he slid the pad of his finger past her clit to brush her G-spot.

"I can keep doing this all night, Katherine. You have to say 'I understand who gives the orders.' That you know you can't always have my dick inside you." Then he sighed as she suddenly climaxed. "Christ, I don't know if there's any point to this."

If she could have answered him then, she would glee-fully have disagreed. And when her breathing finally slowed and her tremors stopped, she looked up, smiled, and said, "I understand, Dominic. Really I do. Completely."

He gave her a forbearing smile. "Until the next time you want to come."

"We'll go see the doctor. That'll help."

He held her gaze, his lashes falling slightly. "We'll be careful till then. Right?"

She nodded. "Right."

He lifted her easily, as if she were a child. "I worry, that's all." He placed her facedown on the bed. "Are you hurt? Was I a brute?" Dipping his head, he kissed her pinked bottom with an angel-wing kiss. "I'm sorry." Another light kiss on his finger marks. "Sorry. Sorry. Sorry." Each apol-ogy punctuated with a kiss. Then his kisses slowly moved up her back and, lifting her hair, he dropped a soft kiss on her nape. "Want a cool cloth on your pretty ass?" he whispered.

Rolling over, she held out her arms. "What I want is you inside me real gently while I'm going to sleep?"

His hesitation was minute, then he said, "So long as it's my definition of gentle."

She smiled, all rosy-cheeked and sweet as candy. "Of course. You're the boss."

He was still laughing softly as he slowly entered her.

After she dozed off, he lay with her for nearly an hour before he left the bed. But after Kate had been sleeping deeply for some time, he slid from the bed, walked into his dressing room, pulled on sweats and a T-shirt, and went downstairs to his library to work.

Martin appeared in the doorway a few minutes later. "Everything all right, sir? Do you need anything?"

Dominic looked up from his computer. "Will you bring me something to eat? I didn't get much supper."

"The chef noticed, sir. Would you like wine?"

"A half bottle. I'm cutting back."

"I'm sure Miss Hart appreciates your support."

Dominic's brows rose.

"I mean since she can't drink, you're adjusting. My daughter's husband did the same thing when Jenny was pregnant."

"Ah, I see. So you're a grandfather?"

"Twice, sir. One of each."

"Congratulations." Dominic smiled faintly. "I admit, it's exciting to think about a child."

"You won't regret it, sir."

Dominic dipped his head slightly. "Now that I'm personally involved I understand that."

"Indeed, sir." The majordomo turned to go, then turned back. "Mr. Roche called twice. I told him you'd given orders not to be disturbed."

"I'll call him. And if you'd send someone upstairs to sit outside my bedroom, I'd appreciate it. Have them come get me immediately if Katherine wakes up. And once you've brought my food, you're free for the night."

"Thank you, sir."

"Do you have far to go?" Martin had been working for him for eight years and he'd never thought to ask.

"Not too far, sir. My son-in-law generally picks me up. Our families live together," he added at Dominic's questioning gaze.

"By necessity? Forgive me, I don't mean to pry, but if you need an increase in wages, I'd be more than happy—"

"No, sir. My salary is very generous. My wife enjoys having the children and grandchildren underfoot." He smiled. "And I agree."

"Should you change your mind, we certainly can be your banker for an additional mortgage for you or your daughter."

"We're quite content, sir. It's a cozy arrangement for everyone."

"I see," Dominic said. He didn't, of course, coming from a home where constant strife had prevailed. "If you're sure, then."

"Absolutely, sir. But thank you." Martin smiled. "I'll

have your supper up directly." He turned, walked from the library, and quietly pulled the door shut behind him.

Amazing, Dominic thought. Martin and his family lived together in harmony. He smiled faintly. He had a lot to learn about families. And not much time. He reached for the phone.

"You called?"

"You sound happy," Max said.

"I am. Did you know Martin lives with his daughter and her family?"

"I did. They live in a semidetached in north London. He bought it when he first started working for you."

"He said he likes the arrangement."

"He dotes on his daughter and his grandchildren."

"Apparently he gets along with his son-in-law as well."

"And apparently you just walked out of a cave."

"No shit. Thanks for taking care of the staff for me. I've never noticed before."

"You pay them top wages. They're not complaining because you don't chat them up."

"It seems that Katherine's opening my eyes to a world beyond—"

"You?"

Dominic laughed. "Yeah."

"She must be sleeping."

"Another early night," Dominic replied, amusement in his voice.

"Get used to it. Liv slept all the time when she was pregnant."

"That's what I hear from everyone. I expect my schedule's going to be erratic."

"We can deal with it. The reason I called was Star Mining is getting anxious. And you're the one who has to make the decision. They're offering you a choice between two palladium deposits. Or both."

"Which ones?"

"The Russian one and the Canadian one."

"I can't go to Russia now. It's too far from Katherine. Remind me again. Where's the one in Canada?"

"Thunder Bay."

"Jackpot. We'll take the leases there." Palladium played a key role in the technology used for catalytic converters that transformed up to ninety percent of harmful gases from auto exhaust into less harmful substances. A number of Dominic's companies were dealing with environmental issues.

"I thought you'd be interested."

"Definitely. The area's only a few hundred miles from Katherine's grandmother."

"Do you know yet when you're leaving for the States?"

"No. I'm working on it. What's the word from the doctor in Rome?"

"Gora's little girlfriend might be early, he said. The baby could arrive any day. Your divorce a day later according to the attorney."

"Jesus. Life's getting way too good. When does the rain cloud show up?"

"Maybe never?"

"That hasn't been my experience. But I'm willing to keep an open mind."

"Never hurts. FYI, I'm planning on going home next week."

"It shouldn't be a problem. As long as your phone's working."

"Always."

A small silence fell.

Then Dominic quietly said, "Did you feel as though you were...fucking born again when Liv was having your child?"

"You're asking me? Someone who's seen more killing than anyone should?"

"So it really is a new world. Not just for me."

"A beautiful new world. Wait and see."

"Everything's too perfect already. It's making me jumpy."

"Once this Gora crap is over, you can relax."

"If everything goes according to plan," Dominic said bluntly.

"I don't anticipate problems. Martin says you're not drinking much. That should help with the edginess."

"It's not about nerves. I just decided I didn't want to be a hard-drinking asshole like my father."

"That's not his only problem."

Dominic laughed. "No shit. The list is long. Look, get some sleep. I'll see you in the office tomorrow."

EIGHT

Dominic's chauffeured black S-class Mercedes pulled up to Justin and Amanda's town house the following night at precisely seven.

"Don't bother, Jake, I'll get the door," Dominic said. "Come back in an hour."

"Will do, boss."

Kate gave Dominic a spiking glance. "An hour?"

"Just in case, that's all," Dominic explained. "I don't want to wait for the car. And Jake doesn't mind sitting here."

Kate bit her lip and frowned. "I thought you said you didn't care if we went to dinner. I could have called Amanda back and made some excuse."

"I really *don't* care. And Jake always watches movies while he waits, so we can stay as long as you want." Dominic opened the back door and offered Kate his hand. "Ready to chitchat?" He smiled. "I know I am."

"Funny."

"I actually *do* want to see the baby."

Jake swallowed his shock, although he told Max later it was one of those moments when you'd always remember where you were when the bomb went off. He'd been driving for Dominic since day one of Knight Enterprises, so he had a pretty good idea of Dominic's previous nonexistent interest in babies.

Kate grinned. "Oh good." She took his hand. "Then it's not just me who's superexcited about seeing the baby."

"Hell, no. We're both feeling the same vibe. Not that we haven't from the beginning," he said, helping her out of the car.

She grinned. "I don't know about vibes, but you were killer sexy."

"And I wanted you way the hell more than I should."

"It was gypsy fate," she said lightly.

"Or just my awesome luck. Jesus," he muttered, pulling her into his body. "Do we have to go inside? We could be in bed in ten minutes and I could be making you feel really good."

"*That's* so tempting," Kate whispered, grabbing Dominic's shoulders and rising on her tiptoes for a kiss. As she looked up though, the façade of the posh four-story redbrick town house came into view and she dropped back down. "Too late," she said with a sigh. "Justin's at the window."

Dominic groaned.

"On the plus side," she said, smiling up at him, "remember, we get to see the baby." She straightened the hem of her embroidered peasant blouse. "Now tell me my clothes aren't *too* casual. This place is pretty fancy." Dominic had chosen green capris and green Bottega Veneta vans to go with the blouse. Coral, green, and white enamel and gold earrings, along with a zebra bracelet in enamel and gold on her wrist added a modest display of luxury.

"You look perfect, baby. Like the really sweet mother of my child." In couture casual that Amanda would recognize.

The brass-trimmed front door opened.

"Showtime, baby," Dominic said and took Kate's hand.

Justin and Amanda greeted them warmly. After the courtesies were observed and the state of London's traffic bemoaned, Dominic and Kate were shown into a small conservatory for drinks.

"None for me." Kate murmured, taking a seat in a tropical-print-cushioned chair near Amanda. "It's still semi-secret, but I'm pregnant."

"How lovely," Amanda replied. She glanced at Dominic. "For you both."

"We're pleased," Dominic said, sitting down in a nearby chair.

Justin served the women nonalcoholic sparkling cider and when he turned from the liquor cabinet to ask Dominic what he wanted to drink, Dominic said, "Cider's fine."

Justin stared at Dominic. "You're kidding."

Dominic smiled. "I'm not kidding."

"Fuck that. Pardon me, ladies. But I'm not drinking alone." And Justin poured two whiskies.

The women were busy talking babies on the other side of the coffee table when Justin handed Dominic his drink.

Justin lifted one brow in a silent what-the-fuck arc and when Dominic didn't respond he said instead, "You'll like this whiskey. It's a forty-year-old reserve."

"I'm sure I will." Dominic smiled. "I happen to own the distillery."

"Since when?" Justin sat down on the coffee table and raised his glass in salute.

Dominic lifted his tumbler. "Almost ten years. Cheers."

And then he took a drink of the full-bodied, perfumed smoky malt.

"So I've been helping make you rich with this top of the line liquor," Justin said a moment later, his mouth twitching into a small smile.

Amusement lit Dominic's eyes. "You're not the only one. Would you like me to send you a case?"

"Does anyone ever say no?"

"To the whiskey?"

Justin snorted and lowered his voice. "Think you can change?"

"You did." Dominic spoke as softly. "Or didn't you?"

"Yeah, yeah...okay. Although I wasn't in your league. Not even close."

"That makes it all the more sweet. Trust me." Dominic raised his glass. "To marriage and family."

It took Justin a fraction of a second to deal with the stunning wonder of Dominic openly displaying his feelings. Dominic was the most emotionally disciplined man he knew: cool, restrained, remote. Even at private sex clubs where most men exhibited a certain degree of excitement, Dominic never had. But Justin hadn't reached the rarified ranks of the financial world without the reflexes of a bull fighter. "I couldn't agree more," he said, lifting his glass. "To lovely wives and children."

Dominic drained his glass, set it down, and shook his head to Justin's silent query about a refill. Then he leaned forward, caught Kate's eyes across the coffee table, and smiled. "What am I missing?"

Kate grinned. "Nursing schedules. That won't be your bailiwick."

"I can do the diaper changing."

"Listen to that, Justin." Amanda nodded approvingly. "Dominic isn't going to sleep through the two a.m. feeding."

"Sure, make me look bad," Justin grumbled, moving to sit beside his wife on the sofa.

Dominic shrugged. "I'm a light sleeper."

"And I'm not," Kate said, smiling at Dominic.

"Teamwork, baby. Although I have the easy part."

"You could just wake me up when I have to move the baby to the other breast."

"Or I could move the baby myself," Dominic said very softly, holding her gaze. "How would that be?"

Justin grinned. "Jesus, you two. Tone it down."

"I think it's sweet," Amanda said.

Kate's face was bright red. "We just got together. Dominic's been away the last few weeks."

"Not because I wanted to be. But I'm back now." He inhaled softly. "Business," he said flatly. "It can be a pain in the ass." Then he deliberately changed the subject to something other than his recent absence. "Tell us about the children, Amanda." His voice was suddenly smoothly urbane. "We're both interested"—he smiled—"for obvious reasons. In fact, we're thinking about taking notes tonight since we're such novices."

"Would you like to see our angels?"

"Could we?" Kate practically leaped up from her chair. "I didn't know if I dared ask."

"Ask away," Justin said, quickly coming to his feet. "We're the crazy parents you hear about who think their children are perfect."

Rising from his chair, Dominic moved around the coffee table and took Kate's hand. "We already feel that way, don't we?"

She smiled up at him. "Totally."

"Along with our own kind of crazy," he said gently, gazing down at her, remembering how they'd both been baby crazy in Hong Kong. "From the very first, right?" His voice was velvet soft.

Kate took a deep breath and nodded, her eyes filling with tears.

"Hey, hey," Dominic whispered, pulling her close, running his hands gently down her back. "Everything's good."

Justin was thinking he'd seen everything now.

Amanda was thinking how nice it was that Dominic was no longer alone.

And the couple holding each other forgot where they were.

As the silence lengthened, Amanda and Justin looked at each other, unsure whether or not to intrude.

Then a baby's wail shattered the stillness.

"Oh, dear," Amanda murmured. "Bee was supposed to sleep for another two hours."

"It's the baby, Dominic." Blinking away her tears, Kate smiled at him, then at Amanda. "Please, may I hold her? I mean if you don't mind."

"Certainly. Ah...there"—the crying abruptly stopped— "the nurse picked her up. I left a bottle just in case. Come,"

Amanda said, indicating the doorway with a wave. "We'll show off our perfect children."

Kate and Dominic admired the baby first while the nurse fed her. There was no need to simply be polite. Bee was a beautiful baby.

Kate jabbed Dominic in the ribs, grinned, and said under her breath, "What do you think?"

"I think I can hardly wait," he murmured, grinning back. "Although it's going to be a whole new universe for us." He looked up at their hosts. "Sorry. This is all still very new. We're super—"

"Giddy," Kate interposed.

"Pretty much."

That was another of those tagged moments that would go in Justin's memory book. Dominic Knight admitting to giddiness—an inconceivable description for such a ruthless, intensely private man.

Amanda stepped into the small silence. "Let me show you Adam," she offered and led them into an adjacent room.

"What a darling," Kate whispered a moment later, standing by the small bed where the dark-haired toddler lay sleeping, a stuffed bunny under his arm. She glanced up at Justin. "He looks like you."

"That's what my mother said."

"I'd love to hold him, but maybe some other time when he's awake."

"If you'd like, I'll have the nurse bring the baby down once she's finished with her bottle. A sleeping baby is easier to hold than a screaming one."

Kate looked up at Dominic, smiled, then glanced at

Amanda. "I'd adore that. Maybe Dominic could hold her too. We're slightly daunted by the whole situation. Everything's happened so quickly."

"You're not alone. We weren't planning on starting a family so soon after our marriage, but—"

"Amanda forgot a couple pills," Justin said, grinning.

"Because you whisked me away for a surprise weekend." She gave her husband an amused glance. "Although we couldn't be happier how things turned out. And you are too, I can tell," she added, smiling at Dominic and Kate.

"It's a great feeling," Dominic said. "Better than anything, isn't it, baby?" he pulled Kate under his arm and kissed her cheek.

"Way better," Kate agreed, thinking life couldn't be more perfect if she had a fairy godmother with a magic wand calling the shots.

Ten minutes after they returned downstairs, the nurse brought the baby into the conservatory. Kate immediately held out her arms and as the newborn was placed in her lap, her breath caught in her throat. "She's so little," Kate whispered, then glanced up. "Come look, Dominic."

The men were surveying Justin's collection of Highland whiskies. Dominic smiled at Justin. "I have better things to do."

Walking over to Kate, seated on the sofa, he stood for a moment gazing at the captivating picture of mother and child. Then, bending, he gently touched the baby's small hand.

"Oh…look—she smiled." Kate glanced up. "Did you see that?"

"I did," Dominic murmured. "That was a sleepy little smile."

"She's just precious, isn't she?"

"Absolutely precious."

"You don't mind if we have a girl, do you?"

"Whatever you give me, baby, will be perfect."

"Are you sure?"

He squatted down so their eyes were level. "I'm a thousand percent sure," he said quietly. "Don't ever worry about me loving our child. I do already. Okay? You got that? My love for you and our baby is unconditional, world without end."

She nodded, too choked up to speak.

Amanda caught Justin's eye, signaled to the nurse, quickly rose from her chair, and shooed them out of the room.

Dominic and Kate didn't notice.

"Sometimes *love* is too small a word for how I feel about you," Dominic whispered, smiling faintly. "I need a bigger word."

"Supercalifragi—"

"Yeah, like that." Rising, he dropped onto the sofa beside her. "We must have embarrassed them." He flicked his finger at the empty room. "Not that I give a shit."

"You never do."

He shrugged. "I'll teach you how to ignore the world."

Kate grinned. "And I'll let you hold the baby if you're careful."

"Really." He looked amused. "I have your permission?"

"Careful now," she said, gently lifting the baby and

placing her in Dominic's arms. "Oh my lord, now she really looks tiny." Dominic held the baby's head in his large palm for a moment before adjusting the small blanketed form in the crook of his arm.

"They grow fast." Dominic smiled. "I remember Nicole as a newborn. Although she had a full head of dark hair instead of this blond fuzz. She liked the trampoline."

"You're not taking our baby on a trampoline," Kate said nervously.

He looked up and grinned. "Are you in charge of our baby?"

"I am at the moment."

"And looking tempting as hell in mommy mode," he murmured. "Do you suppose they'd care if we left now?" He gave her a playful leer.

She giggled.

The baby jerked.

Dominic shushed Kate with a quick kiss and the baby with a professional little jiggle. And Bee went back to sleep.

Wide-eyed, Kate watched the baby drift back to sleep. "You do know what you're doing."

"More than you, apparently. I can see who's going to be taking care of the baby."

"While you're busy at work no doubt," she scoffed.

"Not a problem. Although you're going to have to stay close because we're going to need your milk." He looked up, brows raised. "You could have the office next door to mine. We could work together on everything. Sound like a plan?"

"Tempting, Mr. Knight," she purred.

"Did I mention, most of my offices have a bedroom for

the nights I work late? Once the baby's sleeping, we could put him or her in the crib, shut the door to the bedroom, and make use of the couch in my office. Interested?"

She dropped back against the sofa cushions and shut her eyes. "Jesus, Dominic, it sounds like heaven."

"I'll give you the heaven of your choice if you agree to work with me."

She opened her eyes. "You mean it, don't you? You're not teasing about Knight Enterprises?"

"I never tease about business. Especially my own."

"You're saying we could take care of the baby together?"

"We could—or, if you don't want to, I could."

She gave him a small stunned look. "You'd do that?"

"I'd do anything for you, Katherine," he said softly. "There's nothing I wouldn't do."

She started sniffling. Shifting the baby to his other arm, he pulled Kate into the solid warmth of his body. "It's okay, baby, cry all you want. Just not too loud or you'll wake Bee, okay?"

She punched him softly so she wouldn't wake the baby.

"Wipe your eyes on my shirt sleeve. There you go. Done deal. Now give me a kiss, then we'll eat and get the hell out of here. I'm actually starved."

"You're always starved," Kate murmured. Grabbing the neck of his ocean blue Cucinelli polo shirt he'd worn in deference to Amanda's style of casual, Kate stretched up.

Dominic dipped his head and met her quick kiss, then smiled from close range. "I'm just making sure I get enough to eat to keep my strength up, baby. You like to fuck a lot." His smile widened. "Ready? Cuz, the sooner we eat, the sooner we leave." Rising from the sofa with the baby in one arm, he held out his other hand and pulled Kate up.

"I was just checking with the cook," Amanda said, bustling back into the conservatory from the hallway, where she'd been keeping watch. "Let me get the nurse for Bee and we'll have dinner."

The table was beautifully laid with fine china, silver, wineglasses, and a colorful display of mostly roses in a tall silver epergne that some artistic florist had created in order to leave the sight lines at the candlelit table free.

Amanda served as hostess with the aplomb of someone to the manor born, directing the progressive courses with an imperceptible glance or gesture. And her idea of casual, as Dominic had known, meant pearls instead of diamonds and a street-length skirt rather than an evening gown. But Justin wore jeans like Dominic and neither man paid any attention to who was serving, only to what was served. Both men ate with a hearty appetite.

"You'll get used to it," Justin said kindly, after watching Kate's gaze follow the young woman who was serving them dinner. "I put myself through Columbia on scholarships and student loans and I barely notice anymore."

"I'm sure you're right," Kate said politely, when she knew she would never get used to servants. In fact, she was wondering where the young woman waiting on them lived, did she have children, how late did she work on an evening like this, how did she get home?

Dominic smiled at the patent fraud in Kate's reply. "Katherine has an anarchist soul, don't you, baby? You don't have to change."

She gave him a grateful smile. "I'm not sure I could."

"Or would want to." He grinned. "Right?"

"Probably," she said very softly, becoming increasingly embarrassed with Justin and Amanda watching them like spectators at a tennis match.

"We'll work something out," Dominic said, equally softly. "I don't want you unhappy. You're not drinking your cider?" he added, a touch of concern in his voice. "Or eating much. Do you feel all right?"

"Really, Dominic, I'm fine." Kate wasn't going to say she didn't like the salmon tartar, although the citrus-dressed watercress was tasty. And mushrooms had never appealed to her. She'd tried to eat around the mushrooms in the risotto without making it too obvious. She *had* eaten the au gratin potatoes and some of the steak, until the sizzling grease made her think about barfing.

"You didn't like the steak?" Dominic asked gently. Both men had had seconds.

"It was wonderful." Kate smiled politely at Amanda. "I just don't have much of an appetite at the moment."

Amanda nodded. "That's perfectly understandable."

"Still, baby, you have to *try* to eat," Dominic urged softly. "Would you like something else? Peanut butter and toast? You like that."

"Not right now. I'm good."

Justin and Amanda were mesmerized; neither had ever heard Dominic speak to a woman with such solicitousness. He'd barely noticed women before—other than as sex objects.

Dominic suddenly turned his gaze on Amanda. "You wouldn't happen to have chocolate milk?"

He might have asked whether she cleaned her toilets herself, she was so shocked by his question. "Ah...we might...I'm not...entirely—"

"I'll go ask the cook." Dominic was on his feet and moving toward the butler's pantry before anyone at the table—mainly Kate—could protest.

Could I please just melt into the floor? Embarrassed to the max, Kate blushed furiously and said in almost a whisper, "Sorry. As you see, Dominic worries about me not eating."

"How sweet of him," Amanda said, having regained her composure. "I'm sure he means well."

Kate sighed. "In his own overpowering way. I'm used to eating a lot of pizza and Dominic doesn't approve."

"Pizza can be nourishing," Amanda politely noted, when it was clear she was actually saying, *Pizza, really?*

Justin smiled. "My mother made pizza from scratch. I grew up on it and I'm not exactly what you'd call stunted." He was a big man like Dominic.

"Maybe you could tell that to Dominic," Kate said, grateful for the reinforcement. "And save me the hassle."

"I heard that," Dominic said with a grin, carrying a large glass of chocolate milk. "We'll get that recipe from you, Justin. And if you drink your milk, baby, I'll do something nice for you."

Everyone at the table understood what he meant.

Pulling up a chair beside Kate, rather than take his seat opposite her and blithely ignoring her *if looks could kill* stare, Dominic handed her the glass. "Drink, baby. It's good for you."

"We'll talk about this later," she said under her breath, taking the glass.

"Be happy to," he replied cheerfully. "Would you like a straw?"

What she'd like to do was smack him. Since that wasn't an option and he damned well knew it, she drank the milk, under Dominic's sunny gaze and the barely concealed amazement of her hosts.

Opportunely, since a patent awkwardness crackled in the air, the cook suddenly walked through the swinging pantry door carrying a baba au rhum magnificently decorated in sugared kumquats and green grapes. She placed it on the table with a flourish, then deftly cut and served her masterpiece. The dessert was as delicious as it looked, topped with mounds of whipped Chantilly cream and rum sauce.

Kate had no trouble finding an appetite for it.

"You liked the baba," Dominic said, glancing at her almost empty plate. "And thanks for drinking the milk," he said quietly.

"Thanks for getting it," she spoke as softly. "That was nice of you."

Leaning over, he whispered in her ear, "I'll be even nicer when we get out of here."

She sucked in her breath as a flutter of arousal stirred her senses and settled with a delectable ripple between her legs.

"Just a few minutes more," Dominic whispered, then looked up, smiled at Justin, and reached for the port decanter Justin was pushing his way.

A few minutes later, as the dessert plates were being taken away and the men were enjoying their port, Amanda understood that if she wanted her question answered, her window of opportunity was quickly closing. "I have to ask," she said, her glance swiveling between Kate and Dominic. "And you may tell me it's none of my business, because of course it isn't, but are you planning on getting married?"

"Jesus, Mandy," Justin muttered, giving his wife a sharp look. "That's a little personal." He glanced at Dominic and grimaced. "Sorry."

"It's all right." Dominic gave Justin an easygoing smile. "We've already talked to a wedding planner. Mrs. Hastings is taking care of things."

Amanda's eyes opened wide. "Really, Mrs. Hastings." She spoke like one would on seeing a Martian for the first time—in a tone of breathless wonder. "She's incredibly difficult and overbearing."

"I'm paying her well. She seems agreeable."

"Agreeable? I didn't think she understood the word."

"It costs a little more, but she understands. We're still not certain exactly what we're doing." Dominic glanced at Kate. "But if we decide on a public occasion, you'll be sure to get an invitation."

"I'm dithering," Kate interjected. "Dominic doesn't like me dithering."

"I'll get used to it," he said, smiling at Kate.

"Like I'm trying to get used to a control freak," she playfully retorted.

Dominic's lashes lowered faintly. "You see the adjustments we're making."

Amanda bit back her startled response.

Justin choked on his port.

And a short time later, as the front door closed on their dinner guests, Amanda looked at her husband, dumbfounded. "Did you *ever* think you'd see the day when Dominic Knight made *adjustments*?"

"Not unless he was adjusting some babe's handcuffs or leg restraints," Justin drawled.

"Exactly." Amanda had been apprised of Dominic's excesses by her husband, who'd known Dominic prior to their marriage. She made a small moue. "Do you think he'll actually marry her?"

"It looks like it. Remember, Dominic's been pursuing Katherine for at least four months. And his previous arrangements with women were in hours."

"Except for Julia."

Justin snorted softly. "You saw them together. He treated Julia like a friend. A best friend, but still a friend. Unlike tonight. Dominic touched Katherine every chance he had. And he and Julia never talked about having children. He really *wants* this child. And if the size of the ring he gave Katherine is any indication of his feelings, he's definitely serious."

"That's true. I've never seen a diamond that large."

"Most people haven't. One like that rarely comes on the market."

"He can afford it, of course."

Justin quirked a brow. "But he's never chosen to buy one before."

Amanda smiled. "So what should I wear to the wedding?"

NINE

They were home by nine, Kate was sleeping by ten, and Dominic had the rest of the evening to himself. Pulling on pajama bottoms, he brought a chair up to the bed, picked up his laptop, and worked on until midnight.

If it was possible to paint a picture of contentment, he thought, this was the living image and he was living proof. His beautiful wife-to-be, who was carrying his child, close enough to touch, and their recent lovemaking had warmed his senses. Add in time for business in the quiet of the night...fuck—he had it all.

Also, Katherine no longer seemed entirely averse to joining Knight Enterprises. He half smiled. At least her refusals were less vehement. That was encouraging.

Whether it was the late hour or Katherine's presence, whether he'd drifted into some quixotic land of starry-eyed musing, he visualized Katherine as his partner both in business at Knight Enterprises and in life. A pleasant conceit that would pretty much fast track his last thirty-two fucked-up years into the realm of transcendent perfection, or, for less warped souls, take on the aura of a religious experience. Assuredly a miracle by any standard.

As if some dark spirit from his past suddenly realized it was about to lose its job, a remorseless voice out of nowhere, grunted, "Uh-uh, dude, that happiness shit is reserved for other people...not you." And all his familiar demons reappeared, warning him against chasing rainbows and about trusting people, reminding him of the countless betrayals in his life, ripping off all the scabs.

His jaw clenched at the memory of all those lonely anchorless years. "Fuck off," he muttered under his breath, shaking away the oppressive feelings, struggling to resist the desolation and punishing cynicism that had once been his life's burden. *"Fuck the hell off."*

Kate's eyes fluttered open. "What time is it?" Her cheeks were flushed, her voice liquid with sleep.

"Sorry, baby. I didn't mean to wake you." He could feel the tension in his body melt away, his fight reflex chill. The warmth in Katherine's eyes was balm against the ruin of his past. "It's a little after midnight," he added. "Go back to sleep."

"Ummm...come to bed." Her fingers slid over the top of the quilt and fluttered in silent appeal. "I need you to hold me..."

"You should sleep," he murmured, polite and virtuous.

"Don't want to," she mumbled with that little bunny twitch of her nose that always made him smile. "I need you..."

So much for virtue. "Give me a minute." He shut his laptop and leaned over to set it on the carpet.

"Hurry..." He looked up at the dulcet whisper.

She'd tossed back the covers and rolled on her side, so the curve of her hip was silhouetted against the bed curtains and her large, ripe breasts were softly mounded one on top of the other, her swollen nipples pink and huge and imminently suckable.

"Jesus, baby...I'm never going to get enough of that," he whispered, coming out of his chair in a surge of honed muscle, his fingers on the tie of his pajama pants. A second later, he stepped over his pants and moved toward the bed.

He kissed and sucked her lush nipples, watched her gently dissolve through two dreamy orgasms, half asleep, deliciously aroused, and when she murmured sweetly, "Thank you, Dominic, I'm going back to sleep," he spread her thighs and inhaled her lush moan as he pushed himself into her smooth, sleek body. She was immaculately soft and beautifully receptive and all his, he thought with naked pleasure. All his demons were laid waste. By wistful desire and hot passion, by mutual appetites beguiled and quenched. By an abundance of happiness.

It turned out to be a lazy weekend. They mostly stayed in bed. The food they ordered was left outside in the hallway; once they moved into the room next door when the staff came to change the sheets and clean the bathroom. Until finally, late on Saturday, they went downstairs for a special dinner Quinn had prepared for Kate.

Uneasy about Kate's lack of appetite, in the wee hours of the night, Dominic had e-mailed Nana for some of Kate's favorite recipes. And Quinn had done yeoman's duty on short notice since Nana's reply hadn't arrived until four.

Dominic and Kate, barefoot and semi-dressed in pajamas, walked into the large, candlelit dining room.

"Everything's so beautiful," Kate breathed as someone shut the doors behind them. "So many flowers." The scent of roses perfumed the air. Torchieres with cascading white roses framed the double entrance doors as well as the buffet on the far wall, where the food was waiting under silver domed dishes. Four large candelabra marched down the twenty-foot-long mahogany table in the center of the room, bowls of white roses were strategically ranked between the candelabra, and two place settings were visible on one end of the polished mahogany surface. She smiled up at Dominic. "You must keep the floral economy going."

"I do now," he said with a flicker of a smile. "These are for you. I usually eat in the library."

"How do you ever get used to this..."—she half lifted her hand—"splendor?"

The chinoiserie wallpaper was a faded azure in the diffused light, the lush apricot-colored moiré draperies covering the soaring windows and puddled on the parquet floor shimmered softly in the candle glow, the large furniture scaled to the dimensions of the enormous, high-ceilinged room diminished in size by the flickering shadows.

"It's only splendid with you here," he said gently, seeing the room with fresh eyes. Or perhaps for the first time. His London agent had purchased the house after Dominic had seen it online. He was rarely here; he generally slept at his office or club when he was in London.

Taking Kate's hand, Dominic moved from the doorway. "Come, see what Quinn put together for us."

The sideboard must have been built for giants. Kate had to stand on tiptoe to survey the domed silver platters and bowls as Dominic lifted the covers one by one. A tureen of tomato soup surrounded by dainty grilled cheese sandwiches, perfectly cooked barbeque ribs with Nana's sauce glistening, crunchy mac and cheese the way Kate liked it, three bean salad, and a towering carrot cake with cream cheese frosting.

Recognizing the familiar menu, Kate turned to Dominic. "You talked to Nana again?" Alarm vibrated in her voice.

"Don't panic. I e-mailed her." He drew her to the table. "And I didn't mention anything but recipes. I told her you were missing her food, that's all." He pulled out a large wingback chair for Kate at the head of the table. "Sit, baby. I'll serve us. See that footstool? Need it closer?" Leaning over, he drew it under her dangling feet.

"I'll tell her about the baby soon." Kate ran her toes over the soft blue velvet on the footstool. "Just not yet," she said with a faint grimace.

"Whenever or never, I don't care. Just so long as you're within arm's length of me twenty-four/seven," he said with a smile. "I have my priorities."

She leaned back and smiled. "I like it just us too."

"Good. Are you as hungry as me? Or is it just because Nana's food smells so good?"

Dominic did the serving honors. Kate preferred not having staff around and he preferred not being disturbed. After carrying over several plates so they each had a full array of food, he sat in a chair to Kate's right. Everything was delicious, wholesome, salt-of-the-earth cooking and he watched with pleasure as Katherine ate with an appetite he hadn't seen since his return.

Although after thirty straight minutes of eating, after numerous servings of ribs and cake, he cautioned, "Maybe you should take a rest. Let your food settle."

"I adore you for doing this," Kate said, licking Nana's

barbeque sauce off her fingers as Dominic pushed a finger bowl her way. "Don't you like carrot cake?"

"I had three pieces, baby."

"There's still lots left."

He smiled. "Maybe later."

"I think I can eat one more of those cute little grilled cheese sandwiches your chef cut into bunnies."

Dominic raised one brow and handed her a small sandwich. "Nana said you liked bunny shapes."

"But these almost look real with those little olive eyes and macaroni whiskers. How does he make them furry looking?"

"Beats me."

She took a bite. "We don't have anything this fancy at home. Nana just uses a cookie cutter," she said, chewing, then swallowing. "You can tell they're bunnies, but just barely." The second and last bite disappeared in her mouth and she shut her eyes in bliss as she chewed. "Oh Lord, that cheese is fabulous," she said a moment later. "Although all the butter the sandwiches are fried in helps too." She wiped her fingers on a napkin Dominic handed her. "You spoil me absolutely rotten, but thank you." She blew him a kiss. "It feels really good to eat."

He caught her kiss and grinned. "I like to see you eat. I'm guessing the baby does too. We'll keep Nana in the loop when it comes to recipes so you have food you enjoy."

"If your chef doesn't mind making such pedestrian fare."

"He doesn't mind."

"You're just saying that. He's probably tearing his hair out."

"Quinn hasn't had hair for years. It's not a problem. So if you want peanut butter and jelly sandwiches, or a bowl of cereal, you've got it, okay? By the way, Nana sent her bread recipe so its bacon sandwiches for breakfast tomorrow."

"Ohmygod! I love you wildly and totally! With mayonnaise?"

He laughed. She looked like a child with her red curls finger-combed messy, her eyes alight, her wide, flashing smile radiating happiness. "Yes, baby, with mayonnaise. Nana sent her recipe for that too."

"You are *so* sweet, Dominic. I don't know how to thank you for thinking of bacon sandwiches."

"If you're finished eating, you could thank me by opening your pajama top," he said softly, a lazy smile lifting the corners of his mouth.

Sitting back in the large cushioned chair, she swiftly unbuttoned the pearl buttons on the blue gingham top, pulled it open wide, and grinned. "Ta-da!"

"Very nice." His voice was velvet soft, his gaze predatory. "I might have to suck on your fantastic tits."

"Here?" She touched her nipples with the tips of her index fingers.

"There, and then we'll move on..."

Drawing her legs up as Dominic's deep voice triggered a lush, heated response deep inside, she rested her head against the luxurious azure-and-white-striped silk of the chair back. "Did you tell them to put this chair here? For me. For this?"

Dominic smiled faintly. "I manage a global empire, Katherine," he said, lounging beside her in a mahogany armchair, perfectly at home in this luxurious room wearing a gray T-shirt and flannel pajama pants. "I can manage one woman."

"Maybe," she purred, her eyes half lidded, the shimmering green aglow with desire.

"No maybe about it, Katherine. Take off your top."

"And if I don't?" Half teasing, a playful lift of one brow.

"Then I will." Pushing his chair back, he stood up, moved the candelabrum down to the far end of the table, pushed the flower bowls in the same direction, and cleared a large space on the tabletop.

She sat up. "What are you doing?"

"I'm going to eat you for dessert."

"Not here!"

"Here, Katherine. That's why I'm making room."

"People might come in," she said restively, making a choppy little gesture toward the door.

"They won't," he said, not looking up, smoothing out the tapestry table runner, pulling it closer.

"They could. Dominic! Stop!"

He glanced at her, inhaled softly, then, standing upright, he turned and walked across the large room to the double doors facing the hall. He locked them, crossed the room, and did the same to the two doors used by the staff. Returning to the table, he held her gaze, one brow raised. "Better?"

"Not really. Now they *know* we're fucking."

He thought of all the times he'd been in private sex clubs, where everyone fucked everyone. Tamping down his small impatience at such unnecessary modesty, he said mildly, "Make up your mind, baby. Locked or open. The fucking part is a given."

"I could say no."

"But you won't."

"I might."

He laughed. "That would be a first."

"Don't be smug."

"It's not about me being smug, baby. It's about you needing to fuck." He glanced downward. "I'm guessing you're going to be wanting this."

She sucked in a breath as his erection swelled before her eyes, wondered if she could resist that gorgeous, huge dick pressing against the soft fabric of his pajama pants. Wished her body wasn't turning liquid with longing so her decision could be made with more confidence.

"Come here, baby. Get your little ass up on the table." His voice dropped to a whisper. "Or do you want me to come and get you?"

A small pause while she struggled with submission, with wanting him more. With wanting him too much—as always. She slid from the chair.

With a smile he moved toward her, bent to kiss her cheek, and, leaning down, picked up the blue velvet footstool. Taking her hand, he led her to the cleared space on the table without speaking, dropped her hand, set the footstool on the tapestry runner, and ran his hand over the smooth velvet as though testing its softness.

Dominic was curiously quiet, intent, looked slightly forbidding in the candlelight, the shadows highlighting his stark features and dark brows, the inky black of his hair— his size amplified in the small pool of light. "Are you sure you want to do this?" She tried to suppress the disquiet in her voice. "I mean we—"

"I'm sure." He glanced back at her. "Take off your

pajamas. Please," he added, a fraction of a second later. *Old habits.* "Or would you like help?"

His voice was softly appeasing, the momentary curtness removed. "I would," Kate said, lifting her chin so he'd know she'd heard him the first time.

He noticed the little stubborn set of her chin, had long ago learned all the conciliatory gestures women liked. He smiled. "My pleasure, baby." Turning to face her fully, he slid her opened pajama top down her arms. Setting it on the table, he smoothly knelt at her feet, eased her pajama pants over her hips, watched them drop to the floor, and brushed his warm palms up the sides of her legs and hips as he rose from his knees. "You're absolutely perfect," he murmured. "Thank you for indulging me."

He'd taken her waist in his hands, his fingertips resting at the small of her back, and she felt both captive and captivated by the splendid man towering over her. "It's my pleasure too," she said in a covetous little whisper. "You have very large hands."

"I do."

He spoke with the calm certainty and assurance, the arrogance that recognized what she was saying. "I hope this doesn't take long." In case she hadn't made it clear.

He smiled. "Some things never change. I just have to touch you."

"That's it." She looked up a very long way, her green gaze warm, shimmering. "Old news. So?"

"So it sounds like I'd better get moving," he said with a small smile, "or you might reach the finish line before me." Tightening his grip on her waist, he lifted her easily, swung her up onto the table, and gently seated her on the footstool. He slipped his hand between her thighs, slid his middle finger lazily up her cleft. "You seem to be ready for just about anything," he said, his eyes fixed knowingly on hers.

She wished she could resist that cool appraising look, but the delicious ache lingering in the wake of his finger was taking on a life of its own, settling in like accumulated memory, reminding her of the sweet, unmerciful pleasure he offered. Then he lightly brushed her clit at the top of his stroke, reflection gave way to lust, she groaned through a fog of sensory overload, and her legs parted in unconscious surrender.

Like any competent general he recognized victory. "A little more, baby?" He pressed down on her clit with a nice blend of precision and force.

And a raw, raging delirium hurtled through her slick, pulsing sex, brought a cry to her lips—a small, choked bleat that quickly disintegrated into the vastness of the shadowed room. Her shudder was blatantly obvious though to her watchful partner, as was her blissful sigh that arrived in its own sweet time like her smile.

When she met Dominic's gaze a moment later, they were both smiling. "Good so far. Not too kinky?" he murmured, his brilliant blue gaze amused.

"How do you do it?" Her brows creased in the tiniest of frowns. "Stay so calm."

An infinitesimal shrug. "Discipline. You, on the other hand," he said with a wicked grin, "are into reckless abandonment." Sliding his palms down her thighs, he gently spread her legs wider, grasped her ankles, and crossed one over the other, leaving her sex fully exposed. "But opposites attract, right?" Brushing his fingers over her glistening, pink tissue, he drew in a small breath. "Jesus, baby, that is one fucking beautiful sight." Then he looked up, smiled an appealing smile, and resumed his conversation. "I predict a rosy future for us."

"If we don't kill each other first."

"Only in a good way, baby," he whispered, stroking her gleaming, pouty sex again, up one side, down the other, his fingers sliding languidly over her slick flesh.

She shivered as a sharp frisson of arousal spiked through her senses. Her heart started pounding, fierce desire commandeered her libido to take off the brakes. And grabbing the sides of the velvet seat, she steadied herself against her sudden nuclear-level need.

He grinned. "You okay?"

"I've been better," she muttered. "And don't tell me to relax."

"Wouldn't think of it." He ran his fingertips over her nipples, closed his thumbs and forefingers over the very tips, and squeezed just hard enough to send a sharp, wild rush of pleasure streaking downward to her sex. "We both want the same thing, baby. We just get there different ways."

She might have answered his goddamn casually disengaged comment if she hadn't been acutely attuned to the lush, incredibly intense bliss melting through her body.

A stirring of his hair brushed her cheek, then his breath warmed her ear. "Take it easy, baby. I'm not going to fuck you right away."

Kate slowly raised her lashes. "I don't need you."

"Not even a little?"

Her sharply indrawn breath ended in a tremulous sigh as Dominic slipped first one finger, then another, into her pulsing cleft, moving straight as an arrow to her G-spot.

"Want to make a deal?" he asked.

She slowly climbed back into the world, blinked. "What kind?"

"You come once now. Then I get to play." He pushed his fingers in deeper, effectively forcing the answer he wanted. Her eyes had closed again, so he whispered, "Yes, no, maybe?"

"Yes, of course," she said in such an ordinary voice he glanced up in surprise.

Her gaze was half-lidded, only marginally focused, potent need blatant, tantalizing. "I'm practicing cool insolence."

But it took her effort to speak, her breathing erratic. "Very nice, baby," he said with a small smile. "But why not just enjoy yourself instead." He ran his fingertips delicately back and forth across her G-spot. "Are we on target?" She gasped in answer. "Here too?" Another light stroke that gave rise to her quiet groan. "How about here?" He gently slid his fingers in palm deep.

No longer expecting an answer since she was feverishly panting, he gently flicked and feathered, massaged and stroked her clit, her G-spot, her slick, drenched pussy, deftly matching his fluid touch to the increasing rhythm of her hips. Effortlessly playing the game he'd played a thousand times before. Until with her usual scorching response time, she was soon shivering helplessly, his fingers were drenched, and the pink flush of arousal was spreading up her throat to her face. "Not too rough?" he whispered.

He knew the answer.

"No, no…oh God, no," she breathed, feeling a weightless, stunning ecstasy, feeling as though she had only to stretch out her hand and touch the stars.

She was close. He could feel the initial little ripples sliding over his fingers. "Want me to go further, baby? Scream if I go too far." He added a third finger. "There—still okay? How about right here?"

Her breath caught as his fingers touched the outrageous limits of sensation. "Yes, yes, oh Jesus, oh God, yes!" Her first hard convulsion suddenly hammered every overdrawn nerve, the unstoppable tidal wave began to gather power, and as the swirling rapture mounted, she quivered, whimpered softly, and tensed, waiting for the full orgasmic frenzy to break.

Her abrupt scream was flawlessly matched by the momentum of Dominic's fingers plunging deeper. As her cry ascended in a seething frenzy, Dominic dipped his head, covered her mouth with his, and appropriated her orgasmic delirium as if he deserved it, as if she yielded all to him. As if he owned her body, soul, and wild rapture.

A natural fit for a man of absolute power.

As her tremors slowly calmed, Dominic held her in his arms, supporting her through her waning tumult, ensuring she didn't slip off her small perch.

Her smile was a little shy when she opened her eyes and, leaning back in Dominic's arms, she tipped her head up and held his gaze. "Thanks for being my eunuch."

Laughter lit his eyes. "Temporarily. You're just more impatient."

"Do you want me to apologize?"

She was serious. "Never, baby." He smiled. "I can take care of myself." Sliding his hands down her back, he took her hands in his and wrapped her arms around his neck. "But if you could slow things down for a while." He kissed her lush pink lips. "I'll have my dessert."

"Would that be me?"

He nodded. "That would be you."

Then he slid out from under her arms, smoothly, she thought, like he'd done it a hundred times before. Gracefully, avoiding controversy. "I don't mind now," she said. And when he glanced back from pulling a candelabrum closer, she smiled. "Playing games."

"Thank you," he said, instead of *I know*. "Are your legs comfortable?"

"Everything's comfortable now that I just climaxed. I'm in love with the world."

He grinned. "You said that in Hong Kong that first night. I'd never heard that before."

"That's because you only knew worldly women."

"I don't know about that." His taste in women always had been democratic in scope. "But I certainly didn't know any fresh as dew young ladies like you."

"So I was a novelty."

"In a thousand different ways." He framed her face in his large hands, leaned in close, and said, whisper soft, "I started believing in miracles." Her wide-eyed innocence was even more enchanting in candlelight, her blooming ripeness more lavish, her lush curves gilded by flickering flame. "You have to tell me when you've had enough though because I'm in"—he inhaled softly—"a strange mood." He smiled. "Maybe it's you as centerpiece on my dinner table."

She grinned. "So at least I'm not the hundredth."

Not here at least. "No," he said. "You're the very first."

"Do I get to feel you inside me this time?"

He softly bit her bottom lip, then said even more softly, "As soon as we're done playing." And at her small frown, he added, "It won't take long."

When he dabbed the first dollop of cream cheese frosting on her nipple, she instantly sat up straight, sucked in her breath.

"Cold?" he said without looking up. But he knew what that little indrawn breath meant. He felt her nipple lengthen and swell under his fingertip and looked forward to having his dessert. Scooping up another little mound of frosting with his forefinger, he took his time covering her nipples, layering the creamy white frosting with exacting care, painting her areoles with the same deliberation, tidying up the borders of her areoles with warm licks of his tongue.

When he'd finished, he stood back to admire his handiwork, anticipating the pleasure in touching Katherine, exciting her, ultimately fucking her. Her skin was pale against the partial darkness of the room, the candlelight a golden sheen on her flesh, her large breasts, larger now with pregnancy, her hips more rounded, flaunting, as if she embodied the glory of womanhood.

And this beautiful, lush woman was *his*: ripe, bellyful,

replete. His own sumptuous fertile enchantress perched on blue velvet, waiting to be fucked.

"How does that frosting feel?" It was a rhetorical question; she was panting softly, her arousal clear. Her cheeks were flushed. "Be a good girl, suck this off first." He pushed his frosted finger in her mouth.

The unspoken implication in his deep, low command spiked through her sex like a hammer blow, her tongue momentarily stilled. She shifted restively on the footstool, moisture flooded her sex, and her body opened in welcome as if he'd already entered her in one hard thrust.

"You want something else, baby?" Her response had been immediate, blatant; he could smell her pussy, the heat, the instant need. "Soon, okay?" he said, withdrawing his finger from her mouth and slipping it into her throbbing sex in a light teasing penetration, with only a soft flick on her engorged clit. "Jesus, that's one stiff little clit." He slid his finger free. "Think you can wait?"

She dragged in a shaky breath, shook her head.

"Look at me, Katherine," Dominic ordered. "Speak up."

She met his bland blue gaze. "I can't," she said fretfully.

"Can't or won't?" he asked, amused.

"Both." She was trembling faintly.

"Sorry, baby, my turn first."

She clenched her thighs against the warmth spreading between her legs. "Please, Dominic!"

"Listen to me, Katherine." He took her chin in his fingers, lifted her head, leaned in close and whispered, "My. Turn. First."

Shutting her eyes, she slid her hand between her legs.

"Uh-uh, baby," Dominic murmured, jerking her arm up. "Do I have to tie your wrists? I will if you can't keep your fingers out of your pussy." He cupped her hand, raised it to his mouth, and bit one of her fingers. "Clear?"

She snatched her hand away. "That hurt!"

"Then pay attention," he said brusquely. "Now hold up one of your big tits. Two hands, baby. There you go. Higher. Higher. I can't reach it yet."

Quickly sitting up straighter, she lifted her breast until she winced.

"That'll do," he said, smooth as silk, surveying her plump breast pushed up into a billowing mound, her hands barely visible beneath the soft, flamboyant flesh. Then he smiled faintly. "Now look what you did."

His coercion always had a predictable effect on her libido; she was quivering, her sex throbbing hard, hard, anticipation vibrating through her senses. She didn't answer him. Couldn't.

"Look," he said again. "Your nipples swelled when you lifted your breast. They're showing through the frosting. You need a touch up," Dominic murmured, smearing frosting over the portion of exposed nipple. "Lift your other tit now. That nipple's visible too." A moment later, the frosting was respread. "Now try to relax. If your nipples swell anymore I won't fuck you." He softly sighed as two pink tips appeared through the frosting. "Jesus, baby, you have zero restraint. What am I going to do with you? And don't say fuck me." He sighed again as her nipples further enlarged. "Oh, what the hell," he muttered. "Put that nipple in my mouth, baby, and I might let you come after all."

She was damned near ready to explode, supersusceptible to the merest touch, so filled with lust she was beginning to twitch. And the moment Dominic's mouth closed on her nipple and he sucked so hard she felt it in her toes, the exorbitant pleasure detonated full-blown, rushed flame-hot upward through her belly, up her spine, in a wild and wilder, fiercely savage orgasm she was helpless to contain. And with a high frantic cry, she trembled and shuddered as the incendiary frenzy swept through her body, rampaged and raged until she abruptly collapsed.

Catching her in his arms, Dominic was filled with alarm, shaken by both the speed and intensity of Katherine's climax. She was incredibly orgasmic, hair-trigger swift. Was this normal? Innocuous? Not normal? Should he stop? Should he make her stop?

But a moment later, as he was grappling with fear and angst, Kate exhaled a long gloating sigh. "Ohmygod, Dominic," she whispered, leaning back, running her fingers down his cheeks, his throat, resting her hands on his broad shoulders. "I can't thank you enough. Really, I saw stars."

He felt an outrageous relief. "That's great, baby. You're okay, then?"

"Try okay times infinity," she murmured on another languorous sigh. "Seriously, don't ever leave me." Her contented smile was sunshine bright.

"I won't, baby." Lifting her hand from his shoulder, he turned her wrist to his mouth and touched his lips to the faint pulse under her skin. "But maybe we should take a break. Your last climax made me nervous. It was too fast, too hysterical."

She made a little pouty moue. "No, it wasn't. It was fabulous!"

He blew out a breath. "I'm just freaking out here a little, baby."

"You just haven't had sex with a pregnant woman before."

No shit. "That's why I want to see a doctor. Get my bearings."

"I'll be your North Star until our appointment Monday," she said cheerfully, as if she specialized in celestial navigation.

"Somehow I'm not reassured," Dominic said drily.

She smiled. "Then compromise. Just suck my other nipple lightly."

He laughed. "Heads you win, tails you win."

"You haven't come yet either," she said sweetly. "You *said* you'd come inside me. You promised."

Oh Christ. Her words, *come inside me*, had a predictable impact on his dick. *Fuck and double fuck.* Reason was taking a fast exit stage left while his erection was taking the vertical route.

"See!" She pointed as his erection swelled. "You want to."

"Of course I want to. I could screw you twenty-four/seven." He sighed. "I'm just trying to be practical."

She looked up at him from under her silky lashes. "Pretty, pretty please…"

He stood up, her hands fell away, and holding her gaze, he said, crisply, "Once, that's it. Then we go upstairs. You have to agree."

"Of course," she said, smiling. "Whatever you want."

His gaze narrowed. "I mean it, Katherine."

"Yes, yes...I understand." She held up her hand. "Scout's honor."

"You better not be fucking with me. I'm this close to saying no." He held up his thumb and forefinger, the distance between them minimal.

"I got it. Once. Don't worry."

But he did worry after her last orgasm. He worried enough to say, "Can I trust you on this?"

"Jeez, Dominic, you'd think we were negotiating world peace. You can trust and verify, okay? Once. No more. I'll be good."

He was momentarily unnerved that he was talking about *not* fucking a woman. Although it didn't take him long to recall that indiscriminate fucking hadn't brought him much happiness—or *any* happiness. "Okay, then," he said, reluctantly, as if he were about to jump off a cliff. Jerking his T-shirt over his head, he untied his pajama bottoms, and a second later, stood nude, rampant and so out of control he found that equally unnerving. He never lost control.

"Oh my God, Dominic," Kate said on a small fevered breath. "You're beautiful! Incredible!" Leaning forward, she reached for his erection.

Quickly stepping back, fevered, his orgasm pounding at the barricades, he swiftly lifted her off the footstool, flipped her over, shoved the footstool out of the way, and said, tautly, "Hands and knees, baby." But he helped pull her up, steadied her briefly, then said in minimum explanation, "I hope you don't mind but the table's too low."

She tossed him a smile over her shoulder, wiggled her bottom like she hadn't come in a month, and asked cheerfully, "Is this a good height?"

"Jesus, baby, as if I need encouragement," he said through his teeth, trying to keep it together, her slick pink pussy gleaming like a vision of paradise, framed by creamy thighs and her perfect ass.

"Fuck me hard this time," she purred, glancing back, her green gaze hot with longing, rotating her hips in a tantalizing little swivel. "I'm so horny. Please?"

"I wish I could, baby." He couldn't remember when *he'd* been this horny. Probably when he was fourteen and jacking off twenty times a day. "But after that last high-octane orgasm of yours, let's take it easy."

She suddenly shuddered. "Dominic, please," she panted, her hips twitching. "I'm fine. I need to really *feel* you *now*! Don't torture me. Just do it!" she wailed.

Dominic dragged in a breath and quickly ran through the mantras he knew for controlling his dick. But little pearly droplets were sliding down her inner thighs, her pussy visibly pulsing. Which meant the goddamn landing strip was fucking open. How could he even think about restraint with her quivering ass and succulent clit his for the taking?

Although still not completely lost to all reason, he entered her cautiously.

To another wail of discontent. "What are you *doing*?" she cried.

"Trying not to hurt you," he muttered, struggling to resist his body's urgent momentum, thinking maybe he lost control when it mattered who he was fucking. When it mattered *a lot*. But ruthlessly curbing his lust, he gripped her hips tighter, controlling her, himself.

If he hadn't been completely blindsided when she shoved her hand back and grabbed his leg at the same time she powered her pretty ass into reverse, he might have better withstood her preemptive strike.

Jesus, she was strong when she was horny, Dominic thought, wondering how vigorously he should guard his nonexistent virtue, or, more to the point, whether he should save her from herself. But he wasn't a monk, nor virtuous, and when she panted, "Harder, harder, harder!" self-discipline aside, it was just too fucking much for any man with a dick and a heartbeat.

"No," he said, even as he plunged into her. But he splayed his fingers wide over her hips, intent on trying to control the momentum, not about to be blindsided again. Thrusting hard enough to steal her breath away, he pushed in until she gasped, until she arched into his downstroke, melted around him, until her little wild desperate cries rose in heated frenzy. Begging, pleading.

But even savagely roused, Dominic knew what he had to do. Not hurt her, not hurt anything, dial it back enough to make sure she wasn't harmed. And he tried. But he didn't stop; she didn't stop. They both pitched and reeled, plunged and thrust, even as Dominic struggled to restrain himself in the frantic, dissolving chaos.

But in Katherine's insatiable mood, it wasn't long before he felt her go still, gasp, begin to convulse around him, and he held himself deep inside her—infinitely polite even in extremis for the woman he loved. His own orgasm tightly curbed, breathing hard, he politely waited and waited and waited until, at last, her orgasm burned away completely.

An explosive nanosecond later, he climaxed like a beast with bared fangs, hard and snarling, grunting and growling, coming with such primal fury he found himself shaking when it was over.

For long, hushed, improbably raw moments, neither moved, Dominic holding up Kate, who was unsteady under the strain of so many powerful orgasms, both still breathless, pleasure still tightly rocking their senses.

But driven by politesse and duty, Dominic finally gave himself a little shake, sucked in some air, then lifted Kate into his arms, sat down, held her on his lap, and gently stroked her back until she slowly opened her eyes. "I'm really sorry, baby," he whispered. "I shouldn't have done that."

She smiled. "Hey, I asked you."

He blew out a breath. "I still shouldn't have. I feel like shit."

She reached up and brushed her fingers down his jaw. "Stop apologizing. I love you. You didn't do anything wrong."

He softly exhaled. "We gotta see that doctor. Then I can stop freaking. But okay, okay," he added at Kate's frown. "Subject closed. I'll dress you and we'll go upstairs." Using a dinner napkin to wipe up some of the mess, he put Kate's pajamas back on as she rested on his lap, then came to his feet and set her back in the chair. "Are you going to fall if I let go?"

She smiled. "I'm stronger than you think."

He didn't argue, but he kept one hand on her shoulder while he pulled on his pajama pants. Ignoring his T-shirt, he picked her up, carried her out of the dining room, past the servants in the front hallway, and upstairs to his bedroom.

She was sleeping before he reached his room.

That's how strong Katherine is, dude. Keep it in mind. After tucking her into bed, Dominic took a quick shower to wake up, made a few calls, then worked on two reports that required immediate answers. That done, he climbed into bed, pulled Kate into his arms, finally relaxed, and soon fell asleep.

He came awake with a start and glanced at the clock. *Fuck...three o'clock.* Lifting Katherine's hand that was tapping his chest, he brought it to his mouth, kissed her palm, looked down, and smiled sleepily. "What's up?"

"I'm hungry."

Mentally shaking himself fully awake, he unwrapped his arm from around her shoulder and slid up into a sitting position. "What would you like?"

"I've been lying here thinking about that mac and cheese. Although I can go and get it if you tell me where to go."

"No, I'll go." He swung his legs over the side of the bed. "You won't find the kitchen in the dark."

"You don't have to heat it. Cold mac and cheese is fine."

He swiveled around as he came to his feet. "Cold? You're kidding."

"I like it cold."

"If you say so, baby. Anything else?" He reached for his robe.

"Maybe one of those leftover sandwiches."

He shrugged into the terry cloth robe. "You're not going to eat *that* cold."

"Didn't you ever eat leftovers standing in front of the fridge? Everything's cold. It's good."

"Can't say that I did." He tied the belt. "But I believe you." Standing at the door a moment later, he said, "Last chance. Any more requests?"

"I don't suppose there're any of those chocolate tea cakes left?"

"Christ I hope not. That was days ago."

"The truffle filling should still be good. Truffles last."

He sighed. "I don't want you getting sick."

"Just check, okay? Truffle filling would be sooo delicious right now."

"I'll see. I'm not promising anything. But I'll bring the rest of the food."

"I *really* want some truffles."

"If it wasn't three in the morning I'd have someone go and get you some, but I think it would be breaking and entering this time of night."

"I didn't mean for anyone to go anywhere."

"So you're just breaking my balls for some stale tea cakes."

She smiled. "Even one would be great—unless there's more."

He laughed. "Okay, stay under the covers so you don't get cold. This'll take me a while."

It took him some time because he'd never been to the kitchen of his London house. He knew it was on the lower level, but after taking two wrong turns and ending up first in the wine cellar and next in what looked to be the furnace room, he backtracked to the base of the stairs and shouted for Quinn.

Eight other members of his staff quickly appeared in various states of undress, some alarmed, others wondering if their employer was roaring drunk because he'd never come downstairs before.

Quinn moved out from the small crowd, buttoning his shirt.

"I apologize for waking everyone," Dominic said. "But Miss Hart decided she was hungry and I can't find the kitchen."

"This way, sir." Quinn motioned to his right.

"Please everyone go back to sleep. I'd like to say this won't happen again but I'm afraid it may. And I apologize in advance for what could become an erratic schedule if Miss Hart continues to get hungry in the middle of the night. She might not always want leftovers."

"Not a problem, sir," Quinn said, waving everyone off. "Follow me."

As it turned out, the kitchen was at the front of the house, and when Quinn flipped on the lights, Dominic gazed with amazement at the enormous space.

"Looks like we're ready for royal dinners."

"As a matter of fact, the kitchen *was* built to accommodate royal dinners. One of Bertie's favorite new millionaires lived here in the eighteen nineties. Bertie made him a peer in return for his splendid hospitality."

"You don't say," Dominic murmured.

Quinn grinned. "I do. If you want a peerage you're going to have to entertain more."

"That's the last thing I want to do." Dominic smiled at his chef, who looked like he could lift a house without breaking a sweat. Max had found him like he found all the rest of the staff and Dominic suspected Quinn might have fired a weapon or two in his past. "I'm not the sociable type."

"I noticed," Quinn drawled, a remnant of his Irish brogue softening his words. "So what do you need at three o'clock in the morning?"

"Some sleep," Dominic said, grinning. "But before that, I need..." And he listed the items Katherine had requested.

He sat at a long stainless steel counter while Quinn assembled the food.

"You sure nothing's to be heated?"

"Those are my orders. Personally..." Dominic's voice trailed off. "But we'd better not. Do you have children?" Demands in the middle of the night reminded him of Melanie's youngsters.

"I do. They're grown now. Great kids. My wife raised them. I wasn't home much."

"Do they like you?" There was something in Quinn's voice that allowed him to ask the question, or maybe just his own family dynamics prompted the query.

"They do. We're good friends. I came home whenever I could."

"Is your family in London?"

"My boy's in culinary school in Paris, my daughter's a teacher in Brighton, and my wife's down the hall, sir. She does your household books."

"Ah—forgive me for not knowing that. Max takes care of the hiring."

"Not a problem. You could be the devil himself for the salaries you pay. There, that's the last of it." The brawny chef delicately arranged the cakes on the tray with his beefy fingers. "Tell Miss Hart the truffle filling is fine, she might want to discard the cake. It's a bit chewy now."

"But it won't make her sick?"

"No, I froze the leftover cakes for the staff. And you can eat cake straight from the freezer, but I zapped them for a few seconds. You don't have to tell her."

"I'm good at omission," Dominic said with a small smile.

"Most men are."

"Survival."

"You nailed it, sir. Would you like help upstairs?"

"No." Dominic picked up the tray. "And thank you for your understanding. I expect this won't be the last time I'm down here in the middle of the night."

"Anytime, sir. And all our best to Miss Hart."

A short time later, Dominic watched Kate eat, politely refused the leftovers, took pleasure in seeing her devour every last morsel—including the cake—and turned back from setting the tray on the dresser to find her sleeping again.

Christ, had she developed narcolepsy? That might be something to ask the doctor. Whether it was normal to sleep all the time.

Sunday, they slept late, read the papers in bed, ate breakfast in bed, then lunch. Kate napped in the afternoon, and Dominic powered up his laptop. And as the weekend came to a close, they lay watching a movie on TV—where else— in bed.

TEN

Really, Dominic, someone should warn you about being constantly tired when you're pregnant," Kate mumbled as Dominic shook her awake Monday morning. "Jeez, you're dressed!" Dominic was sitting on the side of the bed in full CEO kit. "What time is it?"

"It's late, baby," he said. "I figured with your shower last night I could let you sleep in. But we have to move." Sweeping the covers aside, he stood, leaned down, consciously averted his gaze or his clothes would be back off, lifted her into his arms, and carried her into the bathroom. Seating her on the marble vanity, he put some toothpaste on a toothbrush, kept his eyes on her face, handed the toothbrush to her with a glass of water, and said, "Brush. Quinn packed your breakfast. You can eat in the car. I'll wait for you in the dressing room."

A short time later, he heard the toilet flush, heard the tap run, then silence. For too long.

He was on his way back to the bathroom when Kate walked out into the bedroom, a stunning image of soft, pink curves and ripe tits that had Dominic quickly weighing his options.

"I think I dozed off," Kate murmured, rubbing her eyes like a sleepy two-year-old.

Having curbed his libido by sheer, bloody-minded will, Dominic smiled faintly. "CX Capital might not get their money's worth today."

"Or for the foreseeable future if I can't shake myself out of this perpetual drowsiness."

"Is that my cue to repeat my classic line about working for me? Anytime, baby. Just say the word." He opened the door to the dressing room wider.

"Jeez, if you don't wear me down, Mother Nature will," Kate said, moving past him into the dressing room. "I should ask Amanda if she spent the entire nine months sleeping or thinking about sleeping."

"We'll ask the doctor this afternoon. I'll pick you up at three. Don't sit down," he said quickly. "We have to get you dressed and into the car."

If any of Dominic's acquaintances had been asked whether they could picture him as personal assistant to a woman, they would have stared at the questioner in disbelief.

But Kate had no way of knowing that Dominic's thoughtfulness was unique to her, so she accepted his attentions as normal. And with her energy levels close to zero, thank God he didn't mind doing almost everything.

Including feeding her a bacon sandwich in the car so her fingers wouldn't be all greasy when she got to work. "How the hell can you eat bacon in the morning?" he murmured as she savored the sandwich, "and not have that make you sick?"

"Dunno," she said, swallowing the last bite. "Comfort

food? Compulsive behavior? Some Neanderthal genetic trigger? Maybe—"

"I'm sorry I asked," he said, grinning. "Here, have some chocolate milk to wash it down." He held out a small thermos.

"I'll make this up to you someday," she promised, smiling at him as she handed back the thermos. "I'll take care of you."

"You already are, Katherine. You make each day worth living. So let me do this. It gives me pleasure."

"Okay then," she said, grinning. "I guess I'll let you."

He laughed, pleased that she made him laugh when he hadn't had much to smile about in the past. "Maybe someone so wiseass needs a spanking," he murmured, a husky note in his voice.

She looked at him lounging against the black leather seat, impeccably dressed in an ecru-colored suit for the spring weather, his hair slicked back, his teasing smile for her alone. "And maybe I know someone who could do that," she whispered back.

"Jesus Christ, baby." He blew out a breath, dragged in another, glanced at his watch. "Seriously, you have to quit your job," he said on a suffocated breath. "I need you available for me all the time. Oh, shit."

The car pulled up to the curb in front of CX Capital.

"You're not the only needy one," she breathed, her gaze riveted on the explosive rise of his erection, her body instantly responding.

"Jake will help you out." His nostrils flared, his voice was suddenly taut as a bowstring. "I'm not touching you with this goddamn raging hard-on. And I mean it, Katherine," he said curtly, his mouth grim. "You have to quit this bullshit job."

"Because you say so?" Her voice took on a sudden edge.

"Pretty much," he said through his teeth, then looked up as the car door opened. "Thanks, Jake. Give Katherine a hand, will you?"

She moved past him as he swung his legs aside.

"Three p.m.," he said.

"Fuck you."

"We can do that after the appointment," he said crisply.

As she stalked away, he shoved the Prada lunch cooler at Jake. "Catch up to her. If I try she'll toss this."

Once in her office, for thirty minutes of pure rage, Kate stared unseeing at her monitor screen while any number of sharp, pithy responses to Dominic's demand she quit work raced through her mind. Something more creative than *fuck you*. Like a barbed reminder to him that she was an independent woman with a mind of her own. Or perhaps she'd ask him who he thought he was telling her what to do, expressed entirely in dog whistle decibels. Or the real one about her not wanting to be another possession of a man who already had a surfeit of them. While the one about him being a controlling dick always reemerged spotlighted center stage.

She thought about going back to her apartment. About walking out and never looking back like they do in the movies or in nineteenth-century novels where the women always get screwed in the end.

But just then a gangly young man with floppy hair walked into her office, struggling under the weight of a large crystal vase filled with beautiful, white, blowsy David Austin roses.

Her anger melted away like snow at the equator. Disappeared in a heartbeat. Abracadabra-poof-gone. Jesus, love was a goddamn, crazy inexplicable roller coaster ride. But, honestly, no matter how angry she got, no matter how opinionated Dominic might be, it always came down to this: only he could make her feel this happy.

When she pointed, the young man set the vase on her desk, then stepped back and straightened his shoulders as if he were waiting for a reprimand or about to be pinned with some really important medal. His Adam's apple bobbed up and down, he opened his mouth, clamped it shut again, and his face turned ten shades of red. Just as Kate was wondering if he was on drugs this early in the morning, he said in a rush, "I'm supposed to say, 'I'm sorry.' He said you'd know what that meant." Then he turned and literally ran from her office.

Kate hoped Dominic had tipped the kid well because that little speech was way the hell out of that youngster's comfort zone. But Dominic's sweet gesture warmed her heart. Either he was good at this or she was supergullible, or maybe this was what love was all about. Forgetting why you were angry in a split second, making concessions you never would have made before. Being thrilled about having a baby when babies had been only in your long-range plans...as in a decade from now.

Leaning forward, she lifted the florist's envelope attached

to the neck of the vase with a bow and pulled out the card. Contemplating Dominic's uncharacteristically small script on the little card, she read:

A thousand apologies. I'm a total ass. I'll spank you very, very softly tonight to make up for my bad behavior.

Dominic had signed his name and added a happy face for the very first time in his life.

Katherine had no way of knowing he'd never considered the emoticon applicable before, but she smiled when she saw it.

She immediately texted him: *Maybe I'll let you.* And added an animated happy face that not only smiled, but also jumped up and down and waved its arms, because that's the way she was feeling. Superhappy.

So...both of them faced the considerable duties of the day in good moods. Kate even gave a pass to a couple of young kids who were hacking way above their pay grade. *Do this again*, she e-mailed to their personal accounts, *and I'll have the police knocking on your door. No joke.*

Dominic was so cheerful Max almost asked him if he was high.

"I know that calculating look," Dominic said, smiling at Max across his desktop. "Don't ask."

"You can't blame me." Max slid lower in his chair and gazed at Dominic from under his brows. "I've seen you like this before...but never at the office."

Dominic grinned. "Get used to it. Personally, it's better than any eight ball high."

"You're completely gone then," Max said drily.

"Flying high, dude. I couldn't be happier. I might even let fucking Larry off the hook for trying to screw me out of that office building in San Francisco."

"He'll do it again then. He'll figure you're soft."

"Maybe I am right now."

"Hopefully not for long," Max muttered. "Or your bottom line's going to suffer."

Dominic leaned back in his chair, crossed his arms behind his head, and gave Max an easy smile. "Don't worry. I can screw Larry later. He'll try it again. We both know that."

Max slid upright, his worried frown gone. "Good. I thought I'd lost you there for a minute."

Dominic shook his head, dropped his hands, and leaned forward slightly. "I'm not that nice. You know that better than most. Although I'm going to have to alter some of my behavior, or at least be careful where and when I'm a prick. Katherine's coming aboard in case that's news."

"I figured. When?"

"Whenever I can convince her to quit CX Capital."

"Joanna has her check."

Dominic's brows lifted slightly. "Did she want much?"

"Not really."

"Send her a thank-you check then. Twenty percent."

"That should bring a smile to her face."

"Not as big as mine when she tells Katherine she can buy her out."

"Then it's happy times all around," Max drawled. "Since

you're in this don't-give-a-shit mood though," he added more coolly, "just a reminder. Don't forget the video conference this afternoon."

"I'll come back for it. Katherine and I have an appointment with a doctor at three thirty. A woman this time."

"Sounds like the gender matters."

"Yeah."

Now that was the clipped, curt tone Max was used to. "Do you want Helen to stay until your conference is over?"

"No. She can go home at five. It's nothing I can't handle."

Dr. Fuller was young, slim, boyish, her long brown hair worn in a ponytail, her toothy smile attractive. She greeted them at the door to her office and shook hands with a firm solid grip. Waving them to chairs in front of her desk, she took her seat behind it and smiled again. "This isn't an emergency, I understand, but pressing." She'd been persuaded to make the time for this appointment by two prominent doctors she knew; Dominic Knight had been in a hurry and had called in some major favors.

"We don't know anything about pregnancy," Dominic said, with a polite smile. "So we have some urgent questions." He shrugged faintly. "Or at least urgent to us." He glanced at Kate, lightly touched her hand where it lay on her chair arm; his voice took on a tender note. "Do you want to start?"

Kate smiled. "Sure. First, is it normal to be tired all the time? Other than that, I feel fine. Well—except for some morning sickness." She grimaced. "How long can I expect *that* to last?"

The doctor answered Kate's questions, then Dominic's,

which had to do with Kate's lack of appetite and his concerns about how much sex was too much sex. Neither of his questions garnered any hard or fast guidelines, which wasn't very helpful to his peace of mind. But the doctor added at the end, "You needn't feel alone in your ignorance. Everyone does the first time." She smiled. "It's quite a learning curve. Now if you don't have any more questions"—she waited a moment, then came to her feet and waved toward the door—"shall we?"

Dominic went with Kate into the exam room, standing beside her and holding her hand once she was on the examining table.

The doctor smiled at Kate. "Now, tell me if you're uncomfortable." And she began the examination. "Everything looks normal," she said a few moments later, and Dominic helped Kate sit up. "We'll send you home with some vitamins and a pamphlet with suggestions for mitigating morning sickness. And sleep when you're tired, if you can. It's nothing to worry about. Some women just need more sleep when they're pregnant. And we'll see you in a month."

As the doctor left the room, Dominic leaned over and spoke to Kate. "I'll settle up at the front desk while you're dressing. Okay?"

Quickly exiting the examining room, he caught up with the doctor in the hall. "I have a question I didn't want to bring up in front of Katherine."

Dominic Knight would have been a stunning man even without the trappings of wealth and power. But the last two were subtly evident in his tone. "Would you like to go back to my office and speak privately?"

Dominic shook his head. "This is fine. I just wanted to ask about the effects of Depo-Provera on the fetus. The information online is all over the place. Anecdotal and otherwise. Katherine had the injection not long before becoming pregnant."

"Then you know that some studies show no significant difference in birth weight, birth defects, or mortality; others show higher risk. We just don't know because we don't have any controlled studies of the wider population, although the UK has actively been promoting the drug as a contraceptive since 2008. Without undue problems, I might add." She smiled faintly. "I wish I could give you a better answer. Obviously, this was an unplanned pregnancy. Is it a concern for you?"

Maybe it was her expression or tone of voice, but he recognized what the code word *concern*, meant. "I'm not concerned except for the child's safety. Unplanned or not, we're both very pleased about the pregnancy."

"Is your fiancée worried?"

He looked startled, as if his mind had been elsewhere. "We haven't discussed it. If she's worried, she hasn't said so." His mouth twitched faintly. "Katherine's in IT so I'd be surprised if she hasn't already looked into this." He smiled. "I'm probably just overreacting."

"Statistically, it's not a problem—if that's of some comfort."

"Yes, of course. And thank you for seeing us today."

"My pleasure. We'll see you again in a month."

Not if he could help it. His plane was at Heathrow, his pilots on call. He smiled. "I'll make the appointment now."

ELEVEN

D ominic's London operation was in a typically Victorian grandiose mansion on the Thames that he'd bought strictly for the view. His office on the second floor faced the great sweeping curve of the river, the spectacular vista framed in floor-to-ceiling windows he'd had installed after he purchased the property.

There was a security guard at the door and a receptionist behind a counter in the entrance hall. And Dominic greeted them both with a nod and a smile as he escorted Kate to a caged elevator tucked into the curve of an impressive but strange art nouveau/Egyptian motif stairway sweeping up to the next level.

Kate smiled as he slid the wildly ornate and gilded black wrought iron door open for her. "This has to be original," she said, stepping inside.

"Yup," he said, following her in. "We restored it. Expensively. We had to have parts retooled." He pulled the door shut, punched a button, and the cage began to rise. "It's no longer a death trap."

"Good to know." She gave him a teasing upward glance. "Was there a body count?"

"There might be now." He faked a lunge; she squealed, and he grinned. "Don't fuck with the boss, baby. You'll always lose."

"Hey, be nice. I *like* to fuck the boss," she murmured and took a step toward him. "It's one of my all-time favorite activities." She reached for the elevator control board. "Let me press this little button here and—"

"Uh-uh." He brushed her hand aside.

"Why not?" She was genuinely startled.

"This isn't a good time," he said calmly.

"What if I want it to be?"

He gave her a cool look. "Don't start, okay?"

The elevator came to a stop on their floor.

"Maybe I'll just wait outside in the car," she said, her tone pissy.

Forcibly cranking down his temper, Dominic reminded himself that his former selfishness was no longer expedient, that this temperamental woman was the love of his life, the mother of his child, and the virtual sun that warmed his world. "My apologies, Katherine," Dominic said with exquisite courtesy and minor restraint because it was all well and good to rationalize away one's temper, but getting it to disappear completely was another matter. "If you'd give me a pass on having sex right now, I'd appreciate it." He blew out a breath. "I'd appreciate it a whole lot."

"Oh God, I'm so sorry," Kate breathed, contrite and full of regret when she saw how generous Dominic was in accommodating her. "I'm such a selfish bitch harassing you when you have this business call on your mind and it's already been a long day and really...I apologize. My temper is deplorable."

"My temper's not any better." He held her gaze and

smiled. "Look, let's just get through this call and then we can fuck with each other in a good way. Okay?"

She bit back her wisecrack remark and said, "Okay," like a well behaved, understanding, compassionate adult.

"Perfect." Drawing back the elevator door, he waved her out. "Take a left."

The walnut paneled corridor was hushed, gold-framed maritime paintings she now recognized as Dominic's preference lined the walls, and a thick carpet underfoot helped muffle the sound of their footsteps.

"This conference call might take a while. Feel free to sleep through it if you want. I wish I could. Here, this is it." Opening one of two decoratively inlaid doors, he ushered Kate into a large sunny office lined with bookshelves and furnished with two seating areas, one near a fireplace; a large library table with chairs was centered on a floral Isfahan carpet. Across the large anteroom, another set of equally elaborate inlaid doors led to an inner office, its gatekeeper seated at her desk, regarding them through owlish dark-rimmed glasses.

Kate flashed a quick startled look at Dominic, but he was smiling at the stout, gray-haired woman in a purple suit, her pursed lips glossed in startling magenta. "Afternoon, Helen." He pointed at a vase of yellow daisies on her desk. "Are the flowers from your garden?"

"Of course."

"I should know, right?"

"It's been ten years," she said drily, her gaze shifting to Kate. "Now show me your manners."

"I was getting there," Dominic said with a grin. "Helen meet Katherine. Mrs. Langdon, Miss Hart, my fiancée."

Dominic's assistant masked her surprise at the word *fiancée*. "Please, call me Helen," she said with a smile.

"Everyone calls me Kate." Kate did an equally good job concealing her shock on seeing the grandmotherly figure behind the desk. "Most everyone," she added, giving Dominic a teasing smile. "Dominic stands on ceremony."

"I'm surprised." The woman's gaze slid to her employer. "He generally prefers informality in every aspect of his life."

"And Helen keeps trying to teach me manners."

Kate grinned. "Really, you think he's teachable? I haven't noticed that trait."

"Ha!" Helen exploded, jabbing a finger at Dominic, her purple nail polish with sparkles flashing in the light. "Now I have an ally."

"You and everyone else looking to teach me something," Dominic said drolly. "Go for it. Maybe I'm ready to change."

If getting married was any indication, Helen thought, *major change was already on board.* "If that's true, it's about time," she said with a lift of her eyebrows. "I'll say no more."

"I wish you wouldn't." He held her gaze for a telling moment. "Seriously."

"Certainly, sir." But she took affront that he even considered she might disclose his private matters.

A small silence fell.

"No offense, Helen," he said smoothly, his voice the kind reserved for diplomatic impasses that required extraordinary tact. "You understand."

"Yes, of course. None taken." Her pride aside, she was

gratified Dominic cared about a woman enough to be concerned. "Max told me to remind you that Hobbs has joined the consortium and he's always touchy," Helen said, businesslike again, as if the veiled exchange hadn't occurred. "And I'm telling you to try not to swear too much," she added in a brisk, motherly tone.

Dominic made a face.

And for a second he looked like an unruly child, Kate thought.

But a second later, the protective armor he wore for the world was back in place. "Thanks for the advice," he said neutrally. "But moral fanatics are a pain."

"That's your decision, of course," she said coolly.

Dominic smiled. "Thank you, Helen. It's good to know I still have a vote."

Mrs. Langdon's little sniff reminded Kate of Nana.

"Max also said he might be back before the conference is over," she said with composure, as if none of the previous conversation had taken place. "It depends how long the meeting lasts at the naval ministry."

"That's fine. I don't need him. And I don't need you, so go on home. I'll see you in the morning. And I like your purple nails," Dominic said with a flicker of a smile. "They're rockin'."

Kate watched the eyes behind the owlish glasses light up with pleasure.

"I thought it was a nice contrast to my yellow daisies."

"You've got the eye, Helen. It's perfect. Now get the hell out of here. Mike likes it when you're home in time for a drink before dinner."

"Don't forget about Hobbs." Like any mother, she was undeterred by his resistance.

"I'll give him a break the first three times he annoys me. How about that?"

Helen shook her head. "How you manage to make a living is beyond me." But she was smiling as she took her purse out of her desk drawer.

Dominic ushered Kate into his office, showed her the spectacular view of the Thames, then waved her to a green leather chesterfield sofa. "Make yourself comfortable. Helen ordered some food for you."

"Is she a relative?" Kate asked, sitting down. "You don't defer to many people."

He smiled. "Only you, baby."

"And Helen apparently. So?"

"She's not a relative, but she's worked here a long time. If you think I defer to her, I must." Another polite smile and he moved toward his desk. "Now if you eat the good stuff, there are truffles for dessert."

"You're not going to answer me?"

"I thought I did." He turned to face her fully. "I'm not good with feelings, baby. You know that. I like Helen. Maybe that's all it is."

"Okay, if that's all I'm going to get." Swinging her legs up on the sofa, she leaned back against the armrest.

He sighed softly. "I really wish I could help you out, baby. But I just have an empty space where normal people store their feelings." He grinned. "I blame my parents for that like I blame them for my other ten million fuckups. Now eat something and you can have the truffles."

As usual, Dominic was avoiding a conversation about his feelings, so Kate politely gave up. "What if I want to eat the truffles first? You're not the boss of me, you know," she said with a smile.

He laughed. "That's always debatable, isn't it, baby? But this time"—he tapped the box on his desk—"you'll have to get by me to eat these first."

"I might be able to do that," she said, softly, beginning to unbutton her suit jacket.

He swept the box off the desktop, slid it in a drawer, and locked it. "And maybe you won't."

She stopped unbuttoning. "Just so you know—you're being cruel to the mother of your child."

"But good to our baby." Dropping into his desk chair, Dominic loosened his tie and collar button. "And I'll be really nice to you as soon as we get home. So be a good mommy, eat the Caprese salad at least. You like them. Then I'll unlock my drawer."

"You're an appalling tyrant," she muttered.

He smiled. "Do it and you'll get a reward. Two of them—the truffles, then me in the kind of tyrannical mood you like."

She gave him an almost smile, part wicked, mostly sweet. "You do know how to deal, Mr. Knight."

"I do, Miss Hart." His blue-eyed gaze was amused. "Did I mention, you can come as many times as you wish?"

"You know that's one impossible-to-refuse proposition," she said with a smile, mentally tripping through Dominic's garden of sexual delights. "Particularly the many times part."

His voice dropped in volume and he leaned forward slightly, his blue gaze intense, magnetic. "You like that clause? I could put it in all our deals."

"Jesus, Dominic..." She shut her eyes, felt the deep resonance of his voice slide through her body, melt, hot and needy deep inside her, and ignite all her libidinous urges.

He glanced at the clock, wondering if he had time, saw he didn't, flicked on the TV instead, found a noisy game show, and waited for Kate to open her eyes.

When she did, she said, a tad sullenly, "Don't you ever just lose it?"

"With you? Constantly. I just about passed on this conference call."

"But you didn't."

He held her gaze. "Do you want me to?"

"Yes, of course I do—no don't," she quickly said as he reached for his phone.

He looked up. Sat back in his chair. "Your call, baby. And I never do shit like this for anyone but you, so when it comes to losing it"—he smiled—"you're my one-person mutiny, turning my life ass-backward." His smiled widened. "I mean in the nicest ass-backward way."

"Oh jeez..." She took a deep breath, shut down the bitch inside her who wanted her own way this *second*, exhaled, and spoke in her mature adult tone of voice. "An hour, right, and then we can go home?"

"Less. I'll make it less."

"Thank you. And I should eat something good for the baby, shouldn't I?"

"I'd be very grateful."

"How grateful?"

He laughed. "Until you can't stand it grateful."

"Am I too demanding?" Her smile was playful, the twinkle in her eyes teasing. "Just asking, cuz I could try and be better."

H grinned. "So far I've managed to keep up."

"You are sooo unbelievably, totally lovable," she purred. "And I know I'm the only woman who's ever said that to you."

"Absolutely, baby. The very first." *The first that mattered.*

"Okay, then. I promise to behave."

"Only for a limited time, baby. After that we'll play as long as you want."

So Kate dutifully ate the salad, Dominic carried over the small box of truffles, said, "You're the best mommy," set it in her lap, kissed her on the forehead, returned to his desk, and started powering up the bank of TV screens.

"In case you do join the business, baby, you might like to listen to this call. We're putting together a new project near Thunder Bay."

She looked up from selecting a truffle and stared at him. "Canada? That Thunder Bay?"

"Yup. We've leased a six-mile strike of palladium. The mine should be operating in three, four years."

"You know how close that is to Nana."

He kept punching buttons on a console. "I do."

"Was that a factor in your decision?"

He looked up and smiled. "It was *the* factor, baby. The other leases were in Russia. Three minutes and counting. Now two of the investors are decent, no bullshit guys who know it takes time to make money with a project like this.

One, the Hobbs Helen mentioned, is a righteous prick who I may or may not decide to toss. The last investor is an engineer with two other palladium mines."

"Why is he interested if he already has two?"

"Same as me. It's a good deal. And Anton and I get along. We've known each other for a while."

"He's not in the righteous prick category then."

"No."

There was something in his voice. "He's a partner in your vices."

"Was. Don't hold it against him. He's smart and cool-headed. Both useful in some of the places we do business. Now, feel free to speak up if you wish. Would you like to be introduced?"

"God no." She put up her hand. "I'll just watch."

Dominic was pleased she was interested. He thought she would be, but then Katherine could be unpredictable. "Just a word of warning. If Hobbs pisses me off, I'm going to cut him loose. Now I might be blunt so don't be shocked."

"I'm pretty hard to shock."

He smiled. "One of your many charming qualities." He glanced at his watch. "Another minute. And I'd really like you to learn deal making, baby," he said, softly.

"I know. I'll pay attention."

Christ, he felt as though Aladdin's genie had granted him all his three wishes, then thrown in the lamp and the cave filled with jewels as a bonus. "Thanks, Katherine," he said, holding her gaze. "I mean it." Then he hit a few buttons and four screens came on air. "Good afternoon, gentlemen." And Dominic morphed into the carefully calibrated, pleasantly official, cool, discerning CEO. "Is everyone ready to talk money?"

Kate watched, fascinated, as Dominic smoothly laid out the project, the short- and long-term goals, the difficulty of dealing with some countries, those categorized in terms of complexity.

The two older men clearly had worked with Dominic before. They trusted him, their investment, found the time frame for profitability realistic, gave their approval after their questions were answered. Anton spoke with a South African accent, was blond and broad shouldered, handsome in a rugged, weathered way; an experienced mining engineer, his only question had to do with whether he could stand the cold winters in Canada.

"All I want is your money, Anton," Dominic said mildly. "Otherwise keep your ass in Paris."

"Speaking of ass, I saw Danielle—"

"My fiancée's here," Dominic warned him quickly.

"Sorry, mate." Then Anton whistled. "Fuck! Did I hear that right? Fiancée?"

"You heard it right," Dominic said in clipped accents. "Now about the licensing permits."

"Holy shit! I don't believe it. You gotta be kidding!"

"I'm rolling my eyes, here, Anton, in case you're not paying attention," Dominic said. "Do you have any questions about mining?"

Anton laughed. "Christ, don't give me a line like that. It's too fucking tempting."

"Must we have this continuous vulgarity?" the pudgy-faced Mr. Hobbs snapped.

"It's a couple of swear words, Hobbs. Get a life," Anton drawled.

"I have a perfectly fine life," Hobbs retorted, peevish and glowering.

"No you don't. You have an incredibly dull life. When's the last time you had a really fine piece of ass? Although," Anton said with cocky grin, "maybe you can't get it up anymore. You know what they say about men who wear bow ties."

Dominic sighed. "Jesus, Anton, how the hell drunk are you?"

"Do I have to be drunk to know Hobbs might as well kill himself now because his life isn't going to get any better?"

The two older men chuckled; Hobbs turned purple with rage.

"I won't invest a penny if *he's* a partner," Hobbs emphatically asserted, bristling with fury.

"Relax, Hobbs," Dominic said. "Anton's been drinking. When it comes to mining he knows what he's doing."

"There are other mining engineers. Sober ones. Ones who don't feel the need to constantly use vulgarity."

"Everyone swears, Hobbs." Dominic spoke with quiet restraint. "Don't make a big deal."

"I beg your pardon," Hobbs hotly protested. "Medard *insulted* me! It's your decision, Knight. He goes or I go!"

"I'm sorry you feel that way, Hobbs. Maybe next time." Dominic clicked off his screen. "Happy now, Anton? Can we get back to business?"

"Goddamn right, mate. So when's the wedding?"

"Shut the fuck up. I want to go home. Let's get this over with."

The discussion turned to the purchase of mining equipment, the construction of the road and rail line into the wilderness area, the procurement process for licenses. Once the licenses were processed they agreed to meet on site. After that, the next conference call was scheduled, then everyone signed off.

"You have the majority share," Kate said into the quiet of the office as the TV screens went black. "Is that typical?"

"Necessary." Dominic smiled. "No surprise—I need control. I only bring in partners on large projects like this. Setting up a mine takes years. Normally, I'm sole proprietor of any company I buy. That way I don't have to deal with people like Hobbs."

"You were never going to keep him were you?" Kate said.

Dominic shrugged. "Probably not. I don't like him. Max tolerates assholes better than I."

"He seemed like a—"

"Asshole?"

"I was going to say a prissy old lady."

"No, that's his wife," Dominic countered, shutting down his computer.

"You're kidding. He has a wife?"

"Baby, you still don't get it. He has money. He could have several wives if he wanted."

"Really. Several wives?" she said, with dangerous emphasis.

"Relax, baby. It was a general statement. You're about

all I can handle." He smiled. "Speaking of handling"—he abruptly stopped, his gaze suddenly trained on a man in the doorway. "Get out," Dominic said, his eyes slits, his voice cold as ice. "I have nothing to say to you."

"She's a nice little handful," the well-dressed man in the doorway said, a familiar resonance to his voice as he stared at Kate. "Small. You don't like them small, but I'm guessing that virginal beauty along with those big tits made you change your mind. She's a live-in I hear."

Before the man had finished speaking, Dominic was on his feet and halfway to the door. "Ignore him, Katherine," he said, very softly as he passed the sofa. "I'll be back in a minute."

As Dominic shoved him out the door, Katherine heard the man say, "She must be a really good fuck. You've never done live-ins before."

There was no question in her mind who had brought Dominic to his feet like a shot, even though the resemblance was minimal: different color hair, inches shorter, features only vaguely alike. The older man's slight air of neglect, excess weight, and face coarsened by age and drink only broadened the disparity between father and son.

Gramp's cousin Wally had been an alcoholic with that same wastrel look. But Gramps had always said, "Wally's not a mean drunk." She suspected Dominic's father was.

Dominic hustled his father through the anteroom and into the corridor, his grip on the elder Knight's arm brutal. "You're such a prick," Dominic muttered, so pissed at his comments to Katherine that he was seriously thinking of beating his father. "I thought you were in LA."

"Keeping track of me?" Charles Knight was too arrogant to know fear. Or perhaps he still considered his son the seven-year-old he'd left behind. Or maybe the liquor gave him courage.

"I try." *His father had to have flown in last night.*

As if on cue, half breathless as Dominic forced him down the hallway, Charles panted, "I want in on the palladium deal."

"Too fucking bad," Dominic said through his teeth.

Whether he hadn't heard Dominic or didn't care, Charles spoke a little louder. "I have contacts in…the Canadian… parliament. Good ones. Greedy men."

"Jesus, have you lost your fucking mind? You think I've forgotten what you tried to do to me with NASA?"

"It wasn't personal, just business."

"It was fucking personal to me. You tried to bankrupt me."

"That was…years ago." Knight senior was breathing hard. "Get over it. I'm…your father."

"No you're not." They'd reached the top of the stairs. "I should toss you over the railing. No one would give a shit," Dominic growled, taking the stairs two at a time, pulling Charles after him like a rag doll. "Including your latest wife."

"What the fuck…do you know…about marriage," his father gasped, trying to catch his breath. "You never…had a real one."

"Listen up, motherfucker," Dominic said curtly, reaching the bottom of the stairs, swiftly striding toward the outside doors, his fingers like vises on his father's arm. "If you dare contact any of my investors I'll tell your new wife about the little girlfriend you set up in that apartment in Malibu. Nikki might want that Mercedes coupe you gave to what's her name, Tanya. And if that's not enough of a deterrent, I'll have someone break your knees. Don't think I fucking won't." He shoved the door open and swept through it. Dragging his panting father down the outside stairs, Dominic shoved him toward his waiting car. "Don't come back! And stay the fuck out of my business!"

Charles Knight stumbled onto the car door held open by his stone-faced driver.

"Listen up, Franco, if you're stupid enough to drive him anywhere near me again," Dominic said with deadly precision, each syllable crisp and clear so the driver didn't miss a word as he hurried around the front of the car to get behind the wheel, "I'll have your tires shot out. Maybe they'll miss the tires and hit the windshield. Armor-piercing rounds. Got it? I'm more dangerous than my father. He's getting soft in—" Before Dominic could finish, the driver slammed his door and punched the accelerator. As the car sped off into the street, Dominic tilted his head left, then right, to loosen his tight neck muscles. Not that it did much good. He could feel the tension like full-body gridlock. He took a deep breath and turned. Now to apologize to Katherine.

But he stood and waited when he saw Max running down the stairs.

"I was coming up from the garage when I saw you and your old man," Max rapped out as he skidded to a stop in front of Dominic. "How're you doing?"

"Good. He's fucking gone." Dominic lifted his brows. "The bastard was looking for a seat at the table on the palladium deal. How's that for clueless? He thought I should cut him in because he's my father."

"Jesus," Max muttered. "The man's without shame."

"No shit. And he was rude to Katherine. I damn near beat him to a pulp for that."

"Good thing you didn't," Max said bluntly. "That would have been a problem you didn't need."

"Or Katherine. She was more of a deterrent. She probably wouldn't have understood if I'd put my old man in the hospital." Dominic shrugged, then winced as his rigid shoulder muscles screamed their dissent. "The prick was drunk as usual." Dominic sighed. "Who the fuck let him in anyway?"

"The new guy at the door. He's been here only a week."

"He should know better. No one gets in without my approval. Did he miss the lecture for Christ's sake? You'd better put a photo of my father in the security guards' break room. I don't want a repeat of this." Dominic nodded toward the entrance. "Is that the guy?"

Max turned to look. "Yeah."

"I'll have a few words with him."

Dominic crossed the drive, took the stairs at a run, stopped in front of the young man stationed at the door, and met him eye to eye because Max had height and weight requirements for the security staff. "You saw that, so you know you fucked up, right?" Dominic's voice was hard as nails.

The young man looked down and the sun gleamed off his skull with his military haircut. "Yes, sir," he mumbled.

"I should fire you, but Max says you're new. Look at me.

Here's the deal. That was your one fuckup. You won't get another. That was my father I just shoved into that car. He won't ever get into this building again. Clear?"

"Yes, sir."

"No excuses."

"He said he was your father, sir."

Christ, the kid's eyes were wet, his voice wobbly. Dominic sighed. "Relax. My old man's a complete prick. But I suppose you haven't read that memo yet. You probably have a normal family. Or at least what passes for normal."

"I think so." The security guard wondered if it was a trick question; then Dominic's scowl disappeared and he said more firmly, "Yes, sir, I do. I have a wife and a baby too."

"Good for you. Make sure you take care of them," Dominic said, the tenor of his voice softening.

Figuring it was always safe to answer in the affirmative, the guard said, "I intend to, sir."

"Good. Okay." Dominic rubbed the back of his neck in silence for a moment while the young man tried not to breathe too loudly. "If you have any questions—what's your name?"

"Forbes, sir."

"Okay, Forbes, if you have questions, always check with Max, or Leo if Max is gone. Or whoever knows more than you, which is pretty much everyone at this point," Dominic said with a small smile. "And don't fuck up my day again. Letting my father in is at the very top of my bad day list. Max'll be putting a photo of my father in the break room. Memorize it. Are we on the same page now?"

"Yes, sir."

Dominic blew out a breath, let his hand drop from his neck. "How old is your baby?"

"Three months, sir."

Dominic smiled. "Getting much sleep?"

"Enough, sir."

"Boy or girl?"

"A boy."

"Congratulations."

"Thank you, sir."

"Now, don't screw up again," Dominic said brusquely. Then he abruptly turned away, opened the door, and walked inside. Moving quickly up the curved staircase to the second floor, he did some slow breathing as he strode down the corridor, flexed his fingers a few times. Felt a sudden shot of happiness knowing that Katherine was waiting for him.

A few moments later, he stood in the doorway to his office and smiled at the woman who'd given him a life, a future—a really epic future. "That was my father," he said. "I apologize for his rudeness. He was vulgar and offensive. I'm sorry you had to hear any of that. Deeply sorry."

"It's not your fault, Dominic. Don't worry about it."

Dominic smiled. "Thanks, baby. With any luck, we won't ever see him again. Although there're no guarantees. My father shows up from time to time, usually drunk, always wanting a cut of my deals"—he grimaced—"or the whole fucking deal. He doesn't need the money. He's just an asshole. Ready to go home?"

"Sure." She rose from the sofa. "Are you okay?"

"I'm fine."

"You don't look like him."

"Thank you."

"You look like your uncle Jordan with the yacht business."

"I keep telling myself that. Is that enough for now? Or do you need more of an explanation?"

"Whenever or never, as someone once said to me." She smiled. "We could talk about baby names on the way home."

His smile was a slow unfurling of tenderness. "Jesus, Katherine, how did I get so lucky to find you?"

She grinned. "Max found me."

"But I talked you into staying," he said, a ghost of a smile on his lips.

She dipped her head and looked up at him, the green of her eyes filtered through her thick lashes, the warm glow of love unclouded. "So we're both lucky."

As if their luck was suddenly piling up heavenward, Dominic received a call from the doctor in Rome on their drive home. "You have news?" Dominic asked gravely. "When?" His brow furrowed slightly. "Why the delay?" He listened for a few seconds more, then said, "Thank you," hit End, and slipped his phone into his jacket pocket.

"That was cryptic. Problems?" Kate asked, trying to decipher his expression.

He shook his head. "No. Actually, problem solved. The baby has arrived." Ten days ago, although he didn't explain that the doctor had been kept incommunicado until Gora could get there. Nor was he about to go into any detail

when he and Katherine had broken up over his forced marriage. Taking her face in his hands, he suddenly smiled.
"We're free. Care to get married tomorrow?"

"Really?" Her squeal registered with Jake through the
privacy glass.

Dominic laughed, pulled her into his arms, and said
very, very softly, "It's over. All the bullshit of the last three
months is finally over."

"Now you're just mine."

"I always was, but now it's fucking legal."

"Boy or girl?"

"I didn't ask; I don't care. Is that okay with you? And I'm
serious. Let's get married tomorrow."

"At the risk of pissing you off, could we wait until the
weekend? I do have to work tomorrow," she said, her voice
softly tentative.

He knew how she felt about her work; he always had.
Except when he was being selfish. "Sure, baby. The weekend's fine. Mrs. Hastings probably would prefer not being
forced to put on a wedding with only a few hours' notice.
This gives her four days."

"So are you happy?" She twisted in his arms so she
could watch his face.

"Just a little," he said with a grin. "How about you?"

"I'm without words."

"No kidding. Let's celebrate tonight."

"What exactly does that mean?"

"Would you like to go out to dinner?"

"Not really."

"See a play?"

"Uh-uh."

"Visit Justin and Amanda?"

"Keep it up and I might say no to this wedding."

"I'd bet you'd like to come a few times?"

"How many?"

"That's up to you, baby..."

TWELVE

I apologize but I'm going to have a couple quick ones." Dominic turned from the drinks table and gave Kate a smile. "Something to soothe the savage beast after seeing my father." He was quiet for a moment, a sudden exhaustion on his face, then he looked up, saw her, and his expression softened. "I'm glad you're here," he said quietly.

"I wouldn't want to be anywhere else."

"Lucky me." He smiled a little lopsided smile, banishing the touch of sadness in his eyes. "I don't know what it is with my parents," he murmured, his jaw working for a second. "Whether they're just self-involved or malicious, delusional or—shit...I have no idea why they think they can continue to interfere in my life."

She wanted to say, *They're all of the above and psycho too*, but she said instead, "At least your father's gone. That's good."

He half smiled. "Biting your tongue, baby?"

"Sort of—yeah, okay I am. But I don't actually know your parents," she added in the well-mannered tone reserved for lies.

"Best to keep it that way," he said flatly. Then he lifted the bottle in his hand. "Special circumstances. I promise not to make this a habit."

She smiled from the sofa. "Have one for me."

He dipped his head. "It's nice to have an understanding wife."

"And you're going to be my *husband*." It suddenly seemed incredibly intimate and wonderful. "Like wow."

"You better believe it." He gave her a lazy wink. "Four more days, baby, and we're shackled for life."

"You do have a way with shackles," she murmured softly, "that warms a woman's heart—not to mention every other body part."

"One woman." He gave her a quick glance from under his lashes as he poured his drink. "Just one."

"You better believe it," she mimicked. "Or I'll make your life a living hell. Oh, dear," she added with wide-eyed innocence, "should I have waited until after the wedding to mention that?"

He laughed. "As if I don't know it already, baby. But your idea of hell and my twisted version aren't even in the same universe. So do your best—you'll never get rid of me. Once we're married, we stay married. Which reminds me, you should call Nana. Tell her what's going on—marriage, baby, and whatever else you think she wants to know." He set the bottle down.

"With Nana, she'll want to know *everything*, from your dental records to your Myers-Briggs scores. So I'll call her tomorrow. I'm not fully alert this time of night."

"She didn't ask me much when I saw her," he said with a small shrug.

Kate smiled. "I'm guessing she figured you wouldn't be around long enough for her to bother with an interrogation."

"So I should brace myself, you're saying."

"Or decide on whatever degree of omission works best for you."

"Got it." He didn't say that was his specialty. "But Nana *is* going to need time to get ready," he gently prompted.

"I know. Tomorrow—I promise I'll call her."

"Sounds like a plan." He wasn't going to argue. He had a plane waiting in Duluth and a driver cooling his heels in a motel a few blocks from Nana's house. He could have Nana in London in ten hours. "Cheers." He tipped his glass toward Kate, then, lifting it to his mouth, drained the whiskey in one long swallow. Refilling the glass, he said, "Last one," and turned to set the bottle back on the table.

They were in a small, cozy room at the back of the house. A table by the window had been set for dinner, a low bowl of pinks on it scenting the air, a branch of lit candles fluttering in a faint draft. Kate was curled into a corner of the ultrasoft purple paisley chintz-covered sofa, her feet drawn up, her head resting against the sofa arm, her gaze on the man she loved. Her adoring gaze, she silently acknowledged, principles of female independence irrelevant when life was this sweet.

They'd changed into comfortable clothes: T-shirts and sweats, hers, designer, the pale green top decorated with the word *Mummy* in colorful glitter. Dominic wore gray Armani and looked good enough to eat as always, she reflected. He had that hard, athletic body, lean and taut with muscle as if he lived in a gym and worked out hours a day, when he didn't. Although he swam every morning; there was a large pool in the lower level here as well. "You know you can't ever look at another woman," Kate murmured. "And I'm going to become even more irrational as I get fatter."

He turned from the drinks table, his glass in hand. "No worries, baby. I don't give a shit about other women." He dipped his head a fraction. "Just take my partnership deal and everything's kick-ass. I'll never leave your side."

"It *would* solve my jealousy problem."

"And, more important, mine," he said with a grin, walking toward her. "I'm a possessive man."

"Dominic," she warned softly. "Don't start."

Quickly upending his drink into his mouth, he set the glass aside, slid behind Kate so she rested between his legs, and pulled her back into his chest. "Okay, I'm done," he said blandly, bending his head to kiss her cheek. "I'm just staking my claim. You can always say no. If you want," he whispered, sliding his hand down her stomach, cupping her crotch, and gently massaging. "I understand no."

"No you don't—oh, lord…" Softly sighing, she brushed her palm down the back of his hand as he gently stroked her sex. "You're making this really hard."

"Am I supposed to respond to that politely?" His mouth brushed her ear. "Tell me the rules."

A brisk knock on the door echoed in the quiet of the room.

"Damn…" Kate groaned; Dominic's fingers, expert, practiced, were touching her in all the right places, provoking, arousing, turning on all her give-it-to-me cravings.

Lifting his hand away, he rested his arm on the sofa back. "As soon as you eat, baby, it's playtime," he whispered. "Now—we have people waiting. Are you okay?"

She drew in a breath, exhaled, then nodded.

Dominic called out, "Come in." First things first: he wanted Katherine to eat a nourishing meal. After that, they had all night to play, although, realistically, they had about an hour after dinner before she fell asleep. "As soon as we're done here," he murmured, "I'll carry you upstairs."

As Quinn walked in, followed by three servers with trays, Dominic smiled. "Smells good. I'm starved." Rising from the sofa, carrying Kate with him, he set her on her feet.

Once they were seated, Quinn ran through the menu, pointed out the carafe of chocolate milk, mentioned wine was available for Dominic if he wished. When Dominic shook his head, Quinn signaled a server to take away the wine bottles, then smiled at Kate. "I'll have someone in the kitchen tonight in case you're in the mood for leftovers."

Kate flashed a glance at Dominic, felt her face turn red as she looked up at the chef who was the size of a mountain. "Please, that's not necessary. I can get my own leftovers."

"Why don't we leave it at that, Quinn," Dominic said smoothly, holding his chef's gaze for a telling moment so his message was clear: *I want someone in the kitchen at night.*

Quinn nodded. "Very good, sir."

As Quinn and the servers shut the door behind them, Kate whispered, eyes alight, "Ohmygod, blueberry pie."

Dominic smiled. "Nana's blueberry pie."

"I see that." The sugar-coated lattice-work crust was a clue. "Where did you get blueberries this time of year?"

"Dunno. Do you want me to ask?"

"No, but you can push the pie closer to me."

Dominic uttered a low growl.

Kate grinned. "I'm ignoring that." Half rising from her chair, she reached for the pie plate.

"You should eat some protein first."

"It's called meat, Dominic. You're not my dietician yet."

"But I am, baby." He took the pie plate out of her hand and said very softly, "Now be a good girl and sit back down. I promise you can have pie for dessert."

A familiar heated buzz streaked through her senses when Dominic gave orders in that deep, husky voice. When he looked at her like that, all quiet authority and cool restraint, she melted. "Where?" she whispered, shifting faintly on the cushioned chair. "Where exactly...would I be eating my pie?"

He held her gaze as he set the pie plate back on the table. "Wherever you want it," he said, equally softly. "We'll work out the details. There's whipped cream too."

"Jesus..." She dragged in a breath, briefly shut her eyes as a jolt of lust punched her psyche, then exhaled and said, her voice unsteady, "This horniness is unnerving. I'm like... defenseless."

"Relax, baby." Dominic smiled. "It's a helluva gift from my point of view."

"You're sure you don't mind if I become too—"

"I don't mind. I never will. And as soon as you eat, we'll go upstairs and you can call all the shots. Consider my dick yours to command, demand, whatever you want you've got it. But right now, humor me. Eat something good for

you—pork chops, duchesse potatoes, peas and carrots"—
his brows rose—"you actually like those?"

"My favorite," she said, her horniness waning thanks to
Dominic's tactical shift in conversation. "Maybe I'll make
you eat peas and carrots." She smiled. "A quid pro quo for
baby's daddy. What do you think of that?"

He laughed. "I think that'll be a fucking first."

She giggled.

And Dominic's dinner agenda was back on track.

It turned out to be an evening of several firsts for
Dominic—starting with peas and carrots and ending with
him lying with Kate on the sofa, watching two TV talent
shows in a row—or half watching. He took more pleasure
in observing Kate as she oohed and aahed, or said, "No
way!" or, if a contestant was really good, she'd shoot him a
look and exclaim, "Isn't that just fabulous?"

It was easy to reply, "Yes," because his view *was* fabulous, along with his life since Katherine was back—with his
baby. He swallowed hard.

They were actually having a baby.

When the second TV talent show was over, Dominic
tapped the remote and politely asked, "Next request?"

Kate glanced up. "Blueberry pie in bed."

"I thought you forgot."

Kate swiveled around in his arms so her chin was resting on his chest. "Did you really?" she said, her smile and
gaze warm with delight.

"Everything's so brand-new in my world, I'm not sure
what to think. I'm treading lightly as hell so no land mines
go off."

She raised an eyebrow. "Are you saying I'm difficult?"

His mouth twitched. "Why would I possibly think that?"

"Personally, I like to think of it as keeping you on your toes," Kate said with a grin, pushing off his chest and rising from the sofa. "Why don't you bring the pie and I'll carry the whipped cream. How's that sound?"

He laughed. "That sounds like a really great line. Actually one of the nicest things anyone's ever said to me."

"I'm going to fucking smack you."

But she was smiling. "Correction, baby," he said, coming to his feet. "I should have said that's one of the nicest things *you've* ever said to me."

Her smiled widened. "I do appreciate a man of perception."

He pulled her close. "You're going to have to reword that," he murmured, only half teasing—really, not teasing at all. "Personalize the man-of-perception phrase."

"You should talk." She looked up, suddenly slit-eyed. "I'm just saying."

"You haven't answered me," he said coolly, ignoring her reply.

"Oh for heaven's sake." She wrinkled her nose in a little fretful sniff. "I love only you, Dominic. There's no one else. There never has been. Satisfied?"

It still jarred the hell out of him, how much it mattered that Katherine was his alone, how he needed to hear her say it; he'd always been the least possessive man on the face of the earth. Sharing wasn't unusual in his world of sexual games; a woman was a woman, jealousy unknown. Even with Julia, even though he'd quit chasing during his marriage, he'd never thought of being jealous. "I'm so sorry, baby." He brushed her cheek with his fingertips. "I hope this gets better because I'm even freaking myself out I'm so bloody possessive."

She exhaled softly, slid her arms around his waist, and smiled up at him. "Let me know if it does," she said with a sigh. "Or better yet, let me know how to deal with my possessiveness in some semi-sane fashion."

"So we're both crazy."

She smiled. "Let's hope it doesn't affect the baby."

"Sorry. I'm possessive about him or her too."

"Then you better get over it." Her mouth stirred in a flicker of a grin. "We have to act like adults if we're going to be parents."

"Okay, gotcha. Act like adults." His grin turned wicked. "I hope that doesn't mean no blueberry pie and whipped cream."

"Cute. I don't believe I said uptight, doctrinaire, conservative adults."

"Whew. Good news."

"As if," she purred, running a finger down his chest. "You couldn't do it."

He lifted one brow. "Better than you."

"I'm so not interested in this stupid argument." *Because he was right.* She took a step back and changed the subject. "Get the pie."

"Yes, ma'am." He smiled. "Or how about I get you," he said, moving in a flash and scooping her up in his arms, "and we'll both get the pie?"

She gave him a teasing smile. "Do I have a choice?"

"Uh-uh. Maybe later…"

THIRTEEN

I'm bleeding."

Kate's whisper detonated like a bomb in Dominic's brain, adrenaline instantly flooded his body, and he came out of a dead sleep in a nanosecond. Rolling over at lightning speed, he hit the light switch, then rolled back, hoping—half asleep—he'd misunderstood.

But Kate's face was ashen, her eyes huge with fear.

"Something's wrong," she breathed, shoving the quilt aside.

Dominic looked down, and for a flashing moment the world came to a halt, his gasp stifled mid-utterance, his heart shuddered to a stop. The puddle of blood under Kate's legs was dark and ominous, spreading before his eyes. It seemed like several years passed at a crawl, although only a second elapsed. "Don't move, baby." His voice was deliberately calm and measured as he grabbed his phone from the bedside table. "Just stay right there." Punching in Jake's number, he slid off the bed. "I'm calling for the car."

Picking up his sweats from the floor, he shoved in one leg, then the other, jerked them up, swearing, *"Fuck, fuck, fuck,"* under his breath as Jake's phone rang, once, twice, three, four—*finally*. "I need the car out front *now*," Dominic said, his words, low, intense, rife with command despite his guarded tone in earshot of Kate. He didn't wait for an answer, already shoving his phone into his pants pocket, bending to pick up his discarded T-shirt. Pulling his shirt on with a few quick jerks, he stepped into his black-and-white-checkered Vans and swiftly moved toward Kate. "Jake'll be here in a minute." He spoke in a carefully modulated voice, the kind you'd use to placate a child's nightmare. "So don't worry. Jake's a fucking race driver. We'll be at the hospital in no time." Jerking the quilt from his side of the bed, he flipped his hair out of his eyes with a quick brush of his hand and began wrapping the comforter around Kate.

"Hey, hey, *clothes*!" She banged on his arm, every childhood warning about car accidents and clean underwear clawing through her fear like some Freudian attack dog. "I need clothes!"

Fuck that. There wasn't time. But after a quick glance at Kate's horrified expression, Dominic muttered, "Okay, okay," sprinted back and swept up her T-shirt and sweats from the carpet. A second later, he lifted her from the blood-soaked section of bed, set her down away from the stain, said, "I'll do this," and swiftly dressed her. But blood almost immediately appeared on her sweats, the spot widening with alarming speed. "I'm going to grab a few towels," he said, outwardly composed, fear twisting his gut. "I'll be right back."

In his absence, Kate was trying equally hard to stay calm, forcing herself to focus on positive action—*get to the hospital, get to the hospital*—rather than totally losing it. But she'd seen the blood on the bed, could feel the continuing flow: something was terribly wrong. She should have eaten better, drunk less caffeine. She shouldn't have worked such long hours those first months. She should have made better choices about—Christ, take your pick from a long list of her maternal inadequacies. Swamped with guilt, she thought of all the things she could have done better, *should* have done better; she beat herself up for not following the most fundamental rules everyone knew about rest and eating well, about vitamins—Jesus, she'd never even taken one. *This was all my fault.* Frantic, she promised whatever spirits were listening, to be a better mother from now on. She'd follow all the rules—every single one, she vowed; she'd write a list, Dominic could give her stickers like he'd threatened. *Just make the bleeding stop. Please, please, make it stop.* She was terrified of what was happening.

"You have to tell me everything's going to be okay," she said in a little frightened voice when Dominic came back carrying an armload of towels. "Just say it."

"I would have anyway, baby." Bending down, he kissed her tenderly. "Don't worry. Everything's going to be fine. We're going to take care of this. I promise." He knew what he had to say; he would have lied to God and the devil and every Brueghel demon in purgatory to make Katherine happy. Standing upright, he swallowed the *oh fuck* that almost escaped when he saw all the fresh blood and forced a smile instead. "I'm going to wrap you up like a mummy now, so don't complain. I don't have time for complaints. Check back with me in the morning when the complaint department opens."

She laughed.

And for a flashing second he felt better—a relative term in the face of disaster. But he didn't have time to waste on introspection; swiftly swaddling Kate's lower body in several towels, he covered her in the quilt, picked her up in his arms, and moments later was racing down the upstairs corridor. As he reached the top of the stairway and started running down the steps, for the first time since he'd bought the London house he was grateful for Martin's insistence on a night porter. The man immediately came to his feet when he saw them. "Get hold of Max. Have him call St. Mary's Hospital and Dr. Fuller," Dominic said in a voice just loud enough to carry; if not fearful of upsetting Katherine he would have shouted. "The numbers are all on my desk phone. Tell the doctor to meet us at the hospital. Open the door now, then *run*."

Regardless of Dominic's tempered tone, the hall porter recognized manifest calamity with his employer racing down the stairs carrying Miss Hart. He rushed to open the front door, then turned and sprinted for Dominic's study.

Dominic swept through the opened door and down the small flight of steps, scanning the street for the car. Jake's quarters were above the garage in the mews behind the house. Minutes away. *Where the fuck was he?* Tense, anxious, his nerves on edge, Dominic paced as they waited for the car, murmuring all the useless platitudes expressed at times like this when one's world was collapsing and you had to pretend it wasn't: "Jake'll be here soon, baby, don't worry; you're doing fine; the doctor's on her way. Are you warm enough? Cold enough? When this is over we'll go sleep on a beach somewhere for a week. How about that?" But he was scared shitless. He knew how quickly a person could bleed out. "A beach sounds heavenly," Kate murmured. They were both trying to deal with the crisis responsibly. No visible panic or despair. But raised by a grandfather like hers, Kate *also* knew how quickly a person could bleed out. And when she asked, "How far is the hospital?" her voice trembled despite her best intentions.

"Not far, baby." Jesus, Katherine's face was faintly sheened in sweat, her voice unsteady. Was she going into shock? "Jake can get us there faster than an ambulance," Dominic said as calmly as he could. "We'll be there soon."

"Oh, God," Kate blurted out as a palpable runnel of blood seeped from her body. "I'm really scared." She didn't say she was afraid of losing the baby, as if voicing the words might tip the hand of fate. "Tell me this can be fixed, Dominic." She winced as her stomach clenched. "Tell me!"

He came to a stop at her sharp cry. "Everything's going to be fine." He spoke with assurance, perjured himself without a qualm. "I'll make sure of it, okay?" He understood what she wanted to hear because he wanted the same thing: their life back to normal—happy, content, fucking heaven-on-earth normal. "Dr. Fuller will take care of you. She's good. Everyone says she's the best. She'll know what to do," he murmured, saying whatever he had to say to soothe Katherine's fears, lying through his teeth. "As soon as the car gets— Christ *at last*—here's Jake. We're on our way, baby." *Thank God.* Katherine was white as a sheet.

The car came to a screeching halt at the curb. Jake leaped out, quickly buttoning the last button on his jeans, his shirt undone, his feet in flip-flops. Racing to open the car door, he said, breathlessly, "Where to?"

"St. Mary's Hospital. Don't stop for lights," Dominic said crisply as he slid into the backseat with Kate.

As the door slammed shut, Dominic adjusted Kate in his lap, then watched Jake sprint around the front of the car and slide behind the wheel.

"I must have done something wrong. Oh hell, I did everything wrong." Kate's voice was quivering, her best efforts at rationalization inadequate against her building hysteria, all her fearsome misgivings suddenly spilling out in a rush. "I should have taken better care of myself, gone to see a doctor earlier, not—"

"Don't, baby," Dominic whispered, as Jake rocketed away from the curb. "Don't blame yourself. You didn't do anything wrong." *He probably did. They shouldn't have been fucking so much. He should have been more sensible.*

"Are we going to lose the—"

"We don't know," he interrupted, not willing yet to acknowledge the possibility. Still holding out hope. "We're clueless. Let's wait for the doctor to tell us what's going on, okay?" But he was struggling with increasing dread. Katherine had bled through the towels and quilt; he could feel the blood saturating his sweats. The word *hemorrhage* was lighting up his brain. "Push it, Jake," he said, sharply. "Use the sidewalks if you have to."

Jake punched the accelerator and the car shot forward.

"I'm really sorry," Kate whispered.

"Baby, it's not your fault." Concern and sympathy shimmered in his gaze. "Don't even think that. We'll be there soon. Dr. Fuller will take care of you."

Fortunately, the city was quiet at that time of night. Jake drove full out, slowing down only marginally as he approached the busiest intersections, then leaning on the horn as he swept through the red lights, almost side-swiping a dozen cars that didn't get out of the way quickly enough. Seven endless minutes later, he careened into the emergency entrance on two wheels, slammed on the brakes, and skidded to a stop.

"I'll get the door," Dominic snapped. "Run. Tell them we're here." Thumbing the handle, he kicked open the door, swung his foot out on the pavement, and came out of the backseat in a powerful surge. "You're safe, baby. Look, help's on its way."

Max's call had mobilized a medical crew that came streaming out the door and escorted them into a cubicle, where Dominic deposited Katherine on a gurney. Turning to the doctor, who had a lean runner's body and thankfully didn't look exhausted like doctors often did in the middle of the night, Dominic spoke in an undertone. "Katherine has lost a *considerable* amount of blood." His gaze flicked downward to his bloody sweats, then to the quilt to emphasize the full extent of the loss. "Is Dr. Fuller here?"

"On her way." The doctor turned to Kate. "We're here to take care of you until she arrives. Just try to relax. We'll handle this. Do you know your blood type?"

"O negative."

"That's mine too if you need any," Dominic said tersely.

The doctor looked at Dominic. "We'll see." Then he nodded at a nurse and turned back to Kate. "We're going to set you up with an IV. Just a precaution. Nothing to worry about." He glanced at the blood pressure reading now that Kate's arm had been cuffed, spoke to another attendant. "Tell Sarah to bring two." Then he addressed Kate. "When did this start?"

Wired to the max, Dominic answered first. "Katherine woke me ten, fifteen minutes ago. We don't know. Do you have any idea, baby, when you started bleeding?"

She shook her head. "I thought I was dreaming at first."

"How far along is the pregnancy?"

"Three months," Dominic said, wanting to hold Katherine's hand but concerned he'd be in the way. "We just found out recently." Dominic stood at the foot of the gurney instead, keeping his bloody clothes from Katherine's line of sight, feeling his pulse rate spike as Katherine's blood pressure continued to drop on the heart monitor. "You can stop the bleeding, right?" he said curtly, his piercing blue eyes on the doctor.

The doctor took a moment too long to answer. "Stopping the blood shouldn't be a problem."

Dominic felt pure terror at the delayed response. His instinctive reaction was to hit the fucker, jar a better answer out of him, force the doctor and the world to yield to his authority. But he knew better than to resort to violence with Katherine's life in jeopardy. So he reined in his explosive temper; only a faint tick along his jaw indicated the extent of his self-restraint. "Should we call in additional specialists? I have people who can do that." Each word was blunt with command, despite the softness of his tone. "My wife has to be taken care of appropriately and expeditiously. Do we understand each other?"

St. Mary's catered to the wealthy and titled, so it wasn't as though the doctor hadn't dealt with demanding patients before. But this man had a tough, ruthless quality to him quite different from the lordly arrogance of the plutocrats. Maybe it was the hard muscled body or the stone-cold look. Or the sense that he could flick a switch in a second and become dangerous. "Dr. Fuller should be here soon. She's the very best. In the meantime," the doctor said neutrally, "I suggest we get the IV going."

Dominic's shoulders rose and fell on a deep breath, his slow raking stare fixed on the doctor for an overlong moment. Then he gradually unclenched his jaw. "Forgive me," he said gruffly. Returning his attention to Kate, Dominic suddenly felt the earth shift under his feet. *Christ.* She was even more deathly pale, her breathing so slight it was barely visible. All noise vanished, the people in the room disappeared, dread rose up like a black shroud and engulfed him.

"Dominic."

Kate's faint whisper dragged him back; he blinked against the brilliant light. "I'm here, baby." Putting a smile on his face, he shouldered people out of his way and moved to Katherine's side. "Hey," he whispered, sliding his strong fingers through hers. "How's my girl?"

"I need you," she whispered, her eyes enormous, glistening with unshed tears.

"You have me—now and always." Dominic's fingers closed over hers. *Even with this tragedy unfolding, he had Katherine to love. And she loved him back. He couldn't ask for more.* "Now look at me, baby, here, squeeze my hand. They're going to stick you."

When Dr. Fuller arrived shortly after, the IV was in place and Katherine's color and blood pressure had improved. But the bleeding hadn't stopped.

"Looks like we have a problem here," she said briskly, coming into the room, snapping on surgical gloves. "How are you feeling Katherine?"

"Scared. Worried. Really scared."

"That's understandable. Now let's see what's going on, shall we?" After a brief examination, Dr. Fuller looked at Dominic first, her expression grave. Then she turned to Kate and spoke in a subdued voice. "I'm afraid you're in the process of miscarrying."

Dominic had suspected as much, but hope was a powerful emotion. The doctor's statement was a punch in the gut.

Kate's tears escaped, slid down her cheeks. "Can you— save—the baby?" Her voice was whisper soft. "Can you stop it?" She looked at Dominic. "Dominic, tell her to stop it."

She was begging him. The hope in her eyes hurt. "Sure, baby," he said gently, putting aside his anguish and distress. "Let me see if they can do something." He turned and met Dr. Fuller's gaze. "Is there any alternative, even the remotest possibility—some new research? I know you have special-ists here, but if there's someone else—anywhere...I have planes around the world, or I can charter aircraft—fly peo-ple in if—"

The doctor shook her head. "I'm sorry. The blood loss is so extreme there's no longer any chance of a viable fetus. I know it's not any consolation, but a miscarriage at three months is not uncommon." Dr. Fuller's mouth firmed for a moment. "Katherine *is* hemorrhaging though, which isn't normal. We have to take her into surgery right away."

He turned to Kate. "It's too late," Dominic said in a ragged whisper. "You heard."

Kate's eyes were great pools of despair. "Oh God, Dominic," she said in a small, broken voice. "No . . . ."

Leaning over, he put his mouth near her ear. "I love you, Katherine. More than anything. But right now, they have to stop the bleeding. Okay?" He couldn't talk about the baby; it was unbearable. He would have had a family for the first time in his life. But without Katherine, he had nothing—no life, no hope, no happiness. So he wiped away her tears with his shirtsleeve, stood upright, gave her hand a little shake, and murmured, "How about I see if they'll let me in surgery? That way I'll be there with you."

"Did I do something wrong?" The pain in her eyes was heartrending. "I did, didn't I?"

Her voice was so weak, the hairs on the back of his neck went up. "No, baby, you didn't do anything wrong." *If anyone had, it had been him.* "You heard the doctor." He spoke in a soothing tone, wishing he could say, *We have to get you into surgery NOW.* But knowing he'd frighten her if he did, he just kept on talking in his fake calm voice. "This is common, the doctor said. It happens to others too, not just us. Give me a little smile now. I'm right here beside you. I'm not going anywhere. You couldn't get rid of me if you tried."

She gave him a shaky smile. "I need a kiss."

Before he'd met Katherine, he'd always avoided public displays of affection; even in private there were doors that remained permanently closed. And now with ten strangers watching he said, simply, "You got it, baby," and gave her a tender, lingering kiss. Raising his head a short time later, he smiled and said, soft and low like he did when he was indulging her, "Better?"

She half smiled.

"Ready to get this show on the road?"

A small nod.

There was relief in his expression, then a slow, lovely smile. "That's my girl." Turning to survey the small company in the room, Dominic said in his blink-free, master-of-the-universe voice, "I'll need some scrubs. I'm coming into surgery with Katherine."

FOURTEEN

Katherine went through nine units of blood before they were able to stop the bleeding, the sense of panic in the surgery the most frightening experience Dominic had ever undergone: nurses and staff ran in and out, the doctors snapped orders, and everyone stood grim-faced over the operating table, the sense of all-guns-blazing urgency acute.

Kate's veins kept collapsing, forcing a frantic search for a new usable vein, until finally, with both Kate's arms a roadmap of puncture wounds, an IV began functioning properly.

A cheer went up around the operating table, the sound, paradoxically, striking terror in Dominic's soul. Katherine's life had been teetering on the brink.

It wasn't as though Dominic hadn't seen his share of dicey situations in lawless regions of the world; he could sit still and listen to someone threaten to kill him without blinking.

But this was different.

Spine-chillingly different.

Sweating-bullets different.

This was personal. Because Katherine was the miracle he still wasn't sure he deserved. She'd transformed his gray, soulless existence, set it ablaze with light and joy, brought him happiness and casually laid it at his feet. And he loved her with a kind of fanaticism felt only by those who'd never loved before. She was his world, his life, his heart and soul.

Only with enormous self-control and sheer bloody will did he keep from physically threatening every doctor in the operating room if they didn't do their fucking job and *stop* the bleeding.

They finally did, almost an hour later, and he experienced such a sense of relief, he understood how an inmate on death row feels when he receives a last-minute reprieve. He couldn't move for a second, his body in full meltdown, his breathing arrested, his heart on pause. Only his brain was lit up in a celebratory fireworks show.

Once his breathing was restored, he moved from the periphery of the group toward Katherine, saying, "May I?" when he was already straight-arming his way in without waiting for an answer. He needed to touch her.

Shouldering the last person aside, he reached Katherine just as the anesthesiologist was taking off the mask from her nose, leaving red marks on her pale skin. Beautiful red marks, Dominic thought, gazing down. Everything about Katherine was beautiful, he reflected with that crazy-in-love, adrenaline-spiked happiness he felt only with her.

"She won't come out of the anesthesia for some time yet," Dr. Fuller said.

He didn't look up. "The bleeding won't start again?"

"No."

"You're sure?" Dominic lightly touched Katherine's cheek in the faintest of caresses, then glanced up, wanting to see the doctor's face when she answered. Needing certainty.

"I'm sure. We found the breach in the vein and closed it."

He felt all his muscles loosen in a neat, smooth sweep. "When can she go home? I can hire nurses, doctors, whatever she needs."

"Perhaps in two days. She's going to be a little weak at first."

Ignoring his heartache, he asked the question that still lingered despite all that had occurred. "There was no way to save the baby was there? Not even the slightest chance. Not with that kind of bleeding."

"No. Your—"

"Wife."

"Your wife was fortunate to arrive here so quickly."

"Even then"—he stopped, not willing to contemplate how close he'd come to losing Katherine.

"Yes, the bleeding was very difficult to stop. We rarely see hemorrhaging like that."

Dominic forced down his rising panic. "Is this episode cause for concern? In the future, might this happen again?"

"We don't have those answers. I'm sorry. I wish we did. Each pregnancy is unique, the reasons for anomalies like this unknown."

"I understand. I appreciate your expertise in this case. Thank you," he said quietly. "We both thank you."

"You're very welcome. Now, Katherine will be in the ICU for some time," Dr. Fuller said. "It's perfectly routine. But it'll be an hour at least before she's fully awake. Do you have any further questions?"

"No—yes, actually, one. When can Katherine travel? I'd like to fly her home as soon as possible."

"I'll be in tomorrow to see how Katherine's doing. Why don't we wait until then? Will that do for now?"

Dominic nodded, understanding the message. The doctor was leaving. "Certainly. Thank you again."

Ten minutes later, Katherine was settled into a room in the ICU. He'd hired private nurses for each shift in addition to those normally on duty and once the private duty nurse arrived, Dominic walked out into the hall, leaving the door ajar so he could see Katherine.

Then, pulling out his phone, he started making calls.

Beginning with Nana.

"I apologize for calling so late, but I wanted you to know Katherine's in the hospital. She just came out of surgery, she's fine, don't worry." That Katherine hadn't been so fine a short time ago, he kept to himself. "She's in the ICU and has nurses with her. I'm standing outside the door. I can see her. She's sleeping peacefully."

"It sounds as though Katie lost the baby. I'm so sorry."

"Katherine told you?" Dominic's voice registered surprise. "She said she hadn't."

"She didn't have to. You were so worried about Katie eating food she liked, I didn't have to be a rocket scientist to know what was going on. I'm already packed. My cousin, Monty, will drive me to the airport. I told him I might be going to London. With the baby coming, I figured you'd do the right thing and marry Katie."

"I want you to know I would have married Katherine much sooner, but for some major problems." He didn't say more since Katherine seemed reluctant to tell her grandmother much. Personally, he considered Nana shock proof.

"Then your stock with me goes up a few notches. I was wondering what was going on. Katie was avoiding my questions."

"She's concerned about what you think. I told her you'd give her a pass on anything at all. Just call and tell Nana, I said."

"*You* should have called. I worried."

"I couldn't interfere with something so significant. Katherine wouldn't have understood."

"So you're soft and mushy underneath all that power."

"Only with Katherine—well…and a few others too." He thought of Melanie's family and Nana too. He admired her cranky charm, her unconditional love for Katherine, and her razor-sharp ability to understand what was important in life.

"As long as you're soft and mushy with my Katie, I'm satisfied."

"Did I hear a slight threat in that comment?" Dominic quizzed, a faint mirth in his voice.

"Not a slight threat, my boy, a big one," she said in her school principal voice that meant business. "I read how the jet set lives. It's not a formula for a lasting marriage. I expect you to remember your wedding vows. And if you don't, you'll answer to me. Now, nuff said. When's the wedding?"

Having just been lectured for one of the few times in his life, and by someone he chose not to cross, Dominic spoke with the utmost politesse. "As soon as you get here. Although I wish you were coming just for our wedding." He took a small breath, never fully prepared for the stabbing pain when he thought of the loss of their baby. "Katherine really needs you now. She's desperately unhappy and grieving. We both are."

"Offering sympathy seems so inadequate at a time like this. I wish I could do more," Nana said softly. "Had Katie been pregnant for—"

"Three months."

Nana sighed. "That's not unusual. If something's going to go wrong, it often happens about then."

"The doctor said as much. Would you mind telling Katherine that? She's upset, thinking she'd done something wrong. We were both very much looking forward to having a child." He paused for a second again and his voice was rough when he spoke. "It's hard to take."

"I know. I also know with time you'll get through it," Nana said bracingly, having lived through enormous personal losses. "And Katie will too. She's strong."

Dominic half smiled. "She is. Definitely."

"I heard that. She giving you trouble?"

"All the time."

"Good for her. A change from the swarm of yes-men in your life. Now let me give Monty a call," she said briskly. "He's a member of the volunteer fire department so he's used to getting calls day or night. Then I'll book a flight and call you back."

Her voice faded as she moved to end the call. "Wait!" Dominic called out. "Don't hang up. You still there?"

"Yup, but the sooner I call Monty, the sooner I'm on my way."

"Don't call your cousin. I have a car and driver at the

Pines Motel. Tomas will pick you up and drive you to Duluth. There's a plane waiting for you at the airport."

"Holy moly. You're almost as sneaky as me."

Is that good or bad? But it wasn't her cranky tone, so he said, "Sounds like you could give me tips."

"I'm sure I could. I've got forty-some years more practice. And believe me, convincing some twelve-year-old fire bug, or some junior high prima donna, or all kinds of other kids who are acting out, to change their antisocial trajectory takes a little creative thinking, a few white lies, and a threat or two. But Katie's not like that at all in case you didn't know."

"I do know. I find it refreshing and sweet—no offense."

"None taken," Nana said, with casual unconcern. "Katie's like her Gramps—a straight shooter. Literally and figuratively. You would have liked Roy. Everyone did." She took an audible breath and her voice abruptly turned crisp. "Back to business. I'll just let Monty know he has to come get my dog, Leon, in the morning. Tell your driver I'll be ready in fifteen minutes."

Dominic heard his line go dead and smiled. Nana was going to be good for Katherine. Hell, good for him too. She could shake anyone out of their gloom and doom stupor, rattle anyone's cage, snap orders with the best of them. Nana would be the perfect no-nonsense one-person support group.

Leaning back against the wall, his phone still in his hand, he shut his eyes, suddenly feeling burned out, exhausted.

"You okay?"

Startled, Dominic looked up and saw Max. He shoved away from the wall, instantly clear-eyed and alert. "Just taking a break. We lost the baby." He blew out a breath. "It really sucks."

"I'm sorry," Max said. "I talked to the nurses while you were in surgery and I saw your bed, so I knew it wasn't going well." Max lifted a small duffel bag he was carrying. "I brought you some clothes. The night porter had gone upstairs after you left, so he clued me in. Katherine must have been frightened."

"She was trying to stay calm and carry on, but yeah, she was. We both were. There was so much blood and it just kept coming." Dominic took another deep breath; the gory sight was etched on his retinas. "They had trouble stopping the hemorrhaging. She was coding out, they kept pumping blood into her. I was fucking terrified." He blew out a breath, then quickly glanced at the half-open door as though to reassure himself. "Katherine's going to be okay, but she's still under. At least an hour more, the doctor said." He rolled his shoulders, grunted at the sharp pain, softly swore, then said, taut and low, "It was worse than Angola. That's how bad it was. But look"—his voice took on a sudden briskness; he'd trained himself to keep on keeping on. "I have to make a few calls. If you'll monitor the flight bringing Nana in and have someone at Heathrow to meet her, I'd appreciate it. The plane should be taking off from Duluth in roughly an hour and a half."

"I'll meet Nana myself."

"Thanks. I don't know what I'd do without you." Dominic ran a quick hand over his eyes. "Jesus. Sorry," he said, exhaling, dragging in a deep breath, standing motionless for a second until his teeth unclenched. "Fuck. How do people deal with something like this?"

"Whatever works. And time, I'm guessing."

Two men who didn't as a rule acknowledge their feelings—out of grief and friendship—were trying.

"I never *wanted* children before." Dominic stared straight ahead at some distant point for a moment, then his gaze flicked to Max and he shrugged. "Not exactly news to you. But with Katherine"—his voice caught, and when he spoke again his voice was barely audible. "Hell, just thinking about her having my baby was the most incredible high."

"That makes this worse. Makes the low even more brutal."

"No shit. Fucking caustic." Dominic flexed his shoulders, regained his balance. "Look," he said, quickly running his fingers through his hair, "let me get changed out of these scrubs, then you can go. I have those calls to make and Katherine could wake up at any time." Dominic took the duffel bag from Max. "And thanks for coming," he said quietly. "Really."

A few minutes later, Dominic walked out of the bathroom down the hall, washed up and dressed in clean clothes. "Who thought of the shoes?" he asked as Max shoved himself away from the opposite wall.

"Martin, of course. He gave orders to the hall porter from his car on the way over to the house. I was gone before he arrived. But Martin was your valet." Max smiled faintly. "And he did well. You look—semi-normal at least. Under the circumstances, no one expects more."

Dominic wore gray dress slacks and an off-white shirt with the collar open and sleeves rolled up. Black belt, black slip-ons, his hair splashed with water and slicked back.

"Semi-normal with Katherine is a hundred times better than my normal without her. Or realistically, more like a million times." Dominic pulled his phone from his pocket. "Save this afternoon on your schedule for our wedding. The suites here aren't very large so the guest list will be small. I'm going to give Mrs. Hastings the good news in a few minutes."

"You're going to wake up the dragon at five in the morning and tell her to pull together your wedding in eight hours. You've got balls."

"Uh-uh—pure necessity. Last night's crisis made it clear I need to be able to take care of Katherine legally. So the sooner we marry, the sooner her position is secure. Not to mention I can't live without her, which trumps legalities till the end of fucking time." He briefly shut his eyes, trying to erase the bloody images from last night, unconsciously shaking his head to dismiss them. "A nightmare," he murmured, half to himself. Then he smiled tightly. "Where was I? Ah—if you'll text me a heads-up periodically on Nana's flight status, I'll know when to expect her in London. That should do it for now." Dominic's nostrils flared briefly, he slowly exhaled. "So...moving on," he said in a low rasp. "What the hell else can we do, right?"

Max nodded. "That always works." His voice softened. "With the life I've lived, I should know."

"Sometimes you wonder how the fuck you *can* move on though. How it's even possible." Dominic was quiet for a moment, then he grunted and raised his hand with the cell phone. "I'd better make my calls. Keep me posted. I'll see you later. And don't worry about dressing up for the wedding." He flicked his finger down his body. "I'm wearing this."

"Leo's going to want to come. Danny too, and"—Max sighed—"Martin."

"And Quinn," Dominic added. "Look, you take care of that guest list. Mine just has Nana on it."

"Helen?"

"Yes, of course. We'll squeeze in whomever you think should be here." Dominic smiled. "I probably won't notice. My focus is pretty single-minded. I know how fucking lucky I am."

"Will Katherine be up to it?"

Dominic did a quick double take, then smoothly adjusted. "If Katherine isn't strong enough, we'll do it tomorrow. I'll tell Mrs. Hastings the schedule is flexible."

"I'd like to see her when you tell her that. Watch the fire coming out of her nose."

Dominic smiled faintly. "No fire, Max. She just ticks up her charges. A very sensible woman, Mrs. Hastings. The kind I can do business with." He started scrolling through his directory. "Katherine might wake up any time. I want to get these calls out of the way." Punching a name, he raised his hand in a wave and put his phone to his ear.

FIFTEEN

D ominic here. I need a few things done."

"Certainly," Martin said. "Our condolences, sir, from myself and the staff."

"Thank you. It's a sad situation. But Katherine's recovering, for which I'm very grateful." He did a quick in and out breath to keep it together, and even then his voice was husky when he said, "I need a number of tasks done." He cleared his throat and his voice firmed. "First, if you'll see that the bedroom is cleaned up."

"It's already done, sir."

"Good. Then I need someone to go to Katherine's apartment and pack up all the baby things—also some of Katherine's T-shirts with inscriptions she won't want to see. They should be put away with the baby clothes. Just let me know where you put things in the event Katherine asks to see them. I have no idea if she will, but if so, I have to know where they are. Personally, I'd prefer giving everything away but I can't speak for Katherine."

"Consider it done, sir."

"Oh, and Mrs. Hastings will be getting in touch with you. I'll be waking her up soon to arrange our wedding. If Katherine's health allows, I'd like to get married this afternoon. Max is arranging the guest list—we'd like you to come, Martin. And if there are any additions, talk to him. I'll get back to you once I talk to Katherine. She's still sleeping off the anesthetic. Any questions?"

"No. We'll take care of everything, sir."

"Good. Fine. And I want the shipwreck Veuve. The hospital suite won't accommodate many guests, but bring enough. Katherine and I will have a token toast, but the rest of you should celebrate the occasion properly."

"Yes, sir. That's a very rare champagne."

"You get married only once, Martin."

Dominic's major domo was momentarily taken aback; his employer was casually overlooking his previous two marriages. Although the recent marriage was easily enough dismissed, and Martin had always known that Dominic's feelings for Julia had been affection and friendship, not passion. "I couldn't agree more, sir. A special occasion deserves a special champagne."

And Martin knew exactly how special the champagne was. Dominic had paid 4.5 million at auction for forty-six bottles of the 1830 Veuve Clicquot found by a salvage diver in the Baltic.

"A shame though…" It was a mistake to even think of what might have been. Dominic swallowed hard. "I'll get back to you."

Shoving his phone in his pocket, Dominic bent over, his hands braced on his knees, and waited for the onslaught of desolation to pass. *Breathe in, breathe out, come on…get a grip. Get a fucking grip.* Easier said than done, but several moments later, his shaky emotional defenses back in place, he stood upright, moved to the door of Kate's room, opened it slightly wider, and said quietly, "I'll be back in five minutes. Everything okay?"

The nurse at Katherine's bedside smiled. "She's sleeping comfortably."

"I won't be long."

Easing the door shut, he turned, strode down the hall, took the elevator to the main floor, and walked outside. Moving away from the entrance door, he traveled down the sidewalk to the end of the block. Then he went around the corner and punched the wall until his knuckles were raw meat. And for those few seconds of blinding pain, the awful sadness was seared, white hot and incandescent, from his brain.

Hearing a gasp, Dominic turned. "Move along," he growled. "None of your fucking business."

The wide-eyed young man, a hospital employee, Dominic assumed from his name tag, quickly hastened away.

Resting his forehead against the brick wall, his arms hanging loose at his sides, blood dripping onto the pavement, Dominic struggled to contain the violence of his rage. He wanted to scream the world to a standstill, reduce the wall to rubble, hit someone—*anyone*. But he knew Katherine needed sympathy and love right now—not his hotheaded wildness. And that quiet reminder resonated in his brain, irresistible and compelling under the ferocity of his anger, until finally, *finally*, the rage subsided. Everything slowed down like it always did afterward: each breath seemed to last a half hour; the world reemerged from the indistinguishable gray-blue haze; he felt as if he'd had the air knocked out of him.

Gingerly pushing away from the wall, he winced as he shook the blood from his hands, looked down and winced again. Jesus, that's some shredded flesh. Fortunately, the sight of blood wasn't unusual in a hospital and the few people in the entry way when he walked back in didn't look alarmed. But he entered the first bathroom he found, washed his hands in cold water, held paper towels over his knuckles until the bleeding stopped, and grimaced when he saw himself in the mirror, his shirt front spattered with blood. Stripping off his shirt, he used cold water on the blood. His San Francisco housekeeper, Patty, had shown him how, saying: "You fight, you clean up your own mess." Wringing out the shirt, he put it back on and actually smiled when he saw his sopping wet image in the mirror. *Grow the fuck up, dude—like seriously.* Although he gave himself a pass this time. Who the hell wouldn't want to break things after losing their child?

He didn't have the heart to call Martin again. They could bring him another shirt later. He made his way back to Katherine's room, pushed the door open slightly, and stuck his head into the room. He glanced at Katherine and spoke softly. "Still sleeping?"

The nurse nodded.

"I'm just outside in the hall making a few calls. Come get me when Katherine wakes. Otherwise, I'll be in as soon as I'm finished."

Another nod.

He eased the door shut, moved away a few feet, and called his sister.

"What a nice surprise," Melanie exclaimed.

"I wish." Dominic dragged in a quick breath. "We lost the baby."

"Oh dear God," she whispered. "Oh, Nicky, I'm so sorry. How awful you must feel. And Katherine. How is she doing?"

"Fine now. Not so fine a few hours ago. She was hemorrhaging, the doctors were freaking in surgery. I was watching, fucking terrified." He didn't say more because he didn't want Melanie accidently bringing up the life-threatening events Katherine had survived. He didn't want Katherine further traumatized. "But she's recovering well, she's sleeping. I just wanted to let you know the bad news."

"How are you doing?"

"Honestly? It's tearing me up. My knuckles are all bloody. That's how it is."

"You didn't hurt anybody?" Melanie's voice slid upward in pitch.

"No, just my knuckles. They're a fucking mess, but no one got hurt. So relax." He wiped his face with the flat of his palm, sucked air in over his teeth. "You know, life was going too good. I should have known it wouldn't last. But Jesus, Mel, why did we have to lose"—his voice broke—"our baby?"

"Oh God, Nicky, I wish I were there to help. Do you want me to come to London? Just tell me what you want."

"What I want isn't going to happen." He was silent for a moment. "God I feel like shit," he whispered. "You know what?"

But he didn't speak for so long, Melanie said, nervously, "Nicky, do you need someone there right now to help you?"

"Nah...I was just—thinking—or had been thinking—about Nicole babysitting for us. Like I did for you. I thought how nice that would be. Second generation...all that shit." He blew out a breath. "Me daydreaming—what a joke, hey?"

"You can have other babies, Nicky. I know how trite and insulting it is to say right now, but you can," Melanie said, softly.

"We'll see." He wasn't so sure he wanted to take the chance. "Everything's too raw right now to even think about it. You don't know how much we both wanted this baby. More than anything in the world," he said, his voice cracking again. "Oh fuck." He blew out a breath. "Look, we're coming home soon." Another hard exhale. "Either to Minnesota or San Francisco. It's up to Katherine. I'll let you know."

His voice was normal again at the end. He'd pulled himself together like he always did, Melanie thought. "I'm glad you're coming back. Wherever you are, we'll come to see you and Katherine."

"Thanks. That'd be good. And I don't want Mother to know." He pronounced the word *Mother* with an undercurrent of distaste so subtle that it was indistinguishable unless you knew the history.

"I wouldn't have told her, Nicky. Not in a million years. You know that."

"You'd better warn the kids—the older ones at least. Ellie's probably too young to pay attention. But I don't want to deal with Mother on this."

"That's the last thing you need right now. No one will say a word."

"Good. Thanks." He paused for a moment and when he spoke his voice was strained, tight, his words slowly unwinding. "I've always been able to manage anything, Sis. You know that. I've been doing it my whole life. Make things better. Or make them go away. Crush them if nothing else works. But I was helpless this time." He sucked in a breath. "Absolutely powerless. It was the most goddamned shitty feeling in the world. So," he said, a sudden crispness to his voice, "I'm going to marry Katherine this afternoon if she's feeling strong enough. Life's too precarious. I don't want to wait. You can give us a reception when we come home. I hope you don't mind. Actually, I don't care if you do," he said, with his more familiar mockery.

"I'd do the same if I were you," Melanie said. "You should have married her before if you ask me."

"I couldn't," he said bitterly. "You know that. Or some of it."

"Problems all gone?"

"Yup."

"That at least makes you happy. I can tell."

"Fucking A. No more waiting. I'm literally counting the hours till I'm married like some kid waiting for Christmas."

"But this is better than any Christmas."

"Yeah, like a gazillion times better. At least getting married is a happy occasion even though everything else has gone to hell."

"Katherine's young. You're young. You have plenty of time."

"Thanks, Mel. I know. It's just going to take a while to get over"—he took a breath—"the goddamned sadness. I went shopping for baby clothes. Did I tell you? They were so tiny. Precious, really. Shit—Jesus Christ, I could swear for a couple decades without stopping. But look, I've got to call the wedding planner now and get her out of bed. See if she can pull this together in a few hours."

"I'm sure she can. All it takes is money."

"Hackneyed but true. I'll call you later and you can congratulate me on my new marital status."

"I'd rather talk to Katherine. You I can talk to anytime," she said sportively.

He laughed. "I'll see what I can do."

When he ended the call, he was still smiling. And he thought of how many times his sister had made the world a better place for him. She had the gift of compassion, or maybe just years of practice. Not that his melancholy didn't return seconds later, just as raw and agonizing as before. But he told himself he still had Katherine. He had to count his blessings he hadn't lost her as well. He told himself to be grateful for what he still had.

SIXTEEN

Mrs. Hastings's voice was woozy, but she'd answered so he didn't give a shit how she sounded. "Ordinarily, I'd apologize for this extremely early call, but I'm in a very bad mood, so if you'd just accommodate me without too many questions, I'd appreciate it. That means I'll pay for your disrupted sleep and my disagreeable mood in case my meaning is unclear. Now here's what I need from you. You're going to have to write this down. I'll wait."

Mrs. Hastings's voice was wide awake when she returned to the phone. "I'm in my office," she said. "What do you need?"

He almost kissed her over the phone, she was so imperturbable and obliging. "Miss Hart is currently in St. Mary's Hospital. She's on the mend but I wish to marry her today. Call whomever you have to call to clear the ceremony in her suite. Pay them whatever they want, promise them whatever they need if it's not money. I want the wedding this afternoon. If I have to talk to someone, give me their name and number and I'll call them. Use the prime minister's name if necessary. He owes me a favor. Two, as a matter of fact," he said brusquely. "I'll call him myself if you like. I don't want any opposition on this. Clear?"

She had to swallow hard, but she thought about Dominic Knight's carte blanche offer of money and spoke with a businesslike calm. "Yes, perfectly clear. What sort of reception were you considering? The suites aren't large."

"I'll see that Katherine has their biggest room. I'll do that as soon as we're done here."

"Flowers?"

"Of course. I want pale yellow roses."

She almost choked because he'd wanted white roses for the church and reception before—lots, he'd said—and she'd ordered three thousand. It took her a moment to clear her throat. "How many yellow roses?"

"I have no idea. I want Katherine to smile when she sees them. I want the suite to look cheerful. Order whatever's necessary."

"Very well." She wasn't going to mention what she was thinking: that he still had to pay for the three thousand white roses.

But perhaps her hesitation hadn't gone unnoticed because Dominic said, "Why don't you send the white roses to some nursing homes and assisted living centers? How would that be?"

"Excellent idea." She was beginning to understand why he was a billionaire. He was a brilliantly discerning man. "I believe the reverend is out of town for the next two days. Should I recruit his assistant?"

"Anyone who can read the marriage ceremony will do. If not the assistant, a magistrate. The religious aspect is immaterial. As for the reception, deal with Martin and Quinn once you know the hospital guidelines. I care little about anything but the actual ceremony. Although I'd like the wedding to be as beautiful as possible for Katherine's sake. And if you'd have Ms. Strahan find something suitable for Katherine to wear in bed. Also, have her invoice me for her work on the bridal gown as well as any time she's given to maternity clothes. We won't be needing either." Ignoring Mrs. Hastings's small gasp, he said, "If you have any questions, please don't hesitate to call. I'll be at the hospital with Katherine. And unless you hear from me with a change in plans, we'll see you this afternoon."

He stood for a moment in the quiet corridor, shaking away his fatigue. Although his throbbing knuckles had the potential to keep him awake. They ached like a son of a bitch. He ran his palms over his shirt: not bad, semi-dry.

Moving down the hall to the nurse's station, he said politely, "Who do I talk to about reserving your largest suite?"

He was grateful to find an amenable employee, and an even more amenable hospital administrator who was speedily summoned from his home nearby. In short order, the administrator was able to rearrange some Middle Eastern prince's room assignment to accommodate the wedding plans. Dominic didn't have to use the prime minister's name, although he did mention the hospital's front entry was looking outdated and said he'd be happy to have it refurbished if his bride-to-be could be moved into the hospital's royal suite.

Dominic was exquisitely polite, soft-spoken, and gracious. He was capable of the most polished civilities if he chose. In this case, he wanted complete, unquestioning consent, since Mrs. Hastings was also likely to require further policy adjustments. Once an agreement was reached,

Dominic smiled, rose from his chair, and cordially extended his hand across Mr. Pitt-Ralston's desk top. Quickly coming to his feet, the administrator sensibly overlooked Dominic's bloody knuckles, kept his gaze averted from the torn flesh, and shook his hand.

"I'll have one of my people contact you," Dominic said. "Tell him what you need for the entry remodel and he'll send you a check. You've been very helpful."

"Happy to be of service, Mr. Knight. Our best wishes on your marriage."

Dominic's smile was instant and dazzling. "Thank you. I'm looking forward to it."

Dominic returned to Kate's room, politely chatted with the nurse, then pulled a chair up to the bed. He chose Katherine's right side since the IV was in her left arm, along with the blood pressure cuff and oxygen saturation clip on her finger. The chair was large, cushioned, comfortable; Dominic almost immediately dozed off.

"Hey."

At Kate's whisper, Dominic came awake in a flash, sat up, and smiled. "Hey, baby," he said softly, leaning forward and taking Kate's hand in both of his. "How are you feeling?"

"Sad."

"Me too." He glanced over at the nurse. "Give us a minute."

As the door closed on the nurse, Kate glanced at his knuckles and raised her brows.

"I punched a brick wall."

"They look like they hurt."

"Not as much as all the rest hurts. It was a really nice dream, perfect in fact. You and me and"—he stopped, took a small breath—"you and me is just fine."

Kate's eyes teared up. "You don't have to marry me now that…all this happened," she said, avoiding the painful words too. "We can just go back to—"

He put his index finger over her mouth to stop the words. "You're not getting away. No way, no how. So don't start." He held her gaze for a moment, then dropped his hand.

"I'm just trying to give you an out—"

"For what?" he asked, flatly. "This is a stupid conversation."

She smiled faintly. "Then if you don't want an out, you *have* to marry me now because I'm so sad."

His eyes widened slightly. "Right now?"

"What if I said yes."

He was pleased to see the tiny teasing glimmer in her eyes. "Then we'd do it. And freak out Mrs. Hastings."

"You're always so good to me—generous and…caring and"—her voice broke at the last. "Oh God—I have to—stop crying."

"It's just going to take time, baby," he whispered, wiping away her tears with the sheet. "And a helluva lot of mental adjustment. Since we're both a little crazy," he added with a flicker of his brows and a faint grin, "it might take even longer than usual to crank up the mental adjustment circuits."

She sniffled and gave him a shaky smile. "If you're trying to make me feel better, it's kinda working." She sighed. "Sorta, maybe…"

"I'm trying to make both of us feel better." He swallowed, slowly inhaled, struggled for control. "I figure a minute, an hour, a day at a time." He rested his forehead on her hand for a second, then sat up again, his blue gaze steady. "You and me, babe. We can do anything, right?"

The world shrank and it was only them in their small broken paradise, Dominic's strong warm hands cupping hers. "You and me," she said with a nod, when she didn't feel like she could do much of anything right now. But she wanted to be good to him like he was to her, and he was asking for something when he rarely did. "Although I have one not-so-small request if you don't mind."

He gave her a mute why-are-you-even-asking look. "Just for the record, I never mind. You can have anything. I've told you that before. The offer's still the same."

The small worry line between her brows disappeared. "Oh good. Then I'd like Nana at our wedding."

Dominic grinned. "She should be landing soon. Or she might already be on her way in from Heathrow."

"No!" Kate shrieked. "Really?" Her face brightened. "Ohmygod, Dominic, you're incredible!"

He laughed. "Do I get a kiss for being incredible?"

"You'll get all the kisses I'll ever have!" Kate's voice suddenly went soft and her bottom lip trembled. "How did you know I *needed* Nana?"

"I just figured," he said gently. "And in the way of my own not-so-small request, I'd like to go home after the wedding. Or whenever Dr. Fuller gives the okay for you to fly." He saw her small flinch. "Just think about it, that's all."

Kate sucked in her breath. "My job…Joanna."

"They'll understand. I'll talk to them."

"What about my contract? And Joanna can't handle things alone."

"I'll deal with the contract and Joanna. Let me do this, baby. Please?"

"Home sounds really...wonderful," she whispered.

"Talk to Nana. See what she says. We can go back to Minnesota or San Francisco. Either place is fine with me. And Joanna will understand. As for CX Capital, it's a big fucking organization. They won't remember your name in a week. We both know that."

"So you're saying I can bail."

"I'm saying I'll take care of it."

There was the smallest pause. "Really?"

"Just say the word."

She shut her eyes for a second, then opened them and nodded. "Okay."

He didn't realize he'd been holding his breath. "Let me check with Max on Nana's ETA," he said on a slow exhale, intentionally changing the subject now that he'd been given permission to execute his plans. Texting Max, he waited for a reply, then held up his phone and smiled. "They're on their way into London. Want to talk to Nana?"

Biting her lip, Kate shook her head, trying not to burst into tears. Nana had always been her comfort and solace when life went bad; she could make everything better, or at least livable. When she'd been young, Nana could make the hurt disappear just by saying, "Let's make chocolate chip cookies. Gramps will love them too." And by the time they'd be eating cookies warm from the oven, whatever childhood crisis had brought her to tears had vanished. "I'm so glad she's almost here," Kate whispered, swallowing hard. "Oh God…" Her words dissolved into a gut-wrenching sob and the tears brimming in her eyes spilled over in a flood of anguish.

Leaping up from the chair, Dominic quickly surveyed the usable space on the narrow bed, shoved the safety rail down, slid in next to Kate, and, avoiding the IV line, took her in his arms. Holding her as if she were made of glass, he dipped his head and brought his lips to hers in a feather-light kiss. Then he wiped her cheeks and said quietly, "As soon as Nana arrives, I want to get married. No more waiting." He smiled his beautiful, patient smile. "You have to say yes."

She nodded and sniffled and tried to smile back.

"That's not a tiptop smile—and it's wetter than hell, but hey, I'll take it. You're not the only one who feels like crying." Bending his head, he kissed her cheek. "But it's gotta get better, baby. It can't get worse."

"I hope not…and I hope—you don't mind—a weeping bride," she said in a soggy hiccupy voice.

"Cry buckets. I don't give a shit, just so long as you're my bride." He gave her face another swipe of his shirt-sleeve. "Maybe we should have a tear-wiper standing by," he teased. He gently wove his fingers through hers. "Seriously though, let me give Mrs. Hastings a call. Hurry her along."

Kate glanced up, startled.

Dominic grinned. "I woke her at five this morning. She's been hustling for a few hours already." Dominic saw a real smile that time.

"Now there's an image," Kate murmured.

"Hey, don't knock it. She was nice. Accommodating."

"And adding digits to her invoice as you spoke."

"Who cares? She's doing it. Now I need a real kiss just to get me through the next few *endless* hours until our wedding."

Dr. Fuller walked in on their real kiss and loudly cleared her throat.

Dominic looked up. "Good morning," he said, not moving.

Kate blushed. "Get off the bed," she hissed.

Slowly unwrapping his arms from around Kate, he slid off the bed and smiled at the doctor. "Katherine's feeling better."

"I'm glad to hear that. We'll check her over and if all's well, she can be moved into a room." The doctor looked at the nurse who'd followed her in carrying a chart, then glanced at the bedside monitor. "Blood pressure normal," the doctor said. "Heart rate good, oxygen—excellent. Let's check for bleeding." Her exam was brief and painless. "On the mend," she said, afterward. "We can take off the patches and clip, the cuff. All your vitals are normal again." She smiled. "The resiliency of youth is amazing. Are you getting hungry?"

"Starved."

"You can order what you wish from the menu. The kitchen here is quite good."

"I'm having food brought in," Dominic said.

"I see. Fine. And if you don't feel dizzy, Katherine, you're cleared to walk around with help. We'll leave the IV in until that saline solution runs out. You might be a little sore for a while, so I'll leave a prescription for some pain meds. Do you have any questions?"

"How soon can we try to have another child?" Kate asked in a rush.

"There's no hurry." Dominic's voice was brusque, his fear of losing Katherine too stark.

"Dominic, I'd just like to know," Kate whispered, choking back tears.

"Oh, God, baby, I didn't mean it." Quickly sitting back down on the bed, he cradled her in his arms. "Whatever you want, okay?" For a man who'd made unilateral decisions his entire life, his willingness to yield to Kate on so significant an issue was a remarkable measure of his love. "You decide," he murmured, wiping away the tears sliding down her cheeks.

"Most women feel the way you do, Katherine," Dr. Fuller said, not unfamiliar with the scene. "It's almost a universal desire. So as soon as you have one normal period, you're cleared in terms of your recovery."

"There," Dominic said softly. "That's not so long."

Kate managed a shaky smile. "We can decide together."

"Thanks, baby. I'm just a little worried, that's all." He looked at the doctor. "Is there any way to know if Katherine will hemorrhage again?"

"I very much doubt it," the doctor said. "But it's impossible to offer a blanket assurance."

"Would it help if Katherine were less active if she becomes pregnant again?" Dominic asked, wondering if Kate's nearly sleepless schedule in the early weeks of her pregnancy might have been a risk factor.

"We don't recommend strenuous exercise, but otherwise, a normal lifestyle is perfectly fine. Pregnant women need a modest amount of activity. I wouldn't recommend any Olympic tryouts," Dr. Fuller added with a faint smile.

He'd hire an ob-gyn to live on site if Katherine became pregnant. He wasn't taking any chances. But that conversation could wait. Dominic smiled at the doctor. "Can Katherine be moved into another room now?"

"Absolutely."

"Do we have leave to fly home in the next few days?"

"It shouldn't be a problem."

"I have a doctor who travels with me on occasion. I'll have him come along."

Dr. Fuller nodded. "Then I'm sure you needn't worry. I'll see you tomorrow."

Once the doctor left, Dominic went out to the front desk and asked if Katherine could be moved into a transitional room to avoid the bustle of activity in the royal suite. By now, he expected that Mrs. Hastings had marshaled a small army to bring in all the necessary supplies for their wedding.

Shortly after Kate was ensconced in her room, Martin arrived with food Quinn had prepared. The major domo didn't mention the miscarriage. Dominic had warned everyone not to bring it up or offer condolences. And sometime later, just as Kate was finishing a hearty meal of all her favorite foods, Nana walked in, dressed in her best navy blue pants suit and sensible shoes.

"I hear you're getting married today," Nana said, giving Kate a wink. "I wasn't about to miss that. Did Dominic tell you I've been packed for weeks?"

Kate felt her spirits lift as if by magic, like someone

flicked a switch from the bad to good vibrations. She smiled. "Thanks for coming, Nana."

Nana snorted. "As if you could have kept me away. And Dominic has orders to keep me up to date on your life when you aren't in the mood to answer my questions." She handed her purse to Dominic as she approached the bed. "So fair warning, sweetie. I'm going to be *fully informed* from now on." She opened her arms and leaned over the bed. "Now give me a hug."

Dominic's mouth quirked faintly as he looked for somewhere to deposit Nana's heavy purse. He wasn't normally treated like a bell boy or valet. Walking over to the windows, he set the black leather bag on the wide marble ledge, then turned back to see Nana pulling a chair up to the bed. "Go and get some sleep," she said over her shoulder. "You look tired. I'll sit with Katie."

"You *should* go home and rest for a few hours," Kate said softly. "You've had a sleepless night."

"I'm not going home. I'm fine." Dominic moved toward the bed. "But if Nana's here, I will go and make a few phone calls." When he reached Kate, he bent and kissed her. "I won't be gone long, baby."

"Good," she whispered. "Because I was mostly being polite."

He grinned from close range. "You're still weak. It's affecting your bossy impulses."

"Then enjoy your short holiday from bossiness," she whispered.

"I intend to." He winked. "Gonna miss me?"

"Like crazy."

"There you go. That's what I need. Your kind of crazy."

As the door closed on Dominic, Nana asked, "Who won that fight? Those are some bloody knuckles."

"A brick wall won. I cry when things go wrong and Dominic hits things. And he's always so good to me. I feel guilty because I can't possibly give him as much as he gives me." She took a deep breath. "Dominic really wanted this baby, we both did. This would have been something I could have done for him. He's never had a real family."

"I'm so sorry, sweetie. But life doesn't always go according to plan. Wouldn't it be nice if it did? But even the best laid plans go awry. We can't control everything."

"Tell that to Dominic."

"I think he knows that now if his knuckles are any indication. As for life dealing blows, I've had my share of unhappiness—you know that. First, losing your mother, then Gramps. But I'm not here to give you a lecture on bucking up when your heart is breaking. Although I can offer you a little ray of sunshine if you'd like."

"Please. All I do is cry. I'll take even a tiny ray."

Nana patted Kate's hand. "It's okay to cry, sweetie. You probably will for a long time. I had a miscarriage before I became pregnant with your mother, so I know a little about what you're feeling. But in my case, Gramps took it as a sign—a bad one, because so many of his friends he'd served with in Vietnam were having babies who weren't healthy. His friends knew Agent Orange was to blame. The government knew. They just wouldn't admit it."

"Jesus, Nana," Kate breathed. "How awful."

"You bet your life it was awful—for a whole lot of

families. Gramps didn't want a child of his to suffer because he'd spent a year in a country that was regularly sprayed with Agent Orange. So after my miscarriage, he was even more adamant about not having children. 'No more babies, Lori Lee,' he said. When he called me both names like that I always knew he meant it bone deep."

Kate's eyes opened wide.

"You're right," Nana said bluntly. "I didn't listen. I felt that I had a say in the decision too. So when I became pregnant with your mother, I didn't tell your grandfather until almost five months later. I was always on the thin side and Roy worked long hours, so I thought I might get by with it."

"Wow, Nana. What did Gramps say when he found out?"

"He didn't say a word. He just turned around, walked out of the house, and I didn't see him for two weeks. He slept down at the store. He came back early on a Sunday morning. I'll always remember it. It was summer, the busy time for him, but he stood in our bedroom doorway, looking at me with the saddest eyes I'd ever seen. 'Vinnie's covering for me,' he said, as if I'd asked. Then he went on in that quiet way of his—you know your grandfather never raised his voice. He said, 'I love you, Lori. I wouldn't have come back from Vietnam if I hadn't loved you so much I refused to die. So if you want this baby, I do too. If something's wrong with the baby, we'll just take care of it. That's it. We don't have to talk about this again.' And we never did. Your mother was beautiful and healthy. Roy gave away cigars for nearly a year he was so happy. Now, the reason I'm going on about this for so long is because I don't want you to think what happened means it's going to happen again. And I'm guessing if you talk to other women who have had miscarriages, most of them have perfectly fine families now. I'm not saying you shouldn't grieve for this loss. It's only natural. But it's not the end of everything." She suddenly smiled. "And I'm pretty sure Dominic isn't going to say he doesn't ever want any children like your Gramps did. So that's one less hurdle, sweetie."

"Between you and Gramps, no wonder I'm so stubborn."

Nana winked. "I like to think of stubbornness in positive terms—like persistence and strength."

"And wanting your own way," Kate murmured.

Nana laughed. "Maybe—sometimes. You don't remember your mother much, but she knew what she wanted too. I always blamed Gramps and he blamed me for her bullheadedness. Your dad was opinionated too. So I'm guessing you're genetically predisposed."

"Thanks, Nana. Now I have an excuse." Kate smiled, a new warmth in her eyes. "And hearing about your miscarriage gives me hope. I need that."

"That's why I told you. Consider me here to dispense all the hope you need. When you've lived as long as I have, you have lots of feel good stories. Speaking of feel good—are you excited about your wedding? I sure am. I was beginning to worry."

"Sorry I didn't tell you sooner. But everything was messy for a while."

"I'm not looking for a detailed account. Whatever it was, I'm glad it's over. Love can be messy. Life too. It's hard to order perfection every day of the week. Believe me, I know."

SEVENTEEN

The royal suite was ready by five, giving Mrs. Hastings bragging rights for at least the next decade. She'd accomplished the impossible in twelve hours.

Max took Nana to the lounge to introduce her to the wedding guests and Dominic escorted Kate to the suite so she could get comfortable before the festivities began. Stopping on the threshold with Kate holding tightly to his arm, Dominic regarded the festooned suite with a slight frown. It looked like an over-the-top version of *A Midsummer Night's Dream*.

But Kate was smiling as she surveyed the room, then said, "Oh my…" in breathy delight and his frown instantly faded. "Yellow roses like that morning in Hong Kong," she whispered, glancing up at Dominic. "You *are* a romantic."

"Only for you, baby. I wanted to see you smile."

She winked. "Good work, Mr. Knight."

He dropped a kiss on her cheek. "My pleasure, Miss Hart."

"Not for long—the Miss Hart part."

"No." He smiled one of those smiles that made the breath catch in Kate's throat. "Dreams really can come true."

Then Mrs. Hastings glided over, elegant in a pale blue designer suit and her pearls, not a hair out of place despite the fact that she'd spent the last twelve hours barking orders at scores of people to bring this wedding to the level of perfection expected by a client of Mr. Knight's stature. Which also accounted for a faint wariness in her gaze when she asked, "Will this do, Mr. Knight?"

"Ask Katherine," Dominic said pleasantly. "This is for her."

The suite was a veritable bower of pale yellow roses, their scent perfuming the air, dozens of large baskets and vases filled with sumptuous rose bouquets, miles of ornamental ribbon-trimmed rose garlands and swags all artfully disposed. A long table, placed against one wall, was draped in white, fringed, beaded brocade set with towering, flower-draped silver candelabra, lined with rows of sparkling crystal flutes, adorned with gleaming silver salvers awaiting Quinn's food. Several ornate silver torchieres served as magnificent accent pieces in the embellished suite. And once the whimsical fantasy was complete, the prominent set designer who'd been dragged out of his bed that morning to take charge of executing Dominic's request for a beautiful wedding had offered his display to Mrs. Hastings with a triumphant, theatrical bow.

"It's breathtaking, Mrs. Hastings," Kate murmured, thoroughly enchanted as Nigel intended. "Truly breathtaking."

Mrs. Hastings visibly relaxed; those who were familiar with her air of command would have been surprised. "I'm pleased you like it. Mr. Knight requested the pale yellow roses."

"He knows I like them." Kate looked at Dominic with a twinkle in her eyes. "Don't you?"

"I have a very good memory, Katherine," he said, very, very softly. "I think you know that."

Mrs. Hastings cleared her throat and said, "Ahem," in her more normal magisterial tone of voice. "If I might introduce the minister," she added briskly, indicating an elderly man in black standing near the windows.

"Of course," Dominic said coolly. "Let me see Katherine into bed first. She's still quite weak. Did Ms. Strahan send over something for Katherine to wear?"

"It's in the closet."

A few minutes later, Katherine was settled in bed and Mrs. Hastings waved over the minister. Introductions were made, and Dominic offered his thanks for the minister's response on such short notice. He explained that Max had the guests waiting in the nearby lounge, then politely asked if they might be excused briefly so Katherine could be dressed.

Moments later, Dominic carried over the dress from the closet, and they discovered that the young designer had simply adjusted the design Kate had chosen to jacket length and added a jeweled border to the hem. With the button front, it was a simple matter to slip on even in bed. Smoothing the cream silk with her palms, Kate lightly brushed the glittering jewels. "These are gorgeous. I feel like a princess. Do you like it?" She glanced up when Dominic didn't respond.

Remembering how happy they'd been when Katherine had chosen the dress to accommodate her pregnancy, he'd suddenly been overwhelmed with sorrow. But as Kate's words registered, he quickly smiled. "It's perfect. You're perfect. I couldn't be happier."

"Liar."

His lashes drifted downward slightly, shielding his gaze. "I'm happy about us getting married," he said quietly. "I'm happy about you and me and our future." He hesitated just for a moment, then his eyes suddenly opened and fixed on her. "Thinking about the rest is torture."

"We have to some time."

"Maybe you do. My response to distress is usually some kind of violence." He paused, took a deep breath, forcibly suppressed the hectic tumult and dark animosity in his brain. "But if you want to talk about it, I'll listen."

"You can't talk about it?"

It took him a long time to answer. "No."

"I *have* to talk about the baby."

"I know." He studied her for another lengthy interval. "Go ahead," he finally said. "Talk."

She told him about the feeling of emptiness that wouldn't go away, about her vast guilt, she told him how she'd been picking out baby names and really liked James for a boy if he wouldn't have minded. He shut his eyes for a second when she said that. Toward the end she told him about Nana having a miscarriage before her mother was born. "So maybe it's genetic and the second time's the charm. But that doesn't mean this doesn't hurt like hell," she whispered. "I feel like punching things too sometimes. You're not the only one."

He'd been sitting on the edge of the bed while she talked and he leaned in close now. "Do it. Be my guest."

She smiled faintly. "At least I can't mess up that wrinkled shirt."

"Martin brought me something else. It's around here

somewhere." He opened his arms wide. "Come on, a couple of punches. We'll both feel better."

She punched his chest hard, twice with each fist.

He raised his brows. "Really, that's it? That's all you got?"

She smacked him on the cheek, he fell back on the bed moaning, and she laughed. "God, you're juvenile."

Sitting up, he gave her a quick kiss. "Then you're going to have to teach me to be a grown-up. And I'll teach you how to be a cutthroat businesswoman. We'll merge our skill sets."

She gave him a little sideways glance. "You don't want to talk about this anymore, do you?"

The blue of his eyes was unfathomable. "No."

"Okay, I'll save the rest for later, but one thing more right now. The miscarriage might have had something to do with the contraception shot. It could have. You can at least acknowledge that, can't you?"

He let out a little breath, looked down at his hands for a moment, then his gaze came up. "Yeah," he said. "I thought about it. That would have been my fault."

"It's not anyone's fault, Dominic. It's just a possible factor."

"Look," he said, "I'm going to get dressed now if that's okay with you."

She smiled. "Thanks for listening."

He nodded, slid off the bed and walked away.

She watched him strip off his shirt, toss it into the closet, put on striped dress shirt, quickly button it up and tuck it in, his movements swift and sure, his smooth efficiency always fascinating to witness. There wasn't a wasted motion, as if he was used to dressing quickly—not a thought she cared to dwell on.

He slipped into a Prince of Wales flint gray sport coat Martin had brought over, left the tie on the hanger, then adjusted his cuffs, buttoned the sport coat, shut the closet door, and turned back to Kate.

"You're prettier than I am," Kate said with a smile.

His dark, longish hair was messy, ruffled like always, as if he perennially stood in a breeze. His stark beauty was casually worn. His tall, broad-shouldered form was strong and muscular, his physical perfection implausible, miraculous.

"Not even close, Katherine," Dominic said softly. "You're so beautiful, you take my breath away. You're the best present life has given me." For a second, his eyes narrowed. "I'd like to lock you away"—his nostrils flared briefly—"but I know I can't." His mouth twitched into a small smile. "Although I'm not giving any guarantees."

"Nana might be packing heat," Kate quipped. "So watch it."

"According to Max she is."

"Oh, God," Kate moaned. "Why am I not surprised?"

"Because she's seventy-five, makes her own rules, and knew she was traveling on a private plane, that's why."

"You could have taken it away."

Dominic laughed so long, Kate's mouth was pursed tightly before he finally stopped.

"It wasn't that funny," she said with a little sniff.

"Yeah, it was. Nana told Max to not even consider taking her handgun away. He told her he wasn't that stupid and a cordial détente was reached. That means doing things Nana's way. Which also helps to explain the trouble I have keeping you in line."

"I'm sorry," she said, sugar sweet. "Did you say—keep me in line?"

"We can talk about it later, after we're married."

Her brows rose. "Or we could talk about it now."

"Why don't I go and get our guests?" He moved toward the door.

"Coward."

He grinned. "I prefer to think of it as diplomacy," he said, grasping the door knob. "You shouldn't get agitated. You're still recovering."

But Kate was smiling when the door shut on Dominic.

EIGHTEEN

During the ceremony, Nana stood on one side of the bed, Dominic on the other, Kate's hand in his while the minister read the vows. The guests were those from Dominic's house and office staff who couldn't be ignored, along with the set designer, Nigel Bell, and Mrs. Hastings, who'd been included out of gratitude for their masterful accomplishments. The room was packed.

Max frowned at Nigel when the designer took out his cell phone and started taking a picture of the bride and groom and even a man of Nigel's bravado understood the danger. He quickly put away his phone and Max's attention returned to the ritual being performed.

The ceremony had reached the point where rings were exchanged. The minister waited while Dominic took two rings from his jacket pocket, handed one to Kate, then leaned forward slightly.

"Look inside," he said quietly, as if they were alone in the room, the world, his focus exclusively on Kate.

She turned the wide gold band in her fingers and read the inscription: *Katherine loves Dominic*. Followed with a colorful enameled happy face.

"I hope you don't mind," he said softly. "I presumed."

Her smile was warm with love. "It's perfect."

"Your ring is inscribed *Dominic loves Katherine*, happy

face. See?" He held out her wedding band of square-cut diamonds.

"No property of?" she murmured, a teasing note in her voice.

"I figured that's what the wedding bands mean. Mutual property of."

A mischievous smile this time. "Good call."

Leaning in even closer, Dominic said brusquely, "I'm serious, Katherine."

"You better be"—her brows lifted in warning—"because I'm *super*serious about that."

Of all the audacious qualities in their relationship, perhaps the strongest was the obsessive nature of their love. It was enigmatic and amazing, exuberant and chaste, a bona fide miracle Dominic in particular recognized, having been alone so long.

Nana cleared her throat and Dominic looked up. "I'm an old lady. I don't like to stand too long. Could you have this discussion later?"

Kate flushed with embarrassment.

Dominic's mouth twitched, but he suppressed his guffaw, thinking it likely would offend the minister. "Forgive me, Mrs. Hart. It was inconsiderate of me to make you wait." Then he nodded for the minister to resume the service.

This time it was Nana's mouth that twitched and she wished Roy were still alive. He would have liked Dominic. Roy had been equally unflappable. And she looked up for a second to send her husband a message, because she talked to him a lot and she wanted him to know: *Our baby girl is getting married to a nice man, Roy. Are you smiling?*

When the service was over and the minister pronounced the conventional phrase, "You may kiss the bride," Nana waited politely until Dominic had kissed Kate before she said, "Gramps wanted to give you a kiss too." She kissed Kate on her cheek. "And one from me, baby girl," she whispered, and kissed her again.

"Don't cry, Nana, or I'll cry," Kate whispered, seeing the tears in her grandmother's eyes. "And tell Gramps thanks."

"He knows." Nana blinked and smiled. "Now, I don't know about you," she said, her voice suddenly brisk, "but that champagne from the bottom of the Baltic has me intrigued." She looked at Dominic.

"Coming up, Nana." He'd no more than spoken than one of Quinn's servers appeared, carrying a tray with four glasses.

The minister didn't stay long and whether it was his departure or the fact that half of the bottles of champagne already had been consumed, the reception turned lively. The recorked champagne was excellent even after having lain in six hundred feet of water for almost two hundred years.

Nana was enjoying herself, entertaining Nigel and others with stories of fishing in the Boundary Waters and comparing notes with Nigel on lures; he made his own colorful ones for trout fishing. Even Mrs. Hastings was seen to actually smile a real smile when Nana complimented her on not only the entire wedding but also her pearls. "Family heirlooms?" Nana inquired graciously. At which point Mrs. Hastings explained her necklace's history at some length to Nana's interested nods and smiles. Decades of making polite conversation with parents who thought their children were geniuses had honed Nana's diplomatic skills. She wasn't always bluntly outspoken.

Having drunk their token toast and eaten from Quinn's splendid smorgasbord, accepted congratulations from all their guests, and chatted with everyone, Dominic and Kate relaxed on the bed, enjoying the rising level of conversation and congeniality. His jacket and shoes discarded, Dominic held Kate in his arms, content, deeply satisfied, relieved that their relationship was legally validated, that they were married at last. He'd never been a man who'd waited for what he wanted.

That his pleasure was partially clouded by the loss of their child was only normal. But *Katherine's mine*, he reflected adoringly. *Now and forever.* That certainty helped mitigate the pain.

Recognizing Dominic's sudden quiet, Kate turned slightly to look up at him. "How are you feeling?" At his blank expression, she said, "Sorry. Wrong question with you. Are you okay?"

"Yes. And don't get pissed, but I was just thinking that you're mine." He smiled faintly. "Till the end of time. Too corny?"

"Uh-uh. It's sweet. And I know what you mean about having someone." She ran her thumb over one of his shirt buttons, then looked up and her voice dropped in volume. "You had your sister and I had Gramps and Nana"—she paused.

"But you always felt—"

"Just a little bit alone," Kate finished softly.

"Yeah." His eyes were grave. "Sometimes more than just a little."

She smiled. "And now we're not alone."

He slid his finger under her chin and lifted her face. Their eyes met. "And now we're not alone," he whispered, and slowly, unhurriedly, touched her mouth with his. And in the lush pleasure and ripening silence, they committed to memory the sheer beauty and magic of the moment.

Afterward, Dominic surveyed Kate with slight puzzlement. "What? Did I do something?" He was beginning to recognize Kate's moods. Or perhaps he loved her enough to pay attention.

She shook her head. "It's just me. I'm feeling really happy and feeling guilty about being so happy. Like it's not right or I shouldn't be so un—"

"Don't," he interrupted softly. "It's a new day, okay? It has to be—or we're not going to get through this."

"I know." She sighed softly. "You're right."

Wanting to trample that sigh into the ground or carry the weight of it himself, he said, straight-faced, "Jesus, let me record this moment for posterity." He made a check in the air, smiling faintly. "You're saying I'm *right*?"

She giggled. "Maybe just this once."

"Uh-uh. Not just once. Now that you're mine and can't get away, I'll start training you. Teach you to take orders. Make you understand that I'm *always* right."

She sat up straight. "That's never gonna happen."

"Hell yeah, it might," he drawled.

"No way."

But she was smiling. "Two games out of three?" he said.

"I set the rules."

"Go for it. You still don't have a chance."

Her face flushed. "We'll see about that."

"After everyone leaves," he said, pleased he'd averted another outpouring of tears. At least for now.

Although he knew neither could ever forget their irretrievable loss.

But they didn't have a chess play-off that evening because once everyone left, Kate was too fatigued. Nana kissed her good night and left with Max, who was driving her back to Dominic's house. Mrs. Hastings and Martin saw that the suite was cleaned up quickly and quietly before leaving. Then Dominic helped Kate get ready for bed and held her until she fell asleep. He still had two calls to make before they could leave London, so he waited until she was sleeping deeply before he slipped from the bed and walked out into the hall.

Justin picked up on the first ring.

"I need your help with Katherine's contract at CX Capital," Dominic said. "We're leaving London in a day or so. The good news is that I'm married as of five hours ago. The bad news is we lost the baby. We're at St. Mary's Hospital. The doctor says Katherine can go home day after tomorrow."

"I'm sorry about the baby. It must hurt like hell."

"Yeah, it's killing me."

A silence fell, thick and dry as dust.

Measurably nervous, Justin spoke first. "If I'm not out of line to say it, congratulations on your marriage. I know Katherine is"—he hesitated, rejected words having to do with love considering Dominic's history—"important to you." Under different circumstances, Justin would have made a quip or two about Dominic and marriage.

"Thanks, I appreciate it," Dominic said, as if Justin's nerves weren't vibrating through the phone. "I've been wanting to marry Katherine for quite a while. Now, if you need our attorneys to step in at CX Capital, let Roscoe know," he said crisply, back on topic. "If you need more than attorneys to clear this up, if I have to talk to someone, let *me* know."

"I don't expect problems." Justin quickly adjusted to Dominic's businesslike tone. "Bill's a good guy. I'll explain the situation to him. It's completely understandable. And if there's anything else I can do to help with—whatever..." His voice trailed off.

"Thanks. That's all I need at the moment." Dominic suddenly sounded tired. "I'll give you a call later, make sure everything went smoothly. *Ciao*."

When he spoke to Joanna, her response to the news of Kate's miscarriage was wholly female; she offered sympathy without inhibition and restraint. "Oh, how awful! Are you sure Kate's all right? Does she want someone to sit with her? How terrible for you! I can't imagine anything sadder when you were looking forward to the baby. Just tell me what I can do to help."

If he weren't so wiped, Dominic might have considered smiling at the gender difference. Instead, he said in as friendly a tone as he could conjure up under the circumstances, "Thanks, Joanna, but we're both semi-managing the pain. We were married a few hours ago though so there's pleasure in that."

"Married! How wonderful. I wish you happiness."

"Thank you. We'll be leaving London in a day or so. I just wanted to let you know. Katherine's sleeping now. It was a long day for her. I'll tell her I talked to you. She gave me permission to speak to you about her leaving. Are we good?"

"Yes, of course."

"I'll tell Katherine you've been considerate about her circumstances. Please accept my appreciation for your understanding." He paused briefly and his exhaustion was evident in his voice when he added, "You can expect some new clients from time to time. And I'm not doing it to be nice. You're good."

"Thank you. That's very kind of you. But before you hang up, I'd like to come and see Kate if she's up to it."

No don't, in case you screw this up. "I'm sure she'd like to see you," Dominic said instead, because Katherine was his wife now; he could deal with anything knowing the permanence of that bond. "I'll tell Katherine you'll be over."

With those two necessary calls accomplished, Dominic returned to the suite and spent another hour on his e-mails. Then he found pajama pants and a T-shirt Martin had packed, put them on, and opened the rollaway bed he'd had brought in.

He stood motionless for a moment, his gaze on Kate, debating whether he'd disturb her if he joined her in bed. He smiled faintly. What the hell—it *was* his wedding night.

A yogi couldn't have done it better; he moved each muscle with slow, exquisite restraint as he climbed into bed, put his arms around Kate, and gently drew her against his chest. She sighed once as she snuggled closer.

He smiled. Jesus Christ, that was an impossibly beautiful sound.

A second later, he was sleeping.

NINETEEN

Kate was feeling so good the next morning, she was ready to leave. But Dr. Fuller insisted on one more day in the hospital.

So Dominic settled in, not in the mood to let Kate out of his sight, not sure he'd ever be in the mood, after having nearly lost her. Quinn brought in their breakfast, Martin came in with casual clothes for both of them, and Nana and Leo arrived shortly after ten.

"I came in to say good morning and see how you're feeling," Nana said.

"I'm feeling like I'd like to get out of here, but the doctor said no. Tomorrow though," Kate said from the bed, "I'm free to go."

Nana glanced at Dominic. "And then?"

"The plane's on the tarmac. I'm just waiting until Katherine feels strong enough."

"I'm good," Kate said. "Whenever."

Nana shot a look at Dominic, sitting next to the table with their breakfast remains. "You staying here all day?"

He nodded.

"In that case, if you don't mind, Katie, Leo's going to take me on a rush tour of the museums. He claims he can do it in four hours."

"Take your time, Nana. Dominic will entertain me, won't you?"

He smiled. "I can't think of anything I'd rather do."

Five minutes later, they were alone again and Dominic glanced up from pouring himself another cup of coffee. "Want some? No?" He dropped in four sugar lumps and leaned back in his chair. "Nana must like museums if she's doing the whirlwind tour."

"It's the teacher in her. She sees it as an intellectual obligation." Kate smiled. "I'm not saying she doesn't like art and culture, but the duty part comes first. If there're five museums in town or ten, Nana's going to see them. Are you sure Leo doesn't mind?"

"He doesn't mind. He paints in his spare time, so he's a great tour guide."

"Leo paints?"

"He's really good. He had his own show last year in Sydney and sold out. Meticulous landscapes—photo realism. Impressive stuff. I have one of his landscapes in the dining room in Hong Kong."

"I didn't see it."

"The small dining room." His brows flickered. "Mother requires the formal one."

"Ah—I see."

He grinned. "So polite, baby."

"We've been married only a day. I'm still on my best behavior."

He laughed. "So I should stay alert."

"Not you, your mother. You need someone to protect you."

"And you're taking on the lioness role."

"You betcha." Cupping her fingers and miming claws, she playfully growled.

Dominic grinned. "Now *that* little scene is definitely on my wish list. Should we invite Mother to our wedding reception back home?" At Kate's sudden grimace, Dominic's expression sobered. "Don't worry, baby. I won't let her near you. You've led too sheltered a life to take on the wicked witch. Leave her to me."

"Maybe if I had Nana at my side," Kate said, offering up a tentative smile.

"You don't need Nana, baby, you've got me. No one, including Mother, will ever hurt you." He didn't say, *I'd kill for you*, because he didn't want to freak her out. But there was no question in his mind. "So what do you want to do?" He lifted the remote from the table and raised a brow.

"Take me for a walk down the hall. I'm tired of lying here."

She held Dominic's arm and they walked to the gift shop, where Kate bought some magazines and candy bars.

On their way back to the suite, Dominic gave the bag a little shake. "You must be feeling better. You have enough candy bars for—"

"Me?" She shot him a quick stare. "Is that what you were going to say?"

He laughed. "For you and Miss Bossy both." He winked. "Glad you're back in form, baby. But if you're feeling generous, I'll take one of those pecan things."

"Things?" she said in a little hum. "As in you never eat candy?"

"I don't much. Is that a problem?" He grinned. "Remember who's the real boss before you answer."

She swung her arm and punched him hard.

"Ow, Ow!" he yelped. Flicking his glance sideways to a couple who'd come to a stop at his sharp cry, he turned to Kate with a private little smile. "Playtime, baby?" Then he swept her up in his arms and rolled his eyes at the open-mouthed couple. "A little too much coffee," he said as he strode past them. "It happens every time."

"You're such an exhibitionist," she hissed, hugging him hard, giggling against his neck.

"Always, baby," he murmured, dipping his head and nuzzling the warmth of her hair. "So don't fuck with me in public."

"Maybe I don't care." She looked up at him with a smirk. "What do you think of that?"

That flicker of teasing in her eyes never ceased to make him think of how lucky he was. How the odd, magical evening in Hong Kong had changed his life. "I think it sounds like a match made in heaven," he said softly. "You and me together."

Her eyes filled with tears. "Kiss me," she whispered. *"Right now."*

"Because somehow we found each other in this spectacularly messed up world, right?"

Choking back her tears, she nodded.

He stopped and kissed her in front of the elevators with a dozen people standing by.

But he didn't notice.

Nor did she.

Because Katherine was his world, and he was hers.

Their kiss ended to a round of applause.

Dominic looked around. "We just got married," he said with a smile.

"He means I finally caught him." Kate grinned. "And it wasn't easy."

"She likes to kid. I had to kick her boyfriend's ass and haul her off," Dominic said, walking away.

"Young Americans," someone remarked, matter-of-factly.

An elderly man was smiling as he watched Dominic's departure. "I envy the young chap. A Californian I'd say with that accent."

"That explains the complete lack of manners," a thin, pursed-lipped woman observed, not amused. "And the sandals."

"You're in big trouble," Kate quipped. "Embarrassing me like that. Is it too late for an annulment?"

"It was too late six months ago, baby. Look surprised. I was too. But what can I say . . . Cupid's arrow hits and it's all over." He grinned. "Want me to write a song?"

"Not if there's a cupid in it."

"I could pay someone to write a song."

"Or you could just keep smiling at me like that and I'll forget about your embarrassing me."

This was where he *could* have argued about who started what. "Thanks, baby. I appreciate your understanding."

"Okay, now I'm worried. What do you want?"

"You, permanently, right here." He shifted her slightly in his arms. "Nothing much," he said pleasantly. "One simple request. All the rest is negotiable."

"Okay, yes." No hesitation, a big wide smile.

His eyes creased with pleasure. "Smart girl." Because none of it was negotiable, not really.

After they reached the suite, it turned out Kate wasn't as strong as she thought she was, or perhaps she'd become overfatigued yesterday; she spent a good part of the day napping. Dominic worked on his laptop, looking up to check on her breathing every few minutes because he still hadn't gotten over the frightening events in the operating room. He wasn't sure he ever would.

Nana and Leo returned that afternoon with glowing commentary on the various museum art shows they'd seen, Max arrived shortly after with some reports for Dominic, and Joanna stopped by after work. When Quinn brought in dinner, Joanna stayed and ate with them. It was a festive evening, the food exquisite, Dominic's wine cellar superb, going home the topic of conversation. Joanna was completely circumspect about the details of her agreement with Dominic. And when she gave Kate a check equal to half their business, Kate took one look at the sum and said, "Heaven's no. That's too much. Tell her, Dominic," she added, showing the check to him. "I couldn't possibly take that much."

He glanced at it. "Are you sure?"

"Of course I'm sure. I know what we had in the bank."

Dominic's gaze was bland when he spoke to Joanna. "Why don't you send another check later?" He turned to Kate. "Is there some sum you think appropriate?"

"A third of that."

Dominic smiled at Joanna. "Simple enough. And I know

better than to get into an argument with Katherine over money," he said with a significant lift of his brows. "She's the authority on those matters." He glanced at both women. "Is everybody happy now?"

Since Max had delivered Dominic's check to Joanna, he was well aware of the dynamic playing out. Nana wasn't a participant in the game, but she hadn't been born yesterday, or even last year, and she knew somehow Dominic was involved. But since he obviously was seeing that Kate wasn't obliged to stay in London, she was on board. When it came to having Katie back home, she and Dominic were equally selfish.

If Katie had wanted to stay in London, Nana wouldn't have interfered.

Fortunately, that wasn't an issue.

TWENTY

The next day, Dr. Fuller was delayed in making her rounds. After they'd been waiting some time, Dominic checked with the desk and was told the doctor was dealing with two emergencies. "She'll be in just as soon as she can," he explained to Kate on his return. "Some crisis came up." He frowned and pointed at a chair. "You're not allowed to pace."

Kate wrinkled her nose. "I feel fine."

"Sit, damn it. I don't want any problems."

"You're not the boss of me," Kate said with a grin. "Or at least not yet."

"Jesus, Katherine, you're not feeling that good." He gave her a startled look. "Are you?"

"Remember, the doctor mentioned the resiliency of youth. I feel great. But I'll sit down if you're going to scowl like that. In the interests of—"

"Pleasing me?" he said smoothly.

"I was going to say not pissing you off when I want to leave London."

Dominic laughed. "What was I thinking? Although it sounds as though I have leverage for a while."

"For a limited time." But she sat, folded her hands in her lap, and smiled up at him. "Enjoy it while you can."

He raised his hands, formed his fingers into a picture

frame, and grinned. "Let me savor the moment. Big inno-cent eyes, submissive pose, even Martin inadvertently con-spired by bringing you that little white blouse and flowery skirt." His grin widened and he dropped his hands. "Are you sure you're feeling okay? Not feverish or anything?"

"Very funny. Can't I be practical or sensible?"

"Really?"

"Is that so hard to imagine?"

"From my temperamental darling?" Then he saw her swal-low hard and added, "I can imagine it just fine, baby. Really."

"I want to go home, Dominic," she whispered.

The sadness in her eyes tore at his heart. "Oh God, I'm sorry." Quickly closing the distance between them, he sank to his knees and folded her hands in his. "I shouldn't be teasing you. As soon as you have the doctor's okay, we'll pack up and go." Leaning forward, he kissed her cheek. "Now let's find something to do until Dr. Fuller shows up. Take our minds off"—he paused—"all the bad stuff."

She didn't answer for so long, he was beating himself up for being so bloody unfeeling.

"Sure," she finally said and his heart started up again.

"Want to look at some magazines?" His voice was ultrasoft, afraid he'd startle her if he spoke too loudly with her gaze focused somewhere over his shoulder. "Or maybe watch TV, or would you like to see some of my reports? Max brought over a couple of—"

"Show me the reports."

She was looking straight at him, the bruised spirit in her eyes plain to see, but she was unmistakably back in the world and he felt that restless spark of electricity and joyful possibility he always felt with her. "You sure?" he said gently, because he'd fucked up once already and he wasn't going for twice in two minutes.

"You said you'd teach me how to be a cutthroat businesswoman." A current of sadness still resonated in her voice. "If you'd said hard-assed I would have said, too late." She almost smiled for a second. "But cutthroat? I need lessons there. If you have time."

For one lunatic second he felt as though he'd been offered the keys to paradise and every picture he'd ever imagined of Katherine working beside him rushed by in brilliant flash frames. "I've got time," he said, keeping his voice steady. "I'll go get the paperwork."

In the next half hour, Dominic walked Kate through two deals he was working on, one a software start-up, the other a communications network in India that required a steep learning curve on the flexibility of governmental policy. He was a good teacher, thorough, patient, knowledgeable. And Kate hadn't earned the designation hacker genius for nothing. She was quick; he didn't have to repeat himself. And when Dominic flipped over the last page of the contract, she said, "That's not so bad. You didn't lose me. Although if I were you, I'd think about brokering the deal yourself and save the fees."

"I've been working with Naren for years."

"That explains his exorbitant fee. It's way above the norm. If you don't want to piss off a business colleague, someone else could point out the discrepancy to him."

"Want the job?"

"Sure. I can be bad cop to your good cop."

He smiled. "Perfect. I'm guessing you're going to help improve my profit margins in the future."

Leaning back in her chair, she opened her arms wide and grinned, the sadness gone from her eyes. "I'm guessing you're right."

His smile was doting; there was no other word for it. "Welcome aboard Knight Enterprises, Mrs. Knight." He leaned over and kissed her as she sat beside him. "You don't know how happy this makes me. I don't like being away from you."

"You might get tired of me underfoot every day. Seriously, Dominic."

"I am serious. If there really is a valley of the shadow, I've been there, and now that I've passed through it I'm not letting you out of my sight."

"Good." She gave him a cheerful, sideways glance. "Because that was me being tactful before."

"Fuck that." He grinned. "This may be a dangerous obsession but I like it, so screw tact."

"And it's not as though we're not both a little crazy. I figure obsession just goes with the territory."

Her smile was sweet Jesus beautiful. "Exactly," he said. "A perfectly rational explanation for you and me—us."

Kate's smile suddenly died at the word *us*, and the despair that was never far away crashed over her like a ton of bricks. "You have to give me another baby, Dominic," she whispered. "Soon. So it won't be just us."

Something cold tightened at the back of his neck and slid down his spine, paralyzing his nerves. *Soon.* He hadn't seen this coming; he needed time.

"You have to say yes." Her breathing was fast, the pitch of her voice rising. "You *have* to."

God no, I can't take the chance. "Yes, of course," he said, knowing he'd give her anything at all to make her smile again. Reaching over, he lifted her from her chair and placed her on his lap. "You just have to tell me when you're ready." He'd hire every top specialist in the world, set them up next door, buy the whole fucking street of homes if necessary to house them and keep Katherine safe.

She nodded. "I'll—send you—an invitation," she said in a shaky whisper.

He traced the curve of her bottom lip with his index finger and smiled. "I'll be waiting."

Kate sucked in a breath. "I'm not going to cry all the time." Her mouth trembled. "Really, I won't. I promise."

"Let's get the hell out of here," Dominic said brusquely. "We don't have to wait for the doctor. I'll leave her a message."

"Can we do that?"

She looked so hopeful he would have built the pyramids for her single-handedly to satisfy that hope. "Sure we can." He rose from the chair with her in his arms. "You didn't have a purse, right?"

He was suddenly looking into an unflinching stare.

"I don't carry a purse. Were you thinking of someone else?"

Dominic laughed. "Jesus, sorry. It won't happen again. And I didn't marry any of them, okay?" he added, because, at the moment, Katherine in temper trumped Katherine in tears.

Her gaze narrowed.

"Julia asked *me*." His shoulder lifted faintly. "I explained all that. You're the love of my life, Katherine. You always will be. So you don't have to go apeshit about something that's ancient history."

"It better be." Then she smiled a little. "Remember obsession *can* be dangerous."

"I'm pretty fucking aware of that, thank you very much. And *you* remember, Mrs. Knight," he said with a lift of his brows, "that jealousy's a two-way street; I'm ruthless as hell and if you don't behave, I'll whip your creamy ass."

A real smile this time. "Why don't I try to be good then."

"Try?" He hadn't raised his voice but he didn't have to.

She looked at him blink-free. "I'll try as hard as you do. How about that?"

His jaw unclenched. "I can live with that. So," he said, his voice suddenly mellow, "if you're done jerking my chain, let's get the fuck out of here. I'm going to set you down for a minute while I give Jake a call. He's around here some-where." After placing her on her feet, he hit a name on his cell, then looked up and smiled at the woman who made his sun come up in the morning and his stars shine at night. "You need your jacket, baby. It's not exactly hot outside. Hi, Jake. We're coming down. Main entrance. Five minutes."

TWENTY-ONE

As Jake drove them away from the hospital, Dominic turned to Kate. "If it's all right with you, we'll swing by the office on the way home. It'll take five minutes for me to run up and collect some papers I have to sign."

"Go for it."

"The office, Jake," Dominic directed. "Some of the palladium leases came through." He smiled at Kate. "Feel like spending next summer at Nana's?"

"Do I ever. There's nothing better than summer up north."

"Find a lake place you like and we'll buy it." He grinned. "I'm not averse to staying with Nana, but just not for long. I like to have you for myself. No one else around."

"Me too, with you. There's nothing better."

"In all the whole wide world, baby...we lucked out." Sliding his arm around her shoulders, he pulled her close. He let out a tendril of a breath, a small stirring of melancholy in his gaze. "I need to know you'll always be there."

"I can guarantee that." She smiled, wanting to erase the small distress in his eyes.

"Reassuring," he said softly. "But seriously"—and his voice took on a quiet gravity—"the entire world could disappear and I'd be happy so long as I had you."

She stretched upward and wrapped her arms around

his neck. "Good," she whispered, her words a warm buzz on his lips before she kissed him lightly. "Because I'm not going anywhere."

He studied her for a second, as though she might be a mirage that would disappear because so much in his life wound up broken. Then she smiled, and he thought maybe this time...and smiled back. "You have a God-given talent for making me happy, baby. And I don't fool myself that that's easy."

"I'm not easy to get along with either, in case you haven't noticed," she said with a little lift of her eyebrows.

He laughed softly. "Where I come from you're practically a saint. You don't fight dirty, no low blows, no sharp edges; you don't even hold a grudge. And you lie like shit, which I find weirdly comforting."

Her green gaze was amused. "So I'm not only saintly, but completely lovable."

"Fucking A, baby," he said with a sudden grin that erased the small furrow between his brows. "No question."

When they reached the Knight Enterprises offices, Kate watched Dominic stride across the gravel drive looking more like a surfer, in cargo shorts, a black T-shirt, and sandals, than a billionaire CEO. Looking beautiful—all raw male and supple strength, tall, broad-shouldered and hers—she thought, feeling outrageously happy. Reaching the stairs, he took them at a run, then stopped at the door to chat with the security guard. The young man smiled at something Dominic said, spoke in turn, and Dominic's expression instantly sobered. A moment later, he nodded and walked through the door hastily thrown open for him.

Settling back in the seat, Kate was just reaching for the TV remote when a green Jaguar sedan drove in through the gate and pulled up near the stairs. The driver got out, walked around the car, opened the back door, and a woman with long dark hair emerged. Since her back was to Kate, her face wasn't visible, but she had the willowy slenderness of youth and as she moved up the stairs, it was clear she also had the sleek, polished patina of money. Her short red summer dress was not off the rack—something Kate had come to recognize after being supplied with a lavish designer wardrobe. The woman's green strappy heels matched the little quilted Chanel shoulder bag—their combined cost enough to feed a family for six months; Kate might not know fashion, but she knew numbers. And the young woman's long swingy black hair had the casual elegance seen only on models in glossy magazines.

Kate leaned forward slightly. "Any idea who that is?"

Jake had a good idea, but since he'd never seen Bianca, the young woman Dominic had been forced to marry, he was able to answer with nominal honesty, "No, I've never seen her before." If the privacy glass had been up, he would have called Dominic and given him warning. As it was, he did nothing; he knew Dominic wouldn't want Katherine involved.

Also, there was a chance Bianca would be turned away at the door.

She *was* stopped. But after what looked like a heated exchange at least on Bianca's part, Forbes escorted her inside.

"Is everyone stopped at the door?" Kate asked.

Jake nodded. "Unless they've been previously cleared."

"Has Dominic always had such major security?"

"Yeah. For quite a while."

"Why?"

"Dominic could answer that better than I." Jake's reply was circumspect and guarded. If she didn't know, Dominic didn't want her to know that his high-profile life was inherently vulnerable to threat. With ransom a business model in some countries, someone as rich as Dominic was a natural target. Add personal enemies to the mix and security was a necessity.

Kate understood that Jake was being evasive, so she didn't press the issue. She glanced instead at the digital clock on the small TV—an unconscious reaction perhaps to the fact that the young woman had not reemerged from the building.

Dressed as she was, Kate doubted the woman was there on real business. Also, she had a disquieting resemblance to Julia—tall, dark-haired, slender. Call it female intuition, but Kate would have bet big bucks that the woman was here to see Dominic.

So she faced a dilemma: politely stay in the car or impolitely interfere.

While Kate was debating the merits in conjugal politesse, Forbes—out of caution—had planted himself between the woman and the stairway to the office floor and waited while the receptionist called Helen. Because this young woman, who'd just cursed and insulted him in Italian *and* English, wasn't getting up to see Dominic without someone's okay.

Helen immediately notified Dominic.

He was just about to leave his office, the folder in his hand, when Helen's voice came through on the intercom. As he listened, his scowl deepened and when she finished, his voice was pure ice. "Have her come up, then send her in. I'll take care of this. I don't want any interruptions. *None*. Katherine's outside, so I need an affirmative from you on that."

"No interruptions," Helen said quickly. "I understand."

"Good." He dropped the folder on the desk, slowly exhaled, and mentally ran through his options. Katherine had to have seen Bianca come in. A problem. Huge. There was no doubt in his mind. Helen would do her best, but with Katherine's temper there were no guarantees she wouldn't be pounding on his office door real fucking soon. So, since the bitch was here, the point was to get Bianca in and out quickly and hope Katherine would understand. Or, more realistically, not get too pissed. He wasn't knocking Katherine's jealousy; he understood the concept viscerally.

He was just hoping to avoid the nuclear fallout.

Taking a seat behind his desk, he flicked a switch under the middle drawer, leaned back in his green leather chair, and waited for his office door to open.

Jesus. Everyone's a drama queen, he thought as the door slowly opened and Bianca came to a stop on the threshold in a pose that would have done justice to a soap opera star.

He felt like saying, *I've seen it done better by real actresses*. But he said instead, his voice as cool as his gaze, "Come in, shut the door, and tell me what you want. You have five minutes. I was just about to leave."

As Bianca shut the door, he flicked a second switch under his desk drawer, and when she turned to face him, he winced at her glossy smile.

She walked toward him slowly, her hips swinging. "Are you happy to see me?"

"No. Shouldn't you be home taking care of your baby?"

"Gora took him away," she said pleasantly, referring to her mafioso boyfriend. "It was part of our agreement. He wanted a boy and I wanted his money."

Dominic thought Gora probably wanted the baby's mother as well, but Gora's motivations weren't relevant at the moment. "I'm not giving you any money, if that's why you're here." His blunt words matched his scowl.

Her smile was smooth and easy, undeterred by his words or expression. "Can't I stop by for a friendly visit?"

"Like hell," he said and the temperature in the room went down twenty degrees.

"My, my, such a scowl. If you're going to be cross for no reason"—another practiced smile, Eve in the garden of Eden, unaware she was ruining the world, or in this case fucking up Dominic's life—"why don't we say I came to give you an invitation to my birthday celebration next month. Papa's rented the Villa Borghese for the night. All of Rome will be there." She strolled around the side of Dominic's desk as if she had all the time in the world, as if he did, then stopped within inches of his chair, extracted a gilded envelope from her purse, and handed it to him. "I thought, Why not invite my husband to my birthday celebration?"

"Ex-husband." Dominic took the envelope and dropped it in his wastebasket.

She didn't even blink. She sat down on Dominic's polished desktop, slowly crossed her legs, and twitched her short skirt a little higher over her gleaming thighs. "You're still my husband in Italy," she said, soft as silk. "They don't recognize your divorce."

"That's where you're wrong." He was telling himself not to strangle her, the price was too high. "The divorce papers have been stamped and filed." His blue gaze took on a sardonic edge. "You pay enough in Italy, or anywhere, and they get the job done in a hurry. The minister who took my money is almost as happy as I am."

"That's a shame," Bianca purred, reaching down to stroke his hand, which was resting on his chair arm, smoothing the fine dark hair on his tanned fingers. "I was hoping we could become better friends."

"I'm not interested." Rather than jerk his hand away, he took a small restraining breath and let the scene unfold. Although if she got on her knees, the stage curtain was coming down fast.

"Maybe I can change your mind," she whispered, lightly circling his middle finger. "You like whips. I like whips. You like violence with your sex. I think I might be the woman you've been waiting for." Raising her hand, she slid her warm palm up Dominic's arm. "Gora's too old to play."

"Are you sure?" Dominic repressed his impulse to flinch. "No one does violence better than Gora. I know that for a fact."

She pursed her mouth. "Please. He likes me to play the innocent young maid."

He met her sultry gaze. "And you'd rather play with whips."

"With you I would." She leaned forward slightly more so her full breasts were on display, reached out with her other hand, and trailed the pad of her finger over Dominic's bottom lip. "I hear you can last all night. That you have a world-class dick."

"That'll do," he ambiguously grunted, slapping her hands away, pushing his chair back, and getting to his feet. "Tell your family to look somewhere else to mend their fortunes. I'm not interested in aristocratic whores."

She jumped off the desk, her dark eyes flashing in anger. "How dare you? You bourgeois prick!" she snapped, glowering at him. "My noble family is eight centuries old!" She stamped her foot. "We have royal blood in our veins!"

Oh fuck. Did she just stamp her foot? Was he still in the soap opera? He shut his eyes briefly, told himself this farce was almost over, and kept his temper under control. "Look, just cut the crap. I don't give a shit if you bleed purple. Stay the fuck out of my life. And if you want my advice, I wouldn't tell Gora you were here. Don't delude yourself that you can handle him. You can't. So tell your folks I'm not buying whatever you're selling, and if you show up again, you're toast." His voice took on a vicious edge. "Now get your ass out of my office."

He took a couple steps back because she had sharp nails, her fingers were twitching, and some of the Italian women he'd known were quick tempered and physical. Although, mostly, he wanted to make sure he didn't touch a hair on her head. She might scream assault, then he'd have to deal with attorneys, a lawsuit, and more bullshit from the Danellis.

When she didn't move, he smiled tightly. "Tell Gora hi from me."

That fucking got her moving.

She suddenly twirled on her spike heels with a pirouette he had to admire for sheer kinetic flow and balance. Then she flounced off like that soap opera star he'd first seen in his doorway.

Reaching under his desk drawer, Dominic flicked the switch to unlock the door before she reached it, then flicked a second switch. He was walking toward a bank of bookcases when the door slammed behind her.

Glancing over his shoulder at the sound of footsteps, he saw Max emerge from the adjoining office. "You heard?" The two offices, as well as Helen's post, were wired for situations such as this.

"Yes. Helen warned me."

Dominic slid a disc from an ornate wooden box on the shelf and turning, held it out to Max. "Tell Bianca's family if I hear from or see any of them or their attorneys ever again, the video goes to Gora."

Max took the disc. "Really? To Gora?"

At Max's obvious reluctance, Dominic uttered a grudging sigh. "No, I guess not. Bianca's a little young to die. But Christ, her family has no sense of restraint. *She* thinks because she can turn on a fifty-year-old guy, she can take on the world." He moved back to his desk. "I can understand that naïveté in a sixteen-year-old, but her parents should know better. Tell them they're playing with fire. Make sure they understand." He picked up the folder he'd come for. "The Danellis may think they're the Borgias of the modern world, but tell them I'm the fucking hand of God if they get in my way. And Gora's my weapon. Look, Katherine's waiting, so I'm out of here," Dominic added, striding toward the door. "Better send at least two men with the disc—more if you think it necessary. I don't trust the Danellis and I don't want any of our men hurt. You'll make some copies?"

"Of course. We'll see that it gets there tomorrow."

"Thanks." Dominic paused with his hand on the doorknob. "Why don't you go home for a few weeks? We'll be leaving London most likely tomorrow and we have security in San Francisco. You and I can deal with business over the phone or by e-mail. Okay?" At Max's nod, Dominic turned the knob and pulled the door open. "Give my best to Liv and Conall. See you in a few weeks. I gotta go. I don't want Katherine upset."

Leaving his office, Dominic smiled at Helen. "Think that's the last we see of her?"

"I don't know." Helen's eyebrows shot up in dubious commentary. "You have a lot of money."

"Max is going to scare the shit out of them tomorrow."

"Good luck with that."

"Jesus, Helen," Dominic said with a grin. "You don't think I know how to scare people?"

"I suppose. You do have the knack."

"Raised in my family, who wouldn't?" he said derisively. "At least I got something out of all that grief. So you're better off betting on me than the Danelli family when it comes to cold-blooded intent." He raised the folder slightly. "I'll get this back to you tomorrow. Go home. We're done here. Say hi to Mike."

He was halfway down the hall when he heard the raised female voices. Breaking into a full-out run, he reached the top of the stairs seconds later and saw Katherine and Bianca facing off like cage fighters in the lobby below, Bianca towering over his wife. *Fuck, fuck, fuck.* He plunged down the steps in great leaping bounds, roaring at Forbes to move his ass.

The young security guard was standing paralyzed near the door.

The receptionist, equally unsure how to deal with the two confrontational women, stood behind her desk, red-faced and rigid with indecision.

"I am *too* his wife!" Bianca's face was inches from Kate's, her mouth in a snarl. "You stupid *puttana!*"

"That wasn't a marriage from what I hear," Kate snapped. She lifted her ring hand in Bianca's face. "*I'm* his wife. So back the hell off."

"I'll give you a month! He likes variety! He likes *lots* of women all at the same time! Everyone knows that!"

"Maybe you'll get another chance then," Kate said, looking up, her eyes green ice. "Maybe in a crowd you might get lucky."

"And maybe I can have you killed, you trashy little nobody!" Bianca spat, tightening her grip on her purse chain.

"As if." Kate's voice was brittle with disgust. "I have a Beretta in the car"—her voice was rising—"so get out of my face or I might be tempted to use it!"

Oh Christ, Dominic thought, Katherine must have found the drawer under the seat. *He could see the headlines now*. But he was almost close enough to reach Bianca. *Fuuuuuck*. He lunged for Bianca's arm as she swung her purse at Kate. Catching her wrist in a bone-crunching grip, he jerked her arm back so the catapulting purse reversed course and, ignoring her shrieks of pain, ripped away the purse and flung it across the lobby.

Then he spun her around so his face was inches from hers. Ignoring her anguished squeals, he spoke with barely suppressed violence. "If you ever threaten my wife again, I'll lay waste to your whole fucking family—money, property, your goddamn blue-blooded prestige. Got it?" He tightened his grip. "Fucking answer me."

She haughtily raised her chin and nodded.

He almost hit her for that patrician insolence. But the word *lawsuit* flashed neon bright in his brain, so he released her wrist instead and gave her a hard shove toward Forbes, who'd come out of his trance and was closing in. "Get her the hell out of here," he growled.

Swinging back to Kate, he quickly scanned her from head to toe. "Did she hurt you?" His voice was whisper soft. "Are you okay?"

"I'm okay. But you better tell me you never touched that smug-ass, uppity bitch," Kate muttered, each word seething with distaste, "or you're never touching me again."

"Never, Jesus...not so much as one finger. I swear."

Kate scanned his face with laser precision, then softly exhaled. "What an epic douche bag—and I mean epic, the bitch is nearly six feet tall. Although seriously, Dominic, I'm actually feeling sorry for you for having to marry her. I mean, jeez, I thought I had a mouth. By the way, she didn't like my outfit." She swept her hand over the flowery skirt, white blouse, and tiny, spangled jean jacket. "Too common, she said. Your fault, I told her." Then Kate's shoulders suddenly sagged and her eyes filled with tears. "Although you know what I hate her for more than marrying you? I hate her for having a baby when I couldn't. There's no fucking justice," she whispered.

"Hey." Dominic took her face in his hands and bent his head so their eyes were level. "You'll have a baby," he said very softly. "I promise."

"Yeah, okay."

"That doesn't sound like a ringing endorsement. That sounds like you don't believe me. Come on, give me some conviction. I promise, I deliver, then you take it from there—okay? Tell me that's how it works. And don't you dare fucking give me any excuses, because what happened to us isn't going to happen again." *He even half believed it as he promised her what she most desired in order to stem her tears.*

She smiled just a little. "Okay, you've convinced me."

"That's better. Now let's go home and pack or have someone pack for us and tomorrow morning, we head back to the States. Sound good?"

"Sounds heavenly."

"Stick with me, baby," he said with a smile, taking her hand and moving toward the door. "From now on I have heaven on permanent order."

TWENTY-TWO

W hen they arrived home, they found that Nana was on her way to the hospital to see them, so phone calls were exchanged and, with their plans set for departure tomorrow, Leo and Nana went off for another day of museums.

"Was that rude of me?" Kate asked, after ending her call with her grandmother and setting her phone down beside her chair in Dominic's study. "We were both doing that what-do-you-want-me-to-do thing until I finally said, 'Nana, go. You might not have another chance for a while.'"

"That's not rude, baby. I think she might have wanted to give us some time alone. And, hey, selfishly, I'm on board. I like you to myself."

"Me too." Kate made a little face. "Although maybe it's just because we haven't been together very long. Maybe we'll get bored after a while and—"

"I can make sure you're not bored," Dominic said softly.

She smiled. "I know. I love that about you. But I'm just saying, married couples eventually get hobbies and stuff, don't they?"

"Don't ask me. As for you, baby, just so long as you're still within sight with your hobbies, go for it. But I have no intention of sharing you." He smiled. "Ever."

Kate grinned. "Same page, here. I was just trying not to be clingy."

"I never said I didn't like clingy." Except to the other thousand women who'd briefly entered his life in the years past. Even Julia had been aware there were boundaries. Dominic leaned forward slightly and smiled. "Right now, though, I do have work to do. Join me if you like or you might rather take a nap. You're still really pale, baby."

"Maybe I will lie down for a few minutes." Whether her row with Bianca had sapped her energy or whether this was typical for her recovery, she *was* tired.

"Want me to carry you upstairs?"

She waved her hand no as she rose from the chair.

"I'll be here when you wake up." Dominic pointed at a stack of folders on his desk. "I have to go through these. We'll have lunch when you get up. Any requests?"

She smiled. "Besides chocolate cake you mean?"

"Keep fucking with me, baby, and you'll be feeling this." He held up his hand and winked. "Although I'll be super-gentle," he teased.

She gave him a playful bow. "Then chocolate cake for sure."

He grinned. "Get the hell out of here. I have to work."

She returned an hour later, refreshed. Pushing open the study door, she saw Dominic at his desk, the phone to his ear. He held up his hand, three fingers raised. She mouthed, *I'll be back*, and shut the door. There was no point in disturbing him when he was busy. She didn't need his attention every minute; she could be grown-up and mature. Maybe.

Although, with everyone busy, this was a good time to do a last look at her apartment. Dominic's staff would pack for them, but in case there were things she wanted to bring home tomorrow, she could set them aside.

Martin asked if she wanted a driver.

"I'll walk," she said. "It's only a few blocks."

He looked for a moment as if he might balk, but apparently thought better of it. "Call if you'd like someone to pick you up, Mrs. Knight." And he gave a nod to the houseboy to open the door for her.

It was late morning, the neighborhood was quiet, with people off to work or school, yoga lessons, shopping, whatever wealthy people did with their days. The sidewalks were relatively empty, the sun high in the sky, the air balmy.

When she let herself into the apartment, she stood for a moment in the entrance hall, her back against the door, remembering the evening Dominic had come back—the second time. When he'd asked her to marry him, when he'd told her how happy he was that she was having his baby.

But she blinked away the tears that welled in her eyes and smiled instead because Dominic had promised her more children. And when he said he'd do something, he did. Both his stubbornness and sense of responsibility had been honed in the raging cauldron of his childhood; *No Excuses* had been permanently inked on his psyche.

And right now, with her emotions still shaky, she needed that precious certainty.

Beginning in the reception room, then moving through the flat, opening cupboards and drawers, she selected items to take with her. She started a pile on the bed in her bedroom: a T-shirt with a line from Keats she liked, a pair of turquoise suede chunky heels, the pearls she'd worn that first night in Amsterdam, some tortoiseshell hair clips Dominic had given her, the small crystal vase Dominic had brought over with the white roses and note. Opening the drawer in the bedside table, she lifted out the small card where Dominic had written that he'd try to be a good father. Rereading it, she smiled and slipped it in her jacket pocket.

At the last, she walked into the spare bedroom for probably only the third or fourth time since she'd moved into the flat. Standing just inside the doorway, she surveyed the room decorated in soft robin's egg blue and creamy yellow, the bed with the padded headboard matching the toile bedspread, the small chaise in cream silk, the painted desk, and the splendid yellow silk drapes on the floor-to-ceiling windows that overlooked the garden.

And if the closet door hadn't been slightly ajar, she might have turned and left. She walked over, intending to close the door, saw all her clothes inside, and pulled the door wider. Lord, Dominic had bought her so many gorgeous things; she'd even become semi-comfortable with his largesse. She slid a funky purple blouse that always made her smile off the hanger, a pair of jeans she'd be able to wear again, the flowered raincoat she'd worn in San Francisco. Tossing them on the bed, she moved to the bank of blue built-in drawers next to the closet.

Pulling open the top drawer, her heart skidded to a stop.

She couldn't catch her breath.

Only a soundless tortured cry escaped.

Neatly folded inside the drawer were rows of little new-born clothes for the baby that hadn't been born, for the small life lost. She stroked them one by one, her heart breaking, tears sliding down her cheeks. Then she opened the other drawers, each one filled with precious tiny clothes. All the ones she'd unwrapped that night with Dominic—when he'd told her how happy he was about the baby, how they'd build a life together—the three of them.

And in the very bottom drawer were her at-home clothes he'd bought to fit her growing tummy: the T-shirts with *Mummy* written across the fronts in glitter and paint, the beautiful silk T-shirt with a screen print of Raphael's *Madonna and Child* Dominic had seen in a window and knew she'd like, the soft sweat pants and loose mommy jeans.

She was sobbing openly in great shuddering breaths by the time she reached the last drawer and, scooping up an armful of baby clothes, she sat down hard, held the scented softness to her face, and inhaled the sweetness of baby and the bitterness of shattered hope.

Then, moments later, only nominally aware in the nightmare of her anguish, she emptied the drawers, carried the clothes to the bed, and gently laid the detritus of that small life and her happiness on the spread. It almost hurt to breathe, she was so overcome with despair. Kneeling on the bed, she slowly sank downward and, burrowing deep into the soft pile of clothing like a wounded animal seeking shelter, she wrapped herself in her misery and succumbed to the bleakness of the world.

An hour later, Dominic found her curled up in a fetal position, cocooned in the baby clothes, pale and stricken, her face washed with tears, her body trembling with exhaustion.

She didn't see him, so he quietly backed out of the doorway and moved down the hall into a bathroom. Shutting the door, he immediately called Jake because he'd walked over too.

"Bring the car to the flat," he said. "Quickly."

He didn't wait for an answer, immediately punching in Martin's number. "Notify the pilots to be ready for takeoff in an hour. Tell Leo to bring Nana to Heathrow ASAP. Jake's coming for us. I'll call you from the plane."

He made an abbreviated call to Max. "You and Roscoe will have to take over for a few days. Sorry to throw this at you, but I can't leave Katherine unattended right now."

"We'll manage," Max said, not asking questions. If Dominic was walking away from his business when he never did—or hadn't until he met Katherine—it was serious.

"I'll give you a call when I can."

Then Dominic walked back into the spare bedroom, lay down beside Kate, and took her in his arms. "I'm so sorry, baby." He brushed her cheek with his lips.

"It's over," she whispered with an awful sadness.

"I know." His breath was warm on her temple, his voice soft with compassion. "We'll go home and—"

"Not yet!" A look of terror passed over her face.

"No rush, baby," he said, his voice softly soothing. But he brought it up again, five minutes later, because she was still sobbing and his concern was growing. Her rebuff was almost manic that time, her breathing erratic after crying so long. Twice more he tried to coax her to leave and each time, she doggedly refused.

With patience rarely exhibited for anyone besides Kate, Dominic cajoled once again. "Please, baby. You're going to make yourself sick."

"I'm not leaving."

He recognized the mulish jut of her chin. "We can't stay here indefinitely."

"Why not?"

"Because you've been crying for two hours, baby, and you're shaking." He resisted enumerating the score of other reasons.

"No I'm not."

But she wasn't able to suppress her shudders, her body tightly wound, her senses on emotional overload. "You're too fragile now, baby. You're going to end up back in the hospital if you don't stop crying," he said quietly, and, rolling off the bed with Kate in his arms, he came to his feet. Ignoring her initial shocked squeal, then her indignant screams, *Stop, stop, I want the baby clothes!*, he strode from the room. There was no way in hell he was going to stop, and; moving swiftly down the hall, he mutely endured her wild, pummeling blows and wilder insistence he go back.

"I want the baby clothes!" she shrieked.

"We'll have the clothes sent," he lied.

"No! Damn you!" She pounded him with her fists. "I want them *now*!"

"Later. We don't have time now. We're on our way to the airport."

"God, Dominic, please, please!" she frantically implored, like a martyr in extremis pleading for divine intervention. "Let me just take a few! I'll be quick! I won't keep you! *Please*, Dominic! Don't do this to me!"

He took a deep breath. He'd never heard Katherine begging with such anguish. "Sorry, baby," he murmured. "I'm probably doing this all wrong, but we're getting out, moving on, leaving this misery behind." He knew about soldiering on no matter what. She hadn't had the practice in her family cocoon of unconditional love. "And if crying would help, I'd say go for it. But it doesn't. Not. One. Single. Bit. I know."

"Shut the fuck up," she sobbed. "You don't know what you're—talking about, so just—*shut* the fuck up!"

"I'm not going to. We're going to pick ourselves up and keep on going. I've done it ten million times, baby, so I know it works. We're going to have a good life. This isn't the end of everything. You have to figure that out."

"It feels like the end right now!" she cried, and slapped him hard, wild with wretchedness and heartache, insensible to reason, striking out against her helplessness and despair.

He didn't so much as flinch or miss a stride. "Everything'll look better tomorrow."

"No, it won't, it *won't*, you unfeeling bastard!" Her voice was ascending into hysteria again, the green of her eyes like flickering flame. "Goddamn it! I'm not *going*! Put me down!"

"I'm sorry, baby. I really am." He felt powerless against her pain. His he could manage. He'd had years of practice shutting down his feelings. He'd learned long ago how to lock them away. He was good at it. "Maybe Nana can help. They're on their way to Heathrow now."

"No one can help." Kate's voice was suddenly soft with defeat, her energy draining out of her as if she'd finally resigned to the empty futility of the struggle. "Not Nana, no one. It's really over, isn't it?"

"This part is, baby. I'm sorry." He kissed her gently. "We'll feel better at home, right?" When she didn't answer, he dipped his head again, so their eyes met. "We'll try at least, okay?"

Her lips clenched tight to stop the trembling, she sniffed, then nodded.

"Thanks, baby. I knew you wouldn't let me down."

As they approached the front door, he was grateful her hysteria had passed. Although he had no compunction carrying her out to the car screaming bloody murder either if he had to. *Fuck the world* had always been his tried and true maxim.

On exiting the flat, they found Jake standing by the car, the back door held open.

A look of understanding passed between the two men.

"Heathrow?" Jake asked, as if he were a mind reader.

Dominic nodded. Another exchange of male glances. "Quickly."

"Gotcha."

Dominic stepped into the car with Kate, seated her in his lap, the door was shut, and seconds later, Jake was sliding behind the wheel.

"I'm sorry for being such a hard ass," Dominic whispered. "I'm a little out of my depth here. Fuck—more than a little. But I figure we just tread water till we get it right or somehow make sense of this fucking tragedy."

Kate exhaled in a great rush of air. "I'm not sure it'll ever make sense." She lay her head on his shoulder and sighed softly. "It doesn't feel like it will right now."

"Maybe we should talk to a therapist."

She lifted her gaze. "Do you want to?"

No. "I will if you want to. Whatever you want, I'll do. You know that, baby. Just tell me."

"I don't know," she mumbled. "I don't know how to deal with this pain. Nothing's ever hurt like this before—with no end in sight."

"I could get us some books about"—he stopped, not wanting to say *baby* or *miscarriage*—"what we're going through," he chose. "Others have suffered this loss too. It might help to read about it."

She wrinkled her nose. "I'm too selfish. I don't care about anyone else. I know what I feel and it sucks."

"Then it sounds like you'll just have to rely on me for your therapy," he said, gently teasing.

She giggled, the teeny tiniest feeling-better sound.

"Hey, don't knock it," he said playfully, taking advantage of that small opening. "I have years of experience. I'm so fucking qualified I'll fix us up in no time."

"I always like your fixing up," she said softly. "And thanks for trying to make me feel better."

"That's my job, baby. I'm your husband. Making you feel better is top of my list," he said gently. But he was going to buy some books and read them because he preferred being informed. Particularly with a serious problem like this. "We'll get it right next time, baby. So let's just stay positive, use all our Zen energy to engage with the circle of life and all that surreal, cosmic shit."

She smiled faintly. "How can you always be so reasonable?"

"It's better than the alternative." He held up his scabbed knuckles. "Your tears and my fists. Come on, baby, let's just fix this goddamn mess." Bending, he kissed her flushed cheek. "We'll go back home, regroup, and take it from there. Gimme a yes now and a smile. I know you can do it." He grinned. "You're goddamn perfect. That's why I married you."

Her smile was almost normal that time. "It's not as though you need the flattery with your past history, but you're damned perfect too. I'm very lucky."

"We both are baby." He grinned. "And it's only gonna get better."

At least Dominic certainly hoped so.

TWENTY-THREE

Nana came to San Francisco with them and with her usual ease, settled in with Dominic's family and staff. The second morning after their return, Nana brought Dominic's niece Nicole back with her from Melanie's. Kate was in Dominic's small upstairs office, at the computer—her comfort zone in good times and bad.

Nana waved Nicole into the office. "Nicole was wondering how you were doing, so I told her to come and see for herself," Nana said. "I'm getting a coffee. Anyone else?"

Kate raised her hand, Nicole said, "A Coke for me," and dropped into a brown leather club chair sizes too large for her. For an irresolute moment, she ran her fingers over the smooth chair arm, then looked up at Kate, her eyes the same blue as Dominic's, full of the same concern. "Nicky said we're not supposed to say anything 'cause it'll make you sadder but I want you to know how sorry I am about the baby. Mom says—"

"Jesus Christ," a low growl interrupted. "What the hell do you think you're doing?"

Nicole swiveled around and stared defiantly at her uncle standing in the doorway, scowling like the wrath of God. "You don't always know what women want, Nicky, even if you think you do."

"Don't tell me what I know, you brat," Dominic snapped.

"It's okay, Dominic, really," Kate said, observing the matching scowl on Dominic's niece, stepping in to avoid an uneven fight. Even with her teenage assurance, Nicole was out of her league against Dominic's fury. "We're just going to visit. I'm fine. Nana's bringing us coffee and Cokes." Kate smiled at her overly protective husband. "Don't you have something to do?"

He took a small breath, held Kate's gaze. "You sure?" His voice was tight as a drum.

She smiled. "I am, thank you."

Dominic turned a grim look on his niece. "Mind your goddamn manners now," he said curtly.

Nicole's eyes narrowed, and she was about to retort, when Kate said quickly, "She always minds her manners, Dominic. No worries—okay?"

Nana returned at just the right moment and Dominic stepped aside to let her into the office.

"Coffee, Dominic?" Nana lifted the tray an inch as she walked past him.

"He was just leaving, Nana." Kate smiled at her husband, who didn't look as though he had any intention of leaving.

A taut five count passed.

"I'll be right next door," Dominic finally said brusquely. "In case you need anything."

That morning Kate and Nicole became friends. The young girl was charming and warm, like her uncle, Kate thought. Unlike her uncle, she was completely open about her life, boyfriends, school, her BFFs, siblings. And in the course of the next few days and weeks, Nicole became

Kate's therapist of choice, slowly bringing Kate back into the world with her cheeky, adolescent, anything-is-possible outlook.

Before long even Dominic understood to whom he owed a gift of gratitude.

His took the form of a new silver Porsche convertible.

"Told you," Nicole said to him in private, flashing him a sassy grin.

He gave her a teasing look right back. "I guess you know what you're doing every once in a while. Now don't go and kill yourself. That's an order."

She lifted her chin. "I don't take orders."

"You do from me, baby girl. Or I'll take the keys back." But he saw even then a little too much of himself in that lifted chin. And he made sure that a governor and tricked-out roll bars were put on the car.

Nana stayed in San Francisco for almost a month. She was there for the wedding reception Melanie arranged at Dominic's restaurant Lucia. She waited until Kate was ready to go back to work; she admired the adjoining office suites Dominic had ordered set up at corporate headquarters in Santa Cruz. She mostly stayed until Kate could talk about losing the baby without crying.

Then she said, "It's time for me to go home, sweetie. You have a husband who loves you and a job you enjoy. Not to mention a world of privilege that's in the Cinderella category. Don't forget to keep your feet on the ground though. There's nothing wrong with living in a fantasy world, so long as you remember how to do the dishes."

"I never did dishes at home, Nana."

"That's because Gramps spoiled you."

"You did too, Nana." Kate smiled. "But if you think I should learn to do dishes, I suppose I could."

"Waste of talent, sweetie. Just don't let all the money go to your head, that's all I'm saying. Dominic wants to give you the world."

"He's been unhappy for a long time. He's grateful, that's all."

"I know. I talked to Melanie's housekeeper, Mrs. B. I heard." The two ladies had bonded like twins separated at birth. Of the same generation, both ardent antiwar supporters, Mrs. B's husband had endured the hell of Vietnam too. Both men understood their wives marching to end the war while they were fighting it. Roy had always said, "We're both trying to end this god-awful war in our own way. So keep on marching, Lori. I might get home sooner."

"And you know what Dominic's house is like, Nana. It's nice and in a nice neighborhood, but Dominic's still living like he did at sixteen. He doesn't care about stuff just for the sake of having it. So don't worry, I won't become a prima donna."

"If you do, I'll be the first to tell you to knock it off."

"There you go. My voice of reason."

"So you're okay if I go back home? No break down, no going off the deep end?"

"Nah. I'm pretty good now. Reconciled. Looking to the future. Dominic's okay with having children soon. He told me that in London."

"That's nice," Nana said politely, although she knew better. Mrs. B had heard from Dominic's sister that he was opposed to the idea. Or, at the very least, unsure. "Well, call me when you can. That way I don't have to bother Dominic for news."

"I will, Nana. When I didn't call before that was just because everything was, like, supercrazy. Now it's just normal busy. I'm looking forward to going back to work."

With promises to visit again, Nana returned home the next day.

While Dominic had been keeping up with work late at night after Kate fell asleep, once Nana left, life for the newlyweds settled into a normal headlong pace of long work days and full-steam-ahead involvement in Knight Enterprises.

Dominic still picked out Kate's clothes in the morning because he knew what he was doing and she wasn't wired for coordinating outfits. And at base, she liked that he dressed her, even if they didn't have time in the morning to do more than exchange kisses.

Jake drove them to work each day while both read reports and answered e-mail on the hour-long ride. Dominic woke earlier than Kate to swim his fifty laps, but Kate had begun lifting weights again in Dominic's private gym at work. They always ate lunch together and the door between their offices was never closed.

After a week back at work, Dominic walked into Kate's office, holding a spreadsheet aloft. "How the hell did you catch this? It went through six layers of management. Do you realize how much money you saved us?"

"Twelve million, three hundred forty-six thousand, seven hundred twenty-five dollars, and fifty-two cents."

He grinned. "What are you, a savant?"

She shook her head and flicked her finger at the account review in his hand. "I happen to have an intimate relationship with numbers and letters."

He smiled. "I'm not sure I like the sound of the word *intimate*." Tossing the spreadsheet on her desk, he dropped into a chair. "Enlighten me."

"Relax. It's cerebral, not sexual." She hesitated briefly, having learned the topic was best left out of conversation. "Now, don't get alarmed, but I see numbers and letters in shapes, colors, textures—I even feel and hear them." She smiled. "Kinda like you can see clothes and I can't. Anyway, there's a name for it—I read an article about it once, although I don't know all that much otherwise. Since I've always been this way, it's just normal for me. When I was younger I thought everyone saw what I saw. I discovered in middle school they didn't. And I learned not to talk about it cuz it can freak out people when you tell them you can hear the letter *C* singing—not every day," she added with a small grin. "Sometimes another letter barges in. But I can shut it down if it gets too distracting, lock it down—like you learned to do with your feelings." She gave him a teasing look. "Although you're getting better, aren't you?"

"I think the word is *trying*."

She smiled. "Whatever you're doing, I like."

"Did the twelve mil strike up the chorus then?" Never comfortable talking about his feelings, no matter the adjustments he'd made to please Kate, he redirected the conversation.

"Not exactly." She politely picked up the cue. "When

I'm working all the mental portals are wide open so I see flaws, aberrations, shifting visual patterns in the flow of even high-speed data. It's intuitive, independent of reason, fun. That's why I love computers." She jabbed her finger at the spreadsheet. "The twelve mil error happened to flash by pitch-black in a multi-colored pastel field. It was impossible to miss."

He didn't look startled, but he *was* staring. "Jesus fucking Christ, baby, you're amazing." He laughed softly. "As if I didn't know." Then a thoughtful look suddenly invaded the brilliant blue of his eyes. "Even if I didn't love you madly, I'd make sure you never got away. You're one helluva asset to Knight Enterprises."

She put up her hand and met his gaze. "Just an FYI. I may not want to always work."

"Not a problem," he said quickly, instinctively alert to that watchful expression in a woman. "I don't give a shit whether you work or not. In fact, you know I'd rather you didn't."

"I know. And *you* know I have reservations about leaving the workforce. But when our children are young, I'd like to be home."

It took him a fraction of a second to stifle the gut-deep panic when she talked about having children. "Your schedule's completely up to you, baby. It always will be." He waved his hand at the spreadsheet, intent on getting off the subject of children. "I just wanted to come in and say thanks for this major bonus."

"Glad to be of service, Mr. Knight." She leaned back in her chair and winked. "Is there anything else I can do for you?" Her voice was soft with insinuation. "Seeing how it's almost lunchtime."

She hadn't made any sexual overtures since London and he'd politely let her decide when she was ready. He smiled. "You sure?"

"Why don't you lock the doors."

That sounded sure. "Happy to, baby." He was unbuttoning his suit coat as he walked first to the door to her assistant's office, then to the one between their suites, locking them both. Shrugging out of his coat, he tossed it onto a nearby chair and started unbuttoning his shirt cuffs.

Seated at her desk, Kate could feel the heat rise through her body, warm her skin, and coil with a piquant flutter deep inside. Dominic's skin was dark against the whiteness of his shirt, his long fingers deft on the cuff buttons, his strong wrists flexing easily as he rolled up his shirtsleeves. "What are you doing?" It was a rhetorical question, breathy, soft, shimmering with an underlying excitement.

His long lashes drifted downward slightly and he smiled. "Getting ready for lunch. Don't move. You're fine."

"Do you know how long it's been?" she whispered.

"I do." He flashed Kate a grin as he rounded her desk. "You deserve a little fun."

She gazed at his strained trouser fly. "What I deserve is you and your really fine dick."

Swinging her chair around, he smoothly dropped to his knees, ignoring her comment. "I picked out a skirt today. It must be karma." Sliding her skirt up over her thighs, he nudged her bottom with one hand. "Lift up." When she did, he shoved her skirt up to her waist, then slipped off her panties with a finesse acquired long before he graduated high school. Gently spreading her legs, he brushed his hands up her inner thighs and slid a finger lightly down her pouty cleft. "Gorgeous as ever, baby."

She shut her eyes briefly, moaned, his skimming fingertip instantly recognized by hot memory, desire immediate and demanding as if she were attuned to his merest touch, as if she were programmed to respond. "I need you inside me," she whispered, her voice shaky. Too long deprived, she was suddenly breathless with need, her pulse hammering. "The sofa." Her words no more than a soft rush of air as she braced her hands on the chair arms and began to rise.

Pushing her back down, Dominic held her lightly in place, his forearm on her rib cage. Running his other hand over her mons in a light caress, he slipped one finger inside and delicately stroked her clit.

She gasped, twitching violently.

He jerked his finger out. "Oh God, baby. Sorry."

"No, no, no." And as he began to pull away, she clamped her fingers over his wrist, dragged his hand back between her legs. "More."

If not for his fingers pressed into her crotch, he might have read that as a mixed message. Still, he proceeded with caution after that twitchy gasp, sliding his finger slowly into her sleek flesh, stroking gingerly as if he were touching some rare substance that would disintegrate on contact.

Adjusting speed and pressure with watchful meticulousness.

Until her familiar little whimper brought a smile to his lips. "Feel good?"

"Chocolate cake…" She shut her eyes, smiled. "Taking down the biggest baddest black hat hacker in the world…" Her voice trailed off for a second because he'd just brushed her clit oh-so-softly and the vibration was still humming through her brain. "And you washing my hair. That good," she whispered.

"Same page, baby," he said, his voice husky. She was wet, silky wet, drenched, beginning to move against his finger with impatience, her tiny moans little eddies of breath on his cheek. Jesus, she felt fine, liquid, soft, and yielding. How long had it been since he'd touched her like this? And for an impetuous moment he almost forgot the limits he'd placed on himself.

Almost.

A heartbeat later, he'd locked down his libido again.

And just in time, because she'd buried her hands in his hair and was trying to lift him to his feet.

"Dominic, please, please. The sofa." Her breath exploded in little hot pants. "I need you *now*!"

He tensed. How many times had he responded to her pleas and fucked her until neither of them could move, until their lungs ached for want of breath, until his dick felt like it had been driven over by a truck? He clenched his jaw, and calling on a lifetime of restraint he whispered, "Soon, baby. Give me a second."

Brushing her hands aside, he leaned back marginally to gain better purchase, then pushed in a second finger and slowly stroked her throbbing sex—gently, faultlessly, teasing her G-spot with each pass, waiting until he heard her hot little gasp before resuming the rhythm. His thumb in sync, circling her clit in slow, lazy circles the way she liked. "Better now?"

She didn't answer, and for a moment he considered forcing her to reply. But he reminded himself to behave. This was for her.

Was it possible to simply melt away in a frenzy of lust? Kate dreamily reflected. Was it possible to just dissolve into a puddle of simmering desire? Was this what dying of pleasure meant, this delicious, heavy ache between her legs? Then Dominic touched her deeply again, and she rose into his strong fingers, her breath catching at the dizzying rapture, the intoxicating pleasure rippling outward from his exquisitely placed fingertips.

When she finally took a breath, as though waiting for his cue, he slowly withdrew his hand, gently caressing her G-spot on the way out. And at the last, when only the pads of his fingers touched her, he twisted his wrist and pressed his thumb down hard on her swollen clit.

A jolt of white-hot lust flared through her senses, stars exploded before her eyes, her body quivered in joy. And the world was suddenly awash with endless rainbows.

"Like that?"

His voice was teasing, raspy and low. His hand was softly pumping again, his thumb lightly brushing her clit in his own special hand-jive post-rainbows. And the entire universe of erotic sensation was melting between her legs, hot, feverishly hot, expectation singing in her ears like a heavenly choir. "You know what I'd like even more?" she murmured, superpolitely, seeing how he'd recently delivered the wonders of clit-propelled rainbows.

"Hmmm?" He was sliding his free hand under her short jacket, intent on not answering her question, intent on shifting her attention from what she'd *like more*. Placing his large hand over her breast, his fingers splayed wide to capture the entire lavish tit, he flexed his fingers so they pressed gently into her soft flesh. Then not so gently. Then not gently at all.

Kate groaned deep in her throat—an unmistakably carnal sound, as Dominic well knew; it was a feverish, cream-her-pussy utterance no matter that it escaped in a soft, wispy breath.

Her interest diverted to more riveting sensations, he bent his head briefly and grazed her nipple with the tip of his tongue. "You like it to hurt just a little, don't you, baby."

She shook her head.

He tightened his grip, held her gaze.

"Yes, yes," she whispered, her eyes half closing.

"That's what I thought." Relaxing his fingers, he slid his hand under her breast, raised the heavy weight, gripped the plump flesh just hard enough to draw her slightly forward. He paused, her nipple a hairbreadth from his mouth. "Tell me when it hurts too much. Look at me, Katherine. That's a good girl. Speak up if it hurts. I might stop." He smiled. "Understand?"

His words only further inflamed her, as he knew they would, and trembling with need, desperate for release, she opened her mouth to reply, hesitated under his cool gaze, and prudently said, "Yes."

His fingers tightened, crushing her breast.

She shuddered.

"Too much?" But he didn't relax his grip. Instead, without apology, he took her nipple in his mouth with a brute pressure because he knew and she knew what it did: it sent a flood of flame-hot sensation streaking downward to her wildly pulsing cleft.

She softly groaned, closed her eyes, and quietly trembled as ravenous desire tore through her body, flared, throbbed like a drumbeat in her greedy sex. Her demanding, impatient, seething sex. Her unapologetically needy sex.

But each time she began to peak, he gentled his touch, letting her frenzy calm. Making it last, making her pant and squirm and plead. Doing what he did so well.

Although with Katherine, there always was a point of no return. And when her eyes suddenly snapped open and she looked at him with a prickly green-eyed stare, he smiled. "Relax, baby. I'll get you off now."

"I—don't want—that." Twisting her fingers in his cornflower blue tie, she dragged him close. "I want to feel you—*inside* me."

"In a minute," he lied, prying his crushed tie free, quickly withdrawing his fingers from her heated cleft, sliding his hands under her legs, and easing them over his shoulders. Then, bending low, he blew a soft *"Hello kitty"* on her slick pussy. "Go time, baby." His voice was warm on her flesh for a second before he looked up and grinned. "Try not to scream." Before she could complain or take issue or give him orders he had no intention of following, he opened her sex with his fingers, dropped his head, closed his mouth over her swollen clit, and sucked.

Not too hard, not too soft. Nor too fast or too slow.

The three bears equivalent of *just right*.

For a hovering nanosecond, her expectations quivered in limbo; she wasn't sure she'd settle for this when she wanted *him*. But her long-dormant passions shrieked, *Are you crazy when this feels so fine!*, her orgasmic receptors feverishly agreed, and every bare wire nerve ending wildly sparkled and flashed its consent. That Dominic had just devoted a little extra attention to her G-spot couldn't be overlooked in her decision making. The world began drifting away, nirvana rose on the horizon in all its golden glory, and Kate whispered with genuine gratitude, "Oh God, *thank* you..."

Dominic looked up briefly. "Thank me later, baby, when I deserve it." He knew how to make it better. He'd spent a decade or more mastering degrees of better. "See if you like this." His lips closed again on her throbbing clit, and he caressed it with a delicacy much practiced and richly appreciated in his former life. He knew with charming precision how hard to suck, how much and how long, the exact rhythm for the appropriate level of arousal. And when, as he intended, Kate was soon whimpering in desperation, he twisted his head slightly, slid his tongue up to her G-spot, and delicately sweet-talked her little pleasure center until she was running wet, until she was ready to collapse from the joy of it.

Then Dominic added first one, then two, fingers into her slick warmth, forcing them in a slow, exquisitely slow invasion to that incandescent point where nothing mattered but glorious, beautiful, maddening lust. Cosmic bliss flooded her brain, and with the clarity of empirical evidence, Kate indisputably understood that great sex wasn't always about hard dicks. "Ohmygod, I'm dying..."

Dominic had learned long ago that great sex was a journey not a destination; he also recognized that his wife's *dying* frenzy meant he didn't have much time. Raising his mouth a fraction of an inch, his breath warm on her sex, he said, unnecessarily, "Done playing, baby?"

She was beyond the point of answering, the tidal wave about to crest, and, reaching out, she seized two fistfuls of Dominic's hair and dragged him close. Pushing into his hand and mouth, she panted as the little pulsing shock waves accelerated wholesale, spiked, raced up her spine at warp speed, and spun her irrepressibly to orgasm.

Dominic heard her take a deep breath—knew what that meant. He glanced up through his lashes, smiled faintly against her succulent flesh, sucked her enthusiastic little clit more slowly, and massaged her sumptuous G-spot with a degree more pressure. And a second later, just as Katherine's orgasmic scream was about to explode, he reached up blindly with his free hand and placed his fingertips lightly over her mouth.

Gently warned, she gasped, choked down her scream, flattened the vehemence, and uttered little explosive groans instead as the deep, throbbing delirium stretched and spread, tantalized and penetrated every quivering, long-deprived orgasmic nerve in her body.

Dominic didn't stop doing what he was doing. Nor did he relinquish his precious sense of place until her soft moans finally evaporated into silence.

A rapping on the door shattered the hush. "Do you need help, Mrs. Knight?"

Dominic turned his head, his dark hair brushing Kate's thighs. "Thank you, no." His voice was curt.

"Oh shit," Kate breathed, incapable of opening her eyes with pleasure still washing over her in soft waves.

"Don't sweat it, baby," Dominic whispered, lightly kissing her smooth, silken thigh. "No one will say a word." *He'd see to it.* Motionless, he waited for Katherine's orgasm to completely fade, wanting her to feel every scintilla of sweetness after so long.

She finally opened her eyes. "That was...so...perfect." She ran her hand over his ruffled hair. "Thank you."

He raised his head and brushed his hair off his face with his left hand. "You're welcome, baby." He winked. "It's been a while for you." Sliding his fingers from her soft-as-silk pussy, he eased her legs off his shoulders, set her feet on the carpet, and rolled back on his heels.

"For you too. Let me"—she took a breath, leaned forward, stretched her hand out, and touched his fly.

He moved out of reach. "I have an appointment." He glanced at the clock. "Morgan. Five minutes."

"He can wait. You didn't have any fun. I feel guilty."

He smiled. "How guilty?"

"Not very," she said with a grin, still wallowing in delight.

He laughed. "That's what I thought." Gracefully rising to his feet, he shot her a warm, teasing look. "I love that my baby's back in form." He quickly rolled down his shirtsleeves. "Hot, sexy, impatient."

She smiled, wiggled her skirt down her hips. "Your turn next time."

"Sounds good." Bending over, he picked up her panties and dropped them on her lap. "And don't worry about Christina. No one will say a word." He'd make sure of that.

"I hope I reach your level of dégagé someday," she said, slipping on her lacy panties.

"Stick with me, baby. It's inevitable." Turning, he walked away, picked up his jacket, slipped into it, and ran his hand down his wrinkled tie. "You decent?" He shot her a glance.

She grinned. "Clothes-wise, yeah."

"Hold that thought, baby. We'll check it out at home. Now I'm unlocking Christina's door." He used his left hand, then blew her a kiss, and, opening the door into his adjoining office, disappeared.

"Sorry I'm late, Morgan," Kate heard him say. "Katherine and I were having lunch. There was a little too much mango salsa on the sandwiches. Let me wash my hands and I'll be right with you."

As soon as his meeting was over, Dominic went to talk to Kate's assistant. If Christina was a voyeur, she was going to have to go.

Entering her office from the outside corridor, he walked up to her desk so his voice wouldn't carry. Without reference to her earlier interruption, speaking softly, he said, "Mrs. Knight is to be treated with discretion and respect. I just wanted to make that clear." He used the formal designation for Katherine to underscore the courtesy he required.

"I understand."

"She's not to be embarrassed or discomfited." His voice was brusque, his gaze cool. "No exceptions, no excuses."

"Certainly, Dom—that is, Mr. Knight." The culture had always been informal rather than corporate at Knight Enterprises. But she'd obviously just been reprimanded and opted for a more respectful tone.

"Good. See that you remember that." He turned and walked away, the corridor door closing behind him a moment later with a soft click.

Damn, the office pool was going to have to pay out. Dominic had just taken himself out of the game. In no uncertain terms. Every female employee was going to be devastated. Not that he'd ever hooked up with members of the staff, but that didn't mean every female wasn't hoping she'd be the first.

Dominic was smiling faintly as he returned to his office. He'd never called Katherine Mrs. Knight at work before. He found he liked the possessive terminology. As if Katherine was his to protect and cherish—old-fashioned words, maybe outdated words. Ones he'd never considered before—at least not in personal terms.

He'd never referred to Julia as Mrs. Knight. He'd never really thought of her that way. In fact, Julia had kept her own name after their marriage. Not that he'd noticed until Melanie had mentioned it.

He remembered saying at the time, "That's fairly common isn't it?"

And never given it another thought.

Now, irrationally, he wanted Katherine to belong to him in almost a feudal sense, as though this weren't the twenty-first century. As though such a demand wasn't a bold affront to the modern age and, more important, to her. He grinned. As if he didn't know. As if they didn't fight about it endlessly.

His smile was still in place when he appeared in the open doorway between their offices.

Kate looked up. "What?"

"Just missed you."

"I know what you mean." She glanced at the clock. "It's been twenty minutes."

Ignoring her teasing, he said, "We could go home now."

"Sorry, I have a minimum of three hours work left to do."

"You're the boss. You could make a unilateral decision."

"I have."

He groaned.

"Roscoe's been riding your ass on the Fly Way Jets acquisition," she pointed out. "Get it done."

He grinned. "Yes, ma'am. Can I do anything else for you, ma'am?"

She blew him a kiss. "You did quite enough for me already today. Really, it was lovely."

"My pleasure. By the way, if you'd rather have another assistant, Christina wouldn't mind moving to our Communications Department."

"She's not a problem for me. Unless she is for you?" Kate had seen how her pretty blond assistant looked at Dominic, but then there wasn't a woman who didn't. "Would you prefer I have a male assistant?"

"Fuck no."

That's what she thought. "Then leave Christina alone. I gather you've given her the warning lecture."

His eyes widened slightly.

"Her knock on the door pissed you off. I didn't have to be a mind reader."

"She won't do that again."

"Good. Now, if you don't mind, my Greek chorus is humming in my head so I have to concentrate."

Kate turned her attention back to her computer.

But Dominic stood in the doorway for a few moments more, experiencing a sense of deep contentment. By some blind measure of luck he'd found Katherine in the vastness of the world. She'd taught him to love, given him love, changed his entire life. Made him happy. "Hey, baby," he said, because life changes aside, he was still a confirmed autocrat. "Give me a heads-up when you're ready to leave. Anytime. I can work at home."

She looked up, his message clear. "I suppose I owe you," she said, grinning.

He looked amused. "I suppose you do."

"How about an hour then? I can work at home too."

Their evenings, in contrast to the busy pace at corporate headquarters, were restful. After eating the dinner Patty left for them, they lay together in the living room or bedroom, holding each other, watching TV or movies, talking about their day. It was the simplest of lives, work, home, just the two of them. Until, one evening, Dominic said, "I thought you might like to learn how to surf."

"No thanks," Kate said, still concentrating on the movie.

"That wasn't really a question," Dominic said, brushing her nose with the tip of his finger as she lay in his arms.

Reaching for the remote, she put the movie on pause. "Ask me if I care whether it was or not," she said, looking up and smiling.

"You'll like surfing."

"No I won't."

"How do you know unless you try?"

"I can visualize; the water's cold, the waves are high."

The corporate headquarters weren't at Santa Cruz just for the hell of it. Her view of the beaches was prime. And the tide charts and weather radio Dominic kept in his office were a constant reminder of his passion for surfing. "Look, I'll watch. You surf."

"No, come with me."

She gave him a grumpy look. "Are we going to fight about this?"

"I'm not. Try on your wet suit." He leaped out of bed and walked to the closet. "I had it custom made." *It and five others.*

"Jeez, Dominic. Must you always be a bulldozer?"

He grinned. "Spoilsport. I'll take you up on my board. It'll be fun."

"Then you have to come shooting with me."

"Sure," he said, turning around with a lime green and black wet suit in his hand.

Oh shit. She thought he'd balk.

"Come on, try it on. Maybe you'd like to ... you know— play around afterward."

"Damn you," she muttered. He'd been resisting actual intercourse, wanting her to be fully healed, while she'd been whining about making love for days now. "That's not fair."

"Oh, yeah, that's me, a fucking Boy Scout," he drawled. "Always fair, that's my motto."

"What do you mean 'play around'?"

"I mean I'll fuck you."

Oh God, she felt that little lightning bolt hit right on target. "Now?"

"If you promise to go surfing with me tomorrow."

"Okay."

"There you go. A cooperative wife. I love it."

"And I'd love for you to finally perform. It's not as though I haven't been asking you for, let's see—seven days, ten hours, fifteen minutes. Roughly."

He laughed. "I've been waiting too, baby."

"So this is just a calculated move?"

"I wouldn't say calculated, exactly."

"What exactly would you say?"

"I was just waiting. It's not as though I wanted to." Then his voice went soft. "Seriously, baby. I don't want to hurt you."

"You won't, okay? And right now the wet suit can wait. I can't." She stripped off her pajamas in seconds flat, lay back on the bed, held out her arms, and wiggled her fingers.

He didn't move for a second, a million restrictions jostling in his brain: the doctor's instructions, the fact that Katherine hadn't had a period yet, the unknowns about how long real healing took. The unrelenting fear that he might harm her, that he might have contributed to her miscarriage.

"Jeez, you'd think this was your first time. Look, I won't hurt you," she said with a grin. "I'll be gentle."

But it was Dominic who was gentle, slightly phobic even. He made love to her, with tenderness and moderation, with unselfish benevolence and with what she resentfully characterized sometime later as a maddening calm.

"If only, baby." He was wound tight as a spring, each plunging thrust worrisome, his rhythm of penetration and withdrawal cautious and wary.

"This isn't working for me."

She'd come twice already, but, on his best behavior on this goddamn maiden voyage as it were, he said, pleasantly, "You need a little more excitement?"

"Just a little more of your dick if you don't mind," she said, mimicking his mild tone.

"Bitch." His voice was low, teasing.

She ran her fingernail down his cheek so it left a mark. "So what are you going to do about it, Mr. Knight?"

"Teach you a lesson I suppose."

Dismissing most of his reservations, or temporarily overruling them, he stopped her complaints by giving her what she wanted, deeper and faster, deeper and harder, meeting her frenzied need until she was trembling, straining toward her impending orgasm, panting for air. Then he went motionless inside her.

Her eyes flew open, her mouth formed a little O.

"Beg for it, baby," he said softly.

Her nostrils flared, her lips firmed.

His erection swelled; hostility did that to his dick. "For the nail mark, Katherine."

"Goddamn you," she hissed.

He smiled. "Just beg a little. So you don't scratch me

again." Then he plunged deep, deep, for a second before withdrawing slightly, felt her low, strangled moan on his throat, and whispered, "Sounds like you're almost there."

She bit her lip, shut her eyes, and took a deep, shuddering breath before opening her eyes. "Please, Dominic." The words were almost inaudible.

"I didn't hear you."

"Goddamn you!"

He grinned. "I heard that."

"Please, please, please, *please!*" Her green gaze was flame hot. "Did you hear that?"

"I did. Thank you. Now hang on baby, we're taking you home." And he did, smoothly, deftly, with expertise, his sexually talented dick and her raging-hot libido. He took her over the edge as only he could, once, twice, three times more—and when she finally gasped, "No, no, stop," he didn't.

Because he was horny as hell.

Since he'd suppressed his orgasm through all her screaming climaxes, it was a few overwrought moments more before he was able to consciously disengage and take off the brakes on his dick. And another few seconds after that before he abruptly jerked out of Kate's slick sex and climaxed on her belly so incredibly hard he couldn't breathe, didn't know where he was, hung for endless moments in some wild, brain-scorching limbo.

Katherine's punch dragged him back into the world.

"What are you doing?" she screeched.

He sucked in a breath and snapped, "Waiting for you to have a normal period." Rolling off her, he grabbed his

T-shirt from the floor. "Or any period." He tossed the shirt on her stomach. "You heard the doctor. Fucking relax." Reaching for his sweats, he sat up and wiped off his dick.

"That's not fair."

"For whom? You came often enough. And stop with the fair shit. Raised in my family, that word's not in my vocabulary."

She scowled at him. "You're being difficult or stubborn. I don't know which. For no good reason."

"Jesus, baby," he said, in a low grumble, wiping off her stomach and dropping the shirt on the floor. "You gotta wait. Follow the goddamn rules. Let's not screw this up."

"Again. That's what you mean, isn't it. I screwed it up."

"What I mean is you and I both heard the doctor." He ran a hand through his hair and held it at the back of his neck for a second before he dropped his arm. "Wait for one normal period, she said. So let's just do that, baby," he said quietly. "It probably won't be much longer any-way. Right?" Sliding up against the headboard, he pulled her limp-as-a-corpse body up on his lap and smiled faintly. "What are you a pouty two-year-old?"

She gave him a sulky look. "I thought you liked obedi-ence. Me doing what you want."

His mouth twitched. "I might if you actually could do it."

"Fuck you."

He laughed. "Two seconds. A new record."

She stuck out her tongue. Then, suddenly, as if a cloud had obscured the sun, she was overcome with the unspeak-able loss that had made this argument necessary. Throwing her arms around Dominic's neck, Kate slowly exhaled in a soft woeful sigh. "Do you think I'll ever be healthy again?" she whispered. "So you don't have to be so careful and I don't have to worry? So neither of us has to worry."

"Sure you will, baby." His hand caught her chin and lifted her face to his, his voice when he spoke comforting. "You just need a little patience. You're not good at that, so it's up to me." He dipped his head, kissed her gently, then let his hand drop away. "So let me be the control freak. I do that pretty fucking well." His smile warmed his eyes. "Now, did you make the appointment with Melanie's ob-gyn? If you didn't, you should. Or if you like, I will."

TWENTY-FOUR

I t was a warm Saturday in June, the temperatures on the coast slightly cooler than inland. Dominic had their gear sent ahead to his apartment in Half Moon Bay since his Tesla sports car only had room for two.

He'd been up for hours, practically pacing, although he hadn't rushed Kate after he woke her other than to mention that the waves were better early in the morning.

It was still dark when they left the house.

Leaning against the car door, her legs resting on the console, Dominic driving one handed while idly stroking her bare feet, Kate gazed at the stunningly beautiful man opposite her. The fine contours of his face were illuminated by the glow of the dash lights, his faint smile visible even in profile. "You've missed this, haven't you?"

He shot her a glance, gauging his reply after their argument last night over surfing. "Yeah, it's been a while," he said neutrally.

"It usually isn't?"

"I surf all over the world. So"—he shrugged—"generally I'm in the water more than I have been lately."

"My fault?"

He gave her his finest bad-boy grin. "Let's just say I had a lot better things to do when you were around."

"And now you don't?"

"Don't start with that, baby. Get a passing grade from Melanie's ob-gyn and we're back on track. I'm just more cautious than you."

"And patient."

He shot her another grin. "Always, baby. That's no contest and no problem," he quickly added to curtail any unwanted retort.

"You're quick."

"Fucking A." He laughed. "Survival."

"Am I really that temperamental?"

"Nah," he lied, when, in fact, women had only said yes to him his entire life.

"Maybe Nana and Gramps did spoil me a little," Kate said. "So if you'd like, I could—"

"Baby, you're everything I want. Okay? Don't change a thing." He wasn't questioning personalities or nuances of behavior when he was happy for the first time in his life. "Seriously, don't even change the color of your lipstick or your nail polish," he added, brushing his fingers over her crimson-painted toe nails.

"Goddamn, you *do* know how to make a woman feel good."

"*One* woman," he said gently, reaching out and brushing her cheek with the backs of his fingers. "End of story. Now hang on. We're going to haul ass. The breaks are better at dawn."

He drove far too fast on the freeway, but smoothly, like a race driver, switching lanes effortlessly, moving past slow traffic at speeds so high the other cars looked like they were parked, then hitting it once they outdistanced the city snarl, a chronic condition in San Francisco. And when they reached the two-lane ocean road that skirted the high shoreline cliffs way too close for comfort, he reached over to check her seat belt, then floored it.

Kate shut her eyes at that point in order not to scream and possibly startle Dominic and cause him to career into the ocean. Had she opened her eyes, she would have seen that Dominic was smiling, relaxed, unperturbed by the curvy, roller-coaster terrain. He'd driven this road thousands of times; he knew it blindfolded.

The sun was just beginning to lighten the horizon, he was with his girl, he was going surfing—no way life could get better.

Twenty minutes later, slowing down as he approached the outskirts of Half Moon Bay, Dominic gave Kate a grin. "You can open your eyes, baby."

"I should have a T-shirt made," she muttered. "I survived Highway 1."

His smile was totally boyish. "Fun, hey?"

She gave him a quelling glance. "We have different ideas of fun."

"That reminds me." He held up one finger. "My apartment here is pretty basic. So don't expect much. It's always been just a place to sleep between waves."

"Fuck. And I'm used to the Taj Mahal."

He grinned. "You're just itching for a spanking aren't you? Tell you what. Be a good girl about surfing and I might make it worth your while."

"Now we're talking fun. How much worth my while?"

"Depends how accommodating you are with surfing."

"I won't whine."

"There's a point."

"I won't make you paddle me out."

"Christ, five points."

"What if I actually get up on my board and don't fall?"

"Then you get—"

"Everything?"

"Almost everything. We still need the doctor's stamp of approval. But, hey, baby, don't pout. That's all but one percent of the game."

"Okay. You're on."

He loved her for a thousand reasons, but her competitive spirit was right up there at the top. Katherine Hart Knight didn't give an inch unless she had to. It was that *had to* part that pleased him most and on numerous highly stimulating occasions, seriously blew his mind.

The apartment was small, simple, one bedroom, with furniture that had been well-lived in and boy's stuff everywhere: surfing posters, boards leaning against the walls, bongs in every size and color of the rainbow, a huge TV, a huger refrigerator filled with beer and very little food. But it's best feature was the beach right outside the window.

"We'll go out to eat," Dominic said, when Kate opened the refrigerator and stared at the rows of beer bottles. "Patty keeps it stocked for my friends who crash here when they surf. Now, come on, let me help you with your wet suit. The waves don't wait."

He kept up a steady stream of instructions as he helped her into the skin-tight suit until she said, "I'm in overload, Dominic. Just show me. Okay?"

"Sorry, baby. It's been a while since I've been here. I'm a little wired. Sit a minute while I dress and we'll hit the water."

He slid into his wet suit with the speed and deftness of considerable practice, then picked up both their boards and nodded. "Ready?"

"As I'll ever be."

"That's all I need, baby." He grinned. "Lukewarm cooperation still gets you in the water with me. And I'll take it from there. You'll have fun."

She actually did have fun when she hadn't been sure she would. Dominic was very patient, taking her up on his board the first few times and holding her tight as they rode some medium shore breaks all the way in. Then he showed her how to paddle out herself, somehow kept his board alongside hers when he got up, then lifted her up on her feet and steadied her as she slid in on the beach breaks smooth as silk.

He saw the elation on her face as they reached shore and felt as though the universe had suddenly turned to gold. "Like that?" he said, unclasping her surfboard leash and scooping up her board when she jumped off.

"Wow."

"It's a good wow, right?" Sliding the boards under one arm, he wrapped his other arm around her shoulder and dragged her close. "One of life's great pleasures."

"No kidding," she breathed, smiling up at him. "You've got a convert."

Abruptly dropping the boards on the beach, he wrapped his arms around her and pulled her into the hard length of body. "I knew it." Raising one hand, he slicked back her wet curls, brushed his dripping hair away from his face, and, bending low, first kissed her, then whispered against her mouth. "Welcome to my world, baby. We're gonna have fun."

And from Dominic's point of view, the weekend was pretty much up there with celestial wonders to the nth degree. Kate actually managed the smaller shore breaks almost immediately and consistently improved in the course of the weekend, the sex was better than ever, which was saying a lot considering their history, and his friend Eddie came down on Sunday to join Dominic surfing the big, badass waves—a relative term in the summer but still not for the faint of heart.

On the drive home late Sunday, fighting traffic the entire way, Kate dozed and Dominic kept mentally replaying his superfine weekend memories. Half Moon Bay had always been his sanctuary and paradise, the juxtaposition not without its occasional mind fuck. But it was mostly paradise, and now he had Katherine to share it with. He knocked wood on his head about a hundred times on the way home, just in case.

Life was going way the hell too good.

Then, when they reached home, Kate came awake, sat up, and suddenly smiled a brilliant smile. "Ohmygod, Dominic! My period started!"

Oh fuck. "The wait's over then," he said in that provisional tone a demolition expert would use when saying, *If it's not the red wire, it's been nice.*

"You don't sound very excited."

"Sorry, baby. I am." He put the relevant emphasis and expression into his next words. "That's *really* good news."

Now what the fuck was he going to do?

TWENTY-FIVE

The next week Dominic was noticeably tense. So much so that Max remarked on it. "What the hell's going on? You on someone's hit list again?"

"I wish it were that simple."

"And?"

"And I'll deal with it."

Max knew better than to continue the discussion.

Even Kate finally asked, "Did I say something to piss you off?"

"Sorry, baby," Dominic said, forcing a smile. "Just some deal driving me nuts."

"Can I help?"

Oh yeah, big-time. "Nah...it's manageable. But thanks."

Then Kate went for her ob-gyn appointment with Melanie. Dominic's sister had just said, "Let me take her, Nicky. She's worried and you might not get it. So don't argue."

He had no intention of arguing. He was probably more worried, although for entirely different reasons. They left work early; Dominic dropped Kate off at Melanie's for her four o'clock appointment and then went home. He tried to work, but his mind was short-circuiting and after reading the same page for the umpteenth time, he finally left his office and, hoping to distract himself, went downstairs to work up a sweat in the gym. After a punishing routine that left him dripping wet and breathing hard, he wasn't any more at ease.

Because he knew what Katherine wanted.

And he didn't want what she did.

Not now, maybe never.

He'd showered, dressed in a white T-shirt and khaki shorts, chug-a-lugged two whiskeys to relax, and was pouring a third when Kate returned.

He heard the front door open and close and all his muscles tensed.

She walked into the living room a few moments later and her smile could have warmed the earth for a hundred years.

"So how did it go?" Dominic asked, as if he didn't know from that dazzling smile.

Kate threw her arms open wide, swept him a dramatic bow, and came upright again, jubilation gleaming in her eyes. "For your information, you're looking at a woman who is completely, totally, *awesomely* healthy! I told Dr. Nye that you get the credit, because thanks to you I'm eating and sleeping well. She said to offer you her compliments. She's really nice by the way. You'd like her. She surfs." Then Kate took a deep breath and tears suddenly welled in her eyes. "I was really worried, Dominic. I was afraid there was something wrong with me." She exhaled a shaky little sigh of relief. "But I'm fine. The doctor said it, like, a million times to reassure me."

"That's good news, baby." He tried to smile and didn't quite manage. "I'm glad you're healthy."

She looked at him, digested his tone, and let out a small breath. "You don't seem glad."

He glanced away for a second, then lifted the glass in his hand to his mouth and drained the whiskey.

"Talk to me, Dominic." She gave herself points for keeping the quiver out of her voice.

He set down the glass. A second of silence passed. "I don't know what to say—or what you want me to say."

"Be happy for us. How about that?"

"Look, baby." He paused, searching for the right words, understanding that no matter what he said he was going to piss off the woman he loved. "I know what you want and"—he took a small breath—"I'm sorry as hell, but I'm not sure I care to take the risk." The operating room was a blinding, never-to-be-forgotten terror. "What happened in London is too…recent. You said you were worried—well, I still am. Let's just wait a while. Not rush into things. Think this through."

"Our marriage isn't just about what you want, Dominic." She stood a little straighter and gave him a stare that was halfway to open warfare. "It's about what I want too, and I want a child."

"Even when you know it might—"

"Even then," she said simply, rather than repeat the doctor's assurances.

"You *are* fucking crazy."

"I never said I wasn't." She took a breath, dialed it down, and said with a soft little catch in her voice, "Please, Dominic, do this for me?"

"Don't say that." There was treachery in her quiet appeal, in the heart-rending sincerity of her soft green gaze, in her sweet fuck-me body that he had to pretend he didn't see or he'd buy into her bad idea.

"I'm not going to stop saying it. I'm not going to stop wanting a baby. That's never going to happen. And you promised I just had to let you know when I was ready." She smiled. "You promised, Dominic."

That sweet glow in her eyes was almost his undoing. He wanted nothing more than to make her happy. But to do that she had to be alive. "I've reconsidered the risks," he said in a half lie; he'd never *not* considered them. "And I can't lose you, Katherine. It's as simple as that."

"You take risks every day in your business. And this isn't even a risk anymore. Ask the doctor, she'll tell you."

"She doesn't know. She *can't* know." He'd thoroughly researched the subject, read the medical papers, books, and articles; there were huge unknowns with miscarriage. "And business risks are just about money. Do I give a shit if I win or lose on that? This isn't the same. Not even remotely." He tamped down his rising temper, kept his voice flat. "This is your goddamn life, Katherine. I can't play this game."

"It's not a game for me." She caught her breath as if she was about to say something sharp, then let out a small sigh instead. "I want a family, Dominic. Not in ten years or when you're ready, but now. You heard Dr. Fuller—I'm not the only woman who feels a kind of desperation after losing a child. Try to understand." Her voice suddenly wobbled. "I *want* a baby."

"No." His nostrils flared. "It's too dangerous."

She said, low, silken, "I can change your mind."

Just the sound of that soft challenge made his adrenaline spike. He sucked in his breath, looked for a way out. She was quietly intent, irresistible, and he wasn't made of stone. "How about a compromise?" he said. "We'll tap the brakes, slow down, just think about it for a while—run the odds." They were both numbers people; maybe he could convince her. "It's a huge fucking gamble, baby, and you know it."

"You mean slow down until I stop asking. Compromise the way *you* want." She shook her head. "No, Dominic. No, no, *no*."

The blunt certainty in her voice was like finding out someone had died. There was no going back. He stared up at the ceiling, thought of how Katherine made every day a winning-the-lottery day, how he'd started living only after he'd met her, how the word *happiness* actually meant something now. Then his gaze came down, didn't go any lower than Kate's face just to be safe, and half-weary, half-pissed, he said, "You start this—"

"I know."

"You can't change your—"

"I *know*."

"I'm not sure you do." He'd been locked down so long, practically celibate for weeks, even he wasn't sure he could stop once he started. He held her gaze, his voice taut and moody. "Last chance to back out."

"Save your breath, okay?" she said, fast and snappish, a real edge to her voice now. "You're not the only one with a fucking temper."

"Whoa, baby, pissing me off's not a good idea."

"Fuck you, Dominic. I'm tired of begging. It's my body, okay? Not yours!"

He went very still for a second, beat back his first ten

rash impulses, examined her for another second, his jaw-line taut, then gave a stiff nod. "Have it your way then." He jerked his phone from his shorts pocket, tapped in a name, waited, and spoke immediately when Roscoe picked up. "I'll be out of the office for three weeks. Katherine too. I have to do something for her," he said flatly. "No, it's not a vacation. We have a project." Dominic pointed at Kate and mimed unbuttoning with his free hand.

She didn't move.

He raised his brows, cupped his crotch.

She began unbuttoning her jacket.

"Jesus, Roscoe. No, I can't, no—no to that too. Listen I gotta go. I'll stay in touch."

Dropping his phone near his empty glass, Dominic silently watched Kate undress. She slid her navy linen jacket down her arms and let it slip from her fingers to the floor, then kicked off her white sandals. He drew in a slow breath when she bent over to slide her white linen slacks and lace panties down her legs, the ripe fullness of her breasts emi-nently touchable.

Whether she heard his small inhalation or was engaged in changing his mind, when she came upright, she lazily raised her arms so the swell of her sumptuous breasts shifted upward, ran her fingers slowly through her coppery curls, and rested her hands on her head, offering herself to him in all her flaunting glory. "Ready to begin your project, Mr. Knight."

That was a gloating smile; there was no other word for it. "Very nice, baby. Definitely a fuck-me pose. But don't start celebrating yet. You're going to have to work for it. I don't like to compromise, I like to win. It pisses me off to compromise—especially about this." He pointed at a spot directly in front of him. "Right here, baby." When she just stared at him, he said mildly, "I thought you wanted something from me."

"I might." She dropped her arms, lightly brushed her mons, then slid a finger into her slick cleft. "You might want something from me too."

"Not as badly as you," he drawled. "We both know who can wait in this twosome. So if I were you, I'd get your ass over here."

"Jesus, Dominic, must you be rude?"

"Look, you want something, I'm giving it to you." His voice was curt. "But I'm doing what you want under some real fucking duress and I'm not entirely sure I can control my anger. So watch your step, watch your mouth, and do what you're fucking told. Now get your willful little pussy over here while I make one more call." Picking up his cell, he tapped a name. "Hey, Richie. Yeah, it's been a while." Dominic smiled. "Yeah, yeah, you wish. Look, I'll be down there later. Just wanted to make sure that—okay—it's there...I thought so. Good. No, that's all I need." Dropping the phone on the table, he glanced at Kate. "You have to move faster, baby. I'm in a real pissy mood." He unzipped his shorts. "Take him out. Then get on your knees."

She glared at him. "I'm not doing that. I want you inside me. That's the whole goddamn point of this."

He sighed softly. "Baby, you really don't get it, do you? It's not about what you want. It's about what I want, when and where I want it, how much I want it. And you'll fucking obey or we end this little game of yours right now. I told you, you start this, you won't be stopping it. Personally, I'm for stopping it. I don't like the odds. And I'm sure as hell not happy about putting your goddamn life in jeopardy."

"So, as usual, it's all about what you want," she snapped.

"No, baby," Dominic said on a slow exhalation. "It never has been with you. I've turned my world upside down for you. I'm not knocking it, I'm not even complaining, I'm just—fuck. I don't know, pissed about risking your life." He shrugged, shut his eyes briefly, and his voice dropped in volume. "What the hell—throw the dice. That's what you want—right?"

He suddenly looked bleak and exhausted. "Oh God, Dominic, I'm so sorry," Kate murmured, closing the distance between them, wrapping her arms around his waist, and holding him tight. "I know how much you've done for me, how much you've changed your life for me." Her chin resting on the America's Cup logo on his T-shirt, she looked up at him with liquid eyes. "I apologize for asking this of you."

"But," he said gruffly, his arms loose at his sides, not touching her, his jaw rigid.

"But I want your baby, our baby," she said, so softly he almost didn't hear.

But the fullness of her need was unmistakable. With a sigh, he folded her in his arms, then sighed again because he couldn't say what he wanted to say—not without hurting her. "I still might be a prick about this before it's over," he muttered, struggling with what he saw as dangerously tempting fate. "You've made me a better person, but not a saint, okay?"

"I know how to talk back, Dominic." Her voice was stronger, her mouth lifted in a small smile.

"Don't ask me to be happy about this," he said, on a long tired breath. "I can't."

"I'll be happy enough for both of us. And I promise I won't make waves, I'll do everything you ask. I won't argue or complain. And if this works out"—she smiled shyly—"you know—eventually, I'll be supercareful about eating and sleeping. I'll follow all your instructions. Really, I will."

He slid his hands gently up and down her spine, his expression resigned, his faint smile tender. "You sure I can't talk you out of this?"

She shook her head. "No. I really want this."

"Just so you know, you might not always get exactly what you want during this three-week program." He grinned just a little. "I can be moody."

"Fuck your moods."

"Then again," he said, soft as silk, "your nervy bitch persona"—he smiled a real smile—"always makes me want to get in the ring with you."

Her green eyes shimmered with impudence. "I've noticed."

"And we both know how that works out," he said very softly.

"You." She tapped his chest. "And him." She rubbed her body against his impressive erection. "And me. Very soon, I hope," she purred.

A lifted brow. "That depends."

"On?" Her own lifted brow.

"A couple of nonnegotiable points," Dominic said, his voice suddenly purposeful, his expression instantly intractable CEO. "I'll be hiring some live-in physicians—to stay next door, not here...so relax. But you will follow their directions explicitly and without complaint. You *will not* dispute your sleep or nutritional requirements with me." He held up his finger to curtail the comment she was about to make. "You know what nonnegotiable means, right? Agree or I'm out. There's no fucking compromise on this."

"Very well." The tiniest little sniff. "Whatever you want, I suppose."

"A little late for that," he said drily. "But at least I've made it less of a crapshoot."

"So, then," she murmured, touched by Dominic's willingness, no matter how reluctant, suddenly breathless with happiness. "Ready?"

He smiled faintly. "I have been for—"

"Since you met me?" she said with a grin.

"Yeah, pretty much."

But he didn't lose it completely, because he never really did. Not after a lifetime of disciplined restraint.

"Get dressed," he said, zipping up his shorts. "We're going downtown."

"What should I wear?"

"It doesn't matter." He gave her lush nudity a spare up-and-down glance. "You just can't go like that. I'll meet you in my office." He lifted his wrist enough to see his watch. "Five minutes, baby. The orders start now."

She hesitated, intrinsically resistant to that tone of voice.

"Your call." He glanced at his watch. "Four minutes, fifty

seconds. Either you want it or you don't." He turned and walked away.

Four minutes later she entered his office and his brows rose.

"What?" she said.

"You're going in that?"

"You didn't give me much time. I grabbed this stuff in a hurry. Hey—you're not getting out of this deal." She gave him a hard look. "You said it didn't matter what I wore."

She looked like some beautiful waif, her curls unruly as usual, a pink flush to her cheeks, his plaid pajama pants dragging on the floor, the tiny spangled jean jacket she liked barely covering her big tits.

"The clothes you wore to your appointment were still on the floor in the living room where you dropped them," he pointed out.

"Maybe you shouldn't have said four minutes, fifty seconds and I might not have panicked. We can't all be cold as ice every second." She stood up a little straighter, her lush boobs almost burst out of the jacket, and Dominic decided being cold as ice wasn't going to be particularly easy for him either. "For your information," she said crisply, standing very straight, facing her adversary with eyes like green flame, "I want this baby, so do your fucking best. I'm not losing this round or any round."

He smiled. "Never a dull moment, baby. I'll give you that."

"As long as you fulfill your obligations for the next three weeks, I'll make sure it's never dull." Her smile, like his, was barefaced cheek. "So where are we going?"

"Sit down." He pointed at the table in the center of the room. "I need you to sign something first."

Kate walked to the table, sat, and picked up the single sheet of paper covered in Dominic's bold handwriting and read the contract defining her health regimen should she become pregnant. She looked up. "Sure there's nothing else? Perhaps a twenty-four/seven monitor to watch me?"

"I'll be doing that."

She met his cool blue gaze. "Then I need a piece of paper too."

"For?"

"Your contract. If you want me to follow all these goddamn instructions, daily I might add, for nine months, I have one requirement." She smiled at him. "Surely in the art of the deal, that makes you the winner."

He carried over a sheet of paper, dropped it on the table, took the chair opposite her, and watched her write swiftly.

She shoved the paper across the table. "I'll sign yours when you sign mine."

He read the single sentence in her small half-printed, half-cursive script. Under any other circumstances, he would have considered it a gift from the gods.

I, Dominic Knight, will deposit my semen in my wife's vagina at least three times daily during the next three weeks.

He looked up, one brow raised. "Pretty specific."

"And yours wasn't?"

A muscle flexed over his cheekbone, his gaze cooled.

"You need a pen," she said into the taut silence. She was equally uninterested in compromise.

He took a small breath, leaned back in his chair, and plucked two pens from the canister on his desk. Facing forward again, he looked at her, his expression grim. "Last time. I'm against this."

"Last time. You promised me. Sign."

He tossed her a pen, followed by a swift scratching of pens on paper, then a mute exchange of documents. Kate folded hers up and put it in her jacket pocket. Dominic took his to his desk and locked it in a drawer. Returning to the table, he held out his hand and said with cool sarcasm, "May the games begin…"

"You'll thank me someday." She smiled and took his hand.

"Don't count on it," he grumbled, pulling her to her feet and leading her to the door.

She stumbled on the dragging pants legs.

He stopped, quickly kneeled, and rolled the flannel material up over her ankles. "All we need is a broken leg to make the day complete," he muttered, coming to his feet.

"Don't be so grumpy. Now you're sure what I'm wearing is okay?" She couldn't keep the elation from her voice. She had his word, his signature, and soon—his baby.

"I'm sure. You won't be wearing it long."

"Tell me where we're going."

He gave her a cool look. "Surprise."

Since the lower level at his house was in use, his garage was under the house next door, where his security lived. He didn't take his Tesla this time, but a car she didn't recognize.

It was a burgundy-colored, low, racy sports car, the sound of the engine when he fired it up a low animal growl. Driving it up the ramp, they came out in the driveway, then onto the street so smoothly Kate murmured, "Wow. This has horsepower. What's it called?"

"A McLaren. Six-sixteen under the hood." He tapped the accelerator and the car shot forward.

"Top speed? Gramps raced on the dirt tracks back home. Saturday night at the fairgrounds always emptied the town."

"Two-oh-four."

She glanced at Dominic with raised brows. "Ever take it there?"

He gave her a quick grin. "Once or twice."

"You have to let me drive it. I used to race with Gramps once in a while. He let me do the demolition derby 'cause I wouldn't wreck his good car."

"We'll see. You're on my shit list right now."

"Fuck you."

"Soon, baby." He took his hands off the wheel for a second and made a rude gesture with his fingers.

"Jeez, you're a sore loser."

He scowled. "And you're living in some fantasy land where things always go right."

"Well, they can't *always* go wrong. You know odds as well as I."

"This might not be about odds. It might be something else. Something that always goes wrong."

"If I didn't want this conception to be as immaculate as possible, I'd say have a couple or ten drinks and relax."

He turned and gave her an insolent smile. "I have some-thing to show you. After you put it on, I'll relax."

"Good. At least there's light at the end of tunnel. What is it?"

"Surprise," he said again, reached over, and patted her cheek. "It won't be long, baby."

He was uncommunicative after that, answering her with grunts or nods or one-word answers until she finally said, tightly, "Am I bothering you?"

"Nope." He was weaving through traffic.

The indifference in his voice only made her more angry. "You're just being mean now."

He braked hard, and the cars behind them on the city street hit their horns. He stuck his arm out the window, gave them the finger, then ignored the traffic jam building up in their lane, took her jaw, and turned her head so she could see the fury in his eyes. "One last time, baby. I don't want you to die. I'm not being mean. I'm fucking scared shitless and it pisses me off." Then he released her chin, stomped on the accelerator, and closed up the open space in front of him. "Let's not have this argument again," he said to the road ahead. "It's getting tedious."

"I'm sorry," she said in a tiny voice.

He didn't look at her. "You better fucking be."

Thoroughly contrite, understanding the extent of his concession to her, she fell silent.

He drove to what looked like a hotel or apartment building. A liveried doorman stood outside polished brass double doors; otherwise, there was no sign to indicate the building's function. Dominic parked in the alley behind the building in a no parking zone, smoothly backing into a spot between two huge generators. Then, sliding out of his seat, he came around the car to help Kate out, his expression still forbidding.

"Do I dare say you're in a no parking zone?"

"They won't tow me."

She wanted to ask why, but mindful of Dominic's grim look and her recent crossing of the line, she didn't say a thing. He unlocked a heavy metal door and led her inside to a small amber marble foyer with a single elevator. Punching some numbers on a keypad on the wall, the doors slid open and he motioned her in. There was no control panel inside, and once the door shut, the car rose for some time, then stopped. "We're here," he said, as if she knew what *here* meant and waved her out.

She almost said, *Wow*, but, on her best behavior after his blunt disclosure in the car, she remained mute. But the Roman mosaics on the walls and floor were real. That they were depictions of erotic scenes didn't surprise her, but the fact that they'd been transported in their entirety was impressive.

Dominic walked over and past the mosaics without notice and shoved open two large bronze doors that swung back silently on their hinges.

Another flick of his hand to usher her in.

The doors shut automatically behind them.

"We'll stay here for a few days. This way."

She followed him through a huge living room with a stupendous view of the bay, through a dining room that could accommodate a large dinner party, down a long hallway with several doors to the left of them, into a bedroom at the end of the hall with more splendid views. The Italian modern furniture, unlike his home on Cliffside, was designer coordinated in shades of gray and red, the sofas in muted gray suede, the large chairs upholstered in scarlet silk obviously down-cushioned, an occasional accent piece in chartreuse the only bright color in the very masculine decor.

The atmosphere was one of lifeless perfection.

Even in the bedroom. The large bed was set on a low platform, the dove gray bedspread tailored in something uninvitingly sleek, the pillows simple white squares, the mirror on the ceiling framed in narrow chrome.

"Do you come here often?" she asked.

"Not anymore. You can leave your clothes here." He stood in the middle of the bedroom, his shuttered gaze on her.

"And you?"

"You can leave your clothes here, Katherine. I believe we agreed you would oblige me in this project of yours."

It was a threat no matter how softly put. She reached for the metal buttons on her jacket.

He watched her silently as she took off her jacket, then untied the knot at the waist of his pajama pants and let them slide to the carpet.

"I forgot to ask," he said mildly, as though she weren't standing nude before him. "Are you hungry? Would you like to eat first?"

"I'm fine. Maybe later." She responded as coolly.

He smiled tightly. "Very well." Another gesture, as though he were leading her to her table at a restaurant. He indicated a door, reached it before her, took a key from his pocket, unlocked it, and swung the door open. "After you."

She came to a stop a foot inside the room, wide-eyed, a tumult of emotions racing through her brain: jealousy and resentment, apprehension, insult, incredulity. Then she turned and said peevishly, "Really?"

"We can stop this game right now," he said softly.

"You'd like that wouldn't you?"

"I would."

She surveyed the mirrored room, the chains hanging from trolleys in the ceiling, the manacled cross on one black-leather-padded wall, the sex swing in violet leather, the marble table that wasn't for a normal dinner, the uphol-stered metal bars in the form of an X, the padded red leather gym horses. The shelves filled with sex toys. "Is this supposed to frighten me?"

"I don't know, Katherine. This entire project of yours is a mind fuck for me. Ask me something else. I can't answer that."

"Do you want me to get pissed about all the women who were here before me and walk away?"

"I haven't a clue. I just want to stop. I want to go back home and do what we were doing. That's what I want."

Kate softly exhaled. "You know what *I* want. You prom-ised me."

He stared at her for a moment. "I did, didn't I?" His voice changed, cooled, and his stance shifted as though he was fully in possession of his body in this room, the mag-netic pull of memory intense. Raw. His expression dark-ened. "Let me show you your new toy."

He drew the door shut behind them and she heard it lock. Taking her hand at her small start, as if she might bolt—perhaps some before her had—he led her over to a black-granite-topped table on which a birchwood box had been centered and released her hand. "You might remember we talked about this before we left for London. Open the box. I had it made for you."

She lifted the lid and visibly caught her breath. Inside, resting on white velvet, was a gold mesh and colorfully jeweled chastity belt.

"It's a copy of a Saracen design. Velvet lined. Do you like it?"

"Am I supposed to like it?"

He smiled for the first time since they'd entered his apartment. "Probably not as much as me. Would you like help putting it on?"

"This is impractical if I'm trying to get pregnant."

"Just put it on, Katherine."

"If I don't?"

"I'll do it for you."

Her eyes were little chips of green glass. "For how long, Dominic?"

"I don't know. I don't even know why we're here. But I do know this isn't open to negotiation." His voice dropped to a low growl. "None of this is—unless you want to leave. Now put the goddamn thing on."

She didn't move for a few moments.

He went still, wanting her to cancel, renege, give up this dangerous game.

Then she took a step forward.

He clenched his fists because he felt like hitting something.

She lifted the handmade girdle from the box and held it up briefly, trying to understand the mechanism. Then she struggled with the supple gold mesh while he watched without helping. Until she finally had the jeweled belt buckled around her waist, had drawn the velvet-lined metal strap between her legs, and turned to him to lock the clasp at her back.

He unceremoniously slid his hand between her legs, slipped his fingers over the pierced metal openings front and back, adjusted the requisite shield over her sex, then, standing upright again, snapped the lock into place. "Now if you'll excuse me, I am going to have one drink. Would you like one?"

He didn't wait for an answer; he left her standing there.

She looked around for something to hit him with, but quickly suppressed the feeling. Her period had ended a week ago, so she could play this waiting game for a few more days. Turning around, she located him across the room, standing beside a small bar, pouring himself a drink. "What are my liquor choices?" she asked pleasantly.

Glass in hand, slowly pivoting, he surveyed her as if debating the sincerity of her tone. "Anything you want," he said finally, "so long as we don't need a bartender." But his dick was less concerned with degrees of sincerity. One look at her voluptuous body, lush tits, shapely hips, her pussy locked up tight, and his dick was fully aroused.

She noticed the fly of his shorts was strained.

He saw she noticed. Fuck. It had been too long since he'd allowed himself to seriously screw that breathtaking body. But Katherine could help him out, take the edge off, take care of him with her mouth. With that thought in mind, by the time she reached the bar, he was marginally relaxed. Although his dick was still rocking.

"I don't suppose you have any champagne," she said, when she reached him, glancing at the array of bottles on the mirrored shelves.

He smiled. "I suppose I do." He lightly touched a portion of the mirrored wall, and it opened to reveal a refrigerator stocked with several dozen bottles of champagne.

She pointed at a half bottle. "I don't want to waste."

"Not a problem," he said, and pulled out a bottle of the Krug Clos d'Ambonnay '96.

"Really, Dominic, that's too extravagant."

"I'll help you." He poured her a glass, handed it to her, quickly drained his whiskey, picked up the champagne bottle, and nodded toward a nearby sofa. "We don't have to rush, baby. We have three weeks." He smiled. "We can't count today on the contract. It's almost seven."

She smiled back. "I suppose."

He politely didn't reply as they moved toward the leather sofa.

"I heard that," she teased.

"I made sure you didn't, baby. You wouldn't have liked what I was thinking." He winked. "Round two coming up after a couple drinks."

He sat on the far side of the sofa, as distant from her as possible, and drank out of the bottle. "If you have any questions about any of this equipment, just ask. Most of it is self-explanatory."

"Did you ever worry about catching something?"

He smiled faintly. "Something?"

"An STD."

He shrugged. "You pay for health certificates and guarantees."

"Did you ever get involved?"

"Every fucking time." He paused at her stare. "Sex is involvement, baby, no matter how you do it."

"God, you're a prick."

"And you're breaking my balls. So I guess we're even."

"Hostile sex. Is that what this is going to be?"

He smiled, half lifted the bottle in his hand. "At least we have the right setting."

"So that's why we're here."

"You said that before and I told you I don't know why we're here. I still don't, so save your breath."

"Is this a hotel?"

He nodded.

"I thought you didn't like to stay in hotels."

"I own this one. The top floor is mine. No one has access except me."

"And your staff."

He did a little double take, registering his staff as a presence. Then he said brusquely, "Right. Them too."

"How many?"

"How many what?"

"How many staff do you have here?"

He sighed softly. "If it's important to you, Katherine, I'll find out how many staff I have."

She sniffed. "You're too rich."

"You are now too."

"Am not."

He laughed. "Fuck, you'll argue about anything." He waved the bottle in her direction. "Want more?"

She shook her head.

Raising the bottle to his mouth, he swallowed for a lengthy interval and drained it. Then he dropped the bottle on the floor and came to his feet. "Let's eat dinner. I'm hungry."

Turning, he walked to the door, then swung back. "Coming? You can't get in or out without a key, so unless this room fascinates you for some reason, I suggest you get off your ass."

"It's going to be a long fucking three weeks, isn't it?" she muttered, rising from the black leather sofa and walking toward him.

"The longest, baby. No shit."

When they entered the bedroom, he went to the closet, found a robe for her, and handed it over. "Cotton," he said, so she'd know he'd bought it for her, that it wasn't someone else's. In Hong Kong, he'd discovered her preference for cotton robes.

"Were you planning on coming here?" She surveyed the row of cotton robes hanging in the closet.

He was pulling open a drawer and glanced over his shoulder. "Nope."

"Then these robes weren't for me."

He swung around, a pair of gray sweats in his hand. "Ever hear of the phone?" Without waiting for an answer, he jerked off his T-shirt and dropped it on the floor.

"That fast?" The trip to this apartment hadn't taken more than forty minutes.

"As you see," he said, without looking up. His shorts and boxers discarded, he was stepping into his sweats. "We can eat dinner in the living room and watch TV. Decide what you want." Leaning over, he picked up his shorts, extracted the key to the locked room, slipped it into his sweats pocket, and, dropping the shorts, walked from the room.

Slipping the robe on, she followed him down the hall into the living room. The sun was beginning to set, the view out the windows stunning. "Nice view," she said, figuring the weather was always a safe topic when nothing much else was.

He looked at her for a moment, as if she'd suddenly sprouted two heads. Then his mouth lifted in a mannered smile. "So I've been told." Dropping onto one of the gray suede sofas, he reached for the phone on a nearby table. "Do you know what you want?" he asked, leaning his head back on the sofa pillows, gazing at her, expressionless.

"Your head on a platter?"

He smiled tightly. "Besides that. Would you like a menu? The restaurant downstairs has two Michelin stars. The food's good. Otherwise, just tell me what you want to eat and they'll make it. And don't say chocolate cake right away, because if this insane project of yours is for real, your desserts are going to come *after* you eat something decent."

"I just lost my appetite."

"Then I'll order for you," he said, undeterred by her petulance. "Find us something to watch on TV." He hit a button on the phone and a moment later said, "Let me talk to Wes. Yeah, same to you. Right, it's been a while. Kids good? Nice. Okay, catch you later. Hi, Wes. What's on the menu tonight?" Dominic listened, said, "Fine," "Good," or "Perfect," many times, then laughed. "I happen to be hungry. Funny. I'll let you know. That aside, we'll be needing three meals a day. Sure...hors d'oeuvres, why not?" Dominic was smiling when he hung up. "They're going to cook something for us," he said, glancing at Kate, who was standing by the flickering TV. "Come on, baby, let's not fight all night. Wes's food is great"—he waved at the windows—"the view is even better at night. And I have trouble staying mad at you." He put up a hand. "Not that I'm still not pissed about this whole deal, but just not now. Okay?"

"Okay." Kate sighed, then smiled. "I don't like to fight either."

She was standing in front of a very large flat-panel TV and looking small in contrast to the screen and the huge, high-ceilinged room. Her curls were wild and unruly, framing her face like a filmy nimbus against the lighted screen, giving her an innocent, saintly air. "You okay with that— whatever...my new toy?" he asked, as if saintly thoughts required instant deflection. "It's not uncomfortable or anything? Nothing rubbing? I told them your skin was delicate."

She smiled. "Nothing rubs. They must have listened." Sweeping the robe skirt open, she playfully posed for him, holding the forget-me-not printed material out in flaring wings. "You like it?"

Saintly images instantly vaporized. "Jesus, baby, that is so fucking hot." The multicolored jewels embedded in the gold mesh twinkled and sparkled, as if the lush sight of pale flesh imprisoned by stark metal wasn't sufficient lure to the eye, as if the punitive factor in the locked design wasn't adequate enticement.

"And temporary, I presume," she said, smiling serenely.

"Why don't we say for my amusement between my work shifts."

"You're such a sweetheart."

"Damn right I am. Because you're goddamn crazy and I'm still going along with this." He sighed softly. "Come here. Let me hold you. Tell me this is all going to work out. That this isn't one huge fucking blunder."

He looked so grave and somber, her heart ached. She wanted to tell him that she had a good feeling, that he shouldn't worry. But that would have sounded juvenile and Pollyanna or worse, crazy, like his accusation. So as she moved toward him, she offered modest comfort. "Remember, the doctor pronounced me awesomely healthy. That has to count for something. Even if it's only a fifty percent factor, it's a good beginning. And," she added, going for broke after all because she was bubbling inside with exuberance, "I have a really good feeling about this, Dominic."

He frowned as he held out his arms. "Does that counteract my really bad feeling?"

"Of course." She fell into his outstretched arms like people did in those trust exercises and whispered against his grim mouth, "Good is always stronger than bad in the world. Always, always, Dominic."

He grunted rather than rain on her starry-eyed parade. "Okay, Little Miss Sunshine. Let's try and keep it that way."

Dominic was effortlessly charming over dinner, with a grace acquired over years of experience, asking her about her projects at work as they ate, praising her for two acquisitions she'd vetted for them, even talking a little about his uncle, whom he'd adored.

She responded less easily with her gaze constantly drawn to Dominic's nude torso, or the dark beauty of his face, or the way he moved with such grace when he came out of his lazy sprawl on the sofa to pick up his wineglass or some appetizer with his fingers.

A table had been wheeled in and placed in front of Dominic on the sofa. A chair had been drawn up for her opposite him. So the object of her love and lust was directly in her line of vision. He was ridiculously handsome, tall, lean yet solid with muscle. Politely immoral, indifferent to censure.

As if he knew he was irresistible in all manner of things.

Not just to her, but to everyone, to women particularly. In this apartment especially. And she jealously wondered how many women he'd entertained in this contrived stage set. How many had seen him lounging on that sofa, half dressed, being gracious, looking at them like he was looking at her—his extraordinary blue eyes under his dramatic black brows, warm, seductive, making them wet like he was making her wet?

When he leaned across the table to feed her a spoonful of caviar and said, "Open up, baby," flame-hot desire lit her from within, as every pleasure center instantly came online. "They claim this is an aphrodisiac," he added with a smile, the mother of pearl spoon inches from her lips.

She stiffened, offended by Dominic's casual dispensing of aphrodisiacs. "Is this your normal routine here?"

She wouldn't care to hear what my normal routine had been. "It's a rare caviar, baby," he said, ignoring her question. "Albino Oscietre. Full of vitamins. High protein." He glanced down at his extended hand, then up, held her gaze. "We want you to be healthy. And in case you forgot, it's my rules the next three weeks."

She faced his self-possessed smile, that trick he had of looking detached enough to wait forever, and experienced a moment of helplessness in this game they were playing. "But I get a baby out of it," she said, to rebalance the equation before she opened her mouth.

After a brief, perfunctory smile, he slid the spoonful in her mouth, sat back while she chewed and swallowed, then repeated the process until she'd eaten the small bowl of caviar on ice.

She gave him a taunting look. "What about you?"

"Don't worry. This harrowing experience is keeping my adrenaline pumping." Then he pushed a small plate of Thai lobster her way and began eating his.

Several courses later—fresh pasta with sorrels, carrot soup, beef tenderloin with Périgueux sauce, artichokes with foie gras, spinach with soft boiled eggs and Mornay sauce, fruit salad with red berry coulis, a stunning chocolate soufflé for Kate at the end—Dominic said in gross understatement, "That wasn't bad. Are you done? Should we move on?" He put his arm along the back of the sofa, slid down a little lower on his spine, and smiled. When her face flushed, he said blandly, "I just meant is there something you'd like to watch on TV? A movie? One of your talent shows? Or," his voice was mild, his gaze amused, "would you rather do something else? That padded velvet lining is making your pussy happy, isn't it?"

"I hope it's not a problem?" She forced her voice into a semblance of calm she wasn't feeling, the chastity belt exerting pressure on her clit with such exquisite focus she marveled at the means by which Dominic had calibrated the measurements for his jeweler.

He smiled. "Not in the least." He slid the key out of his sweats pocket and held it up between his thumb and forefinger. "Feel like a little test run before midnight?"

"Where?" she asked.

He didn't misunderstand; she meant *not* his locked room. "Anywhere you like."

"The bedroom." Coming to her feet, she swallowed a gasp as the chastity belt pressed deeply into her sex. She was wet, needy, aching with longing. And he was entirely too beautiful, too irresistible. While Dominic as autocrat always had a predictable impact on her libido.

She shivered.

He saw her little frisson, knew what it meant. Quickly swinging his legs to the side of the table, he rose from the sofa. "A little shaky? Want me to carry you?"

She shook her head, color rising in her cheeks. She was frustrated with herself for being so susceptible while he, as always, was unfailingly controlled.

"How about I carry you anyway," he said, kicking her chair out of the way, scooping her up in his arms, and moving away from the table. "We don't want you hurting yourself three hours before midnight," he said with cool sarcasm. "Or prior to our test run."

She looked up at him, furious. "God, you're hateful."

"I know," he said without pretense. "Could we go home now?"

But they didn't.

And her refusal made him as quietly furious as she.

Taking her into the bedroom, he carried her to the bed, seated her on the edge, then pulled out the drawer in the bedside table.

She went still; a pair of handcuffs dangled from his fingers. "What are you doing?"

"I should think that's obvious."

She made a small complaining sound.

"If only you had a vote," he drawled. "Give me your hands."

An instant later, he was dragging her back across the bed, his fingers snaked around her ankle. "Don't be stupid," he growled.

She kicked at him with her free foot, missed his dick by a hairbreadth, and a tearing second later, she was facedown on the bed, the rough, rasping sound of the metal belt buckle sliding free like a high-pitched protest in the silence. Then a heartbeat later she was flipped over and he was inside her.

Their test run was a wild and wilder act of mutual frustration. He went after her like a rutting satyr, she fought back, disputing his control, ravishing him in her own ferocious way, coming twice quickly, to his annoyance, as if she weren't actively bloodying his back and face and damn near his dick at the time. Intent on ruining her third orgasm, which was about to detonate, he muttered, "Payback, baby," hastily ejaculated into his wife's vagina, per contract, and rolled away.

Deliberately deprived of her orgasm, hot with anger, she took a wild swipe at his face.

His reflexes sluggish with his climax still strumming, he almost didn't catch her hand in time. "Jesus, that's—my fucking—eye," he said, flinging her away. Falling back in a sprawl, he lay with his chest heaving, eyes shut, the sting of her claw marks unprecedented.

Kate was tumbled at his feet where she'd landed, panting from both the tempestuous sex and *extreme* frustration.

A small interval passed, only the sound of harsh breathing breaking the silence.

Then Dominic came up on one elbow and glared at her. "Don't move," he muttered.

As if she could, she thought, glaring back. Although if she could, she would have, just to jerk his chain.

Rolling up on his knees a second later, he leaned down, flipped her on her back, and slid a pillow under her bottom. "There will be *no* redo of these three weeks. So fucking lie still." Tossing a blanket over her, he stretched for the remote on the bedside table, hit a button, and a TV rose from the floor at their feet. "I'd ask you what you want to watch but I'm too pissed. And we're trimming your nails." He glanced at the bedside clock. "You can move in a half hour, not before." Flicking on ESPN, he slowly exhaled, then smiled faintly. "Fuck. At least something's going right." A surfing competition in Bali was being broadcast.

With the pillow under her bottom, starkly reminded of

the endgame, Kate's sense of outrage evaporated and she was suddenly overcome with euphoria. She was winning. Despite Dominic's resistance or what she had to admit was perhaps well-deserved anger, he was losing.

And he never lost.

She glanced at Dominic, expecting him to show signs of anger or withdrawal. Or sullenness. Instead he was lounging against the pillows, his gaze on the screen, smiling, his shoulders relaxed, his legs in a sprawl, his fingers lightly tapping the remote as though keeping time with some internal music. He laughed abruptly, then let out a cheer as one of the contestants moved up to second place. On impulse, he turned to her. "Did you see that? That was fucking awesome." A second later, he was completely absorbed again as the next competitor crested a huge wave.

Encouraged by his good humor, she touched his arm lightly. "I just wanted to say thank you, Dominic, for—well agreeing to this. Really, thanks."

He looked away from the screen, stared at her, his gaze briefly blank until her words registered. When they did, he frowned and said a little impatiently, "I'm not sure you're welcome."

"Nevertheless, I'm pleased."

He gave her a funny look as though he wasn't sure he should acknowledge her pleasure when his mood was so contrary. Muzzling a mean response, he said, "Good. I think," he added sardonically and went back to his program.

She woke up when he lifted her in his arms. "How long did I sleep?" she murmured, drowsily.

"Three hours. It's midnight."

"Where're we going?"

"Guess."

She was wide awake in a split second.

He smiled. "Right. Night games, baby."

But whether he'd become reconciled in the past three hours or was too tired to sustain his anger, when he carried her into the locked room, he said with a smile, "Feel free to sleep through this warm-up exercise. I don't really need you to participate."

His smile and pleasantries aside, they were still in this hard-core playground and she doubted she could sleep. And maybe he didn't really mean it, since he walked to an open doorway, set her on her feet, and pointed. "You might want to use the bathroom before we begin. Take a shower if you like. It's not necessary, but we're probably going to be busy for a while. So"—he smiled—"whatever. I'll wait for you out here."

It was a beautiful large room with black marble and mirrors, two glass-walled showers, an enormous sunken tub, and a separate area for toilets and bidets. Built-in shelves lined one wall with stacks and stacks of white towels, washcloths, shampoos, perfumes, and cosmetics. She half expected a spa attendant to jump out from the shadows and ask her if she wanted a massage.

Kate was grateful Dominic had said a shower was optional. After three hours' sleep, she wasn't ambitious enough. But she tidied up a little and returned to Dominic's playroom.

He pushed away from the entry wall where he'd been waiting. "That didn't take long."

"A little soap, lots of perfume. You'll have to settle for that."

His smile was lazy. "Not a problem. Ready?"

She made a little circle with her finger in a sweep of the room. "This all makes me a little nervous. Just so you know."

He held out his hand. "We'll take it slow."

She didn't move. "That sounds scary."

"Want me to carry you?"

"Where?"

He grinned. "To the moon." Then he shrugged. "Shut your eyes if you want. I'll tell you when you can open them."

She followed his advice because it was easier not to know. And he *was* being nice, his earlier anger gone. "Is this going to hurt?" she asked, as he picked her up.

"It shouldn't."

Her eyes snapped open. "I don't like the sound of that."

He smiled a little. "If it hurts, we'll stop. How about that?"

"Okay." She let her eyelids fall. "I trust you."

"I don't know if you should do that."

But despite his contradiction, his voice was teasing. "Now you're just fucking with me," she murmured, his strong body flexing lightly against hers as he walked.

"Not yet, baby. You'll know when I'm fucking you." He came to a stop, made a small adjustment on something with his elbow, then deposited her onto smooth leather.

The sensation of coolness brought her eyes open. "Oh," she said, turning her head one way, then the other, taking in the apparatus of the violet leather swing, her gaze guarded as she looked up at Dominic.

He moved forward, slid his hands up her ankles, calves, under her knees, spread her legs, and took a step closer, his thighs resting against the seat rim. Then he slid his fingers down to her calves again and, lifting gently, held her legs against his hips. Leaning forward slightly, he activated the swing and it swung back. He moved back, the swing followed. "Pretty simple, right?"

She took a small breath, nodded.

"You really can sleep now if you're tired. I'm going to take it superslow." He smiled faintly. "Last time was pretty high octane." A quirked grin. "Bloody."

She glanced up, saw the naked scratches and abrasions on his face and shoulders. "We'll trim your nails later," he said, reading her gaze. "Or would you like someone to come up and give you a manicure?"

She stifled an emphatic *no*, preferring not to remind him of her previous rage. She shook her head.

He grinned at her restraint. "Worried?"

"In here? Always," she replied honestly.

"We'll have to see about changing your mind, baby," he said pleasantly. "Let's see if you can come a few times."

"Really? You're not mad?"

He raised one brow. "Don't ask me things I can't answer." Shifting her attention to something less controversial, he let her legs drop, cupped her breast, slid his thumb over her nipple, watched it stiffen. "You felt that," he murmured, smiling faintly. "And this?"

She arched her back into his hand as he gently squeezed her nipple, delectable sensation gliding downward to her sex, softly pulsing through her warming flesh, instantly sending out a drumbeat of arousal to the far reaches of her body.

Bending low, he took her nipple into his mouth and sucked gently, barely touching her, the pressure so delicate, she reached up and pulled his head closer.

"Uh-uh," he said around her nipple, reaching up and unclasping her hands. "Don't touch. If you do, I'll stop."

Her hands fell away as if burned.

He tortured her with deliberately light licks and sucks, a grazing sensation of his lips, the occasional delicate scoring of her nipple with his teeth. Twice, a surprising sharp, hard suck.

Eliciting a lush, heated groan from Kate.

But still, he made her wait, framing her breast in his large hands, sucking first one nipple then the other, repeating the pattern for some time until she was flushed and visibly shaking. Only then did he lift his head. "I suppose you want to come now?"

There was something in his expression that made her wary.

"I'm waiting for an answer, Katherine."

"I would like to, yes."

"How much?" His voice was cool, his eyes cooler, the underlying message unmistakable.

"I don't care if I come the entire three weeks. Does that answer your question?"

He went utterly still. "You're pissing me off. You know that."

"I wish I could make it better for you," she said, softly,

looking down for a moment before she met his gaze. "Really I do."

He gave her a tired look. "Old arguments, no good answers." He stared at her for a moment. "What the fuck," he said, suddenly impatient. "You're my constant wet dream, and reservations aside, my dick's psyched. So open yourself for me, baby. Let's do this."

Throbbing with longing after Dominic's torturous attention to her nipples, she quickly obliged. Sliding her fingers over her slick cleft, she drew her pink, pouty flesh open.

"Put him in." A brusque order, hard and flat. Leaning in slightly so she could reach his huge, grandstanding dick, he swept her legs around his waist in one smooth gliding gesture, then took a sharp breath. "Your hands are cold."

"Lucky your dick is on fire."

"Lucky for both of us," he said mockingly.

She glanced up, opened her mouth, changed her mind, shut it again.

"Smart girl." He grinned. "I can always jack off."

"But it wouldn't feel as good," she said, her smile equally impudent. Raising her hips, she wrapped her fingers around the base of his erection and shoved his rampant dick all the way in, smooth as silk.

When he hit bottom, they both softly gasped.

"Goddamn," he said, a second later, half breathless.

"Nice, hey?" Her voice was just a wisp of sound.

He lifted his head slightly so his smile bathed her in sunshine. "Nice like the crown jewels in the Tower of London are nice."

"Or Almond Joys are nice."

He laughed. "Christ, I can't stay mad at you. You're fucking irresistible. What the hell are we going to do?"

"I don't know about *we*, but *moi* is going to love you to pieces. You're way better even than an Almond Joy."

"And I can make *this* way better, baby." Unwinding her legs from his waist, he stood up, grasped her thighs lightly, and set the swing in motion. The fluid friction and sleek oscillation, their hot, frenzied desire quickly gave rise to a breathtaking pleasure, disarming and stupefying to them both.

So different for Dominic as to beggar description; love did that. Made it brilliant and wonderful, not just about lust.

The difference for Kate was in expectation: she'd not considered a room like this could make her love him more. That passions could be heightened, indulged, and overindulged. That too much of a good thing could be heady stuff indeed.

The fact that Dominic brought her to orgasm five times in a row perhaps contributed to her epiphany.

Or maybe love was love in any guise.

It altered perception, blew away foolish discord, opened eyes, and healed hearts. And made even men like Dominic Knight understand the meaning of besotted.

And ultimately, when Kate was finally satisfied, he came in his wife this second time, willingly.

He carried her over to the sofa afterward and held her propped against his chest with one arm while he tossed a blanket on the cold leather. Then he placed her on her back with a pillow under her bottom. "It's probably stupid, but why not, if you don't mind?"

"I don't mind." She sighed. "I don't mind anything you do; I'm so crazy in love I swear I'm seeing pink unicorns. And if you dare laugh, I'll hit you when I get up."

He was carrying over a heavy black leather club chair and dropped it before he spoke. "I have no intention of laughing. And I'm sorry for being such a prick. We'll figure this out somehow," he said, sitting down, sliding into a lazy sprawl. He smiled one of his warm, beautiful smiles, his eyes crinkling in the corners. "We'll make it work."

She blew him a kiss. "God, I love you. It's terrifying in a way." She grinned. "But not very often. Most of the time, it's that Almond Joy thing. Speaking of that kind of happiness"—she grinned—"maybe I even got pregnant that time."

"I'll bet you did. Let's stop."

She laughed. "Goddamn, I'm going to have to whip you into shape." She gave a little wave of her hand. "And I see I have a lot of choices here." Then she made a wry face. "Seriously, you really used those whips?"

He shrugged. "A long time ago, baby. Everything's been sitting here since I met you."

"It's not all bad, I suppose."

He smiled. "I could tell from your screams. I'll show you a couple more things tomorrow. You'll like them."

She looked doubtful. "I don't know..."

"Trust me, baby. I do." He came to his feet. "I'm going to carry you to bed now. You really should rest. And I'm over my tantrum. We'll just have a little fun tomorrow," he said, lifting her in his arms.

TWENTY-SIX

As soon as Katherine was sleeping, Dominic called his personal physician, Yash, and had him begin hiring doctors. Since he was going to be having sex with his wife more or less continuously for three weeks, and considering she'd conceived last time against impossible odds, there was little to no question he'd be needing a full team of obstetricians.

But during the course of the next three weeks, there were times when he thought better of his agreement, wanted to undo it. And he'd turn surly and perform his function as stud with a kind of wounded umbrage.

Fortunately, Katherine was fully capable of standing up to him.

All in all though, it was mostly a whole lot of fun and only a tiny percentage of strife. They both had tempers and in this instance, relatively divergent interests. Neither had expected complete harmony.

At base though, Dominic took pleasure in Kate's audacity. It was what had first intrigued him in Palo Alto, then charmed in Hong Kong and ultimately made her irresistible and the love of his life.

While Kate loved Dominic even more for obliging her.

Despite his reluctance.

So while they occasionally navigated a maze of conflict-

ing emotions, their sexual compatibility was always con-
spicuous for its white-hot lust and passion. Dominic did
what he did well—provoking, tantalizing, intoxicating his
wife's impatient desires, with mesmerizing subtlety, with
matchless expertise, taking her time after time to a seething, frantic, tempestuous climax.

He'd occasionally smile and say, "Baby, slow down once
in a while. You know . . . just for a change."

"Thanks for the advice," she'd whisper, eyes shut, bliss
strumming through her body like a fine orchestral version
of paradise. "Next time."

But she never did.

Not that he had grounds for complaint. After weeks of
sexual temperance while Katherine healed, he had a permanent hard-on, his issue with the reckless gamble not-
withstanding. Although that persistent, chafing dissent
spurred his agenda.

And at some mindless, incoherent level he needed
payback.

"No," he'd say at times when she'd ask for something.
"We're doing this my way. Any questions?"

The look in his eyes always reminded her of that first
night in Hong Kong when she'd told him she couldn't wait
and he'd said, *You have to.* But he'd given her so much since
then, had given so much of himself, was indulging her now
in what she most wished for in the world. She'd smile. "I
won't ask for anything, I promise."

"Except my dick inside you for three weeks," he'd growled.

"Except that," she'd say sweetly into the thundercloud
of his scowl.

So the game was played out his way, on his terms.

Dominic took her shopping and made love to her in whatever dressing room they were in, ignoring her embarrassment. "Don't worry about it. We bought out the store. They don't care. And you want a baby, don't you?" He knew how to stop her objections.

They went out for lunch, often. They were on a three-week hiatus. "So why not?" he'd say. Which meant he screwed her in the bathrooms of a great many restaurants.

He excused them before dessert at Melanie's one night, politely, with a perfectly reasonable excuse, and took Kate home and fucked her. That time for almost two days, practically nonstop. He couldn't even blame his temper that time. His dick was on a roll.

Kate never had a second period. They both knew she wouldn't.

And a few weeks later, when she joyfully said, "I'm way past what should have been my period. I'm going to check," Dominic just nodded, relatively complacent. "Go for it, baby."

She did a small double take at Dominic's easygoing reply. "You don't seem very conflicted anymore."

He smiled. "Maybe I'm getting used to the idea."

Or maybe the fact that Yash had almost all the required doctors under contract offered him a measure of comfort. With the exception of the pediatric surgeon, the medical team was settled in next door or down the street. Dominic had purchased three more houses on the block and with the staff in place, he was feeling as safe as he was going to be.

No surprise, the pregnancy test came back positive. They celebrated with dinner at Lucia.

As they entered the busy restaurant, Dominic turned to Kate. "You're sure? You don't mind company? I can have the place cleared out."

Kate squeezed his hand. "I like the commotion."

"Not a problem then." He would have preferred privacy, but tonight was all about what Katherine wanted. "Hey, Monty." Dominic smiled at his maître d'. "The usual crush, I see. Can you keep us away from the noise?"

"Sure, Nick. Evening, Katherine. We've got you by the windows. Lynn had a couple of the lemon trees moved to block off your table. Or a private room perhaps?" He looked at Dominic. They'd already talked about options for what Dominic had characterized with his usual reticence as a special occasion. Monty knew better than to ask for particulars.

Dominic dipped his head. "The window's fine. Katherine likes people."

"I'm giving Dominic lessons on how the rest of us live," Kate said, lightly teasing, dressed simply tonight in a white cotton sweater, flower print skirt, and sandals, as though conforming to that classless principle.

Monty grinned. "So how's that working out, Nick?"

"Excellent."

"Nothing but praise, Monty." Kate grinned. "That's my plan."

Dominic's plan was to defer to Katherine as much as possible in the coming months, a Herculean task for a man unfamiliar with constraint.

Recognizing Dominic's restlessness, Monty gestured. "This way, guys. Rudy outdid himself tonight."

As a wave of whispers followed in their wake, Kate glanced up at Dominic. "Popular as ever."

"Uh-uh. They're looking at you and wishing they were me."

She smiled. "Liar. You're a celebrity."

"I think the word is *notorious*. Or was," he added quickly as her brows lifted.

"Supersmooth."

"And happily married," he murmured, smiling and relaxed. "Don't forget that."

Thanks to Rudy's creative imagination, dinner was heavenly: a ten-course tasting menu tailored to Kate's palate, punctuated with an occasional amuse bouche to beguile and served with the casual friendliness that was a hallmark of Lucia. Dominic drank sparkling water; he'd ordered chocolate milk for Kate and they smiled at each other across the table—in pleasurable memory, in present delight, in anticipation of the sweet promise of the night ahead.

Kate was charmed by the concern Dominic and his restaurant staff had exercised on her account, the glorious finale to the sumptuous meal a miniature chocolate fastasia: a tower of millefeuille-layered coconut cream, covered in chocolate ganache, and decorated with raspberry coulis and spun sugar. "This is the culinary equivalent of bliss," she murmured, her dessert spoon poised midair, her smile playful. "Did you tell them I liked Almond Joys?"

"I might have at some point," Dominic said. "I'm glad you enjoyed dinner. You ate well."

"The food was fabulous. And I haven't been sick so far."

She smiled quickly, avoiding further reference to the past. "That helps."

"Amen to that, baby. Which reminds me," he added, equally inclined to shift the topic of conversation. "Have you told Nana the news yet?"

Kate's eyes sparkled with amusement. "I did. She said she already knew."

Dominic's brows rose. "Because?"

"Her tea leaves."

He laughed at the outrageous concept. "Fuck. Maybe she could give us some help with our business negotiations."

"Don't laugh." Kate looked at him calmly. "She probably could."

He set down his espresso cup, pushed the saucer away. "You're serious."

"In a way, I am. Nana learned how to read fortunes in tea leaves from her mother. She's really amazing. Don't look so dubious. The idea of fortune-telling's been around for ages." As Dominic continued to stare at her with a polite blankness, Kate pulled out her cell phone and held it out. "Call her. She'll tell you."

Dominic shook his head. "Forget it. I believe you."

"No you don't, but"—she stuck out her tongue and grinned—"I don't care. Because I want you to take me home now and give me the dessert I really want."

He glanced at his watch, then smiled. "We've just been waiting for your go-ahead."

They didn't actually make it into the bedroom the first time because Kate's pregnancy hormones were in total blitz mode with the chocolate dessert having served as foreplay.

"Did you know what that dessert would do to me," she panted, pulling Dominic to a stop on the stairway and reaching for the zipper on his slacks.

"Fuck no," he said, laughing softly. "But we'll definitely have it again." He brushed her hands aside. "But come on, baby, let's get to a bed."

"No." Her fingers were back on his zipper. "I want you to climb on top of me. I'm in a slam-bang, take-me-I'm-yours mood." She looked up when he stopped her unzipping. "Too frank? Outside your repertoire? Don't want to hurt your knees?"

"I'll climb on top of you anywhere, baby." And his repertoire included stairs in worse places than this. But when she quickly lay back on the carpeted stairs, pulled up her skirt, and wiggled her fingers in frantic entreaty, he lifted her up and, sitting on a stair, lowered her until she was straddling his thighs. "But someone has to be practical," he whispered, kissing her softly as he tucked the front of her skirt into her waistband and slipped her panties over the curve of her hips. "We don't want you hurting your back." Picking her up by her waist before she could protest, he raised her over his head, lightly tonguing her sex on her way up. "Umm, nice. Wet. Now kick off your panties, babe," he murmured, effortlessly holding her aloft.

"Jesus, you're strong," she purred, discarding her panties with a flick of her feet. "All that beautiful, hard-core muscle makes me really"—she moaned as he measured her slick cleft with a leisurely lick before dropping her back on his lap.

Eyes closed, she whispered, "Do that some more..."

He smiled, raised her high. "Slide your legs over my shoulders. There you go, baby. That's the way." And holding her steady, he dipped his head, gently drew her swollen clit into his mouth, and even more gently sucked.

A soft moan escaped as she languished in a lush, sensory paradise, ecstasy taking on a physical presence. Dominic's tongue was deft, devoted, ravishing her clit and G-spot in the nicest possible way—the sumptuous pressure hard, but not too hard, deep, but not too deep, and so deliciously slow, oh Jesus—the first small rippling wave began to break and with a tiny scream she started to climax.

Long moments later, when Dominic swung her down onto his lap and held her close, she exhaled softly. "That was lovely—as usual." She looked up at him from under her lashes and grinned. "Thank you."

"Not a problem, baby. You like to come, I like to make you come. We're a good team. Ready to go upstairs?"

She slid her arms around his neck. "Soon."

His blue gaze was indulgent. "Meaning?"

"He didn't have any fun," she whispered, running her fingers over his erection. "We should see if he fits."

"How about we see if he fits upstairs?"

"You shouldn't have said that." Her voice quivered slightly. "My pussy heard."

He sighed. "With your pussy on a roll, I'd better keep my mouth shut."

Taking his hand, she slid it between her legs. "Feel that?"

"You're fucking drenched," he said, his voice a low rasp.

"You should help me out," she whispered.

He took a small breath and said carefully, "If you're sure."

She slid his finger deeper. "Was I not clear?"

He smiled, drew out his finger, and tapped it on her mouth. "Just checking how much of a gentleman I want to be."

She laughed. "Why start now?"

"Cute." He held her gaze.

"I so hate to wait," she purred.

With stunning speed, he unzipped, lifted her up, guided himself into place, entered her sleek warmth, and smoothly eased her down his enormous dick.

"Oh God." Her eyes shut tightly against the brilliant rapture shimmering through every trembling, twitching nerve. And as he shifted his hips to drive in more deeply, the glorious pressure spread outward from his solid presence, swelled through her body, and bathed her senses in seething splendor.

She shivered. "More, Dominic. More, more, more."

Dragging in a harsh breath, he curbed his libido with effort, then slowly raised her as she clutched at his shoulders and whimpered in dissent. "Hey, hey," he whispered. "I'm back." And he inhaled her soft sigh as he guardedly eased her down his erection. Then he sucked in another breath of restraint. "Don't move," he commanded in a deep husky voice, struggling to maintain his self-control with the tight, velvety feel of her enveloping his cock.

Jesus fuck. His nostrils flared. But her pregnancy had him on unequivocal notice as of today: nothing but tame and gentle.

As though to test his good intentions, Kate whimpered and rolled her hips in deliberate enticement. "What if I want to move?" she murmured.

"You can't." Cupping her flushed face in his hands, he whispered, "Move and I'll stop fucking you."

"No." A breathy, suffocated protest.

His gaze was close and uncompromising.

She went still under his hands. "There's a good girl. I'm just trying to keep this from getting out of hand." His smile warmed her lips. "Now let's see what we can do about some personal fulfillment for you."

Having judiciously quelled his lust, Dominic offered Kate pleasure with delicately measured grace. He raised her slowly, slowly, so she felt the sleek, silken friction with lurid intensity, then he lowered her with equal moderation, repeating the gentle flux and flow with tender benevolence until she was warming his throat with little breathy wails that were rising in volume.

"Almost there, baby?" It was a rhetorical question. She was past reply, eyes shut, and panting.

Splaying his fingers wide, he adjusted his grip on her hips, arched his dick upward, felt her heated flesh yield by slow degrees until he reached the ultimate extremity. A brief moment of internal debate—then he pushed in an infinitesimal distance more.

She gasped; the world shuddered to a stop.

"Too much?" He began to lift her away.

"No, no!" Desperate, trembling, she cried, "No, no, please..."

He hesitated, unsure of her message. But then she

pulled his face down, her mouth closed over his and she kissed him frantically, wildly. Her meaning no longer in doubt, he flexed his fingers, tightened his grip, and exerted the most deliberate, unhurried downward pressure.

Lower. Lower.

Careful now.

Almost.

There.

Her orgasmic scream erupted in a high-pitched burst of splintering sound that whirled past his ear, swept upward into the silent stairway, and echoed breathless rapture in repetitive, quivering, frenzied waves.

And brought a smile to his face.

When her breathing was semi-restored, he carried her upstairs and eventually indulged his darling wife's passions several more times, then his, and when she finally whispered, "I think the chocolate's wearing off. I'm going to sleep," he tucked her in and waited until she fell asleep before going downstairs.

He needed a drink to settle his nerves; a shot of whiskey just might help him deal with this pregnancy that may or may not end well.

Very late that night, Kate came awake and, looking up, smiled at Dominic.

He was lying beside her, propped up on one elbow, watching her.

"It's going to be all right," she said softly.

"You can't know that." His lashes lowered briefly, then he sighed. "Nana can't either—fucking tea leaves or not."

"I understand. But I'll be ever so careful. Will that help?"

He lifted one shoulder in a faint shrug. "Sure. It'll help."

A small silence fell in this boyhood room that was hers now too.

Then she opened her arms to him and he drew her into the warmth of his body and held her close. Reaching up, she slid her fingers through the dark silk of his hair and clung to him, suddenly faint-hearted. Both understood the extent of the danger, of the possible dark abyss facing them. There were no absolutes in the world, no assurances of mercy no matter how much one wished. And when Dominic felt the wetness on his chest, he lifted her face to his, brushed away her tears, and murmured, "Don't cry. I'll keep you safe."

"And the baby?" She shouldn't be so unwise as to bring it up, but she was less capable of discretion, or maybe in the dead of night, fear held sway.

"The baby too," he affirmed, willing to challenge the devil himself and all the fiends of hell to protect what was his. "I promise."

The following morning, Dominic woke very early, threw on a pair of shorts, and went downstairs to his office. Shutting the door, he glanced at the clock, quickly computed the time in New York, and dialed a number Yash had given him.

Tea leaves might be all well and good for those who were inclined to believe in the mystical, but he preferred a more pragmatic approach. And he still had the one pediatric surgeon to persuade.

His call was answered with a crisp, "Frank Gregory here."

"My apologies for calling so early, but I wanted to catch you before you left for work. I'm Dominic Knight."

An exasperated sigh. "I've already told your people no. All eight of them."

"I heard," Dominic said mildly. "But I understand your girlfriend can't get a divorce. I can help you with that."

"It's not a situation that can be remedied." The doctor didn't say, *How do you know?* because he had to have been vetted by Dominic Knight before he'd been offered the lucrative position.

"If I *could* get your girlfriend a divorce," Dominic said with measured calm, "would you agree to a ten-month contract? I'll see that you have a house for your girlfriend and son, therapy for your boy—"

"You don't understand." The doctor spoke brusquely, an underlying frustration to his tone. "Giselle won't leave her daughter and her husband is opposed to joint custody. Accepting your offer would mean abandoning Giselle and my son. I won't do that."

"I can make her husband change his mind."

"Money won't change his mind. You have to know that."

"I do." Harold Parks was a billionaire. "Nevertheless, my offer stands. Are you interested? Ten months. Name your fee and your requirements. I can provide you with a full array of services: live-in help, a physical therapist on-site, a nutritionist, occupational therapy. I almost lost my wife with her last pregnancy. We did lose our child. Now Katherine's pregnant again and I'm trying to avoid a similar outcome. You're the best in the neonatal field. I need you. And to be perfectly blunt, you could use my clout and ruthlessness. I can make Harold change his mind about a divorce and cus-tody. In fact, your girlfriend might get sole custody. What do you say?"

"You must be the closer?" Gregory's voice was sardonic.

"No, I'm a desperate man like you. We can help each other."

There were a few seconds of silence. "I would have to be assured that a divorce and custody were possible."

"You have my word." A reply issued with the absolut-ism of immense resources, power, and a take-no-prisoners mentality. "I'll have the papers served tomorrow. I'll have a private message hand-delivered to Harold this afternoon in New York. You should have the signed divorce papers within two days. I'll see that Harold understands the time-line. Do you need to get confirmation from your girlfriend?"

"No."

Dominic's sigh was unmistakably one of relief. "Perfect. Send your requirements to my ADC, Max Roche. I'll give you his e-mail address, or his phone number if you prefer. Whatever you can say to me, you can say to him. I'll also give you my cell and home number. Any questions, con-cerns, call me. And I can't thank you enough." Dominic inhaled softly, then spoke with an almost painful earnest-ness. "My wife is precious to me. I'm sure you understand the feeling."

After the call ended, Dominic leaned back in his chair and let the tension drain from his body. *Done.* The last hold-out talked in. Katherine was safe, or semi-safe, or within the perimeters of modern medicine safe.

He had the best doctors on the planet.

He'd done everything he could.

Stretching the last kinks out of his shoulders, he leaned forward, picked up the phone, and called Max.

"I can hear it in your voice. You got him."

"Yep. Provided we deliver. So I need Danny in New York this afternoon to hand over the video to Harold Parks. I also need our New York attorneys to arrange the divorce papers and serve them tomorrow. I already gave them the particulars. It's not complicated when the wife doesn't want anything but her daughter. Shit, Harold should be grateful."

"Except he loses the fight."

"Better him than me," Dominic said bluntly.

"I guess it never pays to fuck little girls in a hotel room," Max said drily.

"Or anywhere, but certainly not there. How much did the video cost? It took a while to find." Leo had been combing the Bangkok underworld for a month. Dominic knew the rumors about Harold; the vice-ridden world of major money was small.

"It's a big city. But it wasn't expensive. Prices are low in Bangkok."

"Unfortunately even for little girls."

"No shit. But Leo bought the place like you said, shut it down, sent all the"—Max sighed—"wee children home with substantial pensions." Another sigh. "Not that they won't be exploited again. But their families have enough to live large. Their level of greed is the only unknown."

"Yeah—lots of luck with that," Dominic muttered.

"You tried anyway. The rest is up to them. And if nothing else, Parks might think twice before he molests young girls again. Certainly, it should take care of any custody issues with his eight-year-old daughter."

"So one would hope. But make sure Danny leans on Harold hard—I mean till he's squealing. I need this divorce."

"Don't worry. Danny'll make sure he understands."

"Good. I told Gregory to contact you with his requests. Then if you'd give him a list of those services we talked about for his boy. The kid's improving I hear, relearning how to walk and talk after his accident. So get Gregory whatever he needs. He *will* need a house. If our neighborhood won't do, give him what he wants so long as it's within a five-minute drive. That's it, I think." Dominic blew out a breath. "I'm so fucking stoked. He's the best neonatal pediatrician in the world. He can save babies as small as a pound. And this pregnancy is going to be terrifying the entire nine months."

"Is Katherine terrified too?"

"God no. She's mostly all la-di-da and smiling up a storm."

"Then maybe you should relax."

"I'll relax in nine months. Until then, I'll be living my worst fucking nightmare."

"If we can do anything to help, just ask. Liv and Conall will be here tomorrow."

"Thanks, Max. And thanks for pulling up stakes until this is over. I just don't know how much I can be engaged in day-to-day business. I'll work at night when Katherine's sleeping, but otherwise I'm going to be looking after her."

"We'll manage. It's not as though you're incommunicado. We have a question, you're around. By the way, have you met Roscoe's new girlfriend?"

"Once. At Lucia. We had dinner with them."

"I think he's serious."

"*She* certainly is," Dominic said drily. "Add needy too. Although Roscoe likes to take care of women."

"Until he gets tired of taking care of them."

"True. Although I'm the last person in the world to give advice about women. I didn't have a clue I even wanted a woman until I met Katherine. And then I didn't have a choice. A list of pros and cons, similar likes or backgrounds—none of that mattered. I had to have her." He laughed. "You plan and you plan—right?"

"I'm guessing you don't plan love."

"So it seems. I hear Katherine upstairs. She's up early. I'll talk to you later."

A few moments later, he stood in the bathroom doorway watching Kate run a brush through her curls. "Up at the crack of dawn for you. What's on the agenda today?"

She gave him a sideways glance. "Aren't you going to work anymore?"

"I work. Just from home, that's all."

She smiled, put the brush down, and picked up a lipstick. "You don't have to hover over me, you know."

His brows rose. "Actually I don't know that. As I recall, you said, and I quote, *I'll do everything you ask. I won't argue or complain.* Would you like me to go on, because I distinctly remember every fucking word."

"Oh, very well," she murmured, running some pink lipstick over her bottom lip, then the top, snapping the tube shut, and turning to Dominic. "I remember."

"Good. Then we don't have to argue about it." His voice softened. "Want me to find you some clothes?"

Untying her robe, she shrugged out of it, tossed it on the counter, and moved toward Dominic. "Why don't you find me some clothes *afterward*."

He smiled. "You need help with something else?"

"Maybe something to help me wake up," she purred, sliding her arms around his waist, rising on tiptoe, and kissing his chin, then his mouth as he dipped his head.

"As long as you follow instructions." He pushed a curl off her forehead. "I'll make them easy."

"What if I don't want easy?"

"It's not your choice anymore, baby. But the happy ending's still the same." He grinned. "Look at the bright side."

"Goddamn, Dominic, when I come through this pregnancy with flying colors, you're going to pay big-time for making me suffer. For depriving me."

"If you come through this pregnancy with flying colors, baby, you can have the whole fucking world wrapped in a bow. Okay?"

"Oh okay," she said, softly sighing. "But when this is over, I'm going to want your dick wrapped in a bow too. I'm going to want him ready to rock." Dominic had continued to refuse to engage in anything even approaching intemperate sex.

"You won't have to ask him twice, believe me," Dominic said drily.

"So then," Kate said, cheerfully, "are we both marking off the days, or only me?"

Dominic laughed. "Jesus, how about one thing at a time. It's baby production now. There's plenty of time to fuck our brains out later."

"Could I get that in writing?"

"No problem, baby. I'll carve it in stone and set it on your desk. You're not the only one feeling deprived." He quickly put his finger over her mouth. "A general statement, not serious. Don't blow up. I want this baby, but I want you healthy and alive a million times more. So we're going to be adults about this. Think you can do it?"

"Are you suggesting I can't?"

"No," he said quietly, not about to start a new argument.

She sighed, her breath warm on his bare chest. "Sometimes I think I was pampered too much growing up. You're always more sensible."

"There's no such thing as being pampered too much, baby. You were lucky."

He'd been deeply scarred by his childhood. She could hear it in his voice, see it in his eyes whenever the subject was broached. It always amazed her that he'd shouldered the responsibility of his life so young. "We'll pamper our baby, won't we?" She smiled, wanting to erase the raw pain in his eyes. "We'll fight over who pampers him or her most."

"You'll have to show me how."

She almost broke into tears at the simple truth in his statement. "No problem," she said, softly. "You're a fast learner."

"Speaking of fast learners," he murmured, changing the subject like he invariably did when there was an allusion to his childhood, recognizing that offering his darling wife a different kind of wake-up orgasm was sure to end the conversation. "How would you like me to show you some novel sensations?"

She grinned. "So you've been holding out on me."

"Let's just say I was waiting for the right occasion. Prepare to be amazed"—he smiled faintly at her flaring glance—"in a very nice way, baby. Nothing weird." He lifted her up onto the bathroom counter. "Cool on your bottom? Don't worry, you'll warm up. Now shut your eyes. You'll feel the sensations more intensely."

"I get to climax, right?"

"Don't worry, I won't forget." His small smile was intimate, warm, alive with careless charm. "Now, are you going to shut your eyes or keep giving me instructions?"

"Look, done." She clasped her hands in her lap, eyes closed. "Because you're way better at this than me."

"I am." He ran his thumb over her smile. "And you're always willing to learn."

"For your information, Mr. World Class Stud, all that experience of yours is superattractive." She suddenly opened her eyes and grinned. "You don't know how many times I've played that video of you with the whip."

He stared fixedly at her. "I thought that was taken down."

"Don't worry, it was. But like you with sex, I have special talents. I can find just about anything on the Web, deleted or not."

"Jesus. Get rid of it." Surprisingly, the prospect of possible parenthood was making him high-minded.

"I did. I just made a copy for myself. You're my own personal porn star."

The grim set of his mouth eased, his scowl gave way to a playful lift of his brows. "Then maybe you don't need me this morning."

"Or maybe I need you even more."

Leaning over, he kissed her softly. "Good. I like that."

"Show me, Dominic," she murmured, sliding her hand over the hard, ridged muscles of his chest, following the light trail of dark hair to where it disappeared into the waistband of his shorts. Her lashes drifted downward, her hand dropped away, and she sat, eyes closed, waiting.

He stood very still for a fraction of a second, touched as always by her artless simplicity, by her open-hearted trust, by the joy she'd brought to him. Then, conscious of his responsibility to offer her joy in return, of the reason he was standing here about to indulge his wife with the more beneficent of his talents, he gently placed his warm palms on the outside curve of her full, ripe breasts, exerted a very slight pressure, and gently began to caress her.

"Ohmygod—what are you doing?" It felt like a soft electric current was spreading through her body, warming her everywhere, the energy sliding downward, bringing a delectable melting feeling deep inside.

"Hush. Don't talk. Concentrate." And he gently caressed her entire body, her shoulders, arms, slowly, tenderly, moved down her ribs to her waist, his fingertips sliding around to her back, over her bottom, across her thighs, between her legs, until she was almost fainting with desire, filled with bliss, a swelling, glowing need spreading to her sex, up her spine, every cell in her body vibrating with pleasure.

Dominic had mastered the practice of tantra in India long ago, knew how to use his entire body for sex, not just his dick, understood how to promote the flow of subtle energies and magnetism to intensify ecstasy, prolong orgasmic sensation.

"Can you feel that at the base of your spine?" His voice was soft, low, his touch incredibly gentle.

She nodded, unable to speak, with pleasure expanding inside her, the contact of his fingers so light it felt as though he were worshipping her body, adoring her with his touch. A stream of delight rippled through her senses, strangely fulfilling, as if joy and consummation blended, as if the hot deep throbbing inside her marked each beat of her heart. As if she were being gently transported with soul-stirring rapture into a land of sensory enchantment.

When her consciousness was fully aroused, Dominic cupped each breast and, bending his head, gently sucked first one nipple, then the other, milking her slowly and rhythmically until she was so intensely provoked, she was flowing wet, softly panting. And when she finally died away in an uncharacteristically mute orgasm, the all-pervasive ecstasy pulsed, quivered, thrilled every glowing cell in her body for long, blissful, exquisitely protracted moments.

He stood very still afterward, attuned to her body, to his, filled with a deep sense of wonder as always when he looked inward, when he allowed himself to feel life pulsing within himself.

"You're amazing."

Her eyes were still shut, her voice no more than a

whisper, her pinked cheeks and delicate beauty, her breathless innocence always taking his breath away. "And you're my happiness," he said softly. "I'm going to pick you up now. You don't have to open your eyes."

"I may never open my eyes again," she said as Dominic lifted her in his arms and walked from the bathroom. "That was so beautiful, I don't have words to describe it."

"No problem, baby," he said. "It's about feeling, not spelling."

"You are amazing, you know," she whispered, opening her eyes and gazing up at his firm solid jaw, then higher, until she met his smiling blue gaze.

Just well trained. "If you say so," he said pleasantly, then bent to kiss the fine bridge of her nose. "Now, do you want to sleep, have breakfast, tell me how much you love me?" he finished with a grin.

"To the ends of the earth and beyond. Truly, Dominic."

He smiled. "And me, you, past the star line." Placing her on the bed, he pulled a quilt over her and sat down beside her. "So now that you've had your wake-up orgasm, what's on the agenda? Breakfast?"

"Melanie and I are eating breakfast somewhere. I forgot the name of the place. Then we're going shopping for maternity clothes."

"I'll take you."

"Melanie's driving."

"Jake's driving. I'll take you."

"Are you going to control every minute of my life?"

"Every second, baby," he said in a voice that even other CEOs knew better than to question.

"Well…okay, I suppose." She suddenly grinned. "Are you coming into the stores with us? Maternity clothes, Dominic. Your favorite."

He smiled. "I'll wait in the car."

And so her pregnancy advanced, with Dominic in charge, as benignly as possible, and Kate accommodating him with only occasional resistance because they both understood the essential seriousness of the situation. Although when Kate passed the dreaded three-month mark, they both marginally relaxed. And by the time she was six months pregnant and feeling really fine, even Dominic was able to banish the worst of his fears.

The doctors were within shouting distance, and an emergency surgery station had been constructed in the house next door. Kate's monthly exams were all perfectly normal. She was healthy and vigorous, the baby as well.

Although the baby's robust weight gain triggered a new concern for Dominic. Kate wasn't a big woman. What if the baby was too large? He was assured by Dr. Nye and the other six doctors he questioned that he needn't worry.

He still worried.

As Kate's due date approached, she and Dominic rarely went out.

They walked around the block in the morning and evening because Kate was supposed to exercise moderately. Dominic adjusted his long stride to hers, held her hand, and talked of baby things because Kate was completely preoccupied with the child. She bought clothes for the baby with a boundless optimism while Dominic grappled with the awful memories of the baby clothes left behind in London. Kate had one of the bedrooms made into a nursery, and she, Melanie, and Melanie's girls kept busy discussing paint colors, fabrics, and furniture. She seemed completely immune to the past, confident, assured, all her emotional baggage from her miscarriage put aside. He marveled at her complete reversal, but was cheered by her happiness. They picked out baby names, or rather she did. He cared nothing about the name so long as the baby was healthy. Katherine could name it Rock or Plumtree with his blessing.

"You sure now?" she said, looking up at him as she lay in his arms one evening. "You like James for a boy and Rose for a girl?"

"I do," he said. "They're perfect."

Her gaze narrowed. "You're not just saying that to be nice."

Of course I am. "No. I couldn't have done better. And you're the one doing all the work. You should be able to name the baby anything you wish."

She exhaled softly. "Good." Reaching up, she brushed her fingers along his jaw. "Happy?"

"I'm happy as long as I'm with you."

"It's frightening sometimes," she whispered, tears in her eyes. "Loving you so much. You have to belong to me always. Tell me you will, Dominic," she said, suddenly filled with alarm.

"Hush baby, don't cry," he whispered softly. "We'll always belong to each other. And when you get frightened, I'll pull up the drawbridge, close the gates, and shut out the world so it's just you and me." He glanced down, ran his hand lightly over her belly. "And him or her. No one else gets in. Okay?"

She nodded, sniffling. "You'll be glad when I'm not pregnant anymore." She swallowed the lump in her throat. "I won't have these weepy moments."

"I'll mostly be glad when I can stop worrying about you and the baby and everything that can go wrong." He smiled slightly. "Although each passing day eases my concerns a little more."

"Because they can save the baby at this stage."

He nodded. "But I need you to be okay too." That fear was constant. But he drew in a small breath, then grinned because he wasn't going to voice his worries and add to her apprehensions. "Just so you know, I've threatened all the doctors, so I'm anticipating a smooth delivery."

"Maybe you should talk to me about that," Kate said, her eyes instantly alight, a teasing note in her voice. "Seeing as how I'm intimately involved in the process."

"You don't threaten, or I would have." He tapped her tummy very lightly. "Hear that, baby? I've got your support team on their toes and standing by."

"Jeez, Dominic, you're going to piss them off."

"Nah...I was diplomatic." Or rather Max was, along with the bonus checks he'd dispensed. "They don't mind. Don't worry, baby, everyone will treat you gently."

But when Kate went into labor, she insisted on staying at home.

"Absolutely not!" Dominic snapped, moving to pick her up. Which was exactly why she hadn't told him before, although Patty knew because she'd had Dominic's bedroom cleaned so you could literally eat off the floor. "Don't you dare touch me!" Kate screamed, and when he jumped back she said in a more normal tone, "Get the midwives first. This is going to take a while."

"I'm getting Melanie too," he said. "Scream all you want about that. I don't give a fuck."

"Why would I scream?" she said sweetly.

Dominic kept his gaze on Kate as he punched in his sister's number on his cell. "Come over. Katherine's in labor and she won't go to the hospital. I'm calling them now...all of them? Got it—hurry."

The midwife Melanie had used, along with three others, were next door and arrived minutes before Melanie rushed in. His sister managed to calm Dominic, with a soothing tone of voice and a lengthy explanation. Kate had been counting on that and cast a grateful glance at her sister-in-law when Dominic finally sighed in acquiescence.

"Okay," he said. "But if there's the slightest problem, I mean the *slightest problem*, we're going to the hospital." Then he'd scowled at Kate so fiercely she put up her hands in surrender. "You better fucking mean it," he growled.

Jeez, was he a mind reader or am I that transparent? But she and Melanie, the midwives, and Patty had gone over every detail of the delivery a thousand times and Melanie's last two children had been born at home. Kate was relatively confident. Besides, Dominic practically had an entire hospital next door. Plus, she thought, with the mystical confidence that had sustained her throughout this pregnancy, she just *knew* the baby was fine and all the doctors' exams had corroborated that fact. So really, her fake surrender was inconsequential. "I mean it, Dominic, really I do," she said with a smile. "If anything goes wrong, the hospital for sure. Now help me walk."

For the next six hours, Dominic walked with Kate, her hand in his, holding her up when a painful spasm brought her to a standstill, helping her lie down from time to time so the midwives could massage her and help her relax. Melanie ran the remote and kept them distracted with music, TV, or conversation. Until the contractions reached a point where Dominic insisted the doctors be called in. He stared hard at his sister until she backed him up. "Just in case, baby," he said softly, helping Kate back to bed. "They can sit downstairs if you don't want them up here."

Eventually, the contractions were so close together, even Kate didn't mind some help. The midwives and the doctors did their job, everyone working as a coordinated team because Dominic had emphatically warned them that he didn't want any turf battles while his wife was suffering.

Although Kate was amazing and he told her so, kissing her between contractions, wiping her forehead with a damp washcloth, giving her ice chips when she needed them, holding her hand through it all. She endured the pain with a grim stoicism, squeezing his hand hard during the worst of it, while he counted for her, helped her with her breathing, and wished he could suffer in her stead.

And then someone suddenly said, "You're almost there, Mrs. Knight."

Kate shut her eyes, took a deep breath, and almost broke Dominic's fingers.

A moment later, an elated voice said, "It's a girl."

Kate's eyes opened, and she smiled at Dominic and whispered, "You can stop worrying now."

"I love you so much, baby," he whispered, feeling the weight of the world lifting from his shoulders. She was safe; he hadn't lost her. Leaning over, he brushed her damp curls from her forehead, then bent and kissed her gently. "Now I have to get the world wrapped up in a bow for you."

She smiled. "Show me our baby first."

It took a moment for her words to register; he was so grateful Katherine was alive, that she'd survived. Then he looked up, surveyed the busy scene, found Dr. Gregory holding the baby, and raised his brows.

"She's a healthy little girl," the doctor said, knowing Dominic's concern, why he'd been brought in at enormous cost to guarantee the baby's life. He carried her to the bed and gave them their first glimpse of Rosie. "Give us a few minutes to warm her under the lamps," he said. "Just a precaution."

Ten busy minutes later, with everyone quickly doing their job, the baby had been examined, weighed, and dressed; Kate had been bathed and put in a new nightgown; the bedclothes had been changed; and the doctors had confirmed both Kate and the baby were in good health. Then Melanie shooed everyone out of the room. "I'll have some food sent up. And we're all downstairs if you need us," she said before closing the bedroom door.

"Hungry?" Dominic asked, standing at the bedside, his gaze on Kate, his daughter in her arms.

"Not right this minute."

He smiled. "She looks like you." He lightly touched the baby's small hand, and the tiny fingers closed on his thumb.

"You're crying."

This man who'd been alone most of his life looked up, his eyes moist. "I don't cry."

Kate held out her free hand.

He blinked. "Well, maybe just this once," he said, taking her hand.

"We have a family now, you and I," she whispered, as if she knew what had brought him to tears.

"You've given me an incredible gift, Katherine." The blue of his eyes was luminous with love, his smile for her alone. "Ring the bells, fire the cannons, send out messengers far and wide to proclaim the miraculous birth," he said with a grin. The baby suddenly opened her eyes and looked up at her father.

"Did she hear me?" he whispered.

"I don't know. You're the one who read all the baby books."

"She's looking at me like she sees me. And she's still holding my finger."

"She's going to be amazing."

Dominic smiled. "Of course. She's yours."

"Ours."

"The amazing part is yours, baby. I'm seriously pleased she doesn't look like me." Then his smile broadened. "One question. Will she always have pink hair?"

"Are you saying it matters if she does?"

"God, no, she can have purple hair for all I care. She's perfect."

"That's what I thought you meant."

He laughed. "Okay, now she really is looking at me. There's no question. Come on, Rosie, let your daddy hold you."

Nana came out and stayed for two weeks, helping with the baby, giving advice as only she could, bringing a real sense of family to the house in Cliffside. And when she left, Dominic devoted himself completely to Kate and Rosie. He stayed home, doing most of the caregiving, letting Kate sleep whenever she could between Rosie's every-two-hours nursing schedule. Their baby was soon plump and chubby, with little folds on her arms and legs, and Dominic refreshed his babysitting skills from his years watching Nicole and Isabelle. It was like riding a bike, you never forgot, and looking after his daughter was a joy he'd never imagined. Very early, whenever Rosie heard his voice and saw her daddy, she'd start pumping her arms and legs in delight. And Dominic's heart would melt.

At three months, Rosie began sleeping through the nights, their parenting schedule became less demanding, and Dominic managed to put in more hours at his computer. Kate slept longer, they actually watched TV again occasionally, and had more than a few minutes to eat their meals. It was practically heaven.

Kate said it first, but then she'd borne the brunt of Rosie's demands in the early months. "Small pleasures, right?" she said, smiling at Dominic across the kitchen table.

"A few minutes alone with you, baby"—he saluted her with his milk glass—"heaven."

"You can drink, you know. I won't be pissed."

"I'm good. I'll drink when you drink. I like milk."

"Thank God for Patty. I'm hungry all the time." Their dinner was the equivalent of Lucia's five-star cuisine: lobster cioppino for an appetizer, toasted goat cheese and fig salad, a perfectly broiled rib-eye to keep Kate's strength up, four small covered bowls of diced organic vegetables, and chocolate mousse for dessert. Patty had tiptoed upstairs before she left, saw that the baby was sleeping, and whispered, "I thought it was quiet up here. Your food's on the table for a change." She tapped her wristwatch and grinned. "Eat fast."

Then one night, a few days after their daughter first slept through the night, Dominic came downstairs and into the living room where Kate was reading.

"Jesus, is that a book in your hand? Is life back to normal?"

"Getting there," she said, setting the book aside, surveying him with raised brows. "Why are you wearing a robe?"

He held out his hand. "Come upstairs and I'll show you."

She rose from the sofa. "Sounds intriguing."

Dominic laughed. "Depends what you mean by intriguing."

She put her hand in his. "I figure you're going to show me."

"I'm gonna try, baby." He put his finger to his mouth. "Provided our daughter cooperates."

She followed him upstairs and into their bedroom, saw all the packages on the bed, and quickly glanced up at him.

"I told you if you came through with flying colors, I'd wrap up the world in a bow. Those are just a token. Go on, open them."

He led her to the bed, then took a seat in a nearby chair. "Open the blue one first."

The gifts were beautifully wrapped in all the colors of the rainbow. "This is where I say you shouldn't. It's so much."

"That's just Nana talking. This is nothing, baby. A few trifles."

She ripped the paper off the blue package and squealed in delight. It was a high-end laptop favored by hackers and not on the market yet. Kate had seen the prototype and lusted after it. Dominic had paid a premium to have one put together for her. "Ohmygod, Dominic. I'm going to be up all night with this."

"If only, baby. Not with Rosie. You need your sleep."

"Jesus, I forgot for a minute. I've been coveting this model."

"I know. They hustled for you. Pump a couple of bottles of milk for me and I'll watch Rosie tomorrow." He grinned. "You can have sex with your new laptop."

"I'm going to take you up on your offer. You're sure, now?"

"Absolutely. Rosie and I get along, you know."

She smiled. "I *have* noticed." She hugged the gleaming laptop. "Thank you so much."

He laughed. "Kiss your laptop, then open the other stuff."

Dominic had bought enough jewelry that he must have made a number of jewelers superhappy. Starting with a huge Bulgari emerald ring with a matching bracelet. "To go with your eyes," he said. Then she opened boxes with several kinds of earrings in every imaginable jewel, a necklace of natural baroque South Sea pearls, and one of gold and Venetian glass beads. "You can wear that one with jeans," he pointed out, "along with these." He handed her a package that contained a pair of Dior black velvet beaded flats with a tree of life design. He had three pairs of custom-made boots for her and four dresses, including two for evening that were short and flirty.

At the last he handed her two envelopes. "This one first," he said. Inside was a photo of a green Porsche 918 Spyder. "It's a hybrid," he said. "Good for the environment and zero to sixty in three seconds." He didn't mention the $845,000 price tag. "And you'll like this one." He watched her carefully as she opened the second envelope.

She read what Dominic had written on the card inside.

> Your hometown needs a new grade school and the last three bond issues failed. We can build a new school for the town and if you agree, it could be named for Nana and Roy.

Dominic had written a check to the school district and left the amount blank.

Tears welled in Kate's eyes. "You don't know how hard Nana worked to try to get those bond issues passed."

Quickly coming to his feet, he sat down beside her and took her in his arms. "I heard. But don't cry, baby. They'll have their school now. Everything's good."

She sniffled. "With Nana and Gramps's name on it."

"Nice, hey?" Grabbing the box of tissues on the bedside table, he set it in her lap.

"It's just perfect." She wiped her eyes. "Really wonderful. All this is wonderful," she said, gesturing at the gifts on the bed.

"They're nothing compared to what you gave me," he said softly. "You gave me love. You gave me an incredible daughter and made me the happiest man in the world. And with my history, that was the equivalent of you dragging me up Everest a couple times."

She grinned. "So I'm something of a miracle worker, you're saying."

"You're the miracle of my life, baby," he said. "And as a small token of my appreciation"—he opened his robe and smiled—"one more gift."

"You remembered." She admired his lovely erection, tied at the base with a white silk bow.

"Of course I remembered. I promise, I deliver." He grinned. "I just wanted to wait until there was…time for you."

"Because I don't like to rush."

He shook his head, laughing. "Because you like to rush—repeatedly. We need time for that." He pulled the bow open and tossed the ribbon aside. "Now at the risk of destroying the romance, condom or withdrawal? Your call." Kate wasn't on birth control yet because she was nursing. Not that she couldn't have been, but they both were overly protective of their daughter's health.

She wrinkled her nose. "Condoms are—"

"An issue, I know. I bought some that weren't latex in case you wanted to give them a try."

"I like to feel you."

"We're both on the same page then. I'm superdependable. In fact, I first became interested in tantra because I wanted to learn how to control ejaculation. So don't worry. And tonight's for you, baby, so give me a menu."

"I'd say instant gratification."

"Menu items one through ten?"

She smiled. "You must be psychic."

But they'd no more than settled into a lovely languorous sexual rhythm with Kate softly sighing in pleasure and Dominic thinking he'd almost forgotten how good he could feel, when the sound of the first little soft snuffle resonated from the baby monitor.

Dominic tensed for a fraction of a second, then resumed his downstroke.

A second louder snuffle reverberated in the silence of the bedroom.

Dominic's withdrawal stroke faltered momentarily before continuing.

Kate looked up at him.

He shook his head, then plunged back in so deeply, Kate's lush groan was a small blast of heat on his throat.

The first little whimper echoed through the monitor speaker. Rosie was waking up.

"Done?" Kate whispered, her brows faintly arched.

Dominic smiled. "Probably."

"You've come a long way from whips and handcuffs, Mr. Knight," Kate murmured, a teasing light in her eyes.

Dominic laughed softly. "No shit. On the other hand," he said, in an easygoing drawl, "you haven't even had the first item on your menu, so shut your ears. I'll make this fast."

And he put into practice some of those skills his wife found so attractive, those adept and very competent ones that persistently and compellingly pressed his hard dick against her G-spot with each plunging downstroke. Encouraged an even more heavenly friction on his slow withdrawal. And just for good measure, he brought her clit into the highly stimulating game with the masterful attention of his index finger.

He wasn't timing it, but if he had to guess, he'd say three minutes before Kate's orgasmic scream momentarily drowned out the baby's whimpers.

Afterward, he politely waited less than usual because Rosie was beginning to really wind up. Gently kissing Kate, he whispered, "Gotta go," and slid from her body and a second later from the bed.

He was hopping into some sweats on the way to the bathroom. After quickly washing his hands, he bolted for the hallway and Rosie's room.

The crying stopped. Two minutes later, Dominic came back into the bedroom with Rosie in one arm, looking very small against his large frame, all baby pink against his bronzed skin. "Say hi to your mommy," he murmured to the chubby-cheeked baby staring up at him. "She's just waking up too."

While Kate slowly returned from her very first orgasm in a long time, Dominic changed Rosie into the diaper and jammies he'd carried in. Then, sitting down on the bed, he propped his daughter against his drawn-up knees so she had a view of the world. Glancing at Kate still half dozing beside him, he said, "You're going to have to top her off with a little milk. But she's okay for a few minutes. Change of scene. She's looking around."

Rolling on her side, Kate touched Rosie's toes. "Hi, sweetie. Can't sleep?"

Dominic grinned. "I think she doesn't want us to have S-E-X."

"Too late," Kate said with a contented smile, running her hand down Dominic's arm, twining her fingers in his. "Thanks, thanks, thanks…"

"I have to make sure both my girls are happy," he whispered. "Not a bad job to have"—he winked—"even without whips and handcuffs."

"Speaking of—"

"Someday maybe, baby. We'll see."

"You don't know what I was going to say."

"Yeah I do. The apartment's still there."

"I'm not completely averse, that's what I meant."

"I know what you meant. I'm just not so sure."

"Maybe I could change your mind." Her voice was a soft purr, her green gaze enticing.

He laughed. "Fuck if you couldn't if you keep looking at me like that." Then he glanced down at Rosie and shook his head. "We can talk about it later. Not now."

"Fine." But somewhere in the back of her mind, a lustful little thought remained Their days there had been a different kind of pleasure—ravishing and ravenous, greedy. He couldn't have forgotten.

When Rosie was ten months old, Kate surprised Dominic by telling him that she'd like to go back to work. So a nursery was set up at the office and they shared child-rearing duties, alternating their schedules to accommodate their daughter. Although when Rosie was tired, only Mommy would do. She'd find Kate, climb up on her lap, put her thumb in her mouth, and promptly go to sleep.

At times when their meeting schedules overlapped, Dominic would bring his daughter with him and if she'd fuss, he'd whisper, "Hush, Rosie, let the nice man talk," then rock her or get up and walk her. Even titans of industry took second place to Rosie and were treated to an astonishing view of a domesticated Dominic Knight, the sight eliciting raised eyebrows, the occasional sulk, and a continuous flurry of tweets and texts sent round the world.

Dominic Knight as doting father, they'd say. Playing nursemaid—can you believe it? Who would have thought?

Unaware of gossip or complicated schedules, disgruntled colleagues or business activities in the world her parents constructed for her, Rosie prospered. She had all the advantages, including two loving parents at her beck and call. Perhaps it was only natural that she developed into a bright, capable, chatty child.

By the time she was two, she was speaking well, or quickly at least, her pronunciation less than perfect. But Rosie seemed unaware and talked up a storm to whoever would listen. Kate watched with a smile when Dominic sat listening to his daughter with the same concentration and interest he'd give to any of his business associates. And she often thought that Rosie was likely the best teacher Dominic would ever have when it came to talking about his feelings, because Rosie's favorite question was "Why, Daddy?" And when he'd answered, she'd say again, wide-eyed and curious, "Tell me why about dat you yike, Daddy." And as he answered all her constant whys and more whys, Dominic slowly learned to define his emotions with a simplicity his daughter could understand.

Rosie's *from the mouth of babes* innocence modulated Dominic's disciplined restraint. The demons from his past slowly receded, the crushing weight of his memories lightened, and he smiled more.

Although on one matter, he was unreformed. He wouldn't allow his parents anywhere near Rosie.

During Rosie's toddler years, one of her favorite activities was having tea with Daddy and her toys. The company cafeteria baked a variety of cookies daily, since Rosie's tastes varied and like so many small children she wanted what she wanted when she wanted it.

The ritual never changed. She'd arrange her toys in a certain order on the floor of Dominic's office, point to Daddy's seat, and wait with the calm patience of a stage director for him to sit cross-legged on the floor. Then she'd show the cafeteria lady where to put the tea tray, smile up at her, say, "Tank you," and sloppily pour the first tiny cup of tea for her favorite doll.

Dominic's appointment schedule was always adjusted on those days when Rosie wanted to play teatime. CEOs waited, politicians waited, his managers waited, ambassadors waited.

Rosie was his precious darling.

Dominic taught his daughter to surf before she was three. He came back up to the beach where Kate was waiting that first day because they'd just learned she was pregnant again and Dominic's protective rules were back in place. He didn't want her in the water. Not that she minded complying when he'd finally agreed to have another child. He was smiling proudly, his plump wet-suited daughter in his arms. And Rosie called out from ten feet away, "Daddy thas I'm a na-thur"—she glanced up at her father.

"A natural, Rosie," he said, bending to kiss her cheek. "You're going to be a great surfer."

Kate felt a small sinking feeling in the pit of her stomach because her baby was small and the waves weren't. But she also knew Dominic would safeguard his daughter with his life. In fact, he'd added a security team that was devoted to her.

Each year in August, they stayed in Kate's hometown. Nana enjoyed having their family around and Kate and Dominic liked the peaceful community and their home on the lake. It was a vacation of sorts, although neither of them were ever completely work-free. But they deliberately lightened their schedules in August.

One morning, Dominic and his daughter were at the bakery to get their breakfast pastries. In northern Minnesota the weather could be crisp even in August and both Dominic and Rosie wore sweaters. She was sitting on her daddy's shoulders, eating a cookie while he paid for the pastries, raining crumbs on his head.

"We got cookie for my bruuver?" She tapped Dominic's

head with her half-eaten pink-frosted sugar cookie. "He yikes cookies."

"Jimmy has a sugar cookie and the chocolate one you picked out. Is that enough?"

"More, Daddy, *more*!!"

Dominic smiled faintly, briefly contemplating what *more* might mean ten years from now when cookies and toys wouldn't be enough. "Pick out some other cookies then. Whatever you think Jimmy would like." At six months, it didn't really matter; the baby put everything in his mouth.

Nor did it matter how many cookies Rosie wanted today or tomorrow or next week. His children could ask for whatever they wanted.

He never said no.

Occasionally, Kate took issue with some wild extravagance, but not often.

Dominic had been denied a childhood. She couldn't fault him for wanting to make up that deficit and give his children what he'd never had—unconditional love and the joy of innocence.

But when James was almost a year old, Dominic sat Kate down in the living room one evening after the children were sleeping. "I'm a little tense," he said.

She'd been aware of his unease since they'd come home, his restlessness patent. "Oh, God, you're sick?" Panic flared in her voice.

"No, no, I'm fine." He wrapped her in his arms. "But I have a serious question to ask you."

She was so relieved, she overreacted with a stupid quip. "If you're going to ask for a divorce the answer is no."

His scowl was instant. "Don't joke about that. And don't ever think you'll get one because you won't."

"Hey!"

He put his finger on her mouth. "I don't want to argue right now, so cool your jets. I want to ask you something important."

For a flashing moment he sounded like Gramps in one of his solemn moods. "Sorry," she said, instantly deferring. "I'm listening."

"How would you feel about not having any more children?" His voice was ultraquiet and restrained.

"How would you feel?"

"I asked you first."

She noticed his stark constraint, the way he watched her like he used to in the past, his emotions veiled. "I don't know. I haven't thought about it. You must have."

He drew in a breath, then nodded. "I'd prefer you didn't."

"Okay."

His eyes opened wide. "Really?"

"Yes, really." She smiled. "I know how hard my two pregnancies have been for you. You've been really sweet accommodating me, giving me our two babies. Why shouldn't I try to make you happy too?"

"You do every second of every day, Katherine," he said softly. "I can't lose you, that's all." He took a deep breath, briefly shut his eyes. "I just can't."

"Then we won't have any more children."

He exhaled, felt the earth settle back on its axis. "Thanks, baby. I'll make it up to you somehow if this is a huge concession. Just tell me how and I'll do it."

"I don't need anything, Dominic. You've given me two beautiful children, a beautiful life—"

"And my heart," he whispered.

She smiled. "That works out then, 'cause you have mine."

He touched her mouth gently, a brush of his finger over her bottom lip. "I never knew I could be this happy. I never knew I could be happy at all until you came into my life."

There was a small silence, the muted TV in the corner flooding the room with a flickering light, the flashing light on the baby monitor a noiseless pulse beat. The children were sleeping upstairs, the world was humming around them, but if they listened hard, the dizzying beat of their hearts rang sweetly in the room, like a rockabilly chorus of love.

"We're lucky, you and I," Kate whispered.

Dominic's eyes were clear blue and very close. "I'm going to see that our luck holds," he said quietly, having searched for her too far and wide to doubt how rare was their love, how tremulous the balance of happiness against personal disasters. Then quietly willful, indisposed to failure, his heart in his eyes—this man who had overcome so much, who wielded boundless power, said with unquestioning confidence, "I promise we'll always be happy." He grinned then. "I can make that happen, you know."

Her smile was so beautiful it almost stopped his heart.

"I know," Kate said, lifting her hand to his face and stroking away the hair at his temples, the musky scent of his shampoo reminding her of that long-ago night in Hong Kong where it all began. "You can do anything."

EPILOGUE

Two years later
Paris, 2:25 a.m.

"Christ, don't they know the time here?" Dominic grumbled, understanding his calls came in from all over the world. Rolling over, he grabbed his phone on the bedside table and hit the answer icon.

"You're not going to like this, but I just saw your niece Nicole."

Dominic recognized Julian Wilson's LA drawl; they'd run into each other yesterday at a business dinner. "So?"

"At the Chandelier Club."

"What?" Dominic sat up and swung his legs over the side of the bed.

"She's with some young dude and she looks like a newbie."

Dominic was striding toward his dressing room. "No shit. Look, have Raoul stall them or lock them in if they're already in a room. Discreetly. No scene. I'll be there in fifteen minutes."

Kate had followed him and was standing in the doorway. "Be where in fifteen minutes?"

He quickly explained in an edited version while he pulled on boxers and jeans. He called it a nightclub.

"Nicole's twenty-two, Dominic. Maybe she's okay."

He pulled a navy sweater over his head. "Nicole has a history of making bad choices." He'd quietly bailed her out of a few over the years.

"Shouldn't that be her parents' problem? I'm just saying. She might not like you barging in at some nightclub."

"I'm not asking her, and her parents don't know what she does. How much did you tell your grandparents about your sex life?"

"There wasn't a whole lot to tell."

"But you didn't tell them anyway. Right?" His voice was muffled as he reached into a closet and pulled out some shoes.

"Gramps would have scared them off."

"From what I've heard about Roy, I'm guessing he'd vetted them already and just let it go." He stepped into burgundy suede desert boots and swiftly tied them. "I'll be back in a less than an hour. Shut the children's doors will you? In case Nicole's screaming at me when we come back."

"Be nice, Dominic. She's not going to like you monitoring her activities."

"I'm not. Fuck—although I should have. Thank God Julian called." He grabbed some car keys from the top of the dresser. He didn't want to take the time for Henri to bring up the car. He stopped for a moment to give Kate a kiss, then patted her bare ass. "Close the kids' doors, then get back into bed, baby. No sense in ruining your sleep."

When he arrived at the club, he braked hard, cranked the Mercedes coupe nose in, straight up to the door, got out, pocketed his keys, and snarled, "Fuck you," in French to the valet who started shouting at him to move his car. "I'm here to see Raoul."

The man backed off like he'd been burned. Raoul owned this high-end sex club and ten others in Europe. He was connected and not to the aristocracy. Dominic had known him a long time, had done a lot of business with him in the past. They were friends, acquaintances, and, formerly, partners in vice.

Raoul was waiting for him in the foyer.

Dominic smiled tightly. "She still here?" He spoke quietly in French.

Raoul nodded. "I didn't know she was your niece. They wouldn't have let her in if we'd known."

"*I* fucking didn't know, so don't sweat it. I don't suppose you have a robe—just in case. I'm going to walk her out of here in about ten seconds."

Raoul snapped his fingers and a bouncer rushed over. "I need a robe. Meet us at Room 14. I want you there before us." He was speaking to the man's back at the last.

The club owner and Dominic walked through the luxurious bar—all glass, onyx, crystal chandeliers, and plush carpets—then through the even more richly appointed main salon with muraled walls, antique furniture, and dim lights. Both rooms were packed with clothed and unclothed bodies, everyone high or drunk, sexual exhibitionism graphically on display.

"You're happily married now, I hear," Raoul said as if people weren't fornicating all around them.

"I am," Dominic replied blandly. Having frequented places like this for years, he didn't react to the spectacle.

"And damned lucky to be. You've got kids, right?" Raoul was pushing fifty, personal-trainer trim, well-dressed, good-looking. He'd been married forever, Dominic recalled.

"They're in Barcelona with their mother. They're great kids. Both at university now. Yours are young?"

"Yes." Dominic smiled. "And precious." He sighed softly. "My niece was sugar sweet too not so long ago. Last I heard from my sister, Nicole was at my apartment in Monaco taking a break after university. There's a fucking snow job," he muttered. "Goddamn little liar."

"Give her a lecture from me too. This is no place for a young girl."

"Who brought her?"

"I didn't see. We'll find out. Want me to bar him from the club?"

"Nah. I don't care what he does so long as he's not with Nicole."

A bouncer was standing at the door to Room 14 when they arrived, a black silk robe over his arm. "Door's open," he murmured.

Dominic nodded, took the robe. "Thanks." Then he turned to Raoul. "I'll go in alone. God knows what she's doing. Appreciate your understanding."

"Anytime, *mon ami.*"

Dominic turned the knob, pushed open the door, walked in, slammed the door behind him, took one look at the naked couple swiftly disengaging at his intrusion, and tossed the robe at the bed. "Put this on," he growled.

Nicole let out a shriek, scrambled up into a sitting position, and pulled the sheet up in front of her. "What are you doing here!" she screamed, all wild huff and indignation.

And far from sober. "Shut the fuck up. I'm taking you home."

She didn't move, her eyes narrowed, her mouth set.

"Put the goddamn robe on," Dominic snapped, then glared at the bastard lounging naked beside her on the bed, smirking big-time. "Who the fuck are you?"

"Who's asking?" A languid drawl behind the smirk, a small shrug that rippled the long black hair on his shoulder.

"Just answer me, asshole." But recognition was slowly dawning as Dominic surveyed the man's tattooed erection. He'd seen that inked dick in Tokyo in the days before Katherine. Even in a group orgy, even concentrating on getting off, you couldn't help but notice something like that. The young heir to the Swiss pharmaceutical fortune had been a wet-behind-the-ears kid at the time. So he'd be twenty-five, twenty-six now and he was either on some pharmaceuticals that kept his dick hard or he was turned on by people looking. "Actually, I know who you are. So stay the fuck away from my niece. Got it, douche bag?"

"And if I don't?"

"Don't push your luck, kid."

"Oooh, I'm really scared."

"Good," Dominic said, ignoring the sarcasm. "You fucking should be." He shot a look at his niece, then at the absinthe paraphernalia on the bedside table. "Christ, Nicole, no wonder you're wasted." She'd fallen back on the bed, her dark hair a tangle of curls on the pillows, her eyes half-shut. Softly swearing, Dominic moved to the bed and man-handled Nicole's arms into the robe, feeling a major sense of déjà vu, remembering all the times he'd struggled to get her into her clothes when she was a baby. "Jesus, asshole," he muttered, glowering at the rich punk who hadn't moved from his lazy sprawl. "Why'd you let her drink that shit?" Wrapping the robe around his inert niece, he tied the belt and picked her up in his arms. Then he abruptly stopped and scanned the room for Nicole's purse—credit cards, phone, ID—all the things you didn't want to leave in a place like this. Ah—there. Walking over to the brilliant pink sofa, he leaned over, grabbed her purse strap with one finger, then strode to the door. Bending slightly, he flipped the handle, swung the door back hard with his foot, and walked out to the echo of wood smashing plaster.

There were two bouncers in the hall waiting to escort him and following his muscle through the crowd, Dominic reached the front door in record time. The men accompanied him outside and down the steps, and after handing Nicole to one of them, Dominic took out his keys, opened the car doors, threw Nicole's purse on the console, and started the car to warm it up. Walking back to the man with Nicole, he took her in his arms, carried her to the car, carefully placed her in the seat, buckled her in, and quietly shut her door. With a word of thanks to the bouncers, he moved around the car to the driver's seat and slid behind the wheel.

As he swung the car back out into the street, he had a quick twinge of alarm.

What if he had to collect Rosie from a place like this someday?

Jesus fuck.

He shot a glance at Nicole sleeping peacefully and softly sighed. *Who would have thought?*

Not that he'd given a flying fuck about the time he'd spent in clubs like Raoul's. Of course he hadn't given a flying fuck about much of anything in those days. Conversely, he had to admit to a rare sense of prudery when it came to Nicole. Maybe it was just that he knew Melanie wouldn't approve, not to mention her father, Matt, who'd probably kill the little rat bastard in bed with her. Bottom line though, Nicole hadn't lived the life he had, she'd had a normal childhood. Raoul's club was way the hell too hard core for her.

She wasn't ready for a place like that.

He drove slowly, so Nicole's head wouldn't slide off the head rest. He took the steep ramp into the underground garage beneath the apartment building even more slowly to keep her from slipping down the seat. But the low roar of the powerful engine in the confined space echoed off the walls in a loud, pulsating rumble.

Nicole came awake. "Where are we?" she asked in a wispy voice, like she was a thousand miles away.

"Almost to the apartment. And don't you dare raise your voice when we get there because the children are sleeping." He pulled into his parking space.

"He's like you, Nicky." Her voice was husky, half asleep or drowsy from the being tanked.

"Jeez, don't say that." Dominic turned off the ignition. "That's the last thing I want to hear."

She turned her head to look at him, her eyes the same

blue as his, clearer now as though returning to the world was a possibility. "I don't mean the sex club." She raised her hand in a small dismissive gesture. "I mean Rafe is smart and funny and he's good to me."

Dominic took a deep breath. "Nicole, honey, you're so damned young. You'll find all kinds of guys who'll be good to you. Pick someone else." He reached over and unsnapped her seat belt. "Now, come on, I'm taking you upstairs." Dominic owned the building on the Ile Saint-Louis, his apartment the entire top floor, the view of Notre-Dame stunning. "Katherine will find some pajamas for you. And no one has to know about this. I told Katherine it was a nightclub."

"She won't say anything to Mother, will she?"

"There's nothing to say. That particular nightclub was too rough. I brought you home. End of story."

"Thanks, Nicky. I mean for not telling anyone."

"You better thank me for getting you out of that fuck-ing bed. Your boyfriend is bad news. Take my word for it, Nicole. You don't know. I do, okay?"

"Okay, Nicky." But she'd noticed the faint vibration of the ringer on her cell phone in her small embroidered purse that had slid off the console and lay next to her hip. She looked away and smiled.

It was Rafe calling.

She knew.

Want to see how Dominic and Kate's story began?
See the next page for a preview of

ALL HE WANTS

the first installment in the All or Nothing trilogy.

ONE

She'd done her research like she always did before an interview. So she knew about him. Thirty-two, Stanford graduate, adventure traveler, and a more or less self-made billionaire who'd stopped counting zeros long ago. Quirky, too, but then so many in the start-up world were. Maybe even a little more than quirky since the death of his wife. But those rumors were confined to obscure blogs in cyberspace and were impossible to confirm.

Not that she cared about the man's private quirks. She was here because his company had recruited her at MIT and working for Knight Enterprises, *the* most innovative, venture-capital company in the world, would be a dream come true.

Arriving last night from the East Coast, she'd expected to meet with one of Dominic Knight's lieutenants at corporate headquarters in Santa Cruz. But an early morning e-mail had sent new instructions. And here she was on a quiet tree-lined residential street in Palo Alto.

The cab driver came to a stop and pointed. "That's it."

She looked out the window, mentally flipped through her Art I memories, and decided it was one of Greene and Greene's rare, turn-of-the-century homes. The structure was surrounded by a beautiful, hundred-year-old Japanese-style landscape specific to the building design. It was an unusual venue for an interview, but no explanation and been given for the site change. Although with the possibility of being offered her dream job, who was she to question the reasons?

She stood for a moment on the sidewalk as the cab drove away, surveying the small redwood building. On her junior year J-term, she'd stayed in a mountain village in Japan, in a temple inn much like this. It was supposed to have been a long weekend but, so enchanted by the quiet isolation, she'd stayed a week. Strange that a street so near a major metropolitan area was this tranquil; she glanced around, unsure for a moment whether she was dreaming, her memories were so intense.

Then a lawnmower powered up somewhere behind her. She shook off her reverie and moved with an easy stride toward the entrance to 630 Indigo Way.

A reception desk had been placed in the center of the foyer and a secretary, who'd been reading, set down her book and looked up. She could have been some teenager taking a day off from school: ponytail, jeans, waist-skimming T-shirt, and flip-flops. The girl bore a startling resemblance to the photos of Dominic Knight. Although, according to his bio, he didn't have children.

Interesting.

The young girl smiled. "You must be Dominic's four o'clock. He's not here yet, but he told me to tell you to go on in." She waved in the general direction of a hallway and went back to her book.

Dominic, not Mr. Knight. Even more interesting. As if it mattered, she reminded herself and gently cleared her throat to get the girl's attention. "Actually, I have an appointment with Max Roche. I'm Katherine Hart."

Kate stood there for a moment, an awkward pause stretching between them while the girl apparently read to the end of a sentence before glancing up. "I think it's Dominic you're seeing. Lemme check." Shoving a pencil in the book to hold her page, she clicked a computer mouse, the screen on a sleek monitor came to life, and she briefly scanned it. "Nope, not Max. Dominic." She pointed again. "Down the hall, last door. I'm supposed to ask you if you want coffee." Then she smiled and went back to her reading.

You didn't have to be a mind reader to know coffee wasn't an option, so Kate followed the suggested route. The hallway was lit by clerestory windows, the lustrous light illuminating a photo gallery of sailing vessels; some large, some less so, all glorious action shots of sleek racing yachts, sails aloft, running with the wind. She stopped for a moment and leaned in close to a photo of two racing yachts. Both were full-rigged, one boat heeling so hard to starboard, waves nearly skimmed its rails. And dangling inches above the water, one hand on the rail, the other reeling in a line, drenched with sea spray, was the CEO of Knight Enterprises, younger, thoroughly wet, a wide, exultant smile on his handsome face.

"That was a World Cup race off New Zealand. Sorry to keep you waiting. It was unavoidable."

The deep, rich voice was at ear level. Jerking upright, she swung around, gasped, breathed, *Holy shit*, then flushed. Dominic Knight in all his dark, sensual beauty was standing there, up close and personal, his quick raking glance so casually assessing she should take offense, not feel a shocking rush of pleasure. She almost gasped at the jolt, but caught herself in time because salivating in front of Dominic Knight would be superembarrassing *and* useless. He did models, aristocratic babes, high-end call girls. Researching his personal life had been like reading *Entertainment Weekly*.

Oh God, he still hadn't moved. Was he testing her sense of personal space? Was this some kind of psychological power thing? If it was, he was winning, because his tall, powerful body, sleek in a navy pinstripe bespoke suit, was *way* too close, *way* too personal. Her heart was pounding, she was having trouble focusing her thoughts, the speech synapses from her brain to her mouth were misfiring, and unless she got herself under control, she was going to blow this interview. *Breathe in, breathe out.* Now say something normal. "The...weather's...great...out...here." Breathless and sputtering. Shit.

His faint smile widened.

Arrogant bastard. But having finally regained her wits, she didn't voice her thoughts.

His gaze amused, as if breathless women were the norm in his life, he said blandly, "I agree. Did you have an uneventful flight?"

Before she could answer his cell phone rang.

He glanced at the display, frowned, and grunted, "Go on in. I have to take this."

Flustered by her response to a man who was even hotter in person than in his photos, feeling more like a thirteen-year-old Justin Bieber fan than a magna cum laude graduate of MIT, she lectured her uninvited inner adolescent as she walked toward his office. *Seriously. What was that all about? Haven't you seen a handsome man before? Get a grip. Better yet, go away.*

The hand-carved door at the end of the hall was slightly ajar; Dominic Knight conducted business casually. How reassuring. She wasn't fond of rules and protocol. Pushing the door open, she entered a low-ceilinged room with such spectacular views of the gardens that all thoughts of her embarrassing meeting with Knight Enterprises' CEO vanished.

Dropping her canvas messenger bag on a chair, she walked to the nearest window wall and surveyed the garden that reminded her of some of the royal gardens she'd seen in Japan: immaculately raked gravel, swirled in traditional wave patterns; large, rainbow-colored koi visible in the clear, limpid water of a nearby pond; artfully arranged boulders; ancient, perfectly pruned yews and pines. A small, arched bridge in brilliant red served as a picturesque focal point in the distance. The garden was a museum-quality work of art, carefully nurtured and maintained. Dominic Knight had an eye for beauty.

"I'll personally nail you to the wall if you screw me on this! You don't say no to me! Nobody says no to me! Now do your fucking job!"

She flinched at the audible fury in Dominic Knight's voice. Each word was implacable, taut with rage, the tone unexpectedly dredging up long-suppressed memories. Jesus, she'd not thought of any of that in years. Her gut tightened like it had as a child and she thought, *This job isn't going to work out. Explosive people are bad karma for me.*

She had plenty of other companies wooing her. She could pick and chose. Retrieving her messenger bag from the chair, she was almost to the door when he walked in.

"Forgive me again. I seem to be repeatedly apologizing before we've even met." But he was still distracted. He'd come to a stop and run a hand through his dark hair, his gaze unfocused.

"That's all right." She slung her bag over her shoulder. "This isn't going to work out anyway."

He looked startled. Then a second later he looked down, his gaze narrowed, fixed on her. "Nonsense. Your assignments are abroad. I won't be there. It should work out just fine." At least he didn't pretend to be confused. He seemed to know why she had reservations about taking this job. Or maybe he just didn't care. "I'm told you're the best and that's what I need."

"Our needs are incompatible." She kept her voice calm with effort, as he towered over her, his sexual charisma practically sending off heat waves, his commanding air intimidating—both seriously affecting her pulse rate.

"Tell me what you need—er"—he paused—"I'm not sure I've been told your name."

"It doesn't matter."

He looked at her as if she'd sprouted another head, then sighed. "Look, could we start over? I'm Dominic Knight. You're"—his dark brows rose in query, a touch of humor in his gaze.

"This isn't funny, Mr. Knight."

"I could call someone and get your name."

"To what purpose, pray tell?" she said, staring him in the eye with her best hard-as-nails look.

He smiled. "Really, *pray tell*? Channeling Jane Austen?" His sigh this time was barely audible. "As to what purpose," he repeated, softly mocking, "why not to our mutual satisfaction?" His voice went down a notch. "Now, tell me your name."

His deep, velvety tone melted through her body, turned on everything that could be turned on, *again*. Jeez, who would have thought using your vibrator before an interview was a requirement?

"I'm assuming you have a name," he prompted, a small smile stirring the corners of his mouth.

Asshole. Was he toying with her? Or did a mouth-watering CEO with a killer body figure every woman would roll over for him if he smiled? Her mouth firmed. "If you must know, my name is Katherine Hart. Spelled H, A, R, T."

His gaze was cool, as was his voice. "Perfect. Thank you."

"Miss Hart to you." She glanced at the door.

He noticed, ignored it. "As you wish, Miss Hart." He loosened his honey-colored tie, undid his collar button. "It's been a long day." He flexed his broad shoulders with a Zen-like grace, exhaled slowly, visibly decompressed. "I've had to listen to too many long-winded people in too many boring meetings. Have you ever noticed that those who do the least complain the most and those who know the least talk the most?" He held her gaze, almost smiled. "Now, what can I do to change your mind?"

Jeez, how could that sudden Zen-like calm be so hot? Or maybe tall, dark, and handsome was rocking her world because she was an adrenaline junky—a prime requirement in her line of work—and just looking at all that magnificent maleness was juicing her. "Nothing really," she said quickly, needing to get away, and it wasn't just bad karma. Men didn't shake her world like this. Or at least they never had. "I just changed my mind." She took a step to her right to go around him.

He moved left and checked her progress. "Change it back."

He was like a solid wall of machismo blocking her way. She tried to keep her voice from trembling. "I can't...Sorry."

He recognized the small flutter in her voice, debated responding, decided against it. "Let's keep this simple," he said brusquely. "I need you in Amsterdam. So don't tell me no."

Jesus, that was either intimidating or damn intimidating. "Please move," she croaked.

"In a second," he said with a flicker of a smile, feeling that this difficult young lady may have finally gotten the message. "Tell me what it's going to take to get you on board. Name your price if that's the stumbling block. Max says you're beyond gifted even for a high flyer, and I need you in Amsterdam. This is important."

"To you."

"Yes. That's the point. You can't say you don't want to work for Knight Enterprises. Everyone does."

"Not everyone."

That small startle reflex again. He really wasn't used to dissent.

"Look, I'm sorry if I said something to offend you." Although there wasn't a hint of apology in his tone. In fact, his annoyance was plain. He ran a hand quickly over his face, as though to wipe away the betraying emotion. "The ball's in your court, Miss Hart."

"What if I said I want to leave?"

The pause was so lengthy, a small moment of panic washed over her before she reminded herself it was the twenty-first century.

A winter chill colored the blue of his eyes. "Do I frighten you?"

"No." She wouldn't give him the satisfaction.

He tipped his head slightly and smiled in the most disarmingly ruthless way. "Good. Then if you'll sit down"—he indicated a chair—"we can discuss my problem, your skill set, and how we might cooperate."

Deciding the chances of her fighting her way out of this office were slight to nil, she sat. "You really don't take no for an answer, do you?"

"I'm afraid not." He dropped into a large black leather chair behind his desk. "It's not unique to a man in my position."

A salient argument, but not one she chose to value. "You're putting me in an awkward position, forcing this issue."

"On the contrary, you've put me in an awkward position. I'm offering you an excellent job. Max mentioned some of our issues in his e-mails. The dark market is making inroads in some of our outlier firms. It has to be stopped. Obviously you were intrigued or you wouldn't be here. Why not accept?"

"Personality clash. I heard you in the hallway."

"Perhaps you don't understand the company's organizational structure," he said with exquisite restraint. "I doubt we'll meet again."

"I disagree. As I understand it, Knight Enterprises' organizational structure is one of authoritarian leadership. You're hands on. You demand absolute compliance from subordinates."

His mouth tightened. "You've done your homework."

"I always do. And I have several other job offers, Mr. Knight. With the worldwide level of corruption, forensic accounting is in great demand." She smiled, sure of her prima donna status in her field at least. "Yours isn't the only company losing money to the dark market."

Her cheeky smile lit up her eyes and he looked at her for the first time as if she were more than just an obstacle in his path. She didn't know how to dress, but then the clothes of the young IT set weren't couture or colorful. Neutral tones went with their left brain functions. But her hair was a riot of red curls and her eyes were a potent green. Strange word. Bright green, he corrected himself. And beneath the drab army green jacket and slacks, he could see hints of a lithe, supple body that went well with her wide-eyed innocent beauty.

His lashes drifted downward an infinitesimal distance.

Hmmm. He hadn't considered that before, too intent on talking her around to his point of view. Not an easy task with Miss Hart. She wasn't docile. Or accommodating.

A provocative thought.

But he was a businessman first; there was time enough

for other things once Miss Hart had done her job. Since he'd lost Julia, he was indifferent to women for anything other than sex, and that was available anywhere. Miss Hart's sexual function was immaterial.

What *was* material lay in Bucharest and, according to Max, Miss Hart was the answer to their problem. "Perhaps we could come to a compromise," he said, determined as always to prevail. "You could join us as a contractor. After you finish this Amsterdam job, you can walk. You're a December graduate. Most of the major firms won't start recruiting for another few weeks. You'd still be in the game."

"I'd have to turn down my current offers."

"I'd be happy to make some calls and get some brief deferments for you. I know everyone in this business."

Nobody says no to me, indeed. How much did she want to piss off one of the most powerful men in the world? "You're persistent." She gave him a polite smile.

"So I've been told. Do you have family?" He preferred employees with a casual attachment to family. They were more likely to work the long hours demanded of them.

"You can't ask that," she said flatly.

His smile was mocking. "Are you going to sue me?"

"I won't have to if I'm not working for you."

His jaw clenched. "You can be a real bitch. Sue me for that too if you want. Now, could we stop playing games? I won't ask you any personal questions, other than will you accept my job offer?" Leaning back in his chair, he unbuttoned his suit coat, shot his cuffs, and waited for her reply.

She couldn't help but notice his hard flat stomach under his white custom shirt. And the fact that he didn't wear cuff links. She liked that. She'd always viewed cuff links as pretentious. *Only an observation*, the little voice inside her head pointed out innocently. *No one's trying to persuade you of anything.*

His gaze narrowed. "What?"

"Nothing." Then Kate pointed. "You don't wear cuff links. Is that allowed when you're a CEO?"

A shrug, a bland, blue stare. "Everything's allowed when you're me. My company is privately held."

Her spine stiffened. As she opened her mouth to speak, he stopped her with a lifted finger, picked up his phone, and hit a button. "I'm calling Max. He's scheduled to fly out at seven. He'll fill you in on all the details en route. As will Werner in our Amsterdam office. Now, in the nicest possible way, I'd like to invite you to work for us. Just the one assignment in Amsterdam. Yes or no, Miss Hart? I'm done fucking around. Just a minute, Max." He held her gaze.

"You're a control freak," she muttered.

"Is that a yes?"

Silence.

"Two weeks, a month, that's it. Money's no object. Come now, say yes." He smiled, a beautiful, charming, practiced smile.

Why did it seem that his smile was offering her the entire world and all its pleasures? *Clearly, a lunatic thought.*

"Very well," he said softly into the lengthening silence, his blue gaze grave. "Give me two weeks of your time. I won't ask for more."

A pause, a last small grimace, a barely discernible nod.

His instant smile could have melted the entire polar ice

cap in under a minute. "Welcome aboard, Miss Hart. I look forward to working with you." He grinned. "At a distance, of course."

He was way too smooth and way too beautiful and way too familiar with getting his way. But, deep down, irrationally, she wanted the job more than anything. And she knew better than to fall under his spell. Screwing the CEO was never wise.

As if, anyway.

Besides, the word *bondage* had come up on one of the murkier blog sites in Europe. Whether it was true or not, a man that rich and powerful?

Anything was possible.

Love a great erotic romance?
Don't Miss these titles from Grand Central Publishing!

Slow Satisfaction
By Cecilia Tan

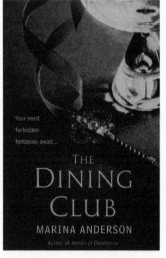

The Dining Club
by Marina Anderson

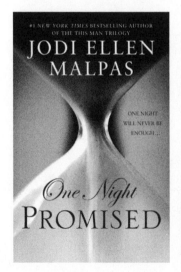

One Night: Promised
By Jodi Ellen Malpas

One Night: Denied
by Jodi Ellen Malpas